MYSTERIOUS TALES OF OLD ST. PAUL

ALSO BY LARRY MILLETT
PUBLISHED BY THE UNIVERSITY OF MINNESOTA PRESS

Sherlock Holmes and the Red Demon
Sherlock Holmes and the Ice Palace Murders
Sherlock Holmes and the Rune Stone Mystery
Sherlock Holmes and the Secret Alliance
The Disappearance of Sherlock Holmes
Sherlock Holmes and the Eisendorf Enigma
The Magic Bullet: A Locked Room Mystery
Strongwood: A Crime Dossier
Rafferty's Last Case: A Minnesota Mystery

Mysterious Tales of Old St. Paul

THREE CASES
FEATURING
SHADWELL RAFFERTY

LARRY MILLETT

University of Minnesota Press
Minneapolis
London

Published by the University of Minnesota Press
111 Third Avenue South, Suite 290
Minneapolis, MN 55401-2520
http://www.upress.umn.edu

ISBN 978-1-5179-1783-8 (hc)
ISBN 978-1-5179-1800-2 (pb)

A Cataloging-in-Publication record for this book is available from the
Library of Congress.

Printed in Canada on acid-free paper

The University of Minnesota is an equal-opportunity educator
and employer.

31 30 29 28 27 26 25 24   10 9 8 7 6 5 4 3 2 1

CONTENTS

DEATH in the NEWS

A Scandalous Tale

There is no suffering comparable with that which
a private person feels when he is for the first time
pilloried in print.

—MARK TWAIN

1
TRUTH AND LIES

ON THE FIRST MONDAY in June 1890 the good people of St. Paul awoke to an astonishing sight, for during the night someone had gone to great trouble to change a sign mounted atop downtown's tallest building. The sign advertised the building's owner and the city's largest newspaper, the *Pioneer Press,* in eight-foot-high block letters. Lighted by arc lamps at night and visible from a great distance, the sign was perhaps the most prominent in all of St. Paul. But instead of the words PIONEER PRESS, the sign had been altered to read LIARS, hardly a message the newspaper wished to convey to its faithful readers.

When police arrived on the rooftop, they found that the vandals had remade the wooden sign by taking down all of its letters except for *I,* an *R,* and an *S.* The *L* and *A* were then fashioned from portions of the leftover letters by means of some crude carpentry work. A wrench, a saw, a hammer, and nails were left behind on the rooftop as evidence of the bizarre crime.

Detective Patrick Donlin, by far the best of a generally indifferent lot of police investigators, was immediately assigned the case, much to his regret, because he knew he would be pilloried in the *Pioneer Press* if he failed to find the culprits. The trouble was, he had very little to go on. The tools were of the most common sort, available from any hardware dealer, and thus impossible to trace. A watchman who patrolled the otherwise unoccupied building

3

during the overnight hours was also of no help, since he reported seeing or hearing nothing out of the ordinary. Nor were any other witnesses found who could shed light on the night's peculiar events.

Even so, Donlin was able to make some guesses. He was pretty sure more than one man was involved in the crime, since the bulky letters, fashioned from hard maple, weighed as much as seventy-five pounds each and would have been difficult for a man to handle by himself. A lantern of some kind would have been needed, and having a second man to hold the light would have made the job much easier. Donlin further theorized that the perpetrators had probably hidden in a vacant office, gone up to the roof through an unsecured door to accomplish their work in the dead of night, then left once the building reopened for the day.

There was plenty of suspicion as to who might have done the deed. Much of it was directed across the river at Minneapolis, whose census officials were engaged in a bitter dispute with their counterparts in St. Paul over the 1890 population count. Although risible irregularities occurred on both sides, the *Pioneer Press* had long contended that Minneapolis was where the real perfidy lay. "There is a dastardly cabal of liars and cheats in the Mill City who will stop at nothing to advance their aims," the newspaper wrote in one of its more temperate editorials, "and a horse-whipping would be too good for them." Was it possible, the newspaper's editors now wondered in bold type, that someone from the "cabal" had taken revenge by disfiguring the sign?

Donlin, however, thought there could be a much simpler explanation for the attack on the sign. A year earlier, three letters had been removed from a saloon sign advertising SCHLITZ BEER in order to spell out a crude word. Two teenage boys were soon identified as the culprits. But the SCHLITZ sign had been small and easily accessible, whereas the PIONEER PRESS sign was neither. Try as he might, Donlin couldn't quite convince himself that mischievous boys on a lark would have gone to so much trouble to fiddle with the newspaper's sign.

A better possibility, he believed, was that someone with a deep personal grudge had altered the sign or hired someone to do it. As Donlin knew from his own run-ins with the press, bad publicity was a dirt storm that could strike anywhere, anytime. Had someone who'd been sucked up in one of those storms now lashed back at the *Pioneer Press*? Donlin considered it likely, but as to who the aggrieved person might be, he had no clue.

The *Pioneer Press*'s chief rivals—the *Dispatch* and the *Globe*—naturally took much amusement in the sign caper. The *Globe* opined that "our local sign shifter is clearly a man of great insight," while the *Dispatch* averred that "readers of our distinguished rival have long doubted its devotion to the truth," adding that "the new sign is quite fetching, and we can only hope the *Pioneer Press* will forever let it shine forth as a beacon to all of St. Paul."

Not surprisingly, the management of the *Pioneer Press* found the incident far less entertaining. The newspaper, with perhaps more enthusiasm than accuracy, liked to trumpet its new edifice as the "largest and most elegantly appointed of its kind in the country," and so the assault on the sign was regarded as a grave insult. In its story the following morning, the *Pioneer Press* referred only to the "ugly defacement of our sign" and offered a one-hundred-dollar reward for information about the crime. The sign was quickly restored, but within a matter of days a far more grievous crime would shock all of St. Paul.

* * *

Newspapering in St. Paul was a rough-hewn business in 1890, its practitioners a largely anonymous group of scribblers who had no particular skills other than the ability to write passably well and hold their liquor. When not preoccupied with loafing and raillery, the newsies dug for shards of interesting information in the mucky soil of the city, driven by editors for whom the greatest of all horrors was a blank page. Accuracy was not essential to the job, and most of the stories that filled the pages of the city's three dailies were amalgams of fact, speculation, and outright invention, usually delivered in a tone of cheeky, deadpan amusement at the follies of the world.

While newspaper editors tended to be a feral breed, always sniffing for the bloody meat of a great story, the man in charge of the *Pioneer Press* did not fit the stereotype. By 1890 Milton Pickett had been the newspaper's managing editor for a decade, and under his direction it became the best-read of the city's dailies. Tall, a bit rotund, and bespectacled, the sixty-year-old Pickett had the punctilious manner of an accountant, and indeed he viewed his newspaper as a kind of ledger sheet where readers could find both the assets and debits of the day. Never married, he had no real life outside of his profession and worked six days a week, taking only Saturdays off while another editor shepherded the big Sunday edition into print.

Despite his prim manner, Pickett had plenty of backbone, and he was willing to take on the rich and powerful, to a reasonable degree. "I am proud to have enemies in high places," he liked to say, "for our newspaper is in the business of serving the people and not their masters." This noble sentiment was tempered by the fact that the *Pioneer Press* lived not by its circulation but by its advertising revenue, which meant big advertisers could count on favorable publicity unless they committed murder in broad daylight. Other prominent men were fair game, however, and three in particular had lashed out so violently in response to recent unflattering stories that Pickett passed on their names to Donlin as possible suspects in the sign caper.

The first was Harley Calhoun, a wealthy hardware wholesaler accused in a lawsuit of cheating a former partner out of thousands of dollars. Calhoun was so angered by the *Pioneer Press*'s extensive coverage of the case that he'd not only confronted Pickett but also gotten into a minor scuffle with the newspaper's hard-nosed publisher, David Whiting, who had only one arm with which to defend himself. A beefy typesetter had finally escorted Calhoun from the building.

Then there was Lemuel Thatcher, a fiery teetotaler and self-avowed prophet who operated a downtown hotel. He'd been skewered as a hypocrite in an article revealing that his property portfolio included two well-known brothels. He claimed to have no idea that the properties were being used for "sinful purposes," an explanation no one believed since he was known to always collect his rent in person. Thatcher had responded to the story by vowing that the "swift sword of retribution" would soon smite Whiting, Pickett, and their "Devil's minions."

Perhaps the newspaper's fiercest enemy, however, was Dr. William Wittemore. A prominent surgeon with a famously wandering eye, he had been the subject of an exposé detailing his habit of chasing after young nurses. Wittemore had confronted Pickett the next day, claiming the story was nothing but "lies, lies, and more lies" and threatening to put the editor down "like a rabid dog."

When Pickett addressed his staff that afternoon, he noted that "Mr. Whiting is outraged by the attack on our sign, and you may be sure he will light a fire under the police department so that they conduct a thorough investigation. Let us hope that investigation bears fruit." Yet there wasn't much fire in Pickett's voice, and he seemed more subdued than angry over what had happened to the sign.

After his brief and not very peppy speech, Pickett called his star reporter, Dolly Charbonneau, into his office and took the unusual step of closing the door so that they could talk in private.

"Between you and me, I have a strong suspicion as to who assaulted our sign," he told her, "and it may be a darker business than anyone imagines."

"What do you mean?"

"It has to do with something I started looking into last week. Something potentially very scandalous. You were off in the Black Hills with that military expedition, or I would have assigned the story to you. As it was, I thought it best to handle it myself."

"What are we talking about?"

"I prefer not to go into the details quite yet. It's the sort of story that could destroy many lives, and I must be very careful. I need help now to put it all together, and that's where you come in. I want you to begin with the old Bellaire Hotel on West Third Street. See if you can find out who owns it and whether a building permit was issued in the past few years for renovations."

"Why are you interested in the Bellaire?"

"I have my reasons. The less you know the better, especially if it turns out I'm wrong, though I very much doubt that's the case. Now, get to it right away and let me know what you find out."

2

RAFFERTY ON THE CASE

TWO BLOCKS NORTH of the Pioneer Press Building stood another of the city's chief architectural monuments—the Ryan Hotel. A neo-Gothic extravaganza built by a transplanted Nevada silver king, the hotel had played a prominent role in the census war after a St. Paul enumerator managed to discover twenty-five men living in the hotel's barbershop. It was a bit of nonsense that Shadwell Rafferty, whose popular saloon occupied a prime space in the hotel, found deeply amusing. "It must be crowded for all those poor fellows," he remarked, "but at least they're well shaven."

Rafferty was by this time already a legend in St. Paul. A giant of man, he was well over six feet tall and wide of girth, with a distinctive scar over his left eye that gave him the look of a jolly pirate somehow marooned a thousand miles from salt water. Rafferty possessed a sharp eye, a clever wit, an Irish brogue that would come and go as the mood suited him, great intelligence, and a bartender's sympathetic view of the frail human animal.

Born in Boston, he'd gone west to St. Paul just in time to sign up for the War between the States, survived three years without a scratch in the killing grounds of Virginia and Pennsylvania, gone farther west to mine silver in Nevada, returned to St. Paul to serve as a policeman, and finally opened his saloon in 1885, the same year the Ryan made its debut. By 1890, he was approaching fifty but still as strong a man as could be found in the city. He had one other mark of distinction, for in recent years he had begun to work as a part-time private detective, and so skilled was he that it was soon said in St. Paul that if you wanted to solve a baffling mystery, Rafferty was the man to see.

Shad's Place, as the saloon was called, had in its five years of existence become the noisy heart of the city, a gathering spot for all manner of thirsty men and even a few women. A bulldog named John Brown served as the establishment's mascot and usually stationed himself like a fierce gargoyle at the end of the long mahogany bar, growling at any fool who tried to invade his territory.

"My pup has an ancestor who was at Harper's Ferry with old John Brown," Rafferty claimed, without a shred of proof, "and I have heard he took a nice bite out of that traitor Bobby Lee."

Rafferty did not work alone. In Nevada he'd met a son of slaves, George Washington Thomas, and the two had hit it off immediately. Thomas was a bit younger than Rafferty, and much thinner, but he was a formidable man in his own right. He partnered with Rafferty at the saloon, tending bar, doing some short-order cooking, and balancing the books, since Rafferty's financial acumen left much to be desired. Although his skin color exposed Thomas to all the usual prejudices, he was a man entirely comfortable with himself, and it was well known that a slur cast in his direction would instantly occasion a two-fisted response.

The strange business with the *Pioneer Press*'s sign became a prime topic of conversation at the saloon that evening. As the liquor flowed, so did a variety of theories as to the identity of the culprit or culprits. Although there was no consensus as to who had vandalized the sign, it was widely suspected that vague "Minneapolis interests" were behind the outlandish deed.

Rafferty, however, had his doubts. "I would not put it past them and yet it seems too clever a thing for men of their ilk," he said from his post behind the bar. "'Tis well known that teetotalling Yankees run the Mill City, with the police as their private army, and they are dry men in more sense than one. They enjoy nothing more than poring over their ledgers in search of a lost penny or finding some novel way to impoverish the working man. In my opinion the sign caper would not have occurred to such a dreary group of men." Rafferty went on to note that all of St. Paul's newspapers had written inflammatory articles about the census war, so why would the *Pioneer Press* have been singled out for attack?

Another theory distilled from the ample flow of whiskey was that the remodeled sign was simply an amusing prank. Rafferty disagreed. "I am of a mind this was the work of a man burning inside with some deep grievance, and such men are never to be taken lightly," he opined to Thomas. "I fear he is a madman and will do worse when the time comes."

Thomas was skeptical. "Well, maybe you're right, but I'm guessing it was just a big joke somebody did on a dare."

"'Tis possible, I admit," Rafferty said. "Time will tell."

One of the saloon's most distinguished regulars, Rutherford Cuddleton, shared Rafferty's concern over what had happened to the sign. Cuddleton was St. Paul's leading defense attorney, a small man with a big voice who regularly held forth at the saloon on all manner of subjects.

"There is indeed something sinister about this sign business," he announced after consuming several glasses of Scotch. "We are dealing, gentlemen, with no ordinary criminal. I say this miscreant has some grand scheme in mind. If I were working for the *Pioneer Press,* I would have reason to be afraid."

"Ah, so what do you think our sign man intends to do?" Rafferty asked.

"I speak for many," Cuddleton replied, raising his glass in a salute, "but I do not speak for the Almighty. Only God knows what this fellow is up to, but I suspect we are in for some dangerous days. Danger has a smell, my friends, and it is wafting into my nostrils."

"Are you sure it's not the Glenturret you're sniffing?" said a man standing beside the lawyer.

"It is not," Cuddleton said, "and I am profoundly offended that you would cast aspersions upon my beloved Scottish friend. But trust me when I say that whoever played with that sign is not done."

* * *

A year earlier, Cuddleton had returned from a monthlong holiday in England bearing a gift for Rafferty. Like Rafferty, Cuddleton was an eager consumer of crime stories, and while browsing in a bookshop just off Baker Street in London he'd come upon a book called *A Study in Scarlet* recounting the remarkable adventures of a detective named Sherlock Holmes. When he presented the book to Rafferty, Cuddleton said, "It's the best damned thing of this sort I've ever read. This Holmes fellow is a regular genius. You wouldn't believe the clever tricks he pulls off."

By a twist of fate, Rafferty would meet Holmes and Dr. John Watson in 1896 during the affair of the ice palace murders, thereby inaugurating a decades-long friendship. But until that fateful meeting, Rafferty knew of Holmes's work only through Dr. Watson's accounts. Rafferty read *A Study in Scarlet* as carefully as a monk parsing the Bible, and he was particularly taken by Holmes's observational skills, to the point that he began trying to "read" everyone he met based on their clothes, bodily features, manner of speaking, and demeanor. "I think I am getting the knack of it," he later told Thomas, "although I am still not sure how this Holmes fellow can tell what a man's profession is just by looking at him."

"Well, wouldn't it be easier if he'd just ask the man what he does?" said Thomas.

"Yes, but what amusement would that provide? I am pretty sure, for example, that you work in a saloon."

"I am dazzled. You are surely the Sherlock Holmes of St. Paul."

"Not yet, but I am working at it," Rafferty said. "I now find myself studying every person I meet down to the shape of their ears and the color of their shoelaces. I am hoping my efforts will lead to some great feat of detection with which I could impress even Holmes himself."

"Maybe it will," Thomas said. "In the meantime, I can deduce by the noisy rumblings of that big stomach of yours that it's time for lunch."

* * *

The day after the *Pioneer Press*'s mutilated sign made headlines, a call came into Rafferty's saloon just before noon. When he picked up the receiver, a woman who identified herself as David Whiting's secretary said the publisher wished to see him that evening.

"Seven o'clock would be suitable," the woman said. "He will be at his home."

The woman had not bothered to inquire whether Rafferty was available for the meeting. He was being summoned, not asked, to meet with the publisher. Rafferty was tempted to say no—a night meeting would take him away from his busy saloon—but he agreed, if only because he was curious what Whiting wanted.

At the appointed hour Rafferty rode a cable car up the steep hill to Summit Avenue and walked over to Whiting's mansion, a

huge granite pile that posed atop the bluffs like a grim Scottish
castle. Rafferty had met Whiting only a few times in passing but
knew of his reputation as an imperious man who ruled the *Pioneer
Press* with an iron hand. When Whiting became the newspaper's
publisher in 1887, a long profile recounted the story of his life, and
Rafferty had read it with great interest, if only because of Whiting's
service in the War between the States.

Raised on a rockbound New England farm that offered endless
work and little hope, Whiting went off to war in 1861 and fought
for two bloody years with the Second New Hampshire Regiment
before losing his left arm to a Confederate sharpshooter at Gettysburg. The loss of a limb served only to double his resolve, however,
and like so many other Yankees he went west in search of the main
chance, landing in St. Paul in 1865.

Gifted with an acid pen, he eventually found work writing editorials for the *Pioneer Press,* where he befriended its publisher, Jasper
Fairchild, and his butterfly of a wife, Margaret. In 1886 Fairchild,
who loved horses far more fervently than he loved his wife, put a
fatal dent in his skull when he was thrown from one of his prized
Arabians at full gallop. His demise left Margaret modestly bereft
but extremely wealthy.

Whiting saw an opportunity and took it. After months of re-
lentless wooing, he married Margaret, an arrangement regarded
as rather scandalous in polite circles as he was ten years her junior.
But money, as Whiting liked to tell his male confidants, does much
for a woman's looks, and he became by all outward appearances a
doting husband, although rumors surfaced that his amorous activities were not always confined to the marital bed.

Margaret happily ceded the job of publishing the *Pioneer Press* to
her new husband, and in that role Whiting quickly proved himself a
tyrant. He hired and fired at whim, remade his predecessor's plain
office into a sumptuous teak-and-leather retreat at great expense,
and subjected his newsroom staff to frequent tirades. Milton Pickett, alone among the newspaper's editors, seemed not to tremble
before Whiting's wrath and even had the courage to say no to him
if the situation warranted.

Rafferty had heard enough about Whiting to know he possessed a volcanic temperament. But like Pickett, Rafferty couldn't be bullied, although Whiting gave it a try as soon as Rafferty was ushered into a bright parlor aswirl with pink-and-white plaster that seemed utterly at odds with the home's dour exterior.

"You are fifteen minutes late. I expect a man to be on time," Whiting said without any preliminaries. He was seated on lushly upholstered side chair and chewing on an unlit cigar. A truncated coat sleeve dangled from his left shoulder.

"As do I," Rafferty said evenly. "Unfortunately, the street railway company had other ideas. There was a problem with the cable grip that took some time to repair."

"Well then, sit down," Whiting said, pointing Rafferty to a white sofa overpopulated with fluffy pillows.

Rafferty pushed aside two pillows to take a seat. As he did so, he glanced up at the parlor's coved ceiling, which was painted with nymphs, fauns, and lissome women in various stages of undress. "I must say, this is quite a room."

Whiting said, "It's all Margaret's doing. Looks like a fancy whorehouse as far as I'm concerned. Now, do you know why you're here, Mr. Rafferty?"

"I am guessing it is not to reminisce about the war, although I believe you were at Gettysburg, as was I."

"Yes, I'm aware of that. A sharpshooter in the Devil's Den got me. It's a wonder a man of your size managed to avoid the shot and shell."

"Luck," Rafferty said. "Sometimes the biggest target is the hardest to hit."

"Well, I wish I could say the same about our sign. As you may suspect, that's why you're here. The sign made quite a target, and there are people who seem to think that defacing it was just a big joke. I am not among them."

Rafferty studied Whiting's face, which looked as though it been sculpted from a block of stone, and doubted whether humor in any form appealed to him.

"So you believe it was no lark."

"Of course not. It was an attack on my newspaper, and I want you to prove who did it."

"Well, I don't know," Rafferty said. "The police are already working on it, and I—"

"The police in this city are a joke," Whiting said, waving his arm in a dismissive gesture. "They will do nothing unless they are paid for their time and trouble, and I have found that I rarely get results for my money. I have already talked twice to that Donlin fellow who's supposedly leading the investigation, and he did not inspire confidence."

"I would disagree, Mr. Whiting. Pat Donlin is the best detective on the force and if anyone—"

Whiting interrupted again. "Well, if he is the best, we are in trouble. That is why I want you to look into this business. Mr. Hill highly recommends you, and that is good enough for me. I will pay you a one-hundred-dollar retainer and a like amount when you identify the culprit."

Rafferty said, "'Tis a generous offer, but I could not guarantee success. From what Pat has told me, there are many potential suspects."

"And that is precisely where the police are wrong. You see, I am all but certain who did the deed, or more likely paid to have it done. All I need is for you to prove it."

"Ah, and who is the prime suspect?"

"Wittemore, who else? Ever since we wrote that story about him running after all those nurses, he has been completely out of control. He all but attacked me in my office and also threatened our editor, Mr. Pickett."

"What sort of threats did he make?"

"I am told he actually threatened to shoot Mr. Pickett down 'like a rabid dog,' or words to that effect."

"Do you have any evidence Wittemore tampered with the sign?"

"That is your job. Once you find the evidence, we will drown the doctor in an ocean of bad ink. He will regret ever insulting the *Pioneer Press*. Now, what do you say, Mr. Rafferty?"

The money was tempting—two hundred dollars would pay for a number of needed improvements at the saloon—and Rafferty agreed to take on the job. "But I must warn you, Mr. Whiting, that I will go wherever my investigation leads. I will not frame Dr. Wittemore for something he did not do."

"Oh, he did it all right," Whiting said. "See my paymaster tomorrow morning and he will give you your retainer. Of course, I will expect regular reports on your progress."

"Of course," said Rafferty, well aware that he'd signed on with a man who was certain to be a difficult client.

3
MURDER

AT TEN O'CLOCK the following evening, Milton Pickett left the offices of the *Pioneer Press* after the newspaper's early morning edition had been "put to bed," as he liked to say. It had been an especially hectic day, and Pickett remarked to a coworker that he intended to "go straight home and sleep the night through." And as far as anyone knew, he'd done just that.

The next day, however, Pickett failed to show up at the office or report that he would not be coming in. This was alarming, since Pickett was highly regular in his habits, and no one could recall the last time he'd missed a day of work. When he could not be reached by telephone, the newspaper sent a reporter to check at his residence, located in a recently built row house in the Seven Corners district at the western edge of downtown. The reporter, who'd brought along a spare house key Pickett was known to keep in his office desk, rang the doorbell and knocked repeatedly but received no answer. He then used the key to gain entrance.

The apartment's front parlor was clean and neat, with no sign of any disturbance, but the acrid smell of gunpowder hung in the air. Feeling a sense of foreboding, the reporter passed through an archway into the dining room, where he came upon a terrible sight. Pickett lay face down on the floor in front of a built-in buffet, a shattered glass decanter and pillow beside him. The reporter rushed over to him but saw at once that nothing could be done. A mass of clotted blood surrounded a wound to the back of Pickett's head, and there was a scorched hole in the pillow, indicating it had been used to muffle the sound of the fatal shot. But the strangest feature of the scene was a broadsheet newspaper page that rested like a small blanket on Pickett's back and that proclaimed itself to be a publication the reporter had never heard of.

When Patrick Donlin arrived to lead the police investigation, he took note at once of the smashed decanter. It suggested that Pickett had gone over to the buffet, which was stocked with bottles of whiskey and gin, and was preparing to pour out a drink when he was assassinated. Donlin made one other quick deduction, based on the fact that the apartment's door gave no sign of being forced. Pickett likely had admitted someone he knew to the apartment, a person he would feel comfortable sharing a drink with.

The coroner would later determine that Pickett was shot with a .41-caliber weapon and that the time of death was probably around midnight. But Donlin and his men found no witnesses who saw anyone enter the apartment about that time, nor did neighbors report hearing a gunshot. "We are drowning in suspects, boys," he told his men, "but when it comes to evidence, we are in the desert."

Pickett's murder prompted headlines so large that only a presidential assassination might have exceeded them in size. Virtually every detail of the crime and of Pickett's final hours, insofar as they could be determined, was treated in the manner of a sacred text requiring elaborate exegesis. At the same time, tributes poured in from other newsmen who hailed Pickett, perhaps with some hyperbole, as a shining star of the journalistic firmament and a man of such splendid character that it was difficult to fathom how the world could go on without him.

But the police, with the cooperation of the press, withheld one crucial piece of evidence from the deluge of publicity that followed Pickett's shocking demise. What the public didn't know about was the sheet of newspaper left on Pickett's body. The masthead proclaimed it to be the *St. Paul Daily Chronicle,* a fictitious publication. A huge headline—LIARS!—dominated the page. The type below consisted of the same word, repeated over and over again. It was naturally assumed that the murderer must be the same man who'd altered the *Pioneer Press*'s sign.

That evening, Whiting called Rafferty. "Well, Wittemore has done it now and he must be brought to justice. I am offering a one-thousand-dollar reward for information leading to an arrest and conviction. That money will be yours, Mr. Rafferty, if you can send Wittemore to the gallows."

"I will do all I can," Rafferty promised. "In the meantime, you must be very careful."

"The secessionists could not kill me," Whiting said, "and Wittemore will have no better luck at it. I will be ready for him if the time comes."

* * *

"I've never seen my people so scared," Joseph Pyle said to Rafferty the day after Pickett's body was discovered. "Half the people in our office have taken to carrying a pistol, and the other half are thinking of buying one. Everybody is wondering who'll be next."

Pyle was a respected reporter for the *Globe,* as well as a close friend and biographer of James J. Hill. Within a few years, Pyle would travel to London at Hill's behest for a meeting with Sherlock Holmes and Dr. John Watson, thereby leading to the renowned duo's first visit to Minnesota to investigate the singular case of the Red Demon.

Now, however, Pyle was on familiar ground, comfortably seated in Rafferty's small office, which offered a quiet retreat from the saloon's noisy bustle. The head of a massive twenty-point buck Rafferty had shot years earlier decorated the wall behind his desk, surveying the scene with cold eyes. Pyle was of medium build, in his thirties, with deep-blue eyes, a curling black mustache, and an unruffled manner. Rafferty had known the newsman for years and regarded him as an excellent source of reliable information. For his part, Pyle viewed Rafferty as the best detective in the city and a man of uncommon wisdom.

"Have you heard the latest?" Pyle asked.

"Ah, you must enlighten me, Joseph. I suspect you know something I don't. I tried to reach Pat Donlin this weekend but could not get hold of him."

"Then I'm guessing you don't know what was found at the murder scene," Pyle said and went on to describe the fake newspaper page left on Pickett's body. "A copper I know filled me in. But that's not the half of it. The very same item came to Bev in the mail this morning. We'll be doing a story about it." .

Wilson Beverly was the *Globe*'s managing editor. "He's scared and I don't blame him," Pyle said. "He thinks the killer may come gunning for him next."

"Is there a particular reason why he believes that?" Rafferty asked.

"There is. You see, Bev believes Dr. Wittemore did the awful deed. Everybody knows he's a dangerous, unstable man, and he went absolutely crazy after we followed up on the *Press*'s story about how he was treating the nurses over at St. Luke's. There is no question in my mind that he could be a homicidal maniac."

"Ah now, that is going pretty far, isn't it?"

"I don't think so. Have you ever met the doctor?"

"I have not."

"Then count your lucky stars. He's supposedly the best surgeon in the city, but he's also known to take a lot of chances. Operate first and ask questions later is his motto, or so I've heard. A doctor I know over at St. Luke's says Wittemore views himself as the king of the hospital and everyone else there as his vassals. He also has a nasty temper and people I've talked to say he's become extremely volatile of late, to the point that he's downright scary. In any case, he had a big run-in with Bev after we did our story. The two of them nearly came to blows. From what I hear, Wittemore had an even bigger scene with Pickett and threatened to shoot him."

Rafferty said, "He did. It seems he also had a nasty encounter with Mr. Whiting."

"I didn't know that, but it's one more reason why Wittemore bears looking at. So do some other people who obviously hated Pickett. There's Harley Calhoun, for one, not to mention crazy old Lemuel Fletcher. But Bev is most concerned about the doctor. You see, there's one other thing you should know. Rumor has it that Pickett was getting ready to run another story that would ruin Wittemore once and for all."

"What kind of story?"

"I'm not sure, but I've heard hints that Wittemore might be addicted to drugs of some kind. Mind you, it's just a rumor. You might want to check with Dolly Charbonneau over at the *Pioneer Press*. If anybody has the juicy details, she'd be the one. Do you know her?"

Rafferty said he did. Delores Charbonneau, who went by Dolly, was the city's only female news reporter. "I'll have a chat with her. By the way, have the police interviewed Wittemore?"

"I don't think so. You know the coppers. They wouldn't dare approach a man of his stature unless they thought they really had the goods on him."

"And right now they don't."

"Correct. Anyway, I understand you're already looking into Mr. Pickett's murder."

Rafferty smiled behind his bushy beard and said, "I see word travels fast in the news fraternity. You're right. Mr. Whiting asked me to see what I can find out."

"Well, I'm glad you're on the case," Pyle said. "I wish you good luck."

"I may need it, Joseph. I am thinking we have an onion before us, and it will not be easy to peel back all the layers."

4
GUNNING FOR THE PRESS

IT WAS SAID OF ROBERT STEVENS, often referred to as "Beautiful Bob," that had he not become editor of the *St. Paul Dispatch*, he might well have found his station in life as a duke or earl, for he liked to dress in a swallowtail coat, ruffled white shirt, colorful ascot, and striped pants as though he was a dandy lately arrived from some dotty corner of England. He was just over six feet tall and still darkly handsome in his early fifties, sporting a full head of jet-black hair meticulously dyed to erase any hint of gray. When he came strolling down the street, an umbrella always in hand no matter how sunny the day, he would greet acquaintances and passersby in a booming voice that, said a friend, was "like hearing Moses deliver the Ten Commandments."

Stevens had once been a well-known playboy, pursuing women of all types and ages so energetically that in the *Dispatch* newsroom he earned the title of "the Great Seducer." His bedroom excursions produced much drama—one jilted woman threw a heavy stapler at him in his office, just missing his overactive groin—but he paid little attention to such "female contretemps," as he called them, and kept right on philandering. Then, in his early forties and deeply in debt, he suddenly married, much to the surprise of his friends. His newfound love was a woman of ample dimensions whose family fortune was said to be her most fetching feature, and as far as anyone knew Stevens hadn't strayed since his marriage.

Despite his flashy apparel and foppish manner, Stevens was a tough-minded, hard-drinking man who viewed the world as a liar's paradise and saw his newspaper as a place where the well-buried truth might occasionally burst into view, "like a wildflower in a field of weeds," as he put it. Even so, Stevens favored moist sensationalism over dry fact, and like Pickett he'd made his share of enemies. More than once, Stevens had found it necessary to defend the First Amendment with his fists, and one especially irate reader had even challenged him to a duel, an opportunity Stevens had declined after stating, with a wink and a nod, that "everyone knows newspapermen have no honor to defend."

Stevens had always viewed Milton Pickett as a stuffy prig and rarely had anything good to say about him. But he nonetheless expressed shock when he learned of Pickett's murder. "It appears some madman with a hatred for the press is now on the loose," Stevens told his shaken staff. "We must all be very careful and watch one another's backs until the killer is found."

The work of putting out an afternoon newspaper like the *Dispatch* began before dawn, and so Stevens was of necessity an early riser despite his frequent nocturnal carousing. On most days he would be in the newspaper offices by seven to review the national news coming in on the wire and begin plotting out local coverage. So it was that on the morning of June 9, five days after Pickett's murder, Stevens left home just before dawn and headed for the *Dispatch* offices.

The newspaper occupied the eastern half of the Union Block, a six-story building on Fourth Street that had been among the largest in the city before the *Pioneer Press* erected a building twice as tall. Stevens had suffered a bad case of edifice envy as a result, and he still chafed every time he looked down Fourth and saw the *Pioneer Press* sign looming above all else. Its defilement had amused Stevens so greatly that he told a friend, "I wish I'd thought of that."

The front doors of the *Dispatch*'s offices didn't open until eight o'clock, so Stevens always used an employee entrance at the rear reached via a narrow alley. The cobblestone alley remained in deep shadows as Stevens approached the entrance. He was only few feet from the door when he heard footsteps coming up fast behind him. Then, as he wrote that afternoon in a front-page story, "I found myself staring down the barrel of a pistol."

Stevens's account of what happened next was chilling. "The man who held the weapon was dressed in a black raincoat and a hood of the same color that disguised his features. 'If this is a robbery,' I said, 'I will give you what I have,' but the man only laughed at me. Then he pointed the pistol at my head and fired, and in that instant I thought I was dead. But the bullet instead flew past my right ear like a buzzing bee, and once again the man laughed derisively.

"'You and your kind must be taught a lesson,' he said in a menacing voice I did not recognize. 'I will not let you get away with sullying my good name.'

"I will admit that I was as frightened as a man could be, for I could feel my assailant's evil presence, like gas rising up from a fetid swamp, and I greatly feared for my life. Still, I tried to reason with him. 'If you believe an injustice has been done,' I said, 'I will be happy to hear you out and make amends if necessary.'

"'I have no interest in talk,' came the reply, and it was then I knew the man intended to assassinate me. My only hope was to seek safety behind the door where I normally enter the *Dispatch* offices, and so I took flight. It was but a few feet to the door, yet it felt like a mile. Another shot rang out and once again somehow missed its mark. I flung open the heavy door just as a third bullet crashed against it with a sharp metallic crack.

"You may be assured that once I closed the door behind me I held fast against it with every ounce of strength in my possession. I waited, for how long I do not know, my heart pounding all the while like the piston of a steam engine. It was only when I heard someone calling out in the alley that I loosened my grip on the door, for I recognized the voice as that of one of our compositors who was arriving for work. I let him in, asking anxiously whether he had seen anyone in the alley. He had not, and when I told him what had happened, he was stunned.

"It is now all too clear that there is in St. Paul a man who wishes to silence the free voice of the press with bullets. He has already taken the life of a distinguished editor at the *Pioneer Press,* and it is only by the grace of the Almighty that he did not take mine as well this morning. So it is that I call upon the police of this great city to leave no stone unturned in hunting down the killer before he strikes again.

"A democracy cannot survive without a free and untrammeled press," Stevens concluded. "The Fourth Estate of this city and the First Amendment itself are under now under assault, and truth will be the ultimate casualty if this murderer is not stopped at once."

At the insistence of the police, Stevens's dramatic account omitted one salient detail. Before fleeing from the alley, the gunman left behind a page from the *St. Paul Chronicle,* with the word "liars" filling every inch of space. It was identical to the page found on Milton Pickett's body and the one sent to Wilson Beverly at the *Globe.* Any lingering doubts that a murderous vendetta now threatened every newsman in St. Paul were soon erased when yet another attack made headlines.

* * *

Mrs. Mildred Ogilvie, whose late husband had insisted she keep the door to their apartment locked at all times, was glad she'd followed that advice when the shooting started in the early morning hours of June 11. Her apartment, in a fourplex just off Summit Avenue, was on the second floor. A short hall at the top of the stairs led to her unit and another one across from her door that had been rented only days earlier by Wilson Beverly of the *Globe.* The gunshots awoke her at two in the morning, and she waited for several anxious minutes before daring to get out of bed and see what the trouble was. She peeked through the peephole in her door and saw Beverly out in the hall with a revolver. Curiosity overwhelming any sense of danger, she cracked open her door and said, "Mr. Beverly, what has happened?"

"Why, someone just tried to kill me!" he said, speaking rapidly as he labored to catch his breath. "I think I might have winged him. I must call the police."

When the first patrolmen arrived, Beverly quickly spilled his story. He said he'd moved out of his Summit Avenue mansion and into the apartment after the attempt on Robert Stevens's life. He'd also sent his nervous wife to stay with her mother in New York for a few weeks as a precaution.

"I figured I'd be safe here, but obviously I was wrong," he said. "I was half-awake when I heard someone fiddling with the door. I got my revolver out, crouched down by the door, and demanded to know who was there. That's when two shots came through the door right over my head. I shot back, and then I heard someone running down the stairs. I don't mind telling you my blood was up and I went right out after the fellow. I saw him at the bottom of the stairs—there's a little lamp there that's kept on all night—and I took another shot at him."

"Did you see what he looked like?" one of the patrolmen asked.

"Don't I wish. All I saw was the back of him, but I can tell you he had on a black raincoat and a hood, just like that fellow that tried to kill Bob Stevens. I started going down the steps after him but then thought the better of it. What if he was waiting outside to assassinate me in the darkness? So I came back up the steps and that's when Mrs. Ogilvie next door asked what was happening."

Beverly began to shake, as though suddenly appreciating just how close he'd come to dying. "I don't know why I crouched like I did. I guess it was just instinct. But if I hadn't, you'd be looking at my corpse. I need a drink."

When Detective Patrick Donlin reached the scene, having been roused most cruelly from his early morning slumbers, he took a full statement from Beverly, who had by then steadied himself with several stout shots of bourbon. Beverly's statement matched the physical evidence. There were three bullet holes in the front door. Two came from the assailant's gun and were found lodged in a plaster wall inside the apartment. The other was from Beverly's .38-caliber revolver and had gone through the door in the opposite direction. Donlin also located Beverly's second round in a door-jamb at the bottom of the steps, indicating that he hadn't managed to wound the attacker.

After retrieving the bullets, Donlin asked Beverly, "Any idea who the shooter was or how he found out you're living here? I assume you tried to keep it a secret."

"Of course, but clearly I did a poor job of it. As to who the shooter was, I can say only that he was a large man. He was about the size of Wittemore, if you know him."

"So you think the doctor tried to plug you?"

"I have no proof of it. But as you must be aware, he's a very peculiar man and he hates the press with a vengeance."

"Yeah, I've heard that, only he ain't the only one who feels that way. I'll have a friendly little talk with him."

"You do that," Beverly said. "The sooner, the better. He frightens me."

* * *

Donlin was still up at ten o'clock when he contacted Wittemore by telephone and asked where'd he'd been at two in the morning.

"Sleeping, if that is any of your business," Wittemore said. "Why do you ask?"

When Donlin explained his reason, Wittemore responded with an angry outburst and hung up after stating in forceful terms that any further questions should be directed to his attorney.

Late that afternoon, after the *Globe* had published Beverly's histrionic account of the attack, Rafferty called Donlin. When he heard Donlin's weary voice on the other end of the line, Rafferty said, "I see by the papers that you had a long night of it. 'Twould seem the newsmen of this city now occupy a shooting gallery."

"Yeah, and ain't that too bad," Donlin said. "You could shoot the lot of them, for all I care."

"Someone is apparently trying to do just that," Rafferty said. "Tell me, if you would, exactly what happened at Mr. Beverly's apartment."

"The papers pretty much covered it all. Somebody tried to shoot him and he shot back. But he couldn't give us a good description of the shooter, so we are just waltzing around in circles at the moment. He offered up Wittemore as a suspect but didn't provide no proof. So I talked to the doc, and, guess what, he says he had nothing to do with it and told me his mouthpiece would speak for him from now on. Ain't that lovely?"

"Ah, you have my sympathies, Pat. 'Tis a hard task you have. But I do have one more question. Did you dig out those slugs that were fired at Mr. Beverly?"

"Sure. How come you're asking?"

"A trifling curiosity."

Donlin cackled. "Ha, I don't believe that for a minute. But if you want to know, they were .41-caliber slugs, just like the one Pickett took in the noggin. Can't be a coincidence."

"No," Rafferty agreed. "It can't."

5

FIRE AND FEAR

Two nights after the attempt on Beverly's life, in the pre-dawn calm of a Monday morning, a fire broke out at the old Bellaire Hotel. By the time a man on his way to work spotted the blaze and called in the alarm, flames were already shooting out the windows and up through the roof. The first pumper crews arrived within minutes and began pouring in water, to little avail. The building's wooden floors and beams provided rich fuel for the fire, which quickly consumed the structure and most of its contents.

"She's a goner," Assistant Fire Chief Billy McNamara declared when the roof collapsed, raining down debris. It took four hours to bring the fire under control, by which time only the lower stone walls remained. Once the ruins were finally cool enough to inspect, McNamara circled around the building and discovered an empty kerosene can just inside the rear door off the alley. A second can was found nearby, leaving little doubt that an arsonist had started the fire.

As fire crews mopped up, members of the city's Insurance Patrol sifted through the ruins, looking for anything of value that could be salvaged. But other than a few pieces of jewelry, including a gold pocket watch that had somehow survived the conflagration, there was little to be found. Surprisingly, the building's owner, whoever he or she was, never arrived to inspect the damages, as would have been expected, and so the salvaged items were removed to the patrol's offices until someone claimed them.

Reporters from the city's three major newspapers showed up at the scene, Dolly Charbonneau among them. She'd made some interesting discoveries about the old hotel after Pickett had asked her to look into its recent history. Now, it was gone—in a fire that, according to McNamara, had been set—and Charbonneau's suspicions began to deepen, for she believed the Bellaire held a secret that was tied in some way to Milton Pickett's murder.

Her story the next morning said the Bellaire had "most recently been used for storage," even though Charbonneau knew that wasn't true. In fact, she'd learned from city records that a private club had purchased the building and renovated it a few years earlier. She didn't yet know the name or purpose of the club, or why it had been of such interest to Pickett, but she intended to find out.

* * *

As the ruins of the Bellaire Hotel still smoldered, Rafferty walked over to the offices of the *Globe* to pay a call on Wilson Beverly. The newspaper occupied a ten-story building on Fourth Street that had been the city's tallest until the *Pioneer Press*'s new quarters rose even higher on the downtown skyline. Beverly's office was on the top floor, and it was there, after an uncomfortable ride in one of the building's bobbing hydraulic elevators, that Rafferty found the editor seated in his office behind a broad flat-top desk.

In Rafferty's experience newsrooms were usually monuments to clutter, but Beverly's tidy desk gave no hint of disarray. A photograph of his wife, Eloise, a Summit Avenue socialite who'd brought money and status to the marriage, occupied one corner of the desktop. The only other item on the desk was a small plaque that commemorated the opening of the Globe Building three years earlier. Other memorabilia were scattered on shelves around the office along with piles of yellowing newspapers, books, and a feathered Cheyenne lance that Rafferty later learned had been a gift to the newly founded *Globe* from George Custer just before he set out for the wilds of Montana.

Rafferty knew Beverly only slightly. A small man not much over five-foot-five, Beverly was about fifty years old, with a slender frame, a fine swatch of sandy hair, and pale-blue eyes. Rafferty thought he would have made a good cavalryman in his day, so long as he didn't find himself following Custer into splendid oblivion. Beverly had come from somewhere out east and worked at the *New York Herald* before migrating to St. Paul. He'd joined the *Globe* as a reporter but quickly rose to the position of editor by virtue of his sharp intelligence and knack for finding good stories.

"Mr. Rafferty, I see you are making the rounds," Beverly said as he stood up from his desk and extended a hand. "Mr. Pyle tells me you are now officially on the case, as it were. Have you found out much so far?"

"I fear I have no big news to report. How are you faring after all the excitement at your apartment?"

"It was the O.K. Corral, wasn't it? I regret that I'm a poor shot or I might have at least winged the fellow. But he knows now that I intend to stand my ground."

"Still, you must take great care. I'm told Mr. Stevens at the *Dispatch* has gone into hiding since his encounter with the gunman. You do not seem quite as fearful."

"Well, I don't know that I'm any braver than Bob, and I don't mind saying I'm frightened. But I doubt the shooter will try to have at me again here."

"'Twould be most unlikely," Rafferty agreed. "Now, as I understand it, you told the police that Wittemore is the man you suspect of attacking you."

"I did. Trouble is, I didn't get a good enough look to identify him, but he was certainly about the same size as the doctor."

"So you must think the doctor was mad enough about that story involving the nurses to kill Mr. Pickett and then go after you and Bob."

"Yes, that could have been his motive, but there may be another one as well. Now, what I am about to tell you must remain confidential for the time being. Will you agree to that?"

"I will."

"Then you should know that Wittemore is not only a skirt chaser. He also has a serious drug addiction, one that could soon lead to his dismissal from St. Luke's Hospital."

"Ah, Mr. Pyle mentioned that in passing when I talked to him earlier. Do you suppose the doctor has succumbed to opium?"

"Cocaine, Mr. Rafferty, cocaine. I have it from an unimpeachable source that he regularly injects himself with a seven-percent solution of that stimulant, after which he becomes highly agitated and extremely unpredictable. I need not tell you how disastrous that could be for a man who is a surgeon, not to mention his poor patients. Indeed, I believe he was under the influence of the drug when he came charging in here to protest our story about his behavior toward the nurses. He seemed dangerously out of control. I damn near had to defend myself with that ceremonial lance behind you."

"That would have been quite a story for your newspaper. Is the *Globe* now preparing to expose his unfortunate addiction?"

"Not yet, but I have Mr. Pyle looking into it. If we can gather sufficient evidence, it will be quite a story."

"And does Wittemore know what you're up to?"

"I think he does, and that's why he came after me."

"What about the other newspapers? Do you believe Mr. Pickett was murdered because the *Pioneer Press* was working on a similar story?"

"That I cannot say, but it certainly seems possible. For all I know, Bob over at the *Dispatch* may also have been aware of the doctor's nasty little habit."

"Well then, I guess I will have to have a talk with the doctor," Rafferty said.

Beverly looked past Rafferty's shoulder toward the busy newsroom, where a huge wall clock reigned as the god of deadlines. "Oh dear, I think I'm already late for a meeting. I doubt there is much else I can tell you in any event. But do let me know at any time if I can be of further help."

On his way out of the newsroom, Rafferty spotted Pyle and stopped by his desk to say hello.

"I see you were chatting with Bev," Pyle said. "Any news to report?"

"Ah, that is your business, Joseph. As for me, I fear I am a spinning top, going round and round to no great effect. Something is off about this whole business. I am in need of a mighty clue."

"And where do you hope to find it?"

"Somewhere back at the beginnings—that craziness with the sign and then Mr. Pickett's murder. I have already talked with half the newsmen in St. Paul, and learned very little, so perhaps the time has come to talk to a newswoman."

6
THE BELLAIRE MYSTERY

AMONG ST. PAUL'S SCRAPPY NEWSHOUNDS, thirty-year-old Dolly Charbonneau was the sole woman. How she'd come to win a place in the *Pioneer Press* newsroom was the subject of much salacious speculation by her glandular male colleagues, many of whom preferred to believe she'd risen from a job as a clerk in the circulation department to her position as a reporter by luring Milton Pickett into bed. The truth was far more interesting.

While Charbonneau was not averse to male company when it suited her, a rather dry old stick like Pickett was hardly her type. Moreover, he'd never made so much as a glancing pass at her. Instead, he'd always treated her fairly, without any of the usual leering male behavior. He was that rarest commodity in the newsroom—a true gentlemen—and Charbonneau viewed him as a second father.

Charbonneau had become a reporter by means of a bold initiative. Tired of the dull routine of clerking, she decided on her own to interview the wife of a man charged with a gruesome murder. The woman had avoided the press up until that point, but Charbonneau, who had a gift for drawing people out, won her over. Charbonneau then worked all night to produce a story so heartbreaking that when she handed it to Pickett, unsolicited, he knew immediately that he'd found a hidden gem. He hired her on the spot, and she quickly produced one big scoop after another, earning a reputation as the newspaper's best reporter.

Although not a great beauty by the standards of the day, her features—including wide-set hazel eyes, a delicate but slightly crooked nose, high cheekbones, sensuous lips, and a dimpled chin—were quite distinctive, as was the thick mass of blond hair that ran down past her shoulders. She was also hard to miss in a crowd, since she stood just two inches shy of six feet. Men of all kinds liked talking and flirting with "the Amazon," as they called her behind her back, unaware of how cleverly they were about to be interrogated. Charbonneau was also a quick and colorful writer, with a sharp eye for telling details.

Pickett's murder had deeply shaken Charbonneau, and she couldn't help thinking it was somehow related to her last conversation with him, when he'd asked her to find out who owned the old Bellaire Hotel. A visit to the recorder's office at the county courthouse revealed that the building was owned by an entity called the Downtown Amusement Corporation, which turned out to be a shell floating in a pea soup of legal obfuscation. But she did discover that the corporation had purchased the building in late 1886 from Lemuel Thatcher. And when Charbonneau checked building records, she found that the former hotel had undergone extensive renovations in 1887 "for use as a private club."

But what kind of club was it and why had Pickett been so interested in it? Just before the club was destroyed by fire, Charbonneau went to take a look at the building. Despite its euphonious name, the Bellaire had ended its hotel days as a flophouse offering wire cages at fifty cents a night. From Third Street, the old hotel looked vacant, its front doors locked and boarded over. Charbonneau walked around to the back of the building, where a walkout basement opened onto an alley. A surprisingly elegant door sheltered by a red canvas canopy gave access to the basement and appeared to function as the main entrance. Charbonneau knocked on the door but received no response.

After the fire, Charbonneau tried to question Thatcher about the Bellaire, but he simply shook his well-bearded head and told her to get out of his office. Charbonneau kept on digging, however, and she finally managed to pry some information out of a source at the police department. "That joint was a private sex palace for rich men," the source told her, "but don't be foolish enough to think anybody will talk to you about it. Many palms have been well greased."

Charbonneau now began to understand why Pickett had sent her out to investigate the old Bellaire Hotel. Clearly, he'd learned something about what was going on there. If the place had indeed been transformed into a "sex palace," then Pickett must have been working on what was sure to be a shocking exposé. Had that story in the making cost him his life? Charbonneau thought it possible. Her next step would be to find out who belonged to the club, since a scandal without names was really no scandal at all, especially when it involved sex and murder.

* * *

Charbonneau was still puzzling over the club and its possible connection to Pickett's murder when she accepted an invitation to join Rafferty and Thomas for a late lunch at the saloon three days after the fire at the old Bellaire. With her own investigation stymied, she decided to share what she knew with her hosts. She recounted her last talk with Pickett and her efforts to learn more about the hotel turned private club, including her fruitless contact with Lemuel Thatcher and the revelations from her police source.

"The place was more or less a private brothel, and there must have been some big money behind it," she said. "The renovations cost twenty thousand dollars, according to the building permit."

"A man could build four or five very nice houses for that," Rafferty said. "Well, I confess I knew nothing about the club. Its members did a remarkable job of keeping it a secret. Have you identified any of them?"

"Not yet, but I think Mr. Pickett must have been getting ready to name names."

"And now he's dead," Thomas said. "Do you think one of the members murdered him?"

"It could be," Charbonneau said. "Mr. Pickett was always ready and willing to expose scandalous behavior. Within reason, that is."

"What do you mean?" Rafferty asked.

"I mean there are untouchables in this city when it comes to scandal because taking them on would be like looking down the barrel of a cannon, only the kind that shoots out lawyers instead of shells. You'd be surprised how easily the *Pioneer Press* could be bankrupted or silenced by someone with sufficient means. But I have to tell you, I have trouble believing the high-and-mighty sorts who established the club would have resorted to murder. They'd just have gone to Mr. Whiting to quash the story. It's happened before."

"I do not doubt it," Rafferty said. "Do you know that Mr. Whiting hired me to investigate Mr. Pickett's death?"

"Did he? That's interesting. I wouldn't trust him if I were you."

"Good advice, I'm sure. The question now is how we go about finding Mr. Pickett's killer."

"Well, I've been dogging the coppers, and for the record they are still saying some lunatic who has it out for all the newspapers killed him and then took those potshots at Beautiful Bob and Bev," Charbonneau said. "But if that crazy man also belonged to the club, then maybe it all starts to make sense. I guess I'd still put my money on Dr. Wittemore. I assume you've heard about the big row he had with Mr. Pickett over that story we did about his amorous adventures at St. Luke's. Maybe the tender flesh of young nurses wasn't enough to satisfy the old goat, so he joined the club for more thrills. The doctor is as creepy as they come and maybe even a little mad."

"Why do you say that?"

"I've heard he just acts like a bug-eyed crazy man sometimes. Goes off into sudden screaming rages, that sort of thing. There are whispers he's using drugs of some kind, but I don't know that for a fact. And, of course, he thinks he sits at the right hand of the Almighty, right next to you-know-who."

Rafferty said, "Ah, he is not the only man who believes that, and he may be disappointed to find he is seated in a hotter place when the time comes. But you are right in thinking he is a good suspect."

"Have you talked to him yet?"

"I am biding my time," Rafferty said. "I doubt he'll be co-operative, so I must play my hand carefully. I need to know more before I can confront him."

Later that afternoon, Rafferty called David Whiting to provide an update on his progress. He then asked the publisher if he knew of any reason why Pickett would have been looking into the activities of a private club that had operated in the Bellaire building.

"Never heard of the club and don't know a thing about that," Whiting said. "Just keep your focus on Wittemore. I am more certain than ever he's our man."

* * *

That evening Robert Stevens made a surprise appearance at Rafferty's saloon, the latest edition of the *Dispatch* tucked under one arm. The editor wasn't a regular patron, and Rafferty hadn't seen him in recent weeks. But when he did stop in, he usually had plenty to drink and plenty to say. Dressed in his usual finery, Stevens headed straight to the bar, where Rafferty and Thomas were busy serving a motley array of eager imbibers. He placed the newspaper on the bar, spread it out, and scanned it with a rueful expression.

"I have found that hiding out like some twitching bunny rabbit does not suit me," he said as Rafferty came over to greet him. "It is also unfathomably dull, so I have decided to resume my usual endeavors, danger be damned. Besides, that fellow who tried to assassinate me was a lousy shot, so I think I'll be safe enough."

"Ah, but what if he proves a better shot the next time around?" Rafferty said. "You were fortunate to survive your encounter with the gunman, as was Mr. Beverly. Your luck will continue here. The drinks are on the house. What will it be?"

"Bourbon," Stevens said, "and please do not stain its heavenly purity with the sin of soda. Your generosity is much appreciated, and I do indeed count myself fortunate to stand before you unventilated by lead. But it was a near thing."

"So it seems. Then again, I have more than once seen a desperate shooter miss at close range in the excitement of the moment."

After Rafferty poured a generous shot of Kentucky Owl, Stevens took a sip and said, "Well, I do not intend to rely solely on luck if I am attacked again. You see, I have a companion that will now accompany me wherever I go." Stevens pulled back his coat to reveal a revolver holstered under his left arm. "Colt double-action and brand new. The fellow over at Kennedy Brothers said it will take a man down just fine."

"That it will if you hit him in the right place. But let us hope it doesn't come to that."

"Agreed. And that's why I stopped by tonight. I want to head off any more trouble, particularly of the kind that involves someone trying to put me six feet under. Imagine the disappointment of our dear readers if that happened."

"Not to mention yours."

"Amen to that. Now, I understand you're looking into Mr. Pickett's most lamentable murder and all the, shall we say, interesting events that have followed. It is well known you are a much better detective than anyone in our beloved police department, which seems to exist largely to give otherwise unemployable men jobs. I am here to ask if you could keep me informed as to any progress you're making. My life could depend on it."

"Well, I would disagree with you at least a little about the police. Pat Donlin is a good detective, and you would do well to stay in touch with him."

"Fair enough. I will do so. But could I also rely on you to tip me off as to what you're learning in your investigation? If I have some reliable information as to who killed Mr. Pickett, I could take appropriate precautions. The betting money, as you probably know, is on that butcher Wittemore, who has no love lost for men of my kind."

"Do you think he's the man who killed Mr. Pickett and shot at you and Mr. Beverly?"

Stevens shrugged. "Maybe, but who can say? There are a fair

number of men in St. Paul who would not shed tears over my death, or Bev's for that matter. I have found that even a whiff of bad publicity is enough to unhinge some people. So what will it be, Mr. Rafferty? Will you help me out in my hour of need?"

Rafferty wasn't sure what to make of Stevens's request. Was he genuinely concerned about his own well-being, or was he simply looking for a source so that the *Dispatch* could get ahead of its competitors as the Pickett murder case unfolded? Rafferty posed the question to Stevens.

"Well, I will admit that preserving my hide is of great interest to me, but it would also be marvelous if we could beat our rivals to the punch with an exclusive story or two. We would pay well for any exclusive information you could pass on."

"If I have reason to believe you are in immediate danger, I will certainly let you know," Rafferty said, "but as the *Dispatch* is not my client, I cannot promise to provide the kind of information you seek."

Stevens nodded and said, "I thought you would say so. Indeed, I hear your client is Mr. Whiting at the *Pioneer Press.* A good man, David, but not always easy to deal with, don't you agree? Well, I will bother you no more. But if you do happen to nail down a firm suspect and you wish to apprise me of that fact, I promise I won't print any news of it in the *Dispatch* unless I have your permission to do so."

"I will keep that in mind," Rafferty said even as he began to wonder whether Stevens's motive for seeking help wasn't really about self-preservation but something far more sinister.

7
ANYTHING GOES

ALTHOUGH THE GOOD VICTORIANS of St. Paul were reluctant to talk about sex, they practiced it enthusiastically, and by the early 1890s the city was home to a dozen or more brothels, ranging from panel house dives where a man's wallet disappeared with his pants to opulent sporting palaces frequented by some of the city's leading men. But men of wealth and influence often found it disagreeable to patronize brothels, even those as elegant as Nina Clifford's, for there was always the chance that some untoward incident might expose them to public opprobrium.

So it was that two men of means decided to establish a secret club, hidden from the fierce prying eyes of decency, where the unruly demands of the flesh could be satisfied in a secure environment. The partners launched their enterprise by purchasing the Bellaire Hotel, which they believed to be a perfect place for their secret enterprise. Next, they began a quiet recruitment campaign targeted at wealthy men of their acquaintance. In a matter of months they found ten men who each agreed to pay an upfront fee of one thousand dollars to join the club. The proceeds were used to refurbish the hotel into a luxurious accommodation that opened, to no fanfare, late in 1887. The partners also took their pleasure at the establishment, which they called the Anything Goes Club.

Designed as a playground of the senses, the club featured an elegant suite with a private bath and oversized bed, several rooms for "female guests," a small kitchen for preparing meals, a well-stocked bar, and a lounge where a member and his escorts for the evening could relax in whatever state of attire suited them. A doorman and a bartender, both imported from Chicago, served at the club, and there was also a porter to clean up after the night's festivities. House rules permitted only one member at a time to use the club, which opened at eight o'clock in the evening and was often booked several weeks in advance. However, the club was always closed on Sundays, when its members could be found in the front pews of their churches, singing holy hosannas with their families.

One of the founders served as the chief procurer, hiring prostitutes from Chicago so as not to raise the hackles of St. Paul's madams. The other founder played a more shadowy role but did provide what he called "erotic plays" by which the members could act out their fantasies. With titles such as "A Night in the Dungeon," "Naughty Schoolgirls," and "De Sade's Delights," the plays proved so popular that club members constantly asked for new ones. The "actresses" in these roles were often only in their early teens, for the club members preferred "tender young flesh," as the procurer liked to say.

The police were well aware of the club from the start but saw no reason to interfere with its peculiar business, since the owners contributed with uncommon generosity to the Patrolmen's Benevolent Fund. They also endowed a more personal charity maintained in Chief Michael Gallagher's pocket. Keeping the press in the dark posed more of a challenge, but the founders were up to the task, and there had been no hint of a public scandal until Milton Pickett apparently got wind of what might be going on.

But with Pickett dead and the club reduced to ashes, the founders believed their secret was safe. True, Dolly Charbonneau was digging around, but what could she really hope to find out? The club's members, for obvious reasons, wouldn't reveal anything, nor would the doorman and bartender, who'd been paid handsomely for their silence before being sent back to Chicago. As for the hired prostitutes, they would be all but impossible to trace in the dusky netherworld of Chicago's notorious Levee District.

"We are in the clear," the club's procurer said to his partner the day after the fire. "All the evidence is gone and no one will ever be the wiser, not even that nosy Charbonneau woman."

But the procurer was wrong. What he didn't know was that another member of the local press corps—a disreputable character who enjoyed nothing more than mucking around in the ooze of sexual scandal—had also taken an interest in the old Bellaire Hotel.

* * *

The *Saintly City Tattletale* was a weekly gossip sheet no respectable man or woman in St. Paul would ever admit to reading, though many in fact did. It was run by an obnoxious little snoop named Monroe Harding, who prided himself on being a sharp pebble in the shoes of the city's high and mighty. Rumor, innuendo, and the occasional minor scandal were the *Tattletale*'s standard fare, but a sensational story that appeared in the June 21 edition shocked even the paper's regular readers.

Beneath a 72-point headline that read BURNED HOTEL A PRI-
VATE RESORT, the story stated that the "resort" was a high-toned
brothel where "rich gentlemen cavorted in sybaritic splendor
with numerous women of dubious repute." The *Tattletale* went on
to report that the establishment, "called the Anything Goes Club,
was owned and operated by a syndicate of men whose names are
well known in St. Paul as they are members of the city's financial
and social elite." The tone of the story suggested Harding knew
who the men were, even though they were not named. Numerous salacious details enlivened the story, which claimed "baccha-
nalias" had occurred regularly within the club's "lushly furnished
quarters."

The story, so titillating that the *Tattletale* sold out its entire printing within an hour, produced outrage in all the usual places. Priests
and ministers thundered from their pulpits that St. Paul was clearly
turning into Sodom and Gomorrah, although one wag remarked
that the latter might actually be across the river in Minneapolis.
Mayor Thomas Reagan called the story "deeply disturbing" and
promised to consider "a full-scale police investigation," which
somehow failed to materialize. Meanwhile, the city's best-known
scourge, an eccentric Summit Avenue millionaire named Ambrose
Harriman, penned a scathing letter to the *Tattletale* in which he
described the club's unnamed members as "scum who dine on the
dirt of depravity with their silver spoons."

Rafferty, who read the *Tattletale* religiously, had a more mea-
sured reaction to the story. Being rich was all about getting what
you wanted, and it came as no surprise to him that a group of
wealthy men craving sexual adventure had used their money to
buy unorthodox forms of satisfaction. Nor was Rafferty surprised
that the club had managed to operate so long without notice. He
assumed the members had paid off the police and anyone else who
might have objected to the club's activities.

Still, Rafferty wondered how the *Tattletale* had obtained its ex-
plosive information. He put the question that evening to Billy Mc-
Namara, who'd stopped by the saloon for a beer and a chaser. The
assistant fire chief was always well informed about the goings-on

at city hall, having secured his own post through political connections, and few rumors escaped his attention.

"Of course I heard talk about the club," he told Rafferty, "but there wasn't much to it. Word was that the big boys who ran the place paid top dollar to preserve their privacy, and money speaks as loudly here as anywhere else."

"And yet Mr. Harding somehow found out about it."

"So he did. Somebody must have tipped off the little guttersnipe. But who it was I can't say. He'd better watch himself, though. The big boys play for keeps, and they can't be happy with him at the moment."

"Ah, I'm sure they are not. Now, one more question, Billy. Was anything at all found in the burned-out building?"

"You mean other than those kerosene cans? I don't think there was much. I heard the fellows from the Insurance Patrol dug out a few pieces of jewelry. There was a nice pocket watch, some sort of commemorative thing, but nothing else of great value."

"That does not sound promising, but maybe I'll have a chat with them when I get around to it. I am scrounging for clues of any kind at the moment."

"Well, good luck," McNamara said. "The big boys are very good at keeping their secrets."

* * *

The next morning, a gray Sunday, David Whiting was on the phone and he wasn't happy. "You have not been in touch with me for three days," he told Rafferty in his usual imperious way. "What have been doing with my money?"

"I have been investigating, as you asked me to."

"How delightful to hear that. Now, perhaps you would be so kind as to tell what you have found out. I do not like being left in the dark. As I have told you repeatedly, I must know everything you do. Is that not clear to you by now?"

"It is," Rafferty said, "but I fear I have little new to report. I am looking at many possibilities and you will be the first to know if I am able to identify Mr. Pickett's murderer."

What Rafferty didn't say was that he'd always been reluctant to share his thoughts while investigating a case with anyone other than Wash Thomas, his one true confidant. Theories were always bubbling in Rafferty's head and some of them, he knew, would turn out to be wrong. Clients—Whiting included—could easily jump to false conclusions if they knew everything on Rafferty's mind.

"You are stalling me," Whiting said, "and I do not like that. I have half a mind to demand my money back. But as you are the only horse I have at the moment, I must keep on riding you. Now then, what about this story in the *Tattletale*? Do you think any of it is true?"

"I would think Mr. Harding had some basis for his story, although he no doubt applied a few colorful embellishments," Rafferty said. "Am I to assume you believe the club had some connection to Mr. Pickett's murder?"

"How should I know? But if you find out anything along those lines, you must let me know at once."

"I will certainly keep you in mind," Rafferty said.

"You'd damn well better," Whiting said before abruptly hanging up.

Whiting wasn't the only newsman to take an interest in the club. Before long both Robert Stevens and Wilson Beverly got in touch with Rafferty to sound him out as to what he knew about the club and its membership. Rafferty replied honestly that he knew very little. But he found it interesting that Whiting and the two editors had suddenly become concerned about the club after ignoring its existence for three years. Had some monetary arrangements been made to keep the press quiet? Or was it simply a matter of fear, since the fancy cats who belonged to the club undoubtedly had legal claws sharp enough to threaten any newspaper.

Yet one intrepid member of the Fourth Estate, Monroe Harding, had finally managed to peek behind the club's carefully constructed veil. How had he done it? Rafferty was eager to know, and so on Monday he walked over to the offices of the *Tattletale* to have a chat with the gossipmonger in chief.

8
THE TATTLETALE

MONROE HARDING was a gnome of a man, short and stocky, with a doughy face, large ears, heavily hooded black eyes, and, as one of his numerous enemies said, "the disposition of an angry wasp looking for someone to sting." Harding, however, was no outsider storming the walls of privilege to expose the unsavory doings of the city's elite. In fact, he knew all too well the social stratum he wrote about because he'd been born into it. The only son of a prominent corporate lawyer, he'd been raised in a Summit Avenue mansion amid the usual trappings of wealth. Yet he'd been a misfit from the start due to his unattractive appearance, angry demeanor, and high, squawking voice, and as he grew older, bitterness ate like a worm at his heart.

After his father died of a kidney disorder, Harding came into a substantial inheritance, which he immediately set to work squandering on drinking, whoring, and losing himself for days at a time in the dreamy haze of opium dens. A year later, Harding's beloved mother developed an aggressive cancer. She was gone within weeks, leaving Harding bereft.

He pulled himself together for her visitation, putting on his one decent suit and shaving for the first time in weeks. But when he went up to the casket to look at his mother's pale embalmed body, her dead eyes seemed to rebuke him, and he broke out in tears. The funeral that followed at House of Hope Presbyterian Church was sparsely attended, and Harding knew why.

His mother, lively and sharp-witted, came from a working-class family, and after her marriage she'd been tossed into a world far different from the one she was used to. She never felt at home among her rich neighbors and liked to make fun of them. "I am stranded among pompous grandees and their fur-bearing wives," she once complained to her son. "I can't stand the lot of them." They, in turn, viewed her as an uncouth interloper and, even worse, a gold digger, and few members of the Summit Avenue crowd bothered to show up for her funeral.

As Harding left the church he had a revelation. Why not take on the snobs and high hats who had no time for his mother and expose them for the rotten people he believed them to be? Thus, the *Tattletale* was born. It had taken a good chunk of his inheritance to establish the paper, which Harding knew would likely have a short life. "It is my icicle," he told people, "but it will inflict many painful wounds before it melts away." He was as good as his word, dishing out so many nasty stories that his first three issues produced a like number of libel suits. But with the mighty Rutherford Cuddleton defending him, Harding intended to stay afloat as long as he could before the law and bankruptcy shut him down.

Unlike the sort of misdeeds Pickett had made a point of exposing in the *Pioneer Press,* Harding concentrated on what he called "news from the boudoir." In so doing he regularly ran afoul of the local guardians of morality even as he built up a surprisingly robust readership. "Sex, sex, and more sex," he once jokingly suggested, was the message that should appear atop the paper's masthead. But as the word "sex" was known to cause fluttering hearts and fainting spells in certain quarters, he instead settled for a more restrained motto: "The Truth Behind Closed Doors."

* * *

Harding's office was on the upper floor of an old stone building on Third Street not far from the burned-out remains of the Anything Goes Club. Rafferty passed by the destroyed hulk on his way to see Harding. It seemed hard to believe the club had operated as long as it had without outside scrutiny, but as Billy McNamara had said, money could buy anything in St. Paul, including silence.

"Ah, it is good to see you," Rafferty said with his usual bonhomie when he strolled into Harding's office. "I trust all is well in the scandal business."

"Never better!" said Harding, who was working at his desk beside a big north-facing window. He wore rumpled clothes and a green visor to protect his eyes. The office was bare of decoration save for several framed letters mounted on a wall near Harding's desk. Rafferty had seen them before but looked them over again.

The anonymous letters promised Harding a dire fate. "I will take pleasure in putting a bullet in your head" read one of the milder missives. Another gleefully contemplated the removal and burning of his entrails. Several others suggested he would soon roast in hell, with Satan giving his case special, sulfurous attention.

"Isn't it nice to have such devoted readers?" Harding said. "Still, I'm guessing you did not come here to read my mail. There must be some other reason, although I can't imagine why you'd be interested in speaking with a poor ink-stained wretch such as myself."

"Ha, now, that is a lie, and here I thought you newsmen were supposed to tell the truth."

"Only if nothing better is available," Harding said with a crooked grin. "I suppose you are interested in the Anything Goes Club. Are you perchance investigating one of its distinguished members? If so, a little quid pro quo might be in order."

"That it might. So let me ask you a question. Are you aware that Mr. Pickett at the *Pioneer Press* was apparently investigating the club when he was murdered?"

Harding was not, and he received the news with great interest. "You have this on good authority, I take it."

"I do."

"Well now, isn't that a succulent tidbit! Makes you wonder if old Miltie took a bullet for his efforts, doesn't it?"

"It does," Rafferty said. "You have been given the quid, now I am looking for the pro quo. I am trying to connect the pieces of a big puzzle, beginning with that altered sign atop the Pioneer Press Building and proceeding to Mr. Pickett's murder and the attacks on Bob Stevens and Wilson Beverly. Somehow, it must all tie together, and the club could be the key. So I am wondering how you found out about it."

"You'll have to keep on wondering. I never reveal my sources. But I can tell you something of interest, provided you keep it a secret until a special issue of the *Tattletale* comes out on Wednesday."

"Fair enough. My lips are sealed until then."

"I will take you at your word. Now, as my exposé made clear, I have a source who is familiar—very familiar, I might add—with the operation of the club. This source has told me that a certain very prominent surgeon with a history of, shall we say, improper behavior was a charter member. I know the name of another member as well, and it is just a matter of time before I'll be able to identify the whole ugly lot of them."

"Ah, that will be quite the story. I look forward to reading it. Am I safe in assuming Dr. Wittemore is the surgeon in question?"

"I can make no comment in that regard, Mr. Rafferty, although I will say I have found that your assumptions are often correct."

Harding was a sly operator, and he began sounding out Rafferty for more information. "I hear Dolly Charbonneau's been looking into this business. I'm curious, have you by chance talked with her of late?"

"I have."

"So you've been busy, haven't you? How much does Dolly know?"

"I can't tell you that. Perhaps you should have a chat with her and compare notes."

"Perhaps I should. Of course, now that I've beaten her to the story, she'll just have to content herself with leftovers. Too bad. I like Dolly and wouldn't mind liking her even better, if you know what I mean. But there's no chance of that, is there?"

"Ah, a man never knows when he might have a lucky day," Rafferty said. "You can always dream."

"Yes," Harding said, staring out the window. "Dreaming is about all I've ever been able to do when it comes to women like her."

9

THE SURGEON

THERE ARE PEOPLE who move through life without doubt or introspection, so sure of themselves they can scarcely comprehend how others clinging to the high ledge of existence might regard falling as a distinct possibility. William Wittemore was just such a man, and when he operated to excise a cancer or repair traumatic damage, he was always perfectly confident that the etherized pa-

tient whose life lay in his hands would come out of the surgery better than ever. But if a patient died on the table, as happened with
bothersome regularity, he knew it was not his fault. Death was
God's work, Wittemore liked to tell the grieving relatives, and he
was no match for the Almighty.

Wittemore's certainty extended into every area of his life save
for one—the primal urgings of his libido. His wife had been unad-
venturous and even indifferent in the bedroom, so much so that
Wittemore separated from her after three stale years of marriage.
He then tried to satisfy himself via regular visits to brothels, but he
soon found it more exciting to seduce young nurses awed by his
magnetic presence. Wittemore saw no harm in such flings, even
though the hospital administrators were unhappy with him, especially after learning he'd had to arrange an abortion for one of
his conquests. But his longings gradually grew so dark and strange
that nothing seemed to satisfy his desires. So it was that when an
acquaintance put forth the idea of establishing a private club devoted to the fulfillment of sexual fantasies, Wittemore jumped at
the opportunity to become a founding member.

Then, out of the blue, had come the story in the *Pioneer Press*
about his behavior with the nurses. It was a vicious attack from
Wittemore's point of view, and he'd stormed into the offices of
David Whiting and Milton Pickett to express his displeasure. Not
long thereafter Pickett had received his lethal comeuppance, and
Wittemore saw no further trouble on the horizon. He was wrong,
as he discovered to his horror after a friend advised him to read the
latest issue of the *Tattletale*.

PROMINENT SURGEON, WEALTHY JOBBER BELONGED TO ANY-
THING GOES CLUB, read the headline. The story beneath said that
"a physician and surgeon known to many in this city was a leading
member of the club and served as its procurer." Another member,
the story claimed, was "the owner of a multimillion dollar jobbing
firm in the Lowertown wholesale district." The story didn't identify
either man but promised more revelations to come. "The *Tattletale*
is prepared to name names in its next edition, and they will come
as a shock to all of St. Paul."

The story touched off a frenzy of speculation among the chat-

tering classes. It didn't take long for Wittemore to rise to the top
of the list as the man most likely to be "the prominent surgeon"
mentioned in Harding's story. There was also much guesswork regarding the identity of the "jobber," but as St. Paul was home to
many wealthy wholesalers, no consensus emerged as to the most
likely suspect.

So rife were the rumors surrounding Wittemore that he was
forced to deny them when reporters from the daily newspapers
came knocking at his door. He claimed to know nothing of the
club and promised to sue Harding for libel if he continued to make
"false insinuations. This Harding fellow is a gutter rat and if need
be I will take every last cent he has and put him out of business
for good. St. Paul will be a better place once he is sent back to the
sewers where men of his kind belong."

"'Tis quite the tale," Rafferty told Thomas after reading Harding's exposé, "but I wonder why Mr. Harding is being so coy. He
must know that Wittemore belonged to the club. Perhaps he has
good reason to fear lawsuits if he starts naming names."

"Or he could be bluffing," Thomas said. "Who's to say he really
knows who the members were? Maybe he's just trying to sell more
papers."

"Well, I would not put it past him," Rafferty said, "and yet Mr.
Harding is the kind of man who has a way of finding out secrets.
He is a digger and I think he struck gold. The question is how he
knew where to dig."

"Someone obviously told him."

"Agreed. I doubt that any of the club members would have talked
to the likes of Harding, so where did he get his information? The
club surely required waiters, porters, barmen, and the like, and I'm
thinking one of them could have spilled the beans. That's where
you come in, Wash. I'd like you to start making inquiries among
the people you know who do the real work in this city. Somebody
may be able to tell you who was employed at the club."

"I can do that," Thomas said. "And what will you be up to?"

"I am feeling some pain in my knee," Rafferty said with a grin.
"Perhaps a doctor could help me out."

Now it was Thomas's turn to smile. "I hear Dr. William Wittemore is an excellent physician. You should see him as soon as possible."

* * *

Two days after the *Tattletale*'s exposé, Rafferty wheedled his way into an appointment with Wittemore. Although Rafferty had a huge circle of acquaintances, he'd never met the doctor, who belonged to that benighted class of men known to abstain from alcohol. When not performing surgeries, Wittemore worked out of an office in his spacious home on Laurel Avenue, and that's where Rafferty went for his appointment.

Like Rafferty, the surgeon was a big man, well over six feet tall, with broad shoulders, a well-sculpted face, surprisingly delicate hands, and hard gray eyes that matched the color of his hair. "I understand you are having some knee problems," he said when he came into the examination room and looked over Rafferty, who had been instructed to strip down to his underwear. "The first thing you need to do is lose some weight."

So much for bedside manner, Rafferty thought. "Ah, I am sure that would help," Rafferty said, "but I fear I am a slave to my appetites, like most men. Speaking of which, I am wondering what you will do now that the Anything Goes Club has been destroyed. Will you and your fellow club members find a new location?"

Wittemore stepped back and stared at Rafferty with the look of a man who'd just found a scorpion in his boot. "That is a lie! Who sent you? Was it that little sewer rat at the *Tattletale*?"

"No, Mr. Harding did not send me," Rafferty said, "but I do have a client. As you may know, I operate the saloon at the Ryan. As it so happens, I am also in the detecting business, which is why I've been asked to investigate the murder of Milton Pickett. You, of course, are the chief suspect in that unfortunate matter, or so the police inform me." In fact, the police had told Rafferty no such thing, but he doubted Wittemore would know that.

"That is utter nonsense," Wittemore said, glaring at Rafferty. "Now, leave at once before I throw you out."

"I fear I am of a size that does not make me easily thrown," Rafferty said, "so let us talk instead. You see, I don't know whether you killed Mr. Pickett. You certainly had a motive but then so did others. Still, it would appear that Mr. Pickett's murder is somehow linked to the activities at the Anything Goes Club. The manner in which you entertained yourself there does not interest me, but the identity of the club's members does. 'Tis possible one of them is setting you up as the guilty party, and I would hate to see a man of your stature go to prison for a crime he did not commit."

Wittemore fingered the stethoscope hanging around his neck as he considered a response. He opted for flat-out denial. "I know nothing of the club of which you speak, and I most certainly was not involved in the murder of that snake Pickett or anyone else."

"Come now, dissembling does not behoove a man of your stature," Rafferty said. "I have no doubt you were a member of the club, just as the story in the *Tattletale* suggested."

"So you are out to ruin me, is that it?"

"No, you seem to be doing that on your own. The philandering, the fits of rage, the cocaine."

"Cocaine? Why, that is another lie! I will not stand for it. Now, you will do me the great favor of putting on your pants and leaving at once. Otherwise, I shall call the police and have you ejected from this office." Yet as the doctor spoke, Rafferty caught a hint of concern in his implacable eyes.

"Well, I wouldn't want to be caught with my pants down, now would I?" Rafferty said, going over to retrieve his bright red slacks, which did not entirely match the rest of his colorful outfit. "But if I were you, Doctor, I'd be very worried. No matter what you say or do, the secrets of the Anything Goes Club are bound to come out, and then your reputation and that of your fellow members will be destroyed. But if you will admit the truth to me, I may be able to help you."

Wittemore's only response was to leave the room and slam the door behind him.

10
THE PORTER SPEAKS

MUCH OF ST. PAUL'S SMALL POPULATION of African Americans lived along Rondo Avenue and nearby streets in an old neighborhood just northwest of downtown. Although no law segregated St. Paul, it was understood that Blacks would be unwelcome in most other parts of the city. Among the neighborhood's many small businesses was an after-hours joint run by a bear of a man named Luther Jones, who kept the place decent with the help of two powerful "assistants." One was a .45-caliber revolver, which Jones always had on his person, and the other was a huge mastiff named Growler, whose bared teeth were generally sufficient to convince an obstreperous patron that leaving might be a wise idea.

Wash Thomas visited the establishment now and then, as did Rafferty, who considered Jones "the one man in St. Paul I would not care to tangle with." Following Rafferty's unproductive visit with Wittemore, Thomas stopped in to have a chat with Jones, who was well informed about everything and everyone in the Black community. After downing an alcoholic concoction of unknown provenance that scoured the lining his throat, Thomas asked Jones if he'd heard anything about the fire.

"Oh, I heard plenty," Jones said. "Do you know George Hall?"

"Sure. What about him?"

"Well, he worked there. Cleaned up after all those rich folks and their lady friends. Said it was a regular whorehouse. I guess if you got money, then whoring is supposed to be real elegant. I say it don't matter how fat your pocketbook is, whoring is still whoring."

"I can't argue with that. By the by, where's George living these days?"

"Big gray house just a block from here, corner of Farrington. Can't miss it."

* * *

The next morning, Thomas went to see Hall in his modest apartment on the second floor of an 1870s-vintage house that had already seen its best days. Hall's wife and two daughters had gone to help out at their church, and so the two men had the apartment to themselves. Thomas had known Hall for a decade or more and regarded him as an exceptionally honest, reliable man. Short but broad-shouldered, Hall was in his early forties, and like Thomas he belonged to several organizations that worked to advance the rights of African Americans.

"I stopped by Luther's joint last night, and he told me you worked at that burned-out club on Third Street," Thomas began as he and Hall enjoyed freshly made coffee at the kitchen table. "I'd be interested if you could tell me all about it."

"You and Shad must be up to something," Hall said. "More detective work?"

"That's right. Shad's been asked to look into the murder of that editor from the *Pioneer Press.*"

"And that has something to do with the club?"

"Maybe. Anyway, we're trying to figure out who belonged to the club besides Dr. Wittemore."

Hall set down his coffee and cupped his hands under his chin as though pondering a weighty question. After a long pause, he said, "There is something you should know. I wrote a letter after I quit my job at the club. I just couldn't stand it anymore, the way those men acted and how they treated those poor girls. It was a sin against God. So I wrote the letter, thinking maybe somebody could put a stop to it."

"What sort of letter?"

"The anonymous kind," Hall said. "I'll show you. I sent copies to all the newspapers—the *Pioneer Press,* the *Globe,* the *Dispatch,* and the *Tattletale.* But the *Tattletale* is the only one that did anything with it."

Hall left the room and returned moments later with two sheets of paper. "You can read it for yourself."

The letter, addressed simply to "Dear Newspaper Editor," described in nauseating detail the activities at the club and said ten "wealthy men" belonged to it. But what made the letter a potential bombshell was that it named William Wittemore and Harley Calhoun as "known members" of the club. The letter went on to state that Dr. Wittemore and a partner who called himself "Gordy Bennett" founded the club and oversaw its operations. "Your readers, I'm sure, would be most interested to learn what terrible things certain big men in this city are doing," the letter concluded. It was signed "A Decent Man."

"Quite a letter," Thomas said after he'd finished reading it. "I can see now where the *Tattletale* got its big scoop, but I surely do wonder why the other newspapers ignored your letter."

"I guess maybe they just weren't interested," Hall said.

"Shad thinks maybe the rich fellows in the club paid off everybody and anybody to keep their dirty little secret. Now tell me, George, what exactly did you do at the club?"

Hall said he was hired as a porter, and it was his job to clean up the club every morning. "I don't mind telling you it was pretty disgusting work sometimes, but the pay was good. I'm not proud about it, but I got a family to feed just like everyone else."

"I understand. Did you know many of the club members?"

"Well, I usually worked in the morning, when most of the members weren't around, but I did run across three of them. One was that Dr. Wittemore. He was there once in a while during the day. He just ignored me, like I was a piece of furniture, but I recognized him from a drawing I saw in the newspapers."

"What about Calhoun?"

"Yeah, I met him once, and I hope I never do again. You know what kind of man he is."

Thomas nodded. "Oh yes, Shad and I know him. He doesn't have much use for Black folks. I think he's still mad the South lost the war. So how did you happen to meet him?"

"I guess he fell asleep after entertaining some ladies one night, and I found him half-naked in the club's lounge when I got there. He woke up and when he saw me he called me every ugly name he could think of. I remember he said, 'Don't you dare tell anybody I was here, or you will be done for. Do you understand that, boy?' I swallowed my pride and said I did."

Thomas said, "I'm not surprised. The man's a pig. Now, I'm curious about the Bennett fellow you mentioned. What do you know about him?"

"Not much, but it's probably not his real name anyway. From what I was told, a lot of the club members used aliases."

"Who told you that?"

"The doorman. His name is Ellis Peters. He'd sometimes be at the club in the morning, and we'd talk about this and that. Anyway, I got to asking him about the club, and Ellis wouldn't say much except that two partners ran the place. I figured one of them must be the doctor on account of he was around so much. Ellis told me the other partner went by the name of Gordy Bennett and was the real brains behind the operation."

"But Bennett wasn't at the club as often as Wittemore, I take it."

"That's right. I only saw him once. At least, I think it was him."

"How did that happen?"

"It was back in May. I was getting ready to leave the club one Saturday morning. Usually, I was gone before then, but somebody had made a really big mess the night before and it took me extra time to clean it up. I was just about to go out the door when a fellow let himself in with a key. I guess he was surprised to see me because he covered his face with his coat sleeve and looked down. I couldn't think of anything to do except say, 'Good morning, sir' and be on my way."

Thomas asked, "Why do you believe the man was Bennett?"

"Well, from what Ellis told me, most of the club members were never there during the day and, anyway, they didn't have keys. So I kind of figured the fellow I ran into must be Dr. Wittemore's partner, and that would make him Bennett."

"George, I do believe you have the makings of a fine detective," Thomas said. "Would you recognize Bennett, or whatever his name is, if you saw him again?"

"I think so."

"That could be helpful. Now, what about Peters, that doorman? Do you think he'd talk to Shad and me?"

"Maybe, but you'd have to find him first. I heard him and the bartender got paid off, very handsomely, and were told to leave town. I think they might be in Chicago. I know Ellis was from there."

"Did you get a payoff?"

"Nope. Somehow, the big men overlooked me when it came time to hand out the hush money."

"No surprise there. What about the fire? Any idea who set it or why?"

"So it was arson?"

"Looks that way."

"That's strange, isn't it? I guess somebody was worried, you know, that they'd be found out, so they just decided to burn the place down."

"You could be right. How about the women at the club? Do you know who they were or where they came from?"

"Ellis said they were all 'imported goods' from Chicago. I don't know how you'd track them down now. But I heard some of them were awful young, just kids really. Makes me mad just to think about it."

"I don't blame you. Do you know who procured the women? Was it Ellis?"

"No, he mentioned once that a club member made those arrangements. I got the impression it was Dr. Wittemore."

"What gave you that impression?"

"Ellis liked to joke around, and he said that the fellow supplying the ladies had performed his best operation yet, or something like that."

"Well, you've been a big help, George. I appreciate it."

"Thanks. But I have to tell you that working at the club sickened me. I'm no innocent babe when it comes to the ways of the world, but I never felt right about doing what I did. The money was good and that's why I took the job. I guess I'm just a whore, too."

"Don't be so hard on yourself, George. There's nothing wrong with trying your best to make a living. It's those men who are disgusting, not you. And, of course, you wrote that letter. Now that the *Tattletale* has seized on it, the whole sordid story is bound to come out. By the way, do you have a new job lined up?"

"Not yet, but I'm looking."

"Well, I'll bet Shad can be of help. He knows damn near everyone in St. Paul. Let's see what he can do. In the meantime, here's something for your trouble," Thomas said, fishing a five-dollar gold piece out of his pocket and putting it on the table. "And if you happen to remember anything else about the club, let me know."

Hall's letter was of great interest to Rafferty, especially because the city's daily newspapers had apparently done nothing to act on it. "'Tis a suspicious business," Rafferty told Thomas. "Your friend Mr. Hall offered up a fat, juicy scandal, and they didn't so much as take a bite."

When Rafferty called Stevens and Beverly, both claimed they'd never seen Hall's letter. "You know how it is," Stevens said. "We get dozens of letters a day. Maybe it just got misplaced or lost."

Beverly offered a similar explanation, adding, "I do wish I had seen it. We could have beaten the *Tattletale* to the story."

But what of the late Milton Pickett at the *Pioneer Press*? Had he received the letter? Rafferty called Dolly Charbonneau but she, too, claimed to be unaware of it. Yet the fact that Pickett had assigned Charbonneau to look into the club's building suggested that he had read the letter. But for some reason, he'd apparently decided to proceed very cautiously in investigating its disturbing allegations.

11
THE TEMPERANCE HOUSE

ON THE LAST DAY OF JUNE, Rafferty went to have a talk with Lemuel Thatcher, the proprietor of the Temperance House Hotel. Both the hotel and its proprietor were among the city's great curiosities. The four-story wooden hotel had originally been built in the 1850s at the bottom of a deep ravine that led down to the Mississippi River. Because of this novel arrangement, guests entered the establishment on its uppermost floor via a rickety bridge that spanned the ravine. "You must think of my hotel as a well of sobriety," Thatcher liked to tell his guests, "for in descending to your room you will escape the drunken corruption of the world above." The city, however, eventually decided to fill in the ravine, an inconvenience that Thatcher overcame by disassembling his hotel and rebuilding it on its new, elevated site.

A man of great energy and definite views, Thatcher operated his hotel in accord with its name. Every room contained not only a Bible but a wall hanging that enumerated the Ten Commandments along with an eleventh that read, "Thou Shalt Not Consume Alcohol on These Premises." At a time when men tended to either drink hard or not at all, Thatcher's establishment filled a righteous niche by catering to God-fearing abstainers who regarded whiskey as nothing other than Satan distilled.

Although approaching his eightieth year by 1890, Thatcher still attended shrewdly to his business interests and also preached occasionally at religious revivals. With his long beard, wild splash of white hair, and piercing dark eyes, he perfectly fit the role of an Old Testament prophet. His hatred of alcohol made him the enemy of all saloons, which he would sometimes burst into without warning to deliver thunderous orations on the manifest evils of demon rum. He'd even declaimed once at Rafferty's establishment. Afterward, Rafferty pronounced it "a very fine speech, except for the part about not drinking." He then offered a rousing toast to Thatcher's good health before escorting him out the door.

Thatcher's reputation as an upstanding Christian had suffered a blow when the *Pioneer Press* revealed his ownership of two downtown properties being used as brothels. Thatcher responded by attacking the "godless men" in charge of the newspaper and claiming he thought the two buildings were being used as boardinghouses for needy young women, an explanation no one believed. Now, it seemed Thatcher had owned what was left of the building where the Anything Goes Club had gone about its unholy business, and Rafferty wanted to know the names of his tenants.

The great teetotaler ran his business from a small office in the hotel. It was outfitted with file cabinets, a roll-top desk, and a lugubrious painting of Jesus on the cross with blood gushing from his crown of thorns. Hanging next to the suffering Son of God was a real estate map of downtown St. Paul, marked with pins that presumably indicated all of Thatcher's properties.

"Ah, Mr. Thatcher, how are you today?" Rafferty asked when he stepped into the office, where Thatcher sat at his desk in a plain black suit. "I trust drink remains a stranger to both you and this fine establishment."

"It does and shall forever be so," Thatcher replied, looking up at Rafferty. "What is it you want?"

Thatcher didn't offer a chair, but Rafferty took one anyway and pulled it up to one side of the desk. "I have been asked to look into the murder of Milton Pickett, and it has occurred to me that you are a likely suspect," Rafferty began. "After all, it is no secret that you hated both the man and his newspaper."

"You speak nonsense," Thatcher replied. "Murder is against God's law."

"So it is. And yet when that story came out in the *Pioneer Press* about you and those two brothels, you vowed retribution, did you not?"

"I vowed only that vengeance would come like a swift sword, as it will for all sinners in the fullness of God's time."

"So you didn't take up a pistol instead of a sword to kill Mr. Pickett?"

"I did not. You may leave now."

"I'll leave when I'm ready. I understand you own that old building on Third Street that burned down. Quite a loss. I trust you were well insured."

"That's none of your business."

"Perhaps not, but I am interested in what went on inside the building. I understand from reading the *Tattletale* that it was the scene of certain activities which might cause a good Christian man like yourself to blush."

Thatcher abruptly stood up and pointed at Rafferty as though identifying a criminal in a lineup. "I have nothing more to say. You are a sinner soaked in rum! Out with you!"

Rafferty didn't budge. "Perhaps I am a sinner, Mr. Thatcher, but that does not change the fact that you rented out the building to a group of wealthy men who used it to cavort with prostitutes. The property you own is your business and I make no judgment upon it. Murder, however, is another matter. I believe there is a connection between Mr. Pickett's murder and what occurred at the Anything

Goes Club. I would like you to tell me who belonged to that club. If you are kind enough to do so, I will see to it that your name does not come up again in my investigation."

"So it is blackmail, is that it?" Thatcher said, reaching into his desk. Rafferty sprang from his chair and grabbed Thatcher's hand before he could level up an antique derringer he'd taken from the top drawer. Rafferty was far stronger than the old man and easily wrestled the gun away.

"Why now, isn't this a prize," Rafferty said, studying the weapon with genuine amazement before breaking it open. "A National Arms derringer, .41-caliber. Haven't seen one of these in ages, and loaded, too. You must be careful, Mr. Thatcher, that you don't hurt yourself with this handy little weapon. Did you know, by the way, that Mr. Pickett was shot with a .41-caliber bullet? A mere coincidence, I'm sure."

"Get out!" Thatcher repeated.

"That is your choice. Of course, the *Tattletale* and every other newspaper in town will have their way with you soon enough. It is no easy thing to be exposed as hypocrite, and I have no doubt your business will suffer greatly as a result."

A tablet and pencil lay on the desktop. Rafferty tore off a sheet of paper and handed Thatcher the pencil. "You must have dealt with someone when making arrangements with the club. If I were to see that person's name written down right now, I would become very forgetful as to how it got there."

The prophet went silent, presumably consulting God as he stared first at Rafferty and then at the sheet of paper. He finally said, "How am I to know that a man of your low habits can be trusted to keep his word?"

"You may ask anyone who knows me. A man's word is gold, and I hoard it. I have no doubt the same is true of you."

There was another long pause as Thatcher considered what to do. Then, without a word, he scribbled something on the paper, folded it, and handed it to Rafferty. "I do not expect to see you again," he said. "Now if you would return my gun, we will be finished."

"I will leave it for you at the front desk," Rafferty said. "And if you ever wish to stop by my saloon again, it will be my pleasure to welcome you."

"Hell and its eternal fires await you!" Thatcher shouted.

"Perhaps, but I am inclined to think most men manage to find hell without leaving this world," Rafferty said. "Well then, good-bye, Mr. Thatcher, and Godspeed to you."

After dropping off the derringer, Rafferty took the sheet of paper from his vest pocket and unfolded it to reveal the name of William Wittemore scrawled in Thatcher's shaky hand. The name came as no surprise. What he read in the next day's newspaper did.

12

A PUZZLING SCENE

"YOU'LL BE WANTING TO SEE THIS," Wash Thomas told Rafferty as he came into the saloon just after noon bearing early editions of the *Globe* and *Dispatch*. "It looks like your investigation may be over."

MURDER SUICIDE, screamed the headline in the *Globe*. DR WILLIAM WITTEMORE KILLS NEWSMAN MONROE HARDING, TAKES OWN LIFE. The *Dispatch* went with DOUBLE DEATH ON THIRD STEET, PROMINENT PHYSICIAN SHOOTS NEMESIS, TURNS GUN ON SELF, DOCTOR MAY HAVE BEEN USING DRUGS. The stories that followed largely agreed on the basic facts. At seven in the morning a cleaning lady found the two bodies in Harding's office. Harding lay behind his desk, with two gunshot wounds to the chest, one bullet penetrating the heart and killing him instantly. Wittemore's body was face up on the floor about fifteen feet away with a bullet wound to the right temple and a revolver beside his right hand. A syringe was found in his coat pocket, seeming to confirm the rumors that he used cocaine and leading the police to suspect he'd been in "an agitated state" when he shot Harding and then himself.

When a detective was sent to search Wittemore's home, he found further evidence of the doctor's guilt in the form of dozens of copies of the fictitious *St. Paul Chronicle* stored in a file cabinet.

The detective made another discovery in Wittemore's home office. Deep indentations in the carpet indicated that a heavy object, almost surely a safe, had once rested there but had recently been removed. It didn't turn up anywhere else in the house, however, and the location of the missing safe remained a mystery.

Chief of Police Michael Gallagher quickly arrived at Harding's office to take charge of the investigation. As a patrolman, he'd acquired the moniker "Merry Mike" because of his unsettling habit of breaking out into laughter while dishing out discipline to some poor miscreant with his nightstick. There were those who thought Gallagher might be a "touch off," but his political instincts were razor sharp and he had risen effortlessly through the ranks to become chief. His gift for city hall maneuvering did not translate into investigative skills, however, and his own detectives dreaded Gallagher's appearance at the crime scene, knowing he would always jump at the supposedly obvious solution even if the weight of the evidence suggested otherwise.

So it had been when he walked into Harding's office and surveyed the carnage. "Well now, a murder-suicide if I ever saw one," he announced. "Isn't that the best kind of a crime? No fuss, no bother, and no need to bring someone downtown and pound the truth out of them. Yes, sir, I will take a murder-suicide anytime and be glad to have it." Gallagher's best detective, Patrick Donlin, wasn't so sure. Donlin had quickly spotted several puzzling inconsistences at the scene and argued for closer consideration of the evidence. Gallagher, however, wouldn't hear of it. "Case closed," he said. "Let us speak of it no more."

Gallagher, however, did love speaking to the press. "This is a tragic case," he intoned to a gaggle of reporters who rushed to Harding's office like blowflies drawn to a corpse. "Indeed, I have not seen another like it in all of my years. Dr. Wittemore was clearly a man obsessed and he took out his rage against Mr. Harding before turning the gun on himself. We believe he also murdered Milton Pickett and attacked the editors of the *Dispatch* and *Globe*." Yet Gallagher said nothing about the Anything Goes Club and offered only a vague motive for Wittemore's homicidal spree. "We know he was upset by recent publicity in the *Tattletale* that threatened to paint him in a bad light, and it must have been enough to derange him. Of course, I do not know if any of the accusations made against him were true. In any case, it does not matter now."

* * *

The chief's account came into question when Patrick Donlin stopped by Rafferty's saloon that night for a drink and, more importantly, conversation. They retired to Rafferty's office to escape the roistering hubbub of the saloon, where a man had to shout to be heard. Rafferty poured out two generous shots of bourbon from his private stock as Donlin settled into a chair.

"I am having trouble believing the official version of events," Donlin began. "I saw things in Harding's office that don't make no sense if it was a murder-suicide like Merry Mike is saying."

"Is that a fact? I am all ears, Pat. What didn't look right to you?"

"The biggest problem is that revolver Wittemore supposedly used. It was a single-action Smith and Wesson thirty-eight and we found it next to his body. But here's the strange thing: the hammer was cocked and ready to go. I ask you, how does a man who just shot himself in the head manage to cock the hammer of his gun again before he drops dead?"

Rafferty shared Donlin's bewilderment. "Ah now, that is a fine mystery, isn't it. The chief and the other detectives must have noticed it."

"Sure, and their explanation is that the first shot wasn't instantly fatal, so Wittemore must have cocked the gun again to fire a second time just before he died."

"Do you think that's possible?"

Donlin took a sip of bourbon and said, "About as possible as me flying to the moon on the back of a pig. What do you think?"

"Unless Wittemore's skull was made of iron, I agree. The chief seems to believe in fairy tales. I wonder why."

"Oh, I can answer that. Merry Mike is just protecting the swells, as he always does. Word has it that some very prominent men belonged to that sex club, or whatever you want to call it, and you can bet they have Merry Mike's ear. They would like the club to be forgotten, the sooner the better. With Wittemore and that pest

Harding out of the way and the club burned to the ground, every-thing gets neatly wrapped up and that's the end of it. Same with Pickett's murder. Merry Mike is sure the doc did it, and as far as he's concerned there's no more to be said."

Rafferty said with a grin wide enough to part his beard, "I am shocked to hear that our sainted chief of police would kowtow to powerful men, but I will get over it. Now then, Pat, what do you really think happened in Harding's office?"

"I can't be sure, but there were other things that seemed very peculiar to me."

"Such as?"

"For one, the position of Harding's body. We found him on the floor behind his desk, flat on his back, with his chair sort of off to the side. What I don't see is how he ended up there."

"Why is that?"

"Here's the problem. Harding was shot twice in the chest, and the slugs went all the way through him and lodged in the floor be-hind his desk. One of the bullets also nicked a back slat on his chair. So he had to be sitting when he was shot, and that means he would have slumped over in his chair, maybe with his head falling on the desktop. There was blood all over the chair and smeared on the desk as proof of that. But we don't find him in that chair. No, he's on the floor, laid out nice as can be like he's ready for the coroner to haul him away, and it just don't make sense to me."

Rafferty could see where Donlin was heading. "So I take it you're thinking the killer lifted Harding from his chair and put his body on the floor after shooting him."

"That's it," Donlin acknowledged. "What I can't figure out is why Wittemore wouldn't have moved the body if he was going to commit suicide anyway. What the hell difference would it make?"

Rafferty thought for a minute and said, "Maybe he moved the body so he could go through the desk drawers."

"Well, if he was looking for something, it wasn't on him when he supposedly shot himself. But just between you and me, Merry Mike found some papers in one of the drawers and stuffed them in his coat pocket without so much as saying a word."

"Ah, now that is interesting," Rafferty said. "Maybe Harding had a list of all the club members and the chief took it."

Donlin responded with a low whistle and said, "Now there's an idea. Of course, if Merry Mike has the incriminating goods, as it were, they'll never see the light of day. He'll just sell his silence for the right price."

"True enough," Rafferty said. "But let's get back to Harding's body. What if the killer was simply trying to hide it? Do you see where that leads? As you said, Wittemore had no reason to do anything with Harding's body if he planned to kill himself. Ah, but if someone else did the deed, and also murdered the doctor, then it all fits together. Harding is shot and his body is placed behind the desk so the doctor won't see it when he's lured to the office on some pretext. He finds someone else there—Harding's murderer—and then he's killed, with his death made to look like a suicide."

"Good Lord, you could be right," Donlin said. "And that actually makes sense because of where we found the doc. He was on the floor just inside the office, next to a little closet that's hidden by a drape. Somebody could have stepped out from behind the drape, shot the doc just after he walked into the office, and then tried to make it look like he committed suicide."

"'Tis a fine theory," Rafferty agreed, "but we are inconveniently lacking any proof of it."

"There's another problem. Why did this clever killer we're talking about leave the gun cocked? That wasn't a smart thing to do."

"It wasn't, but I can think of at least one reason why it might have happened. Maybe Wittemore was still moving a little or making some sounds after he was shot. I have seen such things happen even after a bullet to the brain. If that was the case, the murderer might have instinctively cocked the gun, thinking he'd have to shoot Wittemore again. But the doctor breathed his last soon enough, and when the killer put the gun down by his body, he forgot in all the excitement that it was cocked."

"Could be," Donlin acknowledged, "but I just don't know."

"Nor do I, Pat. I'm just looking for something that makes more sense than the story Merry Mike is peddling."

"Let's say you're right. If it wasn't a murder-suicide and Witte-more didn't kill Harding and Pickett, then who did?"

"I'm working on that, but I would be willing to bet that whoever is behind this bloody business was a member of the Anything Goes Club and will kill again if need be to protect his secret."

"What makes you so sure of that? I mean, Harding was a sleazy character who printed rumors all the time. Who's to say the doc really was in that club?"

"Oh, he was," Rafferty said. "The deceased Mr. Harding, may he rest in peace, did not always get his facts right, but in this case he did."

Rafferty then told Donlin about Hall's anonymous letter and how it had named Wittemore, Calhoun, and the mysterious Gordy Bennett as members of the club. He also recounted how Lemuel Thatcher had scrawled Wittemore's name when asked to identify the person he'd dealt with regarding the club.

"Well, ain't that interesting," Donlin said. "It would be nice, wouldn't it, to know who all the other club members were. Or do you already know and just ain't saying?"

"I don't know," Rafferty said truthfully, "but I'm trying to find out."

"Good, because I ain't. Merry Mike is through with the case and that means I am, too," Donlin said, raising his glass. "Let us have a toast to the truth. I've heard it exists somewhere."

"So it does, Pat," Rafferty said, clinking his glass against Donlin's. "No matter how hard it is to find."

"Well, maybe that safe held the answers," Donlin said nonchalantly

"What safe?"

"I guess I forget to mention it," Donlin said and went on to describe the carpet marks found in Wittemore's office.

"Ah now, that is most intriguing," Rafferty said. "Someone must have been very worried about the contents of that safe. And yet it would seem they didn't have the combination, so they took the whole thing."

"Or maybe the doc himself had it hauled away. Maybe it was just an old safe and he didn't have use for it anymore."

"I doubt it, Pat. If anyone ever needed a place to keep secrets, it was Dr. William Wittemore. No, I am thinking we have been beaten to the punch. Whoever we are after, he is a man who leaves nothing to chance."

13
HANDY JACK

THERE WERE MANY PLACES in St. Paul to purchase a revolver—virtually every pawnshop had a few for sale—but for a new gun Kennedy Brothers Arms Company was the dealer of choice. Long an institution in St. Paul, the company offered an unmatched selection of firearms and sporting goods. General George Custer often stopped by the store on his way west to check out the newest rifles and pistols, although his last visit in the spring of 1876 had not provided enough weaponry to save him from an unfortunate fate in the grassy hills above the Little Bighorn River.

Rafferty, who owned a substantial arsenal, knew the Kennedy brothers well, and a day after his eye-opening talk with Donlin he walked over to the company's store on Third Street to make inquiries. He wanted to know whether Wittemore had recently purchased a .38-caliber Smith and Wesson revolver of the kind he'd supposedly used to kill Harding and himself. But he hadn't, nor had anyone else, since single-action revolvers were already seen as old-fashioned. Rafferty had better luck when he asked a clerk about newly purchased .41-caliber Colt revolvers like the one used to murder Milton Pickett.

Two of the Colts had been bought not long before Pickett met his fate. Robert Stevens had purchased one of them in mid-May, which Rafferty found surprising. When Stevens had displayed a holstered weapon at the saloon, he'd left the impression that he'd armed himself purely as a response to Pickett's murder. Yet he'd actually bought the gun more than a fortnight earlier.

Later that afternoon, Rafferty reached the editor by telephone to sound him out about the revolver. Stevens denied he'd tried to mislead Rafferty about when the gun was purchased. "I merely mentioned that I started carrying it after Mr. Pickett's murder. I did not say when I'd bought it."

"True," Rafferty acknowledged. "But you didn't mention it was a .41-caliber Colt, the same type of revolver that was used to kill Mr. Pickett."

"Don't be silly. Why would I want to kill him?"

"Perhaps he found out you belonged to the Anything Goes Club and threatened to expose you."

"How could I have belonged to a club that I knew nothing about?" Stevens protested. "And even if I knew about that damn club, it wouldn't have interested me, as I have never paid for the company of women. I rely on my natural charms in that regard. If you must know, I bought the Colt because an angry husband threatened me with great bodily harm. I was at the time in his wife's bedroom, a most delicate situation, I think you'll agree. I made a narrow escape, after which I thought it wise to have some protection in the case of further trouble. That is all there is to it."

Could Stevens be believed? Rafferty wasn't sure, since he regarded Stevens as the kind of blustery, fast-talking man for whom lying came as naturally as breathing. In any event, his purchase of the revolver proved nothing. Bullets could rarely be traced to a specific gun in those days, and there were plenty of .41-caliber Colt revolvers circulating in the city. Rafferty owned just such a revolver himself.

Rafferty learned that the other Colt had been purchased at Kennedy Brothers on May 30, a week before Pickett's murder, by a rather disreputable-looking man who gave his name as Spencer Jackson. The name wasn't familiar, but when the clerk described the man, Rafferty knew his real identity at once. Jack Spence, known as Handy Jack, was St. Paul's most notorious hoodlum for hire. He offered a wide range of services ranging from strong-arm robbery to burglary to the collection of overdue gambling debts by means of bruising forms of persuasion. It was also said he'd committed at least two murders, although the police had never found enough evidence to put him behind bars.

Spence usually hung out at a cheap saloon on St. Peter Street, and Rafferty set out to find him there, only to learn that he'd apparently left the city. "I heard he went to Chicago yesterday," the saloon's proprietor told Rafferty. "Nobody seems to know when he'll be back."

The timing was suspicious, and Rafferty wondered whether Spence was somehow involved in the events of the past month. Had he been hired to murder Pickett and perhaps stage the deaths of Harding and Wittemore? It would certainly be the kind of dirty work Spence excelled at. But as to who might have hired him, Rafferty remained in the dark.

*   *   *

Spence, as it turned out, had been paid very handsomely to take a "vacation" in Chicago. The man who paid for the trip had hired Spence through an intermediary for several jobs, beginning with a midnight excursion to the roof of the Pioneer Press Building. The "sign job," as Spence called it, had been the easiest fifty dollars he and a helper ever earned. After that, another fifty dollars came his way for making certain threats at gunpoint. As Spence was accustomed to intimidating people, that job was also simple enough. But his third assignment, again for fifty dollars, entailed some hard physical labor of the kind Spence had spent a lifetime avoiding.

The job was to burgle a house, no challenge for a man of Spence's abilities. But it wasn't the usual sort of burglary. Spence's assigned task was to break into William Wittemore's home, plant multiple copies of the *Chronicle* there, and, most importantly, remove a safe from the doctor's office. Not by coincidence, Spence was told to undertake the job on the night Wittemore left for his fatal encounter with Harding.

There were no witnesses as Spence and a fellow criminal waited under cover of darkness outside Wittemore's house on Laurel Avenue. Once they saw the doctor leave, they gained entry to the home by picking a lock. After planting the evidence as instructed, Spence and his muscular assistant manhandled the two-hundred-pound safe out to a waiting wagon and hid it under a canvas tarp.

An hour later, they reached a spot on Water Street across the river from downtown, where they'd tied up a small boat. Sweating and cursing in the heat, for the night was very muggy, they wrestled the safe into the boat. After refreshing themselves with jolts of cheap whiskey, they rowed out to the middle of the Mississippi a mile or so upstream from the High Bridge and dropped their possession into the fast-flowing waters, never to be seen again.

The next afternoon, Spence was on his way to Chicago to lie low for a while. He wondered a little who'd hired him for so many strange jobs, but curiosity wasn't his strong suit. The money was all that mattered, and now that he had a nice stash of it in his pocket, he planned to spend his evenings in Chicago's Levee District, where the working girls were said to be exceptionally talented.

14
THE WIDOW

St. Paul's elite men gathered at the Minnesota Club, where they could read the latest financial news, make deals, eat dinner, and bemoan the intransigence of the working class, all the while blessedly free from the nagging presence of females. As a mere saloonkeeper, Rafferty was hardly a candidate for membership in the club, which occupied a substantial brick building on Fourth Street, but he did enter its inner sanctum now and then on business. Rafferty had learned that Harley Calhoun was a regular at the club, and it was there that Rafferty found him two days after the bloody doings at Monroe Harding's office.

Calhoun was ensconced in one of the plush chairs in the main clubroom, reading a recent edition of the *Wall Street Journal*. Even seated, Calhoun had the powerful, charged presence of an old bull eager to mate. Broad-shouldered, with a thick stub of a neck supporting his big bald head, Calhoun was known for his ruthless business practices and his racist views, which Rafferty had condemned in several letters to the newspapers. However, Rafferty had never actually met Calhoun before.

"Ah, Mr. Calhoun, I would like a moment of your time," Rafferty said. "It is a matter of some importance."

Calhoun looked up over his newspaper and said, "Who the devil are you?"

"Shadwell Rafferty at your service."

"Rafferty? You're the fellow who wrote those nasty letters about me, aren't you?"

"I would not call them 'nasty.' I was merely trying to enlighten you."

"Is that so? Well, I have no business with you. Go away."

"You might wish to hear me out, Mr. Calhoun. As it so happens, I am investigating certain matters concerning the Anything Goes Club, and as you were a member there, I thought you might be of help."

Calhoun folded up his newspaper, carefully set it aside, and said in an icy voice, "You are misinformed. Now, leave at once before I have you thrown out." Calhoun, who had been born and bred in the South and had fought for the Confederacy, still spoke with the hint of a drawl.

"Ah, as I told another man recently, I am not easily evicted. Nor am I, as you say, misinformed. The club and its affairs are no longer a secret, as you know, and it won't be long before even more of its dirty laundry is put out to hang in public view. When that happens, you may find yourself in a most uncomfortable situation. But if you were to—"

"If I were to what?" Calhoun said, rising from his chair and bumping up against Rafferty. "You are being insolent and I will not stand for it."

Few men in St. Paul were interested in starting a brawl with Rafferty, but Calhoun appeared to be one of them. Rafferty shoved back at Calhoun, and for a moment it looked as though the clubroom's stolid aura of wealth enjoying itself might be disturbed by the unseemly outbreak of a fistfight. But one of the club's usually silent attendants interceded, stepping fearlessly between the combatants. "Gentlemen, this will not do," he said. "Have you forgotten where you are?"

"I have not forgotten, but it seems Mr. Calhoun has," said Rafferty.

"This man is not a member," Calhoun said, glaring at Rafferty, "and he is not welcome here. Escort him out and do not ever let him return."

"I will be happy to leave," Rafferty told the attendant. "The air in here is stuffy and I do not care for it. But Mr. Calhoun will soon have much to regret, and I do not doubt the day will come when he is no more welcome here than I am."

"How did it go?" Thomas asked when Rafferty returned to the saloon.

"It did not go well. Mr. Calhoun had nothing to say and probably never will. I imagine he'll secrete himself behind a wall of lawyers if and when his activities at the club are exposed. But if he did kill to hide his secret, I have no proof of it."

"So where do you go next?"

"I have been thinking about that. 'Tis said hell hath no fury like a woman scorned, and I am hoping that might be true of Dr. Wittemore's widow."

* * *

Two days after William Wittemore's funeral, which was delayed because of the Fourth of July holiday, Rafferty telephoned his widow and asked if she would be willing to speak of the circumstances leading up to his supposed suicide. Jane Wittemore said she was more than ready to talk about "that man," so Rafferty went to see her at her residence. Although electric trolleys had recently been introduced in St. Paul, a cable car line still served much of the well-to-do neighborhood where Mrs. Wittemore lived. Rafferty caught one of the cars on Fourth Street and rode it up the steep Selby Avenue Hill to within a block of her residence on one side of a fine new double house.

When Jane Wittemore met him at the door, Rafferty was immediately struck by her appearance. She was pale and delicate, with skin resembling bone china, short gray hair, and eyes of the same color. Compared to her bluff and hearty late husband, she seemed as insubstantial as a ghost, and Rafferty wondered how the two of them had ever gotten together. But now they were apart for good, a fact that did not seem to trouble Mrs. Wittemore, who turned out to possess a surprisingly forceful character.

"You should know I have gone back to using my maiden name, which is Thompson," she announced after ushering Rafferty into a parlor adorned with outsized vases and potted plants. "There is no honor in that man's name, and I no longer wish to be associated with it in any way. I do not even wish to utter it. Do you know I tried to divorce him but he would not allow it? So I moved out and told him he must support me or I would tell the world about his vile behavior. Now, the world knows anyway, doesn't it? I did not attend the funeral—why would I mourn such a despicable man?— and I suppose I will be criticized for that, but I do not care. Now, how can I help you, Mr. Rafferty?"

"Well, I certainly do not wish to dredge up painful memories, but I have come to believe that your"—Rafferty paused, realizing that the newly minted Jane Thompson probably preferred no references to Wittemore as her husband—"that the doctor was in fact murdered."

"Is that so? It does not surprise me. Was it the husband or boyfriend of one of those tarts he cavorted with?"

"I doubt it, although I am of a mind he was killed because of his connection to the club that burned down recently. I also think his murder was tied in some fashion to that of the newsman, Mr. Pickett. Perhaps you could begin by telling me what you know, if anything, about the doctor's involvement with the club."

"Well, you can be assured that story in the *Tattletale* was hardly news to me. Just before I left the scoundrel, I learned about his disgusting connection to that whorehouse. Indeed, I believe he established it with the assistance of another man."

"May I ask how you found this out?"

"It required no great detective work, Mr. Rafferty. You see, I found a shocking document he'd carelessly left in his study. It indicated he was in the business of procuring women from Chicago to satisfy his terrible lust."

"Exactly what sort of document was it?"

"It was a letter written by the doctor—I know his handwriting well—to someone named Bennett. The letter listed the names of several women from Chicago and said they would be good candidates for 'our little fun club.' I remember those words in particular. The letter described the women, who were obviously prostitutes, in the most vulgar terms imaginable. Next to each one's name was a figure indicating how much her services, if that is what they can be called, would cost. The doctor signed the letter as 'Your Procurer-in-Chief.' It was absolutely disgusting. Naturally, I was appalled and confronted the doctor at once. He tried to explain it away, but I knew he was lying. I walked out on him the next day."

Rafferty was intrigued. "Do you have this letter?"

"No, the doctor snatched it away from me."

"Ah, that is unfortunate. Can you tell me more about what was said in the letter?"

"Let me think. It was mostly about those awful tarts. I do remember the letter began with the doctor saying 'stop the presses,' or words to that effect. I guess he thought the scarlet women he wanted to hire were so exceptional that they should be in the news. Can you imagine that, Mr. Rafferty? How could I have ever married such a despicable man?"

"There are more than a few men who take satisfaction from living a secret life," Rafferty said. "I fear the doctor was one of them. Now, regarding the letter he sent to this Bennett fellow, do you know if he had any acquaintances by that name? Perhaps a Gordy or Gordon Bennett?"

"None that I'm aware of. I suspect it was an alias of some kind."

"You are probably right. Was there an envelope with the letter, perhaps with Mr. Bennett's address on it?"

"Not that I saw."

After a moment's thought, Rafferty asked, "Do you suppose the doctor kept a list of the club's members somewhere?"

"I imagine he did. It was probably in that safe in his office. He never entrusted me with the combination, of course. The police tell me it was stolen from his office."

"It was, and I doubt we will ever find it or its contents. I have but one more question: Did the doctor own a revolver?"

"He always told me he hated guns, probably because of all the bullets he'd removed from wounded men. I certainly never saw a gun of any kind in the house."

Satisfied he had learned all he could, Rafferty thanked her and said he would call again if other questions came to mind.

"It had better be soon," she said. "I plan to leave St. Paul two weeks hence and return to Philadelphia, where my mother still lives. The filthy stain left by the doctor will, I hope, be invisible there."

"Then I wish you the best of luck, Miss Thompson, and I am sorry for all that has happened to you."

"Not as sorry as I am. I thought I married a distinguished man, but he turned out to be utterly depraved. Now, all I wish is to wash him forever from my life."

15

WHAT RAFFERTY SAW

BROTHELS WERE SUPPOSEDLY ILLEGAL in St. Paul, and yet the elaborate Sanborn Company insurance maps used to assess fire risks routinely identified certain downtown structures as "female boarding houses," a well-understood euphemism. The city fathers, who thought it best to keep raging male libidos under at least some kind of control, tolerated houses of sin so long as their operators paid regular fines and kept their employees and clients in line. Newspaper reporters always showed up in court to witness the ritual levying of the fines, taking great delight in describing the apparel of the madams and their saucy manner. Merry Mike Gallagher could usually be counted on to attend the court sessions as well and invariably proclaimed how close a watch the police were keeping over the brothels so as to ensure the safety of the city's decent, God-fearing citizens.

Nina Clifford's establishment on Washington Street was widely considered to be the city's finest, attracting men of high social standing who nonetheless experienced the low urges of the flesh. But another brothel a few blocks to the north drew even more customers. Operated by Marilou Dancer, the brothel offered what one newspaper described, with a touch of humor, as "more modest" rates than those of its haughty competitor.

Rafferty hadn't patronized brothels since his younger days as a soldier, miner, and all-purpose roustabout, but he knew most of St. Paul's madams, and he thought Dancer might be able to tell him something about the Anything Goes Club. Early the next afternoon, he walked up to her establishment on Eighth Street. Known as the House of the Red Curtains because of its heavily draped decor, the brothel occupied a two-story brick building adorned with suggestive cylindrical finials.

"Shadwell Rafferty, it has been awhile," Dancer said when he was ushered into her well-appointed apartment by one of the large if none too bright men who maintained order at the place. "You are a bit early if you hope to see one of the girls."

"Ah, it is you I wish to see, Marilou," Rafferty said. "My wild days are over, I fear."

"Well, that's too bad. I'm sure I could have found a girl to please you."

Dancer was a substantially built woman in her early forties, with sharp eyes that took in men the way a livestock dealer might judge prize bulls. She wore a long red gown with a lacy bodice that displayed as much of her bosom as the law would allow, while diamond jewelry glittered everywhere about her person as a testament to the success of her enterprise. Rafferty wasn't sure how much she cleared every year, but her brothel supposedly had cost twenty thousand dollars to build only a few years earlier, making it one of the most expensive "homes" of its day in St. Paul.

"I do not wonder that you have come to see me," Dancer said, talking a long draw on one of the panatela cigars she favored. "I have heard you are looking into the business with Dr. Wittemore and that Harding fellow. It's too bad the doctor shot himself. He was a good customer for a time, although his tastes were rather exotic."

"So I have been told. What I'm looking into now is that private club he set up on Third Street. Can you tell me what you know about it?"

"You mean other than what was reported in the *Tattletale*? Well, now that Dr. Wittemore has met his end, I do not think it will come as a surprise to you that he was a member of the club."

"Yes, I knew that. Harley Calhoun was another."

"Was he? I hadn't heard that. As to the doctor, I have it on good authority that he was not merely a member of the club but its orchestrator, if that is the right word."

"He procured the women, from what I understand."

"So you knew that? You have been a busy boy, I see. Yes, the girls were all from Chicago. You know how it is there. You can find someone to do anything if the price is right, whereas the girls I hire here have their limits. In any case, I hear the high-class doves from Chicago came up every week. They were put up in rooms at the club and then sent back on the next day's train. It was quite an operation."

"So it seems. Do you know if the doctor had a partner in the enterprise, a cofounder, as it were? It was man who went by the name of Gordy Bennett. Have you ever heard of him?"

"I have not. Other than Dr. Wittemore and Calhoun, or so you tell me, the distinguished gentlemen who frolicked at the club were nothing if not circumspect. Even so, I heard a few rumors."

"I'm sure you did. And what did these rumors have to say?"

"Just that most of the press in this city had good reason to ignore the club's activities. Only the disreputable Mr. Harding, it seems, had the courage to write the truth."

"So you believe the newspapers were bribed to overlook what was going on at the club?"

"Perhaps, but there may have been an even better reason for their silence."

"What do you mean?"

Dancer reached up to Rafferty, gave him a peck on the cheek, and said, "I can tell you nothing more, my dear man. In my line of work, it pays to be discreet, especially when it comes to the activities of wealthy men. Now, I must go about my business. Have a pleasant afternoon."

* * *

As Rafferty walked back to his saloon, he pondered what Dancer had told him and also practiced his Sherlockian skills by trying to remember everything about her appearance. He came up with numerous small details—she wore a brooch shaped like a butterfly just above her bosom, her multi-ringed hands were extremely long and slender, her right eye was partially obscured by a low-hanging lid—but he still didn't see how Holmes would have been able to identify her as a madam. Rafferty had been doing the same sort of mental exercises all during his investigations, and they'd been stored, like valuable keepsakes, in the spacious cabinet of his memory.

He was so preoccupied with his thoughts that he was nearly run over by a wagon thundering down Sixth Street behind a pair of Percherons. "Do you want to get yourself killed?" the teamster shouted as he stood up to rein in the horses before they could trample Rafferty.

"My apologies," Rafferty said as the teamster, a burly man in dungarees and a long-sleeved shirt, glared down at him.

"Well, you just better be careful from now on," the teamster said. As he spoke, he reached down toward the fob pocket in his pants but then suddenly stopped himself. "Damned if I didn't forget my watch this morning. Do me a favor, will you, and tell me what time it is."

Rafferty pulled out his watch and said, "Half past one."

"I knew it. I'm already late," the teamster said, snapping at the reins. "Come on, boys, get a move on."

Although Rafferty was a thinker who could construct a chain of reasoning as well as the next man, he also believed wholeheartedly in the unaccountable magic of inspiration, and every so often an idea would arrive like a comet from some distant reach of the solar system and crash into his brain with startling force. Now, Rafferty had just such a moment. What struck him was an image, the picture of a man rising to his feet, and there was nothing remarkable about it except for the absence of a small but very important object.

Rafferty had spotted the missing item thanks to his study of Sherlock Holmes's observational methods, but he had made nothing of it at the time. And yet now it seemed to open the door to an entirely new view of the "newspaper murders," as they had come to be called. Could it be that he and everyone else had been wrong about the whole business from the start? He thought there might be one way to find out, if he was lucky. So it was that before returning to the saloon, Rafferty stopped by the offices of the St. Paul Fire Insurance Patrol on Cedar Street, across from city hall.

* * *

The patrol had been organized in the early 1880s and was modeled on similar operations in other cities. Funded by the city's insurance companies, its purpose was to salvage valuables from fire-damaged buildings like the Anything Goes Club and guard against potential looting. The patrol's members were mostly strong young men able to perform what could be demanding and dangerous work. Daniel St. Pierre, known as Dash to his friends because he rarely sat still, was a popular member of the patrol and also an occasional patron of Rafferty's saloon.

St. Pierre was sorting through goods in a large storage room when Rafferty greeted him. "Ah, Dash, I have not seen you in a while. I imagine you have been busy with all the fires of late."

"Busy as a bee," said St. Pierre. "Took us three days to recover everything from that fire over at the Mannheimer Brothers store. Lucky the whole place didn't burn down."

"So I've heard. And before that, there was the fire at that building on Third Street."

"Yeah, but we didn't salvage much there."

"But you did find a few things?"

"Very few. We were right on the heels of the first pumpers, but the place was already an inferno so we couldn't get inside. Had to wait until the fire boys finally put it out. By the time we were able to sift through the ruins pretty much everything was gone. About all we found were a few pieces of jewelry, some pots and pans, ceramic bowls, small stuff like that. Why do you ask? Are you on a case?"

"I am, but I would prefer not to go into the details for the moment. Now, about that jewelry. Did any of it look especially valuable or unique?"

"I don't know if anything was very valuable, but we did find a nice gold-plated pocket watch that's obviously a commemorative item. As soon as I have the time, I'll track down the owner. It shouldn't be hard."

"Could I see the watch?"

"Sure. Hold on a sec and I'll get it."

St. Pierre disappeared around a row of shelves and soon returned with the watch. Its face was of the usual kind, but the back was distinctive. It featured the engraved image of a building set beneath the bold numerals of a year. Rafferty stared at the watch, his mind racing. It all seemed to fit together. The altered *Pioneer Press* sign, the three murders, the attacks on newsmen. If Rafferty was right, a very clever man had gone to great lengths to deceive everyone.

"I will need this watch," Rafferty said.

"Oh, I don't think now that I could do that," St. Pierre said. "We have very stringent rules—"

Rafferty cut him short. "Dash, this is about murder. You will get the watch back, I assure you. But I must have it."

"All right, but just don't tell anybody how you got it."

"It will be our secret. And the next time you stop by the saloon, the drinks will be on the house."

* * *

"I think we have our man," Rafferty told Wash Thomas back at the saloon.

Thomas was skeptical. "Well, you may think you have him, but I don't know that a judge and jury would agree. A good defense attorney, I'm sure, would have no trouble explaining away your find."

"I know, but there's also the evidence of your friend Mr. Hall. He saw the man and I'm sure could identify him."

"Yes, and do you suppose his testimony as a Black man accusing a white man of murder would be believed? I have my doubts."

"As do I, Wash. We will need more evidence, and I have some ideas along those lines, beginning with that fake newspaper, the *St. Paul Chronicle.* Where was it printed? Most people don't have an old printing press lying around, but our man clearly had access to one that he could use in secrecy. I intend to make some inquiries about that. I also plan to contact the lovely Miss Dolly Charbonneau."

"She's too young for you," Thomas said with a grin.

"Ah, Wash, you are right. But she is not too young to be of help to us, if she's willing."

16

SECRETS

THE PHONE CALL from Rafferty put Charbonneau in a difficult spot. She wanted to help identify Milton Pickett's killer, but she was uncomfortable with the idea of acting as an intramural spy in the offices of the *Pioneer Press*. She also wasn't sure the kind of careful search Rafferty had in mind would produce anything of value. But she decided it wouldn't hurt to look, so she hung around the newsroom until well past two the next morning, telling everyone she was working late on a story.

Once the last stragglers had left the newsroom, Charbonneau hid out in the women's restroom, listening for the night watchman who patrolled the building. He arrived at half past two, used a special key chained in the newsroom to mark his telltale clock, and then went on his way. He wouldn't be back for at least an hour, giving Charbonneau plenty of time to go about her business. Rafferty believed Pickett had been murdered because he had "the goods" on someone. And if he did, perhaps he kept the incriminating evidence close at hand, or so Rafferty reasoned.

Charbonneau's first stop was at Pickett's office. She'd spent many hours with him there, honing stories under his expert eye, but now the desk where they'd worked together seemed like a big wooden tombstone, more real to her than the one in Oakland Cemetery, where Pickett lay buried. Charbonneau knew the police had already gone through the desk, but she thought she would check it again just in case. She was especially interested in a certain key but didn't find it or anything else of consequence.

The morgue, as the newspaper's library was called, was her next destination. Charbonneau had once spotted Pickett locking the bottom drawer of a file cabinet there and wondered what he was keeping in it. She hadn't found a file key in Pickett's desk, so she used a long scissors to force the drawer open.

Inside, Charbonneau found a large manila envelope, with a name on it that she readily recognized. She unclasped the envelope and removed two documents. One was Hall's anonymous letter. Charbonneau whistled softly. Rafferty suspected Pickett had seen the letter, and he was right.

The envelope also contained a group of handwritten notes clipped together. Charbonneau recognized the handwriting as Pickett's idiosyncratic scrawl. The notes were a revelation. Pickett, it turned out, had done some detective work of his own by finding a vantage point in the alley behind the Anything Goes Club where he could observe the comings and goings without being seen. The notes showed that Pickett had spotted several prominent men in addition to Wittemore and Calhoun entering the club.

Among them was the man Charbonneau now suspected must be Pickett's murderer. Pickett's notes showed that he'd later spoken to the man, who denied being a club member despite what Pickett had seen. "Claimed I saw him there because he was also investigating the club," Pickett's last note said. "Not sure I believe him but will wait awhile before writing anything. Pray he will prove me wrong." The note was dated May 27, four days before the *Pioneer Press*'s sign was vandalized.

Charbonneau put everything back in the envelope and slipped it into her purse. When she got outside, having avoided the watchman, she breathed in the cool night air with a sense of relief. It was just after three o'clock in the morning and the downtown streets were dim and deserted. Instead of going home, she walked two blocks to the Ryan Hotel, hoping to find Rafferty still awake. If he wasn't, she intended to rouse him from his slumbers because he would be intensely interested in what she'd found.

* * *

Less than twenty-four hours after Charbonneau had apprised Rafferty of her discovery in the morgue, Wash Thomas became a burglar. Lockpicking was among his many skills, and he had no trouble gaining entrance to the residence while Rafferty stood guard outside. Thomas made a quick initial search, rummaging through obvious hiding places. Nothing. He took a seat, calm as a burglar could be, and considered other possibilities. To minimize their chance of discovery, Rafferty didn't want him to spend more than a half hour on their illicit mission, and Thomas was nearly out of time when he thought to open the bottom drawer of the cast-iron stove in the kitchen. There, beneath two pans that looked as though they'd never been used, he found a Colt revolver.

Thomas was equipped with one of Rafferty's latest acquisitions, a Stirn & Lyon concealed vest camera. Rafferty had bought the device for the steep sum of ten dollars, thinking it might be useful in "the detecting game," as he called it. The thin circular camera hung around Thomas's neck, its lens designed to peek unobtrusively through an open buttonhole in his vest. Thomas snapped two pictures of the object in the stove and two more showing the stove and its surroundings. Then he left as quickly and quietly as he had come.

When Thomas reported what he had found, Rafferty said, "Well, it is one more indication that we are on the right track, but it is still not final proof of it."

"Not even with the pictures I took and that stuff from Dolly?"

"No, because our man could claim that anonymous letter was all a big lie and that Pickett was simply out to savage his reputation for some reason. As for your photos, he could claim we staged the whole thing after a break-in, and we might be hard pressed to prove otherwise. No, we'll have to keep the photos to ourselves for the present, but I think we can persuade Pat Donlin to secure a search warrant, and lo and behold the gun will be discovered. It will give us extra leverage when the time comes to confront our man."

"And when will that be?"

"Soon," said Rafferty, "very soon. I am building a case, just like our friend Mr. Cuddleton does in the courtroom. The items Dolly found will be of great help, as will the gun. It is clear to me now that the threat of being exposed in the press is at the root of this whole business."

"So you think he murdered three men just to save his reputation?"

"Possibly, or maybe there was something he valued even more—money."

* * *

Although Rafferty hardly moved in the elite circles of St. Paul, he did have one good friend in a very high place in the person of James J. Hill, whom he'd known since they briefly worked together at the old steamboat levee thirty years earlier. Hill had previously introduced Rafferty to "Babs" Goodwin, a wealthy widow whose chief occupation was nosing into other rich people's business. She'd become a valuable source of information for Rafferty, and the next afternoon he paid a call on her at her mansion, which abounded in pillows, ceramic figurines, bad paintings, and cats.

Goodwin, who was well into her sixties and of impressive girth, greeted Rafferty with a smile and said, "My dear Irish bruiser, how nice to see you! Have a seat. Will you drink tea, or shall I have my man uncap a beer for you?"

"Tea would be fine," Rafferty said. "I am, of course, pleased to see you as well. As you have no doubt guessed, I come to you as a supplicant in search of information. There is a woman I'd like you to tell me about."

When Rafferty mentioned the name, Goodwin said, "Why are you interested in her? Are you looking to marry into money, my dear man? I fear her husband might object."

"No, I am merely curious about what she brought to the marriage. I gather she's quite wealthy."

"Oh yes, she is very nicely situated. Did you by chance know her first husband? He amassed quite the fortune but wasn't the least bit handsome in my estimation. Why is it that the plainest men always seem to make the most money? My own late husband, rest his soul, was hardly a looker either. Life would be so much more amusing if all those gorgeous cads out there were also filthy rich, don't you agree?"

"I will not argue the point," Rafferty said. "Now, I believe you were speaking of her first husband."

"So I was. I do natter on sometimes, I'm afraid. Well, he was worth several million, but just like that his life was cut short. Oh, how cruel is this world! The grieving widow remarried just a year later. There were some raised eyebrows, I can assure you."

"And what did her new husband bring to the marriage? Was he wealthy, too?"

"Oh no, he was gold digging and struck the mother lode. He came from a family of the common sort and was living well above his means before the marriage. Do you know she's actually older than he is? In my experience, Mr. Rafferty, a man marries an older women for only one reason, and it is not because he is enchanted by her appearance. He courted her very skillfully, from what I have been told, married her as quickly as he could, and now enjoys the fruits of his labors."

"So he does. But I suppose if there was a divorce, all those lovely fruits would disappear."

Goodwin's eager eyes bored in on Rafferty. "So you believe the marriage is troubled? I must say I am not surprised. However, the man you speak of is not the only one with marital difficulties. Indeed, from what I know divorce is about to become a veritable epidemic along Summit Avenue."

"Why do you say that?"

"Oh, come now, my dear fellow, I know why you're quizzing me. You are interested in that revolting club to which Dr. Wittemore belonged, are you not?"

"I am," Rafferty admitted. "Can you tell me what you've heard?"

"I am told that Mrs. Wittemore has a list of all the club members and has begun naming them to their devoted wives. It is a bit like spreading manure around, don't you think? A brief fling with a housemaid is one thing, but the club is quite another. I don't know the men's names yet, but you will be able to infer them from the expensive divorce proceedings that are sure to come. The offenders will end up paying a steep price for their perverse pleasures. However, I doubt they will ever be formally identified in the press. Money can buy good publicity, but it is even more useful for warding off the bad."

Goodwin would eventually be proved correct, for only the two founders of the Anything Goes Club were ever named in news stories, much to Rafferty's disappointment.

"You have been most helpful," Rafferty said with a slight bow. "I see now that I should have talked to you sooner."

As Rafferty returned downtown on a cable car, he considered what he'd learned from Summit Avenue's champion gossip. The news about Jane Wittemore was interesting. She'd apparently lied to him when she claimed not to know who belonged to the Anything Goes Club. Rafferty wasn't sure why, but he suspected she wanted to remain anonymous, and thereby avoid any legal entanglements, when she identified the club members to their wives. It was a nasty bit of business, but also in some sense a cry for justice, and Rafferty wasn't prepared to condemn her for it.

What Goodwin had told Rafferty about his prime suspect was far more significant. It provided another powerful motive for murder, and Rafferty was more certain than ever that he knew who had murdered Milton Pickett, William Wittemore, and Monroe Harding in a scheme as devious as any he had ever encountered.

17

A KILLER REVEALED

AT THREE O'CLOCK on the afternoon of July 14, six weeks after the "LIARS" sign appeared atop the Pioneer Press Building as the opening volley in what would become an intricate campaign of deception and murder, Shadwell Rafferty stood in the shadows of a doorway, waiting for the man he believed was behind it all to arrive. George Hall was with him, looking nervous but ready to do as Rafferty had asked. They were stationed behind shelves just inside the entrance to a stationery shop. From their vantage point they could see the main doors of the building where the suspect worked, but it was unlikely he'd notice them as he passed by.

At five minutes past the hour their quarry came through the doors, his features clearly visible beneath a black homburg hat.

As the man headed toward the elevators, Hall said, "That's him all right. That's the fellow who tried to disguise himself when I saw him coming into the club."

"You're sure?" Rafferty asked. "Would you testify to it under oath?"

"If I have to, yes."

"Then you have my thanks, Mr. Hall, and I will ask no more of you."

After Hall left, Rafferty used the shop's telephone to make a call, first depositing a silver dollar with the proprietor. Wash Thomas, who been waiting at the saloon with Patrick Donlin, answered.

"We have him," Rafferty said after recounting Hall's positive identification. "You and Pat can come over now and we'll try to get the truth out of him. And bring along a pistol, Wash. A cornered beast is always dangerous."

"So it is just as you suspected," Thomas said. "We'll be there in ten minutes."

Once Thomas and Donlin arrived, they laid plans with Rafferty. It was decided Rafferty and Donlin would handle the interview, while Thomas would hover nearby in case their quarry tried to make a run for it.

"Well then, here we go," Rafferty said to his companions as they walked toward the elevators. "Let us hope he'll cause us no trouble."

"His type usually don't," Donlin said. "They're soft when it comes down to it."

"He was hard enough to kill three men," Thomas noted, "so I wouldn't put anything past him."

* * *

Their quarry was seated at his desk and apparently buried in paperwork when Rafferty and Donlin stepped into the office. Thomas was nearby but out of sight.

"Mr. Rafferty and Detective Donlin, how nice to see you," the man said but didn't stand up to shake hands. "To what do I owe the pleasure of your company?"

"We have come to talk of murder," Rafferty said.

The man's eyes narrowed and his smoothly shaved cheeks reddened slightly, as though a banked fire had suddenly come back to life inside him. "Is that so? As you can see, I am rather busy at the moment, so why don't you come back at a more convenient time."

"It can't wait," Rafferty said. "We have come for the truth. We know what you did and why you did it, and we have more than enough evidence to hang you. But if you will give a full statement and admit your guilt, then perhaps you can save your skin. It is as simple as that."

"Well, that is a peculiar offer if I ever heard one. But as I have done nothing wrong, I must decline. Moreover, I am outraged that you would accuse me of murder. Now, leave this office at once. I have nothing more to say, but I assure you my lawyer will not be at a loss for words when he files his slander suit."

"I think Pat and I will stay for a while," Rafferty said. "Since you are a man who likes good stories, I will tell you one. And you will do me the favor of listening," Rafferty added, a hint of menace in his voice. "Let us begin with an anonymous letter that was sent out in May. The letter described the Anything Goes Club and named Dr. William Wittemore and Harley Calhoun as two of the club's members. As you were also a member of the club—indeed, I believe you were a cofounder, along with the doctor—the letter was very concerning. You, of course, made sure it would never see the light of day."

"I know of no such letter," the man said, "and I most certainly was not a member of that club."

"We will see about that," Rafferty said. "As it was, the letter presented no immediate threat to you, but Milton Pickett did. He, too, received a copy of the letter and decided to look into its troubling allegations. He hid outside the club's entrance for several nights and saw you entering it. He must have been very surprised, perhaps even in a state of disbelief. So he came to you, in what might be described as an act of professional courtesy, and asked for an explanation. I imagine he told you he intended to expose the club and its ugly doings. You lied to him just as you are lying to us now and swore you weren't a member. But Mr. Pickett wasn't convinced and perhaps even managed to verify your membership by one means or another."

"This is ridiculous. You are just throwing out wild guesses without a shred of evidence."

"Oh, we have plenty of evidence, as you will see soon enough. Now, you knew from your talk with Mr. Pickett that you were facing ruin, and so you began devising a murderous scheme to save yourself. As schemes go, I must say, it was extraordinarily imaginative. Step one was the sign caper, which was designed to create a false narrative. Only a madman seething with anger against the *Pioneer Press* could have undertaken such a bizarre feat, or so it was assumed. And who better for that role than Dr. Wittemore? He was incensed over unflattering stories about him that had appeared in the *Pioneer Press* and other newspapers."

"He was all of that, as Detective Donlin well knows," the man said. "It is obvious that he was behind the business with the sign."

"He wasn't," Rafferty said. "No, you hired a hoodlum named Jack Spence to alter the sign, and I imagine you even took some personal pleasure in his handiwork. I also believe you hired Handy Jack to steal a safe from the doctor's home because you were worried what might be inside it."

"And you have proof of all this? If so, let's hear it."

"We will have our proof when Handy Jack returns from Chicago," Rafferty said. "He is the sort of man who can be persuaded to talk if he figures it is to his advantage. And so we can move on to step two—the murder of Milton Pickett. Killing him was essential because you knew that if he identified you in a news story as a member of the club you would be finished in more ways than one. You would lose your job, your reputation, and, most importantly, your wife, whose wealth has given you a most comfortable life. But once she divorced you, as she surely would when she learned you were regularly frolicking with prostitutes at a private club, you would be left penniless and utterly ruined. And you couldn't let that happen, could you?"

"You are offering 'a tale full of sound and fury, signifying nothing,' to quote the Bard. But do go on, Mr. Rafferty. I believe I will own that saloon of yours by the time my lawyer is through with you."

"I doubt you'll be in the saloon business or any other. You'll be in close quarters in Stillwater with the other criminals, if your neck hasn't been stretched by then. As to how you murdered Mr. Pickett, my thinking is that you went to his apartment claiming you wished to make one last appeal to keep your notorious activities out of the public eye. But, of course, you did not come to argue your case. No, your intent was to kill him. The moment he turned his back, you put a bullet in his head."

Donlin now weighed in, reaching into his vest pocket for a legal document, which he slapped down on the desk. "You used a .41-caliber Colt to do the deed. Did Mr. Rafferty mention that we're searching your apartment at this very moment? If we find the gun there, and I believe we will, I will have the pleasure of arresting you for murder."

The man still gave no evidence of concern. "The warrant will be tossed out, I'm sure," he said, "and in any event there is no crime in owning a revolver."

"Perhaps not," Rafferty said, "but the gun is not your only problem. Those copies of the *St. Paul Chronicle* you spread around were printed on an old handpress in the basement of this very building. I was down there this morning with someone you know, and we tried it out. The press leaves distinct marks identical to those on that page you printed."

"Is that a fact? I presume you have witnesses who saw me as I went about this supposed work. Because if you don't, it hardly matters, does it? Anyone could have used that press."

"Not really," Rafferty said. "Only you and a few other people knew it was down there. But let us move on to step three of your plan. Having dispensed with Mr. Pickett, you decided to stage two attacks to make it look as though the press as a whole was still being threatened by a mad murderer with a grudge. I suspect your agent, Mr. Spence, staged one of the attacks while the other did not require any help from him. Am I correct?"

"I like a good story," the man said, drumming his fingers on the desk, "but fairy tales are for children."

"This ain't no kiddie tale," Donlin said, "and you better listen up because it's about to get even better."

Rafferty said, "So now let us consider step four—the murders of Dr. Wittemore and Mr. Harding. I am of a mind you aimed to murder the doctor all along and make his death appear as a suicide. I don't think Mr. Harding played a role in your original plan, but when he began exposing Dr. Wittemore's activities at the club, you realized, clever fellow that you are, that a golden opportunity presented itself for a fake murder-suicide."

"Utter nonsense," said the man, rising from his chair. "Now, unless I am under arrest, I will go on my way."

"Sit down!" Donlin growled. "You ain't going nowhere unless I say so. And keep your hands where we can see them."

"Patrick can be a most forceful man, so I would not cross him if I were you," Rafferty said. "Now, then, where was I? Ah yes, the double murder that brought your grand scheme to its conclusion. I suspect you called on Harding, using some pretext, and shot him dead as he sat at his desk. Then you hid his body behind the desk and awaited the arrival of Dr. Wittemore, who you'd already arranged to lure to the scene. You stepped out from your hiding place and shot him in the side of the head before he could react. But you made a mistake, didn't you?"

"I have no idea what you're talking about."

"Sure you do," Donlin said. "You ended up cocking that single-action revolver you used by mistake. A man who's just put a bullet through his brain ain't going to cock his gun again. You did that."

"I most certainly did not!"

"And I suppose you'll also deny setting that fire at the Anything Goes Club," Rafferty said, "but we know better. You wanted to eliminate any physical evidence that could connect you or the other members to the club. Your fellow members may even have suggested the idea. After the fire, you paid off the club's employees to ensure their silence and sent them back to Chicago. But you forgot about George Hall."

"I don't know anyone by that name," the man said. "He must be a figment of your overactive imagination."

"No, George is very real. He was the club's porter, and he saw you there just before it burned down. You tried to disguise your face, but he got a good look at you."

"Yet another fantasy, Mr. Rafferty. You should be writing dime novels."

"And if I did, you would have to be the villain. But what would I call you? How about Gordon Bennett? There's a nice name."

"If you say so."

"I do. The real Mr. Bennett is, of course, the publisher of the *New York Herald.* He's also known as the Commodore because of his fondness for yachting. You worked for him back in the day, although I doubt you ever sailed with him. But you did borrow his name as an alias."

The man was about to offer another denial when Rafferty asked a question that took him by complete surprise. "What time is it? I seem to have forgotten my watch."

"Me too," said Donlin with a straight face.

The man peered at his two antagonists with disbelief but by habit pulled out his pocket watch. "Quarter to four," he said.

"Why, that looks like a brand-new watch. But I'm wondering what happened to your other one. You know, that fine gold memento you've carried around since 1887, when this building opened. Did you lose it?"

"I don't know—"

Rafferty cut him short. "Could this be it?" he said, producing a timepiece from his vest pocket. "You somehow lost it when you were setting fire to the Anything Goes Club, didn't you? The funny thing is, it survived the fire. I found it at the offices of the Insurance Patrol. Imagine that. By the way, have you ever heard of that Sherlock Holmes fellow who's a famous detective over in England? Well, I've been learning some of his tricks. When I talked with you right after the fire, in this very office, I noticed you had no watch in your fob pocket. I'd say that's quite a coincidence, Mr. Beverly, quite a coincidence indeed."

* * *

Rafferty would later blame himself at least in part for the events that followed. "I should have invited Mr. Pyle to join us when we confronted his boss," he told Thomas that evening. "I believe Joseph and Mr. Beverly were quite close. But Joseph was very agitated after he took me to see that old press in the basement. He couldn't quite force himself to believe what Mr. Beverly had done, so I thought it best not to have him come along with us."

"I do not see that you made a bad decision," Thomas said. "You knew Mr. Beverly might be dangerous, so why put Mr. Pyle at risk?"

"Perhaps you're right. But my biggest mistake was that I somehow failed to take account of that side door in Mr. Beverly's office. How could I miss that? I should have stationed you there right from the start."

The side door was but a few steps from Beverly's desk and opened out directly onto the six-foot-wide gallery that formed a perfect square around the Globe Building's small but very high atrium. After Rafferty brought out the commemorative watch, Beverly offered a wan smile, slowly shook his head, and then without a word stood up and bolted for the door, catching Rafferty and Donlin flat-footed.

"Wash, he's on the run," Rafferty shouted as he and Donlin followed Beverly out toward the gallery.

"Stay away!" Beverly screamed. He produced a small revolver from his jacket pocket and fired four wild shots in their direction, forcing Rafferty and Donlin to retreat back into the office. The rounds went well past them and crashed harmlessly into the upper walls of the gallery. Curious tenants immediately emerged from other offices to see what was happening. They scampered back inside when they saw Beverly waving his revolver around as though trying to summon up a magic spell that would make him disappear.

"I'll get the bastard," Donlin said, raising his heavy police revolver. Rafferty grabbed him by the wrist and said, "Hold up, Pat. You could hit somebody in one of the offices. Besides, he has nowhere to go."

Rafferty was right. Thomas, who "was as good a man in a gunfight as you could ever hope for," as Rafferty once said, was already on the run, hunched over, racing toward the elevators. Beverly was heading in the same direction from the other side of the gallery, but Thomas arrived first and took cover in the elevator lobby. The building's only staircase spiraled down next to the elevators, which meant all of Beverly's escape routes were blocked.

When Rafferty peeked out the office door, he understood the situation at once. "Mr. Beverly, you have no choice but to give yourself up," he shouted. Beverly responded by taking another shot at Rafferty and Donlin, only to miss again by a wide margin. "One left, by my count," Rafferty said. "We will have him soon enough."

Beverly now realized he had run out of options and could see only darkness and destruction ahead. He stopped at a corner of the gallery behind a massive iron column and bent over to catch his breath. He was only a few paces from the elevator lobby where Thomas waited for him. Across the atrium, Rafferty and Donlin stood ready to block any retreat.

"Come now," Rafferty said. "Throw down that gun and you can take your chances with the law. It is your only hope."

"A dying man has no hope," Beverly said, his words echoing across the atrium. "But at least I will give our readers a good story."

Beverly slipped his gun into his jacket pocket, found a foothold on the gallery's ornate iron railing, and hoisted himself up as he held on to the column. "That's better," he said as he stood atop the brass handrail, his left arm wrapped around the column. "A wonderful view from here. What a great day it was for the *Globe* when this building opened. Tallest in the city, it was, but not for long. I wish I could deliver some magnificent final words, but really, who cares? I will let the *Globe* write my obituary. Well then, it is goodbye."

Taking the revolver out of his pocket, Beverly fired its last bullet into his right temple and then fell soundlessly into the atrium. He was dead by the time his body, traveling at forty miles an hour, hit the tile floor at the bottom.

"Well, I'll be damned," Donlin said after he and Rafferty rushed to the railing and stared down at Wilson Beverly's body, blood pouring from his shattered skull.

Rafferty shook his head, saddened by what he saw, and said, "Well, he lived for the news, and I suppose you could say he has now died for it. Let us hope there is a good newspaper in hell."

The BIRDMAN
of SUMMIT AVENUE

A Sentimental Tale

From where then does wisdom come?
And where is the place of understanding?
It is hidden from the eyes of all living,
And concealed from the birds of the air.
—BOOK OF JOB, NEW KING JAMES VERSION

1

THE MAN WHO HATED CATS

THE FIRST VICTIM was Miss Julie, a sleek blue Siamese found strangled to death with a wire in a yard on Crocus Hill. Pinned to her ear was a small card on which the image of a robin, probably cut out from a book or magazine, had been pasted. Beneath the image a single word—SAVED—stood out in bold printed letters.

Miss Julie's owner, a prominent socialite named Barbara Goodwin, was sufficiently appalled by the gruesome event to call the police and demand an investigation. "There is obviously some madman skulking about in the dead of night killing cats," she told the detective who arrived at her door. "Who could do such a barbaric thing? This is 1892, not the Middle Ages. You must find the man responsible. He is clearly a menace."

Patrick Donlin was the detective, and he knew all too well why he had been sent out on such a ridiculous mission. Goodwin, all two hundred pounds of her, had plenty of money and plenty of friends at city hall, among them Chief of Police Michael Gallagher. Known as Merry Mike because of his habit of breaking out into eerie laughter while roughing up criminals, Gallagher was far more solicitous when it came to obliging the rich and powerful.

"Serve the rich well and you will do well," the chief liked to say, and so Donlin had been instructed to investigate Miss Julie's tragic demise. Murder and mayhem of the human sort were Donlin's usual line of work, and he felt embarrassed by his absurd assignment.

But orders were orders and so he went to see Barbara Goodwin at the scene of the crime.

"It is probably the work of some nasty boy in the neighborhood," Donlin offered as he gazed down at Miss Julie, whose tongue hung out beneath grotesquely bulging eyes, the wire still pulled tightly around her neck.

"I very much doubt that," said Goodwin, who viewed Donlin as just another servant to be ordered around. "A boy would not go the trouble of pinning a picture like that to my dear Miss Julie. No, this is the work of some awful man who hates cats. I expect you to find him at once, and when you do, throttle him. He needs to be taught a lesson. By the way, I have already called the mayor and he agrees what an outrage this is."

"I am sure His Honor does," said Donlin. "I will make some inquiries and see what I can find out."

Donlin, however, didn't bother to make any inquiries, seeing no point to it, and went back to his usual business of extracting confessions, not always delicately, from murderers and other miscreants. Then, just three days later, Gallagher showed up at his desk. "Another damn cat is dead," he announced as he handed Donlin a slip of paper with a name and address. "Go see about it. Now, what have you found out so far?"

"I am hard at it," Donlin replied untruthfully, "but I have not yet made much progress."

"Well then, you'd better work harder. I've already had one call from the mayor, and I don't want another one. Understand?"

Donlin nodded and said, "I'll get right on it, sir."

The second victim was Dalliance, a green-eyed American Shorthair found face down in a birdbath just off Summit Avenue. Like Miss Julie, he had an image of a bird, this time a sparrow, pinned to one ear along with the word SAVED. Donlin talked to the cat's owner, another wealthy and influential woman, and she not only demanded action but also insisted she knew who'd committed the foul deed.

"It is that terrible man Ambrose Harriman," she said. "Everyone knows how much he hates cats."

But since there had been no witnesses to Dalliance's demise,

Donlin had little to go on. As for Harriman, well, he was certainly an odd character, what with all the birds that flocked to his property. But a cat killer? That seemed unlikely. The man was at least sixty years old and hardly seemed agile enough to be chasing down felines in the dark.

Still, Donlin decided he'd have a talk with Harriman, just to cover his bases. Before he could do so, however, came the most shocking death of all. Empire, a beautiful black Persian, was discovered hanging from a tree branch on the grounds of James J. Hill's gigantic mansion on Summit Avenue. Attached to his corpse was the same kind of note found with the other two feline victims. Empire had been a favorite of Hill's wife, Mary, who was said to be all but inconsolable when she heard the dreadful news.

Donlin knew that he'd now be under intense pressure to solve the case. Hill was the richest and most powerful man in St. Paul, president of the Great Northern Railway, and if anyone could make waves big enough to capsize Donlin's career, Hill was just that man. To Donlin's relief, the great man was out touring in his private railroad car when Empire met his end. Donlin, however, did secure an audience with Mary Hill. Although she could offer no real evidence as to who had killed her beloved cat, she became the second person to point a finger of suspicion at Ambrose Harriman, who lived only a few blocks away on Summit Avenue. "He is known to be awful man," she said, "and awful men do awful things."

* * *

It was said of Ambrose Harriman that the only people who pleased him were the ones he'd never met. He lived with a staff of four servants in a not especially grand house on Summit Avenue that he rarely left, although he was often seen puttering about in his yard during the summer months. Harriman called his estate Birdwing, and unlike those faux English names the rich often use to infuse their property with a suitable scent of the Old World, the name actually meant something, for Harriman much preferred birds to people.

The estate occupied nearly a full acre and Harriman did all he could to make it a haven for what he called "my flying friends."

Feeders, nesting boxes, and birdbaths were scattered all around the grounds, and there was even a small duck pond to attract migrants coming north in spring or heading south in the fall. Harriman employed a gardener named George York full-time to maintain his avian sanctuary, which in summer became a spectacle of color, movement, and sound as birds of all kinds fluttered about the grounds. York had supervised many plantings and was especially proud of a red mulberry tree, thought to be the only one in the city, its tempting fruit a magnet for catbirds, cedar waxwings, and orioles. In winter, birds unwilling or unable to fly south even enjoyed a small "warming house," as Harriman called it, which was attached to one side of his mansion and heated by means of a special furnace duct.

Cats eager to kill were also drawn to the yard, and Harriman waged a constant battle against their depredations, chasing them away with a broom or spade held menacingly over his head. He also clashed with neighbors whose cats hunted down and killed birds on his estate. If Harriman knew where the offending cat's owner lived, he would deliver the dead bird to their door with a warning that their feline's next incursion might prove fatal. Rumor held that Harriman, with help from York, used cleverly designed traps to catch serial offenders and then dispose of them by tossing them off the High Bridge in a bag. A number of cats in the neighborhood had indeed gone missing over the years, but no evidence was ever obtained linking Harriman to the disappearances.

Tall and gangly, Harriman was often likened, despite his fondness for birds, to a scarecrow, an impression bolstered by his habit of wearing ragged old clothes. Others thought of him more as an old buzzard who saw his fellow humans as little more than ugly carrion. His long face hid behind an even longer beard, while atop his head rose a tangle of gray hair so wild and unmannered that a small bird might have nested there perfectly invisible to the world. His wary gray eyes, sheltered beneath brows of unusual size and luxuriance, were perhaps his most notable feature and would glitter with particular intensity whenever he launched one of his all-but-patented diatribes. He walked with a pronounced limp, reputedly the result of a war wound, but if he had been in battle, he never talked about it.

Although the occasional visitor might experience a rant in person, Harriman preferred to vent his ample spleen in weekly screeds sent to the local newspapers. His letters to the editor were so reliably outrageous and misanthropic that they appeared under a standing title, "Harriman's Harangue," and readers of a certain kind enjoyed them, as they might an ice-cold shower or a dental drill grinding away at a deep cavity without the aid of ether.

Harriman's hatred for cats had inspired one of his most controversial letters. "Dear Sirs," it began, "Of what possible use are cats? They are cold, sneaky, violent creatures who kill for no reason other than pleasure, and their irresponsible owners do nothing to rein in their brutality. Indolence, however, is their natural state, and when they are not hunting innocent birds, they lie about to no good purpose or, in the case of tomcats, roam the alleys crying out for a female or fighting among themselves like the rude beasts they are. Were it up to me, cats on the loose would be hunted down and shot like any other wild animal, their carcasses providing a fine meal for crows and vultures."

So richly offensive and wide ranging were Harriman's letters that one local newspaper, the *Pioneer Press,* eventually compiled a list of everything he hated. It began with apartments ("breeders of crime and immorality"), proceeded past beer ("a foul intoxicant") to children ("little tyrants in the making") and dogs ("filthy creature who eat their own waste") all the way down the alphabet to women ("on the whole, a mistake") and xylophones ("perhaps the most obnoxious of musical instruments") before concluding with zoos ("which would be of far greater value if people were kept behind the cages").

A poor man possessing peculiar views is adjudged a fool, whereas a rich man in that situation is merely seen as eccentric, and so it was that Harriman was tolerated in the manner of some batty old uncle who always makes a scene at family gatherings. Harriman himself cared nothing for public opinion and regarded his weekly letters as a service to benighted humanity. Even so, he held out little hope that his efforts would reduce what he liked to call the "general stupidity of the world."

No one knew how Harriman spent his days, other than tending to his birds, until a carpenter making repairs in the mansion came across a full-fledged stock ticker in the old man's bedroom. It was later revealed that Western Union, at great cost, had installed a private telegraph line to accommodate the ticker, which clattered away all day and sometimes into the night. When the carpenter asked about the ticker, Harrison supposedly replied, "It is the only music I care for and I sleep well knowing that I am making money more often than not."

How Harriman had ended up in St. Paul was a mystery, for he never spoke of his early life and career. Even so, his misanthropic outbursts in the newspapers made him the source of much gossip, and various stories were advanced to account for his bitter temperament. One rumor held that he was "a close relative" of E. H. Harriman, the New York financier and railroad tycoon, but had been ostracized by the family after a scandalous affair with a married woman. It was further claimed that upon his departure from New York, he carried with him a thick stack of bonds issued by an obscure railroad that was subsequently sold at great profit to the mighty Pennsylvania, thereby making Harriman a wealthy man. Yet another version of Harriman's backstory asserted that an unspecified "family tragedy" had caused him to pull up his roots in New York and begin a new life in St. Paul. But rumor can be a fast locomotive pulling empty cars, and so Harriman's personal history—and the source of his extraordinary bile—remained unknown.

When Harrison landed in St. Paul around 1880, his pockets bulging, he immediately purchased his estate, which came with exceptionally large grounds even by the standards of Summit Avenue. The house itself, in the picturesque Italian Villa style and already shuffling toward decrepitude, held no particular appeal for Harriman, but he spent a small fortune transforming the grounds into an avian paradise that quickly became one of the sights of the city. The *Pioneer Press,* against Harriman's wishes, devoted a long and colorful story to "The Birdman of Summit Avenue" and in the spring of 1891 sent it out on the wires to other newspapers around the country.

Harriman refused to be interviewed for the story and even threatened to sue the *Pioneer Press* because of it. But his attorney told him a lawsuit would have little chance of success, and so he closed himself off from the world and hunkered down amid his birds—the only companions that mattered to him. A mynah named Webster was Harriman's favorite, and like his namesake he was quite an orator. The bird could spout portions of the Gettysburg Address, knew the opening lines of "The Raven," and had also mastered such useful phrases as "you are speaking nonsense, sir" and "stop wasting my time." Webster had the run of Harriman's mansion, and the task of cleaning his droppings, which were deposited on the furniture as often as not, fell to Harriman's long-suffering housemaid.

Harriman explained his passionate love of birds in a harangue directed against a "useless little child" who one day trespassed in his yard and tried to chase down the birds there. "Children are a nuisance," he wrote, "and will of course grow up to be no better than their parents. Birds, by contrast, are the only creatures not attached by gravity to the awful stain of this Earth. They are bright and beautiful, and they alone are free. I say woe to any man or beast who would seek to destroy the perfection of their being."

* * *

The "epidemic of felinicides," as one local newspaper called it, garnered considerable attention in the press. Chief Gallagher assured the presumably nervous public that "we will not rest until we find the culprit, if indeed it is not Mr. Harriman." That remark left little doubt as to who Gallagher believed was the guilty party.

Harriman immediately denied he had killed the felines, telling a newspaper reporter, "I have no use for cats. However, I am not in the business of killing them. I do not know who is going after these cats, but I cannot say I am brokenhearted over it. Cats should not be let loose to kill and maim birds at their pleasure, and perhaps these killings will convince more people to keep their wild little beasts indoors."

Meanwhile, the cat killings drew much condemnation from local pulpits. Preachers insisted that God, though perhaps not entirely satisfied with fallen mankind, certainly loved cats. At the Church of God's People, the celebrated Reverend Arthur Killjoy went a step further, assuring his worried congregation that heaven was well populated with felines in accord with "God's love of all His creatures."

"I suppose that means there will have to be mice, too, to keep the cats busy," Shadwell Rafferty observed to his partner, George Washington Thomas, after reading Killjoy's comments. They were seated just before opening time at the long mahogany bar in their saloon, which was the city's most popular gathering place for thirsty men of all kinds. It would be their last time together for several weeks because Thomas was about to head off to Georgia for a prolonged family visit.

"I refuse to believe heaven will be infested with vermin," said Thomas, who unlike Rafferty hoped to join the celestial congregation after his death. "As for cats, I have my doubts. But maybe you should look into these killings. They're certainly strange."

"That they are, but I will leave the felines to fend for themselves," said Rafferty, who combined saloon keeping with occasional detective work. "I prefer the companionship of John Brown"—Rafferty's beloved bulldog and the saloon's mascot. "At least he can growl at a troublesome customer. A cat would merely hiss."

"I guess so. But I will say whoever is killing those cats must be a clever fellow," Thomas said. "I wonder how he hunts them down."

"Well, you will have to keep on wondering. Maybe our noble police force will solve the mystery by the time you get back from Georgia."

* * *

After seeing Thomas off at the Union Depot later that afternoon, Rafferty returned to the saloon to find a message from James J. Hill. The railroad baron asked Rafferty to come up to his mansion that evening for a brief meeting. Hill didn't say what the meeting would be about, but Rafferty sent back word that he'd be there at seven o'clock as requested.

Rafferty had known Hill for more than thirty years, going back to St. Paul's rude frontier days before the War between the States. They had both worked at the Lower Levee at a time when steamboats were still king. Rafferty had soon marched off to war while Hill, who always radiated the authority of a great commander on the battlefield, couldn't qualify for military service because he'd lost sight in one eye in a childhood accident. So Hill had instead marched ahead to build a fortune in railroading.

When Rafferty arrived at Hill's gigantic new mansion on Summit Avenue, a butler escorted him into the great man's study. Hill greeted his old friend warmly, offered a glass of cognac, and then said to Rafferty's surprise, "I cannot believe it, but I must talk to you about cats."

"Ah, I read about poor Empire in the papers," Rafferty said.

"The fact is, I have no interest in cats," Hill stated with his usual vehemence as he lit a cigar and looked out toward Summit and its array of trim lawns and stately residences. Dusk was settling in and the big houses were melting into shadows. Hill's house was the biggest of them, grand beyond measure, but in the dim light of the study it felt dark as a tomb.

Hill continued: "But Mary loves to have the damned creatures around, and the minute I returned from my travels, she told me what had happened to Empire. She is quite beside herself over it."

Rafferty, who was no great fancier of cats himself, nodded and said, "I am sure your wife grew quite attached to the cat. May I ask if the police were consulted after he was killed?"

"Yes, Mary talked with a detective named Donlin. Do you know him?"

"Sure. Pat's a good enough detective, but he's no Sherlock Holmes. Neither am I, for that matter."

Hill smiled and said, "So you have been reading the tales of the English detective, I see. I've actually read a few myself. He's a very clever fellow."

"He is. Too bad he's not here to look into these cat killings."

"But we have you, Mr. Rafferty, and you're the best detective I know. Mary and the police seem to believe Mr. Harriman is behind this business but have no proof. What do you think?"

"Well, Harriman is a strange character, and he's long made his feelings about cats well known. But as you say, proof is lacking. In any event, I'm guessing you would like me to look into this business."

"Yes, as a favor for Mary. These ridiculous killings must stop or she will grow even more agitated. As it is, the police seem to be getting nowhere, so I am hoping you can get to the bottom of it. I will, of course, pay you for your time."

"No need of that. I am happy to do any kind of favor for you and Mrs. Hill. I will just poke around a bit and see what I can find out."

* * *

Late the next morning, Rafferty sauntered down to the Central Police Station, a grim old building on Washington Street, to talk with Donlin. The detective was chewing on a hearty roast beef sandwich at his desk when Rafferty appeared.

"Well, I'll be," he said. "If it ain't the biggest Irishman in St. Paul. What brings you my way, Shad?"

"Cats," Rafferty said as he pulled up a chair.

Donlin set down his sandwich and rubbed his hands over the bib tucked into his shirt collar. "Don't tell me," he said with a sigh, "that you're working for those swells up on the hill."

"I'm afraid so."

Donlin shook his head in disgust and said, "You and Merry Mike both! I can't believe it. Do you know he's been down here three times—three times!—lecturing me on the almighty importance of those damn cats? I must leave no stone unturned, hunt down every lead, give him a daily report, et cetera, et cetera. Well now, I've got a dead man in Frogtown sliced open with a butcher knife and the widow and children destitute, but that don't matter to the chief as much as a few cats."

Rafferty had rarely heard Donlin—a pasty, broad-shouldered man with sad Irish eyes—speak with such passion. "Now, Pat, you know as well as I that the chief has never met a rich man or woman he didn't cotton to. It is not right, but if the world were true and just, there would be no need for coppers such as yourself. Now, why don't you just show me your files and maybe I can help relieve you of the burden of chasing after whoever killed those cats."

"Gladly," Donlin said.

The files were of no great help. Donlin had tried to make a fine showing of himself, traipsing from door to door on Summit Avenue looking for clues, and he'd even hauled in a few suspects whose main point of interest appeared to be that they lived in the vicinity and were known to be petty criminals. Rafferty was acquainted with a fair share of St. Paul's criminal class, but he didn't know a single crook who would bother with killing cats when there was so much thieving, burgling, and purse snatching to be done.

Among the items in the files was Donlin's report on his interview with Ambrose Harriman and George York. The great eccentric admitted to nothing, nor did his gardener claim to have any knowledge of the killings. Harriman also insisted he'd never had a run-in with any of the owners whose cats had been killed. Even so, he made no attempt to disguise his attitude toward felines, telling Donlin, "The world would be a much better place without them."

"Find anything?" Donlin asked after Rafferty handed back the files.

"Well, I can see why some people think Harriman might be the culprit. Your report make it clear he hates cats in all their works, pomps, and circumstances."

"Yeah, they're devils as far as he's concerned. Trouble is, he seems to hate everything and everybody. If you ask me, I'm betting he's our man, although that fellow who works for him probably does the dirty work. Then again, maybe there's just some lunatic out there who's amusing himself by killing cats. All I know for sure is that I'll take a nice clean homicide over this nonsense any day of the week. Well, let me know if you find out anything. I need to get the Merry Mike off my poor back."

"I'll do what I can and keep you posted," Rafferty promised.

That evening, back in his apartment at the Ryan Hotel, Rafferty worked over an old cigar as he pondered just who might go to the trouble of slaying the dearly beloved felines of Summit Avenue. Money did not seem to be a motive, since the cats had not been kidnapped with the idea of demanding a ransom from their wealthy owners. Nor had any of the owners received complaints or threats before their pets were so mercilessly dispatched.

As to who the killer might be, Rafferty kept an open mind. Harriman was certainly the prime suspect, his avowed hatred of cats giving him an obvious motive. But as Donlin had suggested, the killings simply could be the work of a cruel neighborhood boy. In either case, Rafferty wondered how the killer had gone about his business, since catching a cat by surprise in the dark of night was no easy thing. Did he actually stalk the cats, just as they might stalk a bird or mouse? Or did he set and bait traps of some kind? Or did he lure the cats into his home, wherever it was, and kill them there before depositing their bodies on their owners' lawns? And how did he manage to operate undetected in one of the most populous and well-patrolled parts of the city?

Rafferty wanted to ask Harriman those questions and more, and so one afternoon he went up to Birdwing in hopes of speaking with the old contrarian, only to be turned away by a beefy young butler who answered the doorbell.

"Mr. Harriman is receiving no visitors at present," the butler announced.

"Would there be a better time?"

"With Mr. Harriman, there is no better time," the butler replied, and shut the door.

2

THE SECRET LIFE OF ELI TUTTLE

ELI TUTTLE WAS A MAN OF ASHES. Although fire had never seared his flesh, hatred burned inside him like a white-hot furnace, leaving only ashes behind. He smelled them on his skin, tasted their bitter dryness in his mouth, felt them course through his blood like the dust of old bones. Ashes were all he knew and all he thought he might ever know.

Consumed by an unaccountable loss in his past, he saw no future for himself, and gloom seemed to follow him like a shadow. There were whisperings, too, that dogged him. In the harsh orphanage where his childhood lay buried in a tomb of suffering and neglect, he'd been accused of a molesting young boys and other appalling acts. He'd responded by trying to burn the place down, and when fireman found him choking in the smoke-filled basement, all he said was, "Ashes to ashes, dust to dust. Isn't that what God wants?"

He'd been tossed out of the orphanage after that and left to fend for himself, taking whatever menial jobs he could find. But under the cover of his ashes, he'd discovered a knack for deception and thievery. By the time he reached his mid-twenties he'd built up a substantial wad of cash by means more foul than fair, and he thought often of escaping the misery of his birthplace. But the ashes were so suffocating that he couldn't find the will to move on, and more than once he'd put a revolver to his temple and wondered if he should end his misery.

Then, on a memorable day in May 1891, his life miraculously changed. He was working as a hired hand at one of the big summer houses on Lake Champlain when by chance his eyes fell on a story in the Sunday edition of the *Plattsburgh Republican*. MILLIONAIRE'S ESTATE IS FOR THE BIRDS said the headline on the syndicated story, which included a woodcut image of Harriman. When Tuttle saw the image and read that Harriman "hailed from the Lake Champlain region of New York State," he knew who the "birdman," as the story called him, must be, and he also knew that he had at last found deliverance.

He gathered up his savings, bought a new black suit, packed all he could into a suitcase, and left Plattsburgh for good, ready to embark on his new existence. During the long train ride to St. Paul he went twenty-four hours without sleep, using every precious moment to plan and plot. When he finally arrived at the Union Depot and walked out to look at the storied Mississippi River for the first time, fiery joy filled his heart.

Yet Tuttle knew he could not let his seething anger get the better of him. He would have to be patient and calculating because it might take a year or even longer to bring about the time of judgment, as he preferred to call it. A downfall as sudden as Satan's when he was hurled from the vault of the heavens would be too quick and easy. Instead, Tuttle wanted to inflict a slow and painful ordeal. Ambrose Harriman would taste the bitter fruit of shame and loss, and Tuttle intended to watch it happen with the cruel pleasure of a boy plucking wings from a fly.

* * *

Among the idlers, drifters, and adventurers who habituated the saloons of St. Paul, Jack Spence was regarded as the ultimate exemplar of the breed. Known as Handy Jack, he drank, gambled, and fought, and when not engaged in those pastimes, he ran a profitable if illegal numbers game and was also known to be a part-time pimp. Around St. Paul he was regarded as a cruel and dangerous man willing to perform any deed, no matter how dark or dishonest, if there was money in it.

Spence had been implicated two years earlier in the peculiar case that came to be known as the newspaper murders, but he'd managed to slip out of trouble by taking a long "vacation" in Chicago. When he ran out of money after a few months, he returned to St. Paul to resume his usual crooked business. Still, he was surprised when he read the note left for him at the rough saloon on St. Peter Street where he usually spent his evenings. The note said, "If you are willing to do a job, a Double Eagle awaits you. Call at my residence at precisely 11 o'clock tonight if you are interested. A. Harriman, 363 Summit Ave."

"You ever hear of somebody named Harriman, first initial 'A,' up on Summit?" Spence asked the bartender as he slipped the note back into its envelope.

"Must be Ambrose Harriman. You know, that geezer who writes all those crazy letters to the newspapers."

Spence made the connection. "Sure. He's the guy with all the birds in his yard, right?"

"That's him."

"He must be worth a lot."

"Millions probably," said the bartender. "Want another beer?"

"Might as well," Spence said. "Looks like I might be coming into some money soon enough."

Spence idled away several hours drinking and playing euchre

before hailing a hack for the short ride up to Birdwing. A man was waiting for him at the front gate, but he looked much too young to be Ambrose Harriman. The man opened the gate and motioned Spence to follow him.

Once they were hidden from view in small grove of trees, Spence turned to his guide and said, "Now who might you be?"

"That doesn't matter," the man said as he put a gold coin in Spence's hand. "Here is the twenty dollars. There will be another twenty in it for you if do as exactly as you are told."

Spence was suspicious. "Say, what kind of racket is this?"

"That is not your concern," Eli Tuttle said. "Now, here is what you must do."

* * *

Eli Tuttle had come to be employed at Birdwing by dint of a series of events that looked to be accidental but were not. The servant he replaced had nearly succumbed to a mysterious ailment that left him so weakened he could no longer continue to work. Arsenic, carefully administered at the saloon where the servant enjoyed an occasional drink, was the source of his distress, which doctors attributed to a particularly bad case of food poisoning.

Hardly had the sick man left to recuperate at the home of his sister when Tuttle knocked on the door of Harriman's mansion, seemingly quite by chance, to offer his services, using an assumed name. He claimed he had only recently arrived in St. Paul to attend the funeral of a beloved grandparent and liked the city so much he decided to stay. He carried excellent fake letters of recommendation from a previous employer, supposedly in Wheaton, Illinois. So perfect was his manner that he was hired on the spot. Tuttle further insinuated himself into Harrison's good graces by causally mentioning he had been born in the town of Chittenango in up-state New York. By no coincidence, Harriman's forebears hailed from the same village.

"Why, what a small world it is," Harriman remarked upon hearing this news, to which Tuttle responded, "Smaller than we think, or so it would seem."

Once he had secured his place in the household, Tuttle slowly began to explore the mansion. He often tiptoed through the house late at night, looking for ways to make Harriman feel uneasy, as though a shadow was growing around him. One night Tuttle staged a fake burglary, quietly breaking a windowpane to make it look as though he had come in from the outside, and after he'd taken a few small items he left a "present" on an expensive oriental rug in the living room.

Harriman was appalled by what had been done, and as he later recounted in his newspaper harangue, he called in the police to investigate. Patrick Donlin, as it so happened, was the detective who took the report, but he was not as surprised as Harriman by what the burglar had deposited on the rug. He'd seen other cases of excremental insult—it was more common than the public knew—and he understood it to be a particularly ugly way of displaying profound hatred and contempt.

"It is the work of one of those damn cat owners," Harriman insisted. "You see now the kind of filthy people they are."

"I suppose that could be," Donlin said, "and we will see what we can find out. But unless someone saw the break-in, we can't—"

"I know," Harriman said with a dismissive wave. "You can do nothing, which insofar as I can tell is what you police people always do. Nothing, nothing, nothing. That is your line of work, and why you get paid for your idleness and incompetence is beyond me. Well then, be gone. I shall make my own inquiries, and I assure you there will be great trouble when I find out who did this."

As soon as Donlin left, Harriman ordered the rug to be removed and burned. The next day he hired men to install bars on all the first-floor windows, not knowing that the malevolent soul taunting him was close at hand.

* * *

Tuttle had killed cats before, back in Plattsburgh, for the simple thrill of it. But in St. Paul the killings had a strategic purpose as the opening act in Tuttle's campaign of vengeance against Harriman. The killings were also a test of Tuttle's ability to operate unseen in the depths of the night—a skill he intended to put to use later to commit far more terrible crimes

To secure his feline prey, Tuttle built a drop trap out of wood and wire, then refined its workings through trial and error. The trap worked quickly and quietly, but attracting cats was rarely easy, and Tuttle spent many long nights hidden in shrubbery, rope in hand, waiting for his quarry. Scraggly feral cats were his first captures, but plumper house cats eventually sniffed out the food and fell for the bait.

When Tuttle reached in with a long gloved hand to grab a trapped cat, he strangled it immediately with a wire, an act that gave him a powerful sense of satisfaction. Later, in the hours after midnight, he dressed in black and roamed through alleys and back yards looking for a suitable spot to pose the dead felines with an attached note that left no doubt they had been deliberately and cruelly slain. The killing of the Hills' cat, Empire, proved to be a particular stroke of good fortune, since Tuttle had no idea who owned the cat when he hung it on the grounds of the mighty mansion.

Tuttle knew Harriman would be suspected of the killings, but mere suspicion was not enough, and so he'd recruited Jack Spence to tighten the screws. Spence's reputation as an unsavory man for hire made him perfect for the job, and when he told his tale Harriman would be pilloried in public. Killing Harriman would have been as easy as killing the cats, but swift revenge held no appeal for Tuttle. He wanted to experience the far more delicious pleasure of ruining Harriman, step by bitter step, until his life became an unendurable ordeal. The cats were only the beginning, and as Tuttle lay down at night, his mind a buzzing hive of possibilities, he took delight in knowing that the worst for Harriman was yet to come.

* * *

Harriman tried to ignore all the ridiculous whisperings about his supposed attacks on neighborhood cats, but it wasn't long before disturbing new allegations propelled him into the news yet again. The *St. Paul Globe* broke the story, courtesy of a tip from Jack Spence, whose previous appearances in print had all been as a name in the police blotter. Now, however, he was eagerly informing the *Globe* how Harriman had paid him to kill the cats.

"He offered me twenty dollars to do the job," Spence stated, presenting as proof the note he'd received at the saloon. But what Spence said next was even more damning.

"When I called on Mr. Harriman that night, he met me at the front door and told me what needed to be done. I was to use some traps he'd made to catch as many cats as I could up there on his estate. Then I was supposed to bring the cats to him and he'd 'take care of them.' That was how he put it. He said he'd pay me an additional five dollars for each cat I trapped."

"And did you go ahead and do that?" the *Globe* reporter asked.

Spence, who could not be described as man of fine moral sensibilities, then allowed as how he could not bring himself to cause the death of innocent house pets. "I guess it just seemed a rum thing to me," he told the newspaper, "so I finally told him he could keep his money. He wasn't happy about it, I will tell you that, but I guess he just went ahead and killed those cats himself."

Harriman, caught by surprise, denied the entire story. But the note Spence received had been signed with a flourish that certainly looked like Harriman's signature. And while Spence had never been known to make a habit of practicing honesty, the police and the public appeared to believe him.

Although Gallagher liked to stay on friendly terms with men of wealth, Harriman was a special case. In one of his recent newspaper harangues, he'd railed against what he called "the utter incompetence of the police" after someone burglarized his mansion and stole several items of value before committing what Harriman called "a loathsome act." The investigating officers, Harriman complained, "showed little or no interest in looking into the crime but did leave their filthy cigar ashes all over my carpeting," a residue that apparently bothered him far more than Webster's frequent excretions.

Since Harriman had so rudely insulted the police, Gallagher saw no reason to downplay Spence's accusation. "This is a most serious matter," Gallagher intoned the next day as a scrum of newsmen gathered in his office. "Mr. Harriman's denials are beginning to sound ever more hollow. Perhaps it is time for him to own up like a man and come clean."

"Will he be arrested?" a reporter asked.

"That is to be determined, but it is certainly a possibility."

Meanwhile, a flood of letters to the editor lambasted Harriman for his perceived brutality. "Mr. Harriman has brought shame to himself and this city," said a missive to the *Pioneer Press* from Mrs. Robert Fontague, who identified herself as "Chairwoman of the St. Paul Cat Club." She went on to say that "Mr. Harriman would do us all a favor by leaving this city. There is no place in St. Paul for such a cruel and deceitful man."

* * *

"I did not know we had a club for cat fanciers in St. Paul," Shadwell Rafferty said to Patrick Donlin as they dug into a substantial breakfast of sausage and eggs in the Ryan Hotel's café.

"Gives all those rich ladies up on Summit something to do besides trying on their jewels," Donlin said. "But as I've told you, I am sick of cats."

"Well, I cannot blame you. Tell me, what do you think of Mr. Spence's little tale?"

"You know the man. Handy Jack would swear falsely with his hand on every Bible in the city and spit on his mother's grave to boot if he thought it would make him a dollar."

"Agreed. When it comes to telling fables, Aesop has nothing on him. So the question is, why would he lie about something like this unless there was money in it for him? But if he turned down the twenty dollars, as he claims, how does he come out ahead? You and I both know he did not volunteer his story to the newspapers as a matter of conscience."

Donlin shrugged and picked at his last piece of sausage. "I have no answers. I just want this all to go away, the sooner the better."

"Well, unless you've got a genie's lamp at home, I doubt your wish will be granted. Besides, I am beginning to think this business may be about more than just a few dead cats."

"What do you mean?"

"I can't put my finger on it, Pat, but there's a kind of malevolence in the air. I have the feeling somebody is plotting and planning, but as to what end, I cannot say. In any case, I intend to have a chat with Mr. Spence one of these days. Maybe I can wring some truth out of him."

"Good luck with that," Donlin said. "Handy Jack has spent his entire life as a criminal, and he has learned the value of silence. You will not get much out of him."

3

A GIRL AND A BOY

IN ST. PAUL'S DAYS OF OLD the poorest of the poor lived in places no one else cared to occupy. This usually meant home was a make-shift shack located on the treacherous flats of the Mississippi River, where spring floods occurred almost every year. For a small annual rent paid to the landowner, impoverished immigrants could cobble together rude wooden dwellings and live as best they could until the floods came. If a home survived the inundation, it could be cleaned and reoccupied. If not, new living arrangements would have to be found in some other precarious place shunned by the substantial citizens of the city.

Anna Jerabek was among the many children who lived on the flats, in her case upriver from downtown just past an unauthorized but well-used dump. She had arrived in America with her parents, Anton and Adela, when she was three. Czech was her first language, but she quickly learned English when she went to school. She grew into a pretty girl with long blond hair, wide blue eyes, and a look of seriousness that suggested she would find some great path forward in life. "She will be somebody," her mother liked to say. "I am sure of it."

Growing up on the flats, with the big river pushing past beneath high bluffs, was not the worst life a child could have, and Anna never thought of herself as poor. From an early age, she was fascinated by the bald eagles that swooped and soared above the river, hunting for fish. She dreamed of one day flying up on a huge kite to cavort with the eagles, free of all her ties to Earth.

Anna became a proficient reader and at least once a week she hiked up to the public library downtown to find new material. She'd come across a copy of *Birds Through an Opera-Glass* there and thought it quite wonderful. Inspired by the book, she began keeping a notebook with descriptions and drawings of birds she'd seen along the river and elsewhere. In the summer months her afternoons were usually free after doing household chores, and she liked to roam the city in search of birds and adventure. On one of her excursions, in mid-June, she walked all the way up to Summit Avenue to look at the fancy houses there, and that's how she met Ambrose Harriman, who happened to be examining a flower bed near the front gates of his estate.

The old curmudgeon didn't like children hanging around his property, and he approached Anna to shoo her away. As Anna peered through the gates, she saw a bird with a flaming orange throat fly down from a hemlock tree and land in a large birdbath. "Why, that is a Blackburnian warbler," she said in an excited voice to no one in particular. "I am sure of it."

Harriman heard her words and was stunned. Few people he knew could name birds other than the most common species, and yet here was a mere wisp of a girl who had correctly identified a very rare avian visitor. He went up to the gate and said, "You are right, my child. It is a Blackburnian and not a fellow one sees very often around here."

"He's beautiful," Anna said, taking out the small notebook she always carried with her. "I'm so happy to see him. I will add him to my records."

"Your records?"

"Yes. I like to know when all my friends arrive for the season. Here, have a look."

Harriman was astounded to see that the girl kept a meticulous account, complete with comments, of what she called "first arrivals." She'd spotted her first robin on March 16 ("a skinny little male"), a Bohemian waxwing ("so delicate and pretty") a week later, and then in April came an eastern phoebe, a northern shrike, a rusty blackbird, and many others. All told, there appeared to be almost fifty species on her list.

"Aren't birds wonderful?" Anna said.

Something happened to Harriman that hadn't happened in a very long time. He was enchanted. Who was this little bird lover? He swung open the gates and said, "What is your name, my dear?"

"Anna Jerabek. I just turned twelve yesterday."

"Is that so? I hope you had a fine birthday. Do you know that our warbler friend here is named after an Anna? Anna Blackburne was her name. She lived in England."

"I would like to have a bird named after me," Anna said.

"Perhaps one day you will. Now, if you would like, I can show you some other birds who like to visit here."

Anna said she would, and by the time she left the estate she and St. Paul's great naysayer had become friends. She soon became a regular visitor at Birdwing, walking the grounds with Harriman and sharing milk and cookies with him inside the mansion, where Webster also took a liking to her. "Pretty girl," he would say when he flew up next to her. "Pretty, pretty girl."

* * *

Anna Jerabek had surprised Harriman in a good way. The same could not be said of another child who'd taken a liking to Birdwing. His name was Freddie Whistler, and Harriman viewed him as a menace. Freddie was the son of a prominent railroad lawyer named Thurston Whistler, who resided with his family in a stately house a few doors down from Birdwing. The boy, who was ten, liked to roam the neighborhood in search of what his father described as "innocent mischief." Not everyone took so liberal a view of Freddie's activities, and more than one neighbor regarded him as an obnoxious little brat doted upon by his unsuspecting parents.

Although Freddie had been cautioned against trespassing in neighbors' yards, he was not attracted to the idea of obedience, and usually did as he pleased. He'd also made a secret friend at Birdwing who encouraged his trespassings. "The old man is mean to everybody," the friend said. "He deserves to be teased and taunted by a fine boy such as yourself."

A week or so before the cat killings began, Freddie had made a daring incursion into Birdwing, where he climbed an apple tree and began shooting at birds and squirrels with his birthday present, a Chicago model air rifle. Harriman caught him at it and roughly escorted Freddie off the grounds with a variety of threats and imprecations, or so the boy claimed.

Thurston Whistler immediately rose to Freddie's defense, demanding an apology from Harriman for his "rude treatment" of the boy. Harriman not only declined but fanned the flames by calling Freddie "an obnoxious little imp." Further unpleasant words ensued, to the point that Whistler threatened to bring assault charges against Harriman, who in turn promised to file a lawsuit against Whistler for supposed damages caused by his delinquent son. Freddie, meanwhile, was under strict orders to stay away from Birdwing, orders he did not obey.

*   *   *

George York resided in a tidy apartment in Harriman's carriage house along with a coachman who made do with smaller quarters next to his. York was always the earliest to arise, climbing out of bed at the first hint of daylight to prepare Birdwing's grounds for their daily avian influx. He added seeds and suet to feeders, prepared a sugary mix for the hummingbirds, and made sure the bird baths and duck pond were topped off with water. Although York had been in Harrison's employ for only a year or so, he knew the morning routine well.

On the morning of August 5, the air already thick with humidity, York went about his duties in the usual fashion. The carriage house stood at the rear of the estate along a cobblestone alley called Maiden Lane. A row of tall arborvitae screened the alley along with a bower of willow trees that formed the farthest corner of the grounds. Nearby, a large feeder with four roosts sat atop a greased pole designed to discourage squirrels from their usual thieving ways. It was York's habit to begin his rounds by mounting a tall stepladder to restock the feeder. As he did so, he caught sight of something within the bower. He couldn't quite make out what it was because it had rained during the night and mist hovered around the willows.

York went back down the ladder to have a look, and he would

later tell the police he could scarcely believe what he saw. A boy he recognized at once as Freddie Whistler lay face up on the ground, utterly still, his fixed blue eyes staring up at the willows. He wore a cotton shirt but no shorts or underpants. Around his neck a red scarf was cinched so tightly that it had left a deep bruise. An air rifle lay next to the body.

York turned away from the awful scene and ran toward the mansion house. Great trouble, he knew, was about to descend on Birdwing like a hawk diving toward its prey. Once he reached the house, York raced upstairs to Harriman's bedroom and pounded furiously on the door. "You must come out, sir," he shouted. "Something terrible has happened."

By the time the police arrived, Harriman had seen the dead boy for himself. He was shocked, or so it appeared to York, and he ordered his gardener to return to the mansion at once and summon the authorities. He also told York to bring back a blanket to cover the dead boy so that he would not be left half naked for all to see.

Patrick Donlin was the first detective on the scene. He found two uniformed patrolmen stomping around the body like big dumb horses and ordered them to back away. Harriman, dressed in a morning robe, stood nearby with York. Both men appeared shaken. Donlin pulled back the blanket to examine the body. The boy was cold and hard to the touch and clearly had been dead for some time. There were no visible wounds to the body other than the deep red mark left by the scarf. Donlin was especially disturbed to see that the body was naked from the waist down. Had the boy been molested before he was strangled? It seemed all too likely, although it was strange that the murderer had apparently taken the boy's shorts and underpants. Donlin didn't see any obvious signs of a sexual assault, but it would be up to the coroner to make that determination.

"Who found him?" Donlin asked.

"I found him, sir," York said and then explained how he'd come across the body while performing his usual chores.

"And you didn't move the body?"

"No, sir."

"What about the blanket? Was he wrapped in it when you found him?"

"Oh no, sir, he was, well, I'm afraid he was, you know, exposed. Mr. Harriman told me to put the blanket on him."

Donlin shot a suspicious glance at Harriman and said, "Why did you do that? You were interfering with a crime scene."

"I did not think it proper that the boy should be left naked to the world."

"Well, the dead don't much care about being proper," Donlin said as he put the blanket back over the boy. "Did you do anything else to the body? Remove his shorts for some reason?"

"Of course not. As far as I know, he is lying just as Mr. York found him."

"That's right," York chimed in. "That's just how it happened."

Donlin said, "Do either of you know the boy?"

After a slight pause, Harriman said, "We do. His name is Freddie Whistler. He lives just a few doors down."

Donlin had a flash of recognition. "He's the kid who sneaked in here awhile back, right? You shooed him away and then his father got mad at you. He claimed you roughed him up."

"It was a false claim. I did nothing to the boy."

"Maybe, but now here he is, dead, with most of his clothes gone," Donlin said. "How do you suppose that happened?"

Harriman said, "I have no earthly idea."

"Did either of you see him on the grounds last night?"

Both Harriman and York said they hadn't. "I can only guess he came here with his rifle to shoot at things," Harriman said. "There was full moon, I believe, so he had enough light."

"Are you sure you didn't catch him at it?"

"Do not be ridiculous," Harriman said. "I am not in the business of murdering children, if that is what you're getting at. Neither is Mr. York, for that matter."

A tall, mustachioed man in a dark suit and a black bowler hat strode up to the group, and the patrolmen standing by gave brief salutes.

"So there's been a murder, I'm told," Chief Michael Gallagher said as he bent down to pull back the blanket over Freddie's body. Although he was about as hardened as a man could be, Gallagher recoiled slightly when he saw the body. "Why, it's just a boy," he said to Donlin. "Now, tell me all you know."

* * *

Minutes after Gallagher arrived, Mathilda Whistler, the boy's mother, came running up and when she saw the small covered form encircled by policemen she burst into tears. "That is not Freddie, is it?" she cried and fell to her knees.

Donlin bent down to try to comfort her. He had two children of his own and could not imagine how he would react if either of them died. "I'm afraid it's Freddie," he said, wrapping an arm around her shoulder.

"I must see him," she said, lunging toward the body. Donlin didn't want her to view the boy in his strangled, half-naked state but didn't feel he could stop her. He pulled down the blanket just far enough to reveal Freddie's face, causing his mother to begin shaking and sobbing. "My little boy, my little boy" were at first the only words she could choke out between sobs.

"What happened?" she finally asked, daubing at her eyes with a handkerchief Donlin gave her. Her voice had turned flat and hard so that almost seemed someone else was speaking on her behalf.

"Unfortunately, it appears he was murdered," Donlin said. "But I promise you we'll find whoever did it."

Mathilda Whistler's face went blank, as though she couldn't comprehend Donlin's words, and then she looked up at Harriman, who stood behind the circle of police.

"You killed him! You killed him!" she screamed as she rose to her feet. She rushed toward Harriman with murderous intensity, and he backed away just as two policemen intercepted her.

His face drained of blood, Harriman said, "No, no, I did not kill your boy. I would never do such a thing."

"Murderer!" she said and began chanting the word as though it was a magical incantation.

As two burly officers struggled to control Mathilda Whistler,

Gallagher finally stepped in and told Harriman to retreat back to his mansion. "We will talk later," he said in a tone that suggested the interview would not be pleasant. Meanwhile, Donlin instructed the officers to take Mathilda home as gently as possible, since he didn't want her to be present when the coroner came to poke and prod at the boy's body.

Thurston Whistler, it was soon discovered, was in Duluth on a legal matter, and it was midmorning before the police were able to reach him with the terrible news. He said he'd return to St. Paul on the first available train, and like his wife he immediately assumed that Harriman was responsible for the ghastly crime. "I will see him hang if it's the last thing I ever do," he promised. "You may be sure of that."

* * *

Back inside his mansion, Harriman felt overwhelmed. How had the boy come to be murdered on his property? It seemed inconceivable, and he could only assume some madman wandering in the night had spotted Freddie and attacked him, perhaps driven by perverted lust. It was almost too awful to think about but Harriman knew he had to. The crime had occurred on his property, and the victim was someone he'd only recently chastised, perhaps too firmly, for trespassing. Unbelievable as it seemed, Harriman realized he would be the prime suspect. So it was that before Gallagher and Donlin came to grill him, Harriman placed a call to Rutherford Cuddleton, who said he would come up to Birdwing as quickly as possible.

Gallagher and Donlin soon came knocking at Harriman's door. A heavyset young butler in maroon livery admitted them and led them into a parlor furnished with tall wooden chairs, two settees, and an étagère populated by small ceramic birds. More birds took flight in the room's greenish-yellow wallpaper.

"We're here to see your boss," Gallagher said, eying the decor with disbelief. "He really likes his birds, don't he?"

"I will tell him you're here, sir," the butler said and left the room.

It was several minutes before Harriman, looking sad and gaunt, made his appearance, Webster perched on his shoulder. "Useless. Useless, I say," the bird squawked, staring at Gallagher with ominous black eyes.

"Be quiet!" Harriman commanded. "You must excuse Webster. He is not at all polite sometimes."

"Then why don't you send the damn bird away," Gallagher said.

Harriman ignored the request and took a seat across from the two men he knew were about to interrogate him. He said, "I will, of course, assist you in any way I can in your investigation, but I fear there is little more I can tell you."

"I'll be the judge of that," Gallagher said, chewing at a cigar that looked to have spent the entire morning in his mouth. "You can start by giving us the lay of this place. We met that fellow York already. He's your gardener, right? Now, who else works here?"

"There's my butler, Mr. Newman, and Mr. Edmonds, my coachman. I also employ a maid, Mrs. Lagerquist."

"And do they all live here?"

"Mr. Newman and Mrs. Lagerquist have rooms on the third floor. Mr. York and Mr. Edmonds have apartments in the carriage house out back."

"And would they all have been here last night?"

"Yes. But if you think any of them—"

"I will think as I please," Gallagher interrupted, raising his voice, "and you best remember that. Now, I imagine you are about to tell me that you were sleeping like a babe last night and heard or saw nothing. Can anyone prove that was so?'

"How? My staff does not watch me sleeping."

"So you have no alibi?" ·

"I do not see that I need one."

"Is that so? Well then, why don't you show us your bedroom."

"My bedroom? Why would you want to see that?"

"Never mind why. Just show us."

"I will not!" Harriman said. "You are being ridiculous."

Donlin said, "No, we ain't, Mr. Harriman. I noticed there's a hole and big crack in one of your upstairs windows, like someone maybe shot a BB through it. That window faces right out to where your gardener found the boy and his air rifle."

"Do you get it now?" Gallagher said. "Because I do. It's simple. That shot woke you up. You went over to your broken window and saw Freddie out in the yard with his air gun. You got mad, real, real mad. So you decided to go out and teach the boy a lesson."

"I did no such thing."

"Then you won't have no objection to us taking a look at that window."

Harriman wasn't sure what to do. He knew nothing about a broken window, but if Gallagher was telling the truth—

Before Harriman could complete his thought, Gallagher was back at him. "Yeah, the way I figure it, you went out, grabbed the boy, diddled with him because you're a pervert of some kind. Then you killed him because he could identify you. You even took his shorts as a nasty little souvenir. That's what happened, ain't it?"

"That is an outrageous lie!" Harriman said, glaring at the chief, "and I will not stand for it. How dare you accuse me of such a thing! You may leave now. I have nothing more to say to you, but my attorney undoubtedly will."

"Foolish! Foolish!" Webster suddenly blurted out. "Away with you, sir!"

Gallagher looked at the bird in a way that suggested he'd like to dine on him for dinner. "Shut that goddamn bird up or I will," he said.

"You will do no such thing," Harriman said. "Now, once again, I must demand that you leave."

"We'll go when we're good and ready," Gallagher replied. "So you've already hired a shyster. That's what guilty men do. Well, he won't do you no good. You'll hang for what you've done. You killed that poor boy and I intend to prove it."

It was all Donlin could do to hold his tongue. Donlin regarded himself as a skilled interrogator who knew how to probe for inconsistencies and lies in a suspect's story. The chief, on the other hand, seemed to think that bashing Harriman with a hammer would somehow force him to admit guilt.

"Mr. Harriman will not hang for anything," said a booming voice behind Gallagher. The chief spun around and saw Rutherford Cuddleton, all five feet four inches of him, step into the room. "Mr. Harriman is my client, and neither he nor I will tolerate your baseless allegations. Mr. Harriman, however, will provide you with a full and honest statement once I've had a chance to go over matters with him. Now, I think we are done here."

"Oh, we ain't done. We're just starting," Gallagher said with a growl. "You can talk all you want, but there ain't a jury in the world that will think twice about seeing your client swing." Gallagher, who despised lawyers in general and Cuddleton in particular, stood up and laughed in in his peculiar menacing way. "You won't get this filthy murderer off," he said as he came straight toward Cuddleton. At six feet two, the chief towered over Cuddleton, but the lawyer held his ground like a fearless little terrier confronting a bear.

"We shall see about that," said Cuddleton. "You are a bully, Chief, and bullies always get their comeuppance in the end."

"Why, you dirty little pipsqueak, I ought to—"

The chief, who liked nothing better than delivering a good beating, was on the verge of doing something regrettable when Donlin interceded.

"Come on, don't be foolish. It's time to go. If Mr. Harriman killed that boy, we'll get him for it."

"Damn right we will," Gallagher said as he tried, unsuccessfully, to stare down Cuddleton, "and this fat little mouthpiece won't save him."

* * *

After the chief and Donlin had gone, Cuddleton sat down next to his new client and said, "You are in grave trouble, Mr. Harriman. The chief, albeit a brute, is quite right that a jury will want desperately to see that someone hangs for murdering that lad."

"You must know I did not do it," Harriman said.

"No, what I must know is how to win an acquittal if you are indeed indicted and brought to trial, which is very likely. Now, why don't you tell me everything you can about this business."

Harriman did so and eventually got around to mentioning the broken window. Cuddleton immediately understood its significance. "We must have a look for ourselves," he said.

When they went out to gaze up at the window, Harriman felt a sour churning in his stomach. "It is my bedroom window," he said. "But I am a heavy sleeper and I assure you I did not hear the glass break."

Cuddleton said, "Well, it's a problem for us. Let's see if we can find a BB in your bedroom."

It didn't long to locate the pellet, which lay on the floor beneath the shattered windowpane. Heavy drapes, which Harriman said were almost always drawn shut, shielded the window and stopped the BB from penetrating farther into the bedroom.

Harriman stared down at the little projectile and said, "What should we do with it?"

"I am afraid we must leave it," Cuddleton said, "however tempting it would be to make it disappear. The law is the law, and it must be followed. We cannot tamper with evidence, but we must do some reconnoitering before the police come stomping through here. Who knows what other evidence might be lying about."

"So you think the police might be coming back? I've told them all I know."

"That doesn't matter. Our ogre of a police chief, if he has half a brain, will request a search warrant for your house and its grounds posthaste and anon. And once the police arrive, they will scour every nook and cranny to see what wonders they can find."

"I have nothing to hide," Harriman insisted.

"If that is so," said Cuddleton with a slow shake of his head, "I must account you the rarest of men."

4

A TIGHTENING NOOSE

THE NEWSPAPERS OF ST. PAUL—the *Pioneer Press*, the *Globe*, and the *Dispatch*—became instantly obsessed with Freddie's murder, as did the entire city. Day after day stories poured out beneath screaming headlines, and no feature of the case was too small to be overlooked. Much was made of the possible sexual assault but in the carefully coded language of the day. The killer, wrote the *Dispatch,* "may have intended to gratify certain perverse desires," and everyone knew what that meant.

Thurston Whistler drove much of the coverage. He stated to any reporter who would listen that he believed Harriman had assaulted and then murdered his son. "The man is a perverted fiend and if the law does not bring him to justice, I will," Whistler told the *Pioneer Press,* which assigned its top reporter, Dolly Charbonneau, to the story. When pressed by Charbonneau to explain what he meant, the lawyer said, "I mean that I will kill him myself if I must. Is that clear enough for you?"

Charbonneau also managed to obtain an interview with Mathilda Whistler and wrote a heart-wrenching story about how she "keened day and night, inconsolable at the loss of her beloved little boy." And like her husband, she believed Harriman was the murderer. "Why, oh why did that evil man do what he did to my little Freddie?" she was quoted as saying. "God's wrath awaits him, and he will burn in hell as surely as Satan does."

Gallagher, meanwhile, was doing all he could to paint a dark halo of guilt around Harriman. "He has not been at all cooperative in this matter," Gallagher told the *Globe.* "He has refused to answer questions and has no alibi for his whereabouts at the time little Freddie was murdered. When all the evidence is in, I do not doubt for a moment that Mr. Harriman will have much to answer for. The noose is tightening, as far as I am concerned."

The *Globe* went on to write: "Thus far, Mr. Harriman has offered no public statement in regard to Freddie's murder. However, his well-known attorney, Rutherford Cuddleton, averred to our reporter that 'there is not so much as a scintilla of evidence linking Mr. Harriman to this terrible crime. He has told the police all he knows, which is very little. There is a presumption of innocence in our legal system, but in this case there is instead a presumption of guilt directed at my client.'"

For its part, the public had little use for an abstraction like the presumption of innocence. Anger and disgust rolled across St. Paul like a mighty wave and crashed up against the old stone walls of Harriman's house. "It is all too obvious who committed this foul deed," said a letter writer to the *Dispatch*. "If there are still red-blooded men in this city, they should find a tall tree and hang Ambrose Harriman from it at the first opportunity. Animals of his type deserve nothing better."

* * *

Patrick Donlin had been a detective for fifteen years and although he was no Sherlock Holmes, he possessed what Rafferty like to call "good eyes." He noticed small things, and he'd been the only copper on the scene to spot the hole in Harriman's bedroom window. But had that broken window precipitated Freddie's murder, as Gallagher clearly believed? It seemed like a good enough theory—Harriman rushing outside in white-hot anger to attack the boy in response to the BB shot—but the more Donlin thought about it the less sense it made.

The biggest problem was that Freddie was an agile ten-year-old while Harriman was a man of about sixty with a pronounced limp. Could he really have chased down Freddie in the dark and killed him? That seemed unlikely. Or had Harriman, perhaps armed with a pistol, managed to sneak up on Freddie before strangling him? It was possible, Donlin supposed, but he still had trouble seeing how a codger like Harriman could have pulled off the feat.

As for the "sex angle," as Donlin liked to call it, he wasn't so sure about that, either. Donlin had dealt with men who assaulted children and knew that they often led what otherwise looked to be perfectly normal lives. A recluse like Harriman, who rarely left his property and seemed to have no great human attachments, did not strike Donlin as the type who in his old age would suddenly decide to bugger a child. Yet Donlin also knew that when it came to sex, many men had secret longings and hidden urges, and maybe that was true of Harriman.

Another big question in Donlin's mind was what Freddie had been doing at Birdwing in the middle of the night. When Mathilda Whistler was able to talk, she said Freddie had gone to bed at nine as usual and that she assumed he was asleep in his bedroom when she awoke the following morning. It was only after she discovered he was missing that she went out to look for him and saw the commotion at Birdwing. Once the coroner established that Freddie had been killed between about midnight and 2:00 a.m., Donlin needed to figure out why and under what circumstances Freddie had left home and gone to Birdwing, air rifle in hand, at so late an hour.

As Donlin puzzled over the case, he knew he'd also have to figure out a way to keep Gallagher from mucking up his investigation. The chief always favored simple, obvious solutions over any other kind. Not given to deep thinking or careful investigation, he liked to wrap up criminal cases, especially the ones that garnered extensive newspaper publicity, as speedily as possible. "Do not hesitate to arrest the first available suspect," he liked to say, "and you'll rarely be wrong."

Unfortunately, he often was wrong, as the case of the newspaper murders had so amply illustrated two years earlier. Donlin knew the chief would waste no time in pinning Freddie's murder on Harriman while the press howled for blood. But Donlin wanted to dig a bit deeper before sending Harriman to the gallows, no matter what Gallagher thought.

* * *

Like almost everyone else in America that August, Eli Tuttle had closely followed the saga of Lizzie Borden in Massachusetts, and he was deeply impressed by her homicidal achievement. Tuttle took great pleasure in the thought of planting an axe so deeply in Harriman's skull that bits of his brain would come flying out like spilled oatmeal. But, of course, he couldn't do it. Blood lust was an urge to annihilate, and his urge was different. Above all else, Tuttle wanted Harriman to suffer before he died, to feel the sting of scorn and revulsion as his days wound down to a shameful date with the gallows.

Tuttle had framed Harriman for the murder of Freddie Whistler with that end in mind. He'd thought at first that killing a child might be difficult, but as he choked the life out of Freddie, the boy's terrified eyes bulging out like marbles, Tuttle felt no pangs of guilt. His own life, he believed, would have been much better had it been cut short at age ten, as Freddie's was. Instead, Tuttle had endured endless days of pain and abandonment in an orphanage where there was much discipline but little love. Besides, Freddie was just like all those rich boys Tuttle had known, the ones who laughed at his shabby clothes and called him ugly names. How sweet it would be, Tuttle thought, if he could go back and kill every last one of them.

Tuttle had wanted Jack Spence to take care of Freddie, but the thug who was said to be up for any dirty job had unaccountably turned him down, despite being offered one hundred dollars. "I don't kill kids for no amount of money," Spence said and walked away. So Tuttle, who had quietly befriended Freddie, convinced the boy to sneak out of his home at midnight and come to Birdwing. The lure was a chance to gain revenge against Harriman by killing a great horned owl known to hang out around the estate. "The old man loves that owl," Tuttle told Freddie, "and he'll be furious when he finds out somebody shot it. But he won't be able to prove a thing against us. It will be our secret. You see, I hate him just as much as you do."

Being just ten, Freddie was easily manipulated, and when he arrived at Birdwing, ready for his great adventure, Tuttle easily overpowered and strangled him. Afterward, Tuttle removed the boy's shorts and underwear, hoping to deceive the police into thinking he'd been molested. Then Tuttle fired a shot from Freddie's BB gun at Harriman's bedroom window to provide a motive for Freddie's murder. Later, when he talked alone to the police, Tuttle expressed mild doubt that Harriman could have murdered the boy but added, "He is a very strange, secretive sort, and I guess you can never really know a man like that, can you?"

Nor did Harriman know what lay in store for him once the police searched his house, as Tuttle assumed they would. On his secret rounds through the mansion, Tuttle had salted away a number of incriminating items he hoped would be sufficient to send Harriman to the gallows for Freddie Whistler's murder. Yet even though Tuttle had done all in his power to frame Harriman for the crime, he feared it might not be enough. A clever lawyer like Rutherford Cuddleton was a moth who could eat holes in any case unless it was armor-plated, and so there was at least a chance Harriman might slip free of the noose.

As he considered his situation, Tuttle suddenly realized how he could deliver one final, terrible blow to Harriman, and he wondered why he hadn't thought of it earlier. It would bruise his withered old heart so deeply that nothing could allay the pain. He would die a bereft and shattered man, and no amount of lawyerly wiles would save him from his awful fate.

* * *

Oblivious to the agent of vengeance in his household, Ambrose Harriman tried to keep to his routine in the days after Freddie's murder, and he visited frequently with his one true friend, Anna Jerabek. But he began to worry that his attachment to the girl would be all too easily misconstrued. If people believed he was capable of killing Freddie, then what would they think of his relationship with Anna?

"We must be careful, my child," Harriman said to her one afternoon as they wandered through the spacious grounds of Como Park. In those days much of the park was still undeveloped, and there were patches of wild woodland where birds of many species found refuge. With the aid of Harriman's binoculars they'd spotted a pileated woodpecker at work, the bright red crest atop its head a blur as the bird used its pointed beak like a tiny jackhammer to pound into a tree in search of insects.

"Why is that?" Anna asked. "Have we done something wrong?"

"No. But there are people who believe I'm an awful man. You know about the boy who was murdered, don't you?"

Anna nodded solemnly. "Mama says she thinks you did it, but I know better."

"Oh, my child, what a wonderful heart you have! I have done bad things in my life, but I would never murder anyone. I am sorry to hear your mother feels as she does."

"I will convince her she's wrong. "

"I do not doubt that you will. You are an amazing girl, and I care for you more than I have cared for anyone in a long, long time. But it will be best if we do not see each other for a while. Otherwise, people will start talking, and I would be very upset if any trouble came your way."

"But I like being with you," Anna protested. "You're my best friend."

"And I will always be yours," Harriman said, gripping her hand. "I promise I will see you again as soon as I can. Come now, I will take you home. Your mama will be worried if you're not back by dinnertime."

Edmonds was waiting for them with the landau, and they rode back in style to Harriman's mansion. Anna loved being in the carriage and dreamed of having one of her own someday, along with a fine house and a big yard where birds would always sing. Once they neared the river flats, Harriman told Edmonds to stop and let out Anna. A fancy carriage on the flats would be an unusual sight, and Harriman did not want anyone to see him with Anna.

"Be safe and well, my dear," he said as she stepped out. "We will see each other as soon as my troubles are over."

5

A VISIT TO BIRDWING

A GOOD BARTENDER, Shadwell Rafferty liked to say, was only as good as his ears. Serving up beer and whiskey required no great skill, but listening was an art that had taken Rafferty years to fully master. By the early 1890s, he'd been in the saloon business long enough to have heard hundreds of men expound on one topic or another. The duplicity of women, the ungratefulness of children, the stupidity and arrogance of bosses, the idiocy of politicians, and, perhaps most vexing of all, the failure of everyone else to recognize the speaker's innate brilliance were all topics that Rafferty knew well. A nod of agreement, a sympathetic word, or a pat on the shoulder were the balms Rafferty applied to the wounded souls who bellied up to the bar. They in turn responded by making his establishment such a great success that on most nights Rafferty had to use his commanding bulk to carve his way through the crowds like a ship cutting through sea ice.

The saloon was also a great engine of gossip and Rafferty always paid close attention to it, for he knew rumor was a scented wind that often blew in ahead of a storm. The murder of Freddie Whistler naturally inspired much talk from the assembled drinkers, who were always a mixed lot. On any given night a learned judge in a bespoke wool suit might be standing at the bar next to a house painter in dungarees or a retired lumberjack in a checkered shirt carefully nursing his glass of Theodore Hamm's finest lager.

Among the saloon's regulars, one figure stood out, although not because of his physical stature. Rutherford P. Cuddleton was short, rotund, and perpetually disheveled, and nothing in his appearance suggested his status as St. Paul's leading criminal defense attorney. Yet the force of his character was so incandescent that Rafferty compared him to "one of Mr. Edison's lightbulbs, for he always seems to be shining brightly." Cuddleton specialized in seemingly hopeless cases, and more than once he'd won acquittal for a guilty criminal by means of some intricate feat of legal legerdemain. Despite his warm-sounding name, he was a razor-sharp dagger in the courtroom, and in courthouse parlance to be "cuddled" was to be subjected to a cross-examination so withering that a ceremonial disembowelment might have been more pleasurable.

His theatrics made him a favorite of the newspapers, which always alerted the public to an impending performance. "Mr. Peter Brown, of the contracting firm which bears his name, will be cross-examined tomorrow afternoon by Rutherford Cuddleton in the courtroom of Judge Kelly," a typical item read. "Fireworks are expected." When the time came for Brown or some other poor soul to be filleted, the courtroom would invariably fill with spectators, among them a small group of elderly women who staked out seats in the front row and saw no harm in mixing a little blood with their knitting.

"'Twould be easier to proclaim innocence from sin to Lucifer at the gates of hell than to face Mr. Cuddleton in a courtroom," Rafferty once said. Yet at the saloon, with a glass of Glenturret in hand, Cuddleton could be quite charming.

Cuddleton was on his third dose of Scotch when he casually mentioned that he had been hired by Ambrose Harriman. "I was engaged by the gentleman none too soon. Judging by what I have read in the newspapers, the police and the public already seem to have made up their minds when it comes to poor little Freddie's murder."

"Ah, so the police must regard Mr. Harriman as their prime suspect," Rafferty said.

The lawyer shook his head in disgust, took a swig of his Scotch, and said, "The police can usually be counted on to pursue the innocent in lieu of finding the guilty, and they are entirely mistaken in thinking my client had anything to do with the boy's murder. I shall take great pleasure in making fools of them."

"I don't doubt that you will try, but the police must have something that makes them suspicious."

Cuddleton said, "Perhaps we should talk in private for a moment, Mr. Rafferty. Be a good fellow and bring that bottle of Glenturret along to your office. I have a proposition for you."

Once they'd settled in Rafferty's office—where a big flat-topped desk acted as an anchor amid a swirling sea of papers, books, mementos, and miscellaneous flotsam—Cuddleton said, "The police do not merely regard Mr. Harriman as a suspect. He is in their minds the guilty party, and I would not be surprised if he is arrested soon and charged with murder."

"On what basis?"

Cuddleton described the crime scene to Rafferty and revealed that newspaper accounts had omitted two important details— Freddie's missing clothes and the broken bedroom window. "The police are keeping that information to themselves as they try to build a case against my client. Their next step will be to obtain a search warrant for Mr. Harriman's mansion, and I fear they may well find more incriminating evidence."

"What sort of evidence?"

Cuddleton leaned in toward Rafferty and said, "What I am about to tell you must be kept in the strictest confidence. Mr. Harriman called me late this afternoon and said he'd made a startling discovery quite by accident in a dresser drawer in his bedroom. It was a red silk scarf all but identical to the one used to strangle the Whistler boy. Mr. Harriman told me he had no idea how it got there, as he had never seen it before."

"Do you believe him?"

"That hardly matters. What I do believe is that the scarf would be powerful evidence of guilt if Mr. Harriman goes on trial."

"What did you advise Mr. Harriman to do?"

Cuddleton shrugged and said, "I merely advised him to consider how it might look if the police were to find the scarf."

"I see. And if the scarf were to disappear, you would know nothing about that."

"Correct again, Mr. Rafferty. But regardless of the scarf, I must assume that Mr. Harriman is an innocent man. If so, the scarf was planted by someone out to frame him for murder."

"Someone with ready access to his mansion," Rafferty noted. "Do you have any idea who it might be?"

"That, Mr. Rafferty, is what I hope you can find out. I have a sense that there is some buried secret behind all that has happened of late, beginning with those strange cat killings. I would like you to help so that Mr. Harriman does not end up on the gallows."

"As it so happens, I have been looking into the matter of those dead cats on behalf of Mr. Hill," Rafferty said.

"So you already have a client, is that it?"

"An informal client, I would say, as I was merely doing the work as a personal favor."

"Then I see no reason why you should not work for me on behalf of Mr. Harriman. Everyone knows you are the best detective in this city, and I can think of no one better to ferret out the truth. There will be a hundred dollars in it for you and another hundred if you can find the real murderer. What do you say?"

Rafferty was doing very well with his saloon. Even so, one hundred dollars with the prospect of double that to come was a most attractive offer. And the case of Freddie Whistler's murder was certainly intriguing. Rafferty made a quick decision. "All right, I will do it, but under one condition. If I find convincing evidence that Mr. Harriman is indeed guilty, I will not hesitate to state so publicly, and you can keep the extra one hundred."

"Fair enough," Cuddleton said. "Where would you like to start?"

"With Mr. Harriman and his servants."

"Very well. I will arrange an interview. Have you ever been in his mansion?"

"No."

"Well, you will be in for an experience. I will let you know when I have arranged a time for the two of you to talk."

* * *

The mansions occupying the high bluff from which Summit Avenue derived its name were a mixed lot. Some of the smaller ones had been built as early as the 1850s, when St. Paul was more of an idea than a place, but as the city grew so did the size of the houses from which the wealthy could gaze down with satisfaction on the less deserving classes below. James J. Hill's sandstone fortress was the largest of them all, its roof vast enough to shelter an entire colony of more modest dwellings. Ambrose Harriman's home, built of gray limestone and dominated by a pagoda-roofed tower, was on the lower end of the grandeur scale. With its narrow crowned windows and delicate detailing, the house by the 1890s already seemed to be from an age gone by.

A day after accepting Cuddleton's proposal, Rafferty paid an early evening call on Harriman while assistant bartenders took charge of the saloon. Rafferty had been in quite a few of the fancy homes on Summit, but Harriman's was indeed an "experience," as Cuddleton had promised. A stout, youngish butler in crisp maroon livery answered the doorbell and escorted Rafferty through what he later described as "the biggest damn birdhouse in St. Paul." There were no live birds in cages, as he expected to find. Instead, the walls in every room were papered in elaborate patterns featuring peacocks, snowy egrets, orioles, cardinals, and a host of other birds Rafferty couldn't identify. Ceiling murals, obviously executed at considerable cost, continued the avian theme, while every shelf, mantle, and table served as a roost for a stuffed or sculpted bird. The only exception to the avian theme was a framed drawing, hung amid an otherwise blank expanse of wall, that offered a panoramic view of a town identified as Plattsburgh, New York.

Since reading the early adventures of Sherlock Holmes, Rafferty had tried his best to emulate the great detective by becoming more observant. He stopped for a moment to examine the map, which looked to have been mounted only recently judging by the absence of dust around its frame. "Is there some significance to Plattsburgh?" he asked the butler.

"I wouldn't know, sir. The picture went up just a few weeks ago."

"I noticed that," Rafferty said, pleased that his deduction had been confirmed.

Rafferty's attention turned to a stuffed hawk perched atop a high bookcase and presumably looking for prey in the carpet. "I had heard Mr. Harriman loves birds, but this is almost beyond belief," he said. "It must be strange working in such a house."

"I do not find it to be a problem, sir."

"Ah, and you would be?"

"Adam Newman, sir, at your service."

"A pleasure to make your acquaintance, Mr. Newman. Do you receive a lot of visitors here?"

"Not many, sir."

Rafferty said, "Yes, I've heard Mr. Harriman is something of a recluse. He must have been shocked by Freddie Whistler's murder."

"I am not at liberty to speak of such things," Newman said by way of an answer that really wasn't one. "Now, if you will follow me, sir, I will bring you to Mr. Harriman."

The house tour ended at a small, tiled breakfast room with a bank of tall transomed windows sporting stained-glass bluebirds. Harriman was seated at a table by the windows, reading the morning newspapers with the aid of spectacles that teetered precariously at the tip of his long nose. A foot-high brown bird with a yellow beak and feet sat on Harriman's right shoulder and said as soon as it saw Rafferty and the butler, "Get to the point, sir. Get to the point." It then took wing and flew off into an adjoining room.

"Webster always offers good advice, doesn't he?" Harriman said in a high, nasal, and instantly irritating voice. He wore a black silk kimono adorned with flying cranes and a heavy wool muffler around his neck even though the day was warm and muggy. His white hair, a maze of curls and tangles, appeared as though it hadn't been visited by a comb in weeks, and his long beard was just as unruly. To Rafferty, he looked like some crazy old wizard out of a fairy tale.

Harriman dismissed the butler, then fixed his dark eyes on Rafferty and said, "That thief Cuddleton, who claims to be an honest lawyer—an oxymoron if there ever was one—told me you would be here at seven and so you are. It is a good thing you are on time, sir. Lateness is rudeness, as I see it, and nothing else. Have a seat then and tell me what you want."

Small talk clearly was not on Harriman's agenda, so Rafferty, taking a cue from Webster, wasted no words. "Mr. Cuddleton has hired me to look into the murder of Freddie Whistler. As you are a suspect, I would like—"

"You would like me to deny any involvement in it, I suppose," Harriman interrupted. "Well, of course I deny it. Why, the very idea is patently ridiculous."

"Perhaps, but the fact remains there are those who believe you began by killing those cats—as a sort of practice, I suppose—and then moved on to bigger quarry."

"Lies!" Harriman said, slapping a hand on the table. "Lies, lies, and more lies! I have many enemies in this city, and they are all people of the worst sort, not that many good people are to be found in this cruel world as far as I am concerned."

Rafferty was struck by the vehemence of Harriman's words. "Why are you such a bitter man, Mr. Harriman? What has the world done to you?"

"Everything bad that can be done to a man," Harriman responded before quickly turning his head away as though afraid some powerful emotion might betray him. "But I do not wish to speak of such things. As I said, I am the victim of a dark plot. That fellow who claimed I hired him to kill cats is at the center of it. He made up the entire story."

"You're speaking of Jack Spence. Why would he make up such a thing?"

"Somebody paid him, I imagine, to spread vile falsehoods about me."

"Who do you think that was?"

"You are the detective, sir, not I. Go out and investigate."

Rafferty could see why Harriman had few if any friends. The man was insufferable. Still, Rafferty plowed ahead. "I have been looking into the matter of the cats, and as you know the police suspect you killed them just as you killed Freddie Whistler to keep your birds out of harm's way."

"It is all nonsense, pure and simple, and the police are perfect fools if they think otherwise," Harriman said. "As I have said repeatedly, I had nothing to do with killing those damned cats, however much I despise felines in general. As for the Whistler boy, I most certainly did not murder him."

"I hope that is so, Mr. Harriman, but if it is not, the truth will inevitably come out. The police are busy digging away, and the newspapers probably have half a dozen men at work sifting through every last detail of your life in search of something to incriminate you."

"The newspapers, sir, are in the business of lying, and were it not for the letters I send them regularly, I doubt you would find a scintilla of truth in all of that wasted ink."

"Very well, let us return to the subject of Freddie Whistler. There was an incident some weeks ago when he sneaked onto your grounds and shot at birds. Was that the last time you saw him before his body was discovered?"

"Of course it was. He was a nasty little imp as far as I am concerned, but that does not mean I wished to harm him in any way. I simply wished to keep him off my property."

"And you had no idea he had come back on the night he was murdered—no idea whatsoever—even though he shot a BB through your bedroom window?"

"So Cuddleton told you about that, I see."

"He did. He also mentioned that silk scarf you found in your bedroom."

Harriman looked suspiciously at Rafferty and said, "Mr. Cuddleton should learn to speak less and think more. I have nothing to say about any scarf."

"May I ask who besides you has access to your bedroom?"

"My housemaid and my butler."

"What about the other servants?"

"They would have no reason to be in my bedroom. Now then, what is the point of this tiresome interrogation, Mr. Rafferty? As I have stated to the police, to Mr. Cuddleton, and now to you, I had nothing to do with the Whistler boy's death, and I have no information as to who might have killed him or why. It is that simple."

"It is not simple at all, Mr. Harriman. You are in a very serious situation. Trouble is bearing down on you like a highballing freight, and you are standing square in the middle of the tracks. The police are not the utter fools you make them out to be, and, if Mr. Cuddleton is right, they intend to search every inch of your home and grounds for evidence. I assume you've disposed of the silk scarf, but if the police find anything else that links you to Freddie's murder, you will be a candidate for the gallows."

"They will not dare do such a thing," Harriman said. "Why do you think I have engaged Cuddleton? Because I like the man? No, it is because he is being paid very good money—my money, Mr. Rafferty, my money!—to put all of this nonsense to rest. I presume he is now paying you to investigate. He seems to think you are the best detective in the city. Well then, as I have said, do your work and find the real criminal."

"I will do my best," Rafferty said, "but I need your cooperation. Assuming you did not kill Freddie, then someone—presumably the murderer himself—has gone to great lengths to paint you as the guilty party. Do you have any idea who would want to do so? A businessman who believes you cheated him? An employee with a grudge? Someone you attacked in one of your letters?"

"I am unaware of anyone in St. Paul who would go so far as to commit murder just to bring me down, but one never knows, does one?"

"I suppose not. What about family members? Are you on poor terms with any of them?"

Harriman paused—the first time he had done so, Rafferty noted with interest—and there was a note of agitation in his voice when he finally answered. "As for a family, I have none."

"No children or brothers and sisters?"

"None that I wish to speak of."

"You are estranged from your family, I take it."

"Take what you please," Harriman said curtly. "I will say no more about it."

Wondering if Harriman might be hiding something, Rafferty

pressed for more information. "Perhaps you can can tell me a little about your life before you arrived in St. Paul. I believe I read somewhere that you were born in New York State."

"That is of no consequence," Harriman insisted.

"I saw a map of Plattsburgh, New York, hanging on the wall in another room," Rafferty said. "Is that where you come from?"

"My early life is none of your concern, nor anyone else's, for that matter. Now, sir, I think you have taken up enough of my time. All you need to know is that I am innocent of any wrongdoing. The police, who are the very definition of village idiots, have no case, yet I have been forced at great expense to hire an attorney to defend myself against their ignorance and incompetence. Why don't you find that Spence fellow and pound the truth out of him? He'll know who's behind this dirty business."

"I am not in the habit of beating confessions from people, Mr. Harriman. I leave that to the police."

"Then that is exactly what the police should be doing."

Webster suddenly returned. He landed smoothly on Harriman's shoulder and said in a voice that sounded eerily like that of his master, "Nonsense, sir, nonsense. Seeds now."

"Yes, Webster, you shall have your dinner," Harriman said as he stood up. "There is no more to be said at the moment. Cuddleton will keep me informed as to your activities."

"I am sure he will. There is just one more thing. Would it be possible to talk to Mr. York about the discovery of Freddie's body?"

"The police already spoke to him at length."

"Yes, but I have a few questions of my own."

Harriman let out a sigh and called for the butler. "Very well, I will have Adam ring up Champ and let him know that you wish to have a few words. You will find him in the carriage house."

"Champ? I'm afraid I don't know who that is," Rafferty said.

"It's Mr. York's nickname. Apparently, he's won several chess tournaments in his day or some such thing. Of course, chess is nothing but—"

"A waste of time?" Rafferty offered.

"Precisely. Now, I bid you a good day, sir, if such a day is ever to be had," Harriman said. With Webster still occupying a shoulder, Harriman limped toward the door. Rafferty wondered about the limp—an old war wound, perhaps?—but said nothing as the cantankerous old man left the room.

* * *

The carriage house was a rambling wooden affair with steep roofs rising over a series of bargeboarded dormers. Its big swinging doors were wide open and Rafferty went inside, where he found a man working on a hose fitting. Another servant was grooming one of two big roans that occupied stalls to the rear. A handsome landau carriage was parked nearby next to a sleigh used for winter excursions.

"Ah, you must be Mr. York," Rafferty said when the man tending to the hose looked up. "Or should I call you Champ?"

York was a short, thin, jittery-looking man who seemed barely able to fill his overalls. He had a weather-beaten face, short-cropped black hair, and the gnarled hands of a laborer. Rafferty put his age at about thirty, or perhaps a little younger. He hardly looked like a great chess player, but then again it was always hard to tell about people.

"Champ is what I go by, so that would be fine," York said. "Mr. Harriman said you wished to speak with me. And you are?"

"Shadwell Rafferty. I am doing a little detective work for Mr. Harriman. I promise not to take much of your time, but I do I have a few questions about the boy who was found murdered here. You discovered the body, did you not?"

"Yes, and it was a sight I hope to never see again."

"I do not blame you. It must have been a great shock. I am just wondering if you had ever seen the boy here before."

"Well, there was that time we caught him trying to shoot birds."

"I understand that made Mr. Harriman very angry."

"Oh, I wouldn't say that, sir. He was just a little upset, that's all."

"Didn't the boy claim he was manhandled?"

"I do not wish to speak ill of the dead, sir, but the boy wasn't telling the truth."

"And Mr. Harriman escorted him off the grounds, is that right?"

"Yes, sir, that's what he did, and he told him never to come back. Too bad he did."

"Did you see the boy or hear anything unusual the night before you found his body?"

"No, sir. I go to bed early."

"And you have an apartment here in the carriage house?"

"Yes, sir. I'm upstairs, and Ted has a room next to the stalls."

"Do the two of you often go into the mansion itself?"

"Hardly ever, sir. That is Mr. Newman's domain."

"Yes, I've met him. He is not a very talkative fellow."

"He's the great stone face, that's for sure," said the servant who'd been grooming one of the carriage horses and now came up to join the conversation. "Say, what's going on, Champ? Who's this big fellow?"

Rafferty introduced himself and said, "I am looking into certain matters on behalf of Mr. Harriman. May I ask who are you, sir?"

"Theodore Edmonds," the man responded with an engaging smile as he shook Rafferty's hand. He was tall and well built, perhaps in his late twenties, and seemed more outgoing than York. "I'm the coachman, groomsman, and jack-of-all-trades hereabouts."

"Pleased to meet you," Rafferty said, thinking at once Edmonds might turn out to be a better source of information than the taciturn gardener. "As you may have heard, I've been asking Champ about the Whistler boy."

"Oh, what a terrible thing that was," Edmonds said, shaking his head. "I told the police all I know, which isn't much. I was sound asleep and didn't hear a thing. Same with Champ. I guess the boy came back here wanting to shoot something and some pervert attacked him. That's about all I can figure."

"I've heard Mr. Harriman despises children," Rafferty said. "Isn't it possible he became so angry with Freddie that he went out and attacked the boy for shooting out his bedroom window?"

York started to reply but Edmonds cut him short. "Well, that's what the papers are saying, but I don't believe it for a minute. Mr. Harriman has a temper all right but there's no crime in that, is there? And I know for a fact he's got nothing against children. He's very sweet on that girl who comes around here."

Rafferty's ears perked up. "What girl is that? "

York shot a quick glance at Edmonds and said, "I see no reason to talk about that, Ted. It's got nothing to do with anything."

Edmonds said, "Well, I was just trying to help out Mr. Harriman. He's got a softer side people don't know about. Besides, it's no big secret about the girl."

Despite repeated attempts by York to shush him, Edmonds told Rafferty about Anna Jerabek and her frequent visits to Birdwing. "I call her the bird girl," Edmonds said. "She knows all about them, just like Mr. Harriman. That's why he likes her so much."

"What is this girl's name?" Rafferty asked.

But York all but dragged Edmonds away before he could answer. "We have said enough, Ted, more than enough. Now, Mr. Rafferty, both of us have work to do before the sun sets. I trust you will have a pleasant evening."

Edmonds shrugged and said, "Well, I'm the junior clerk in this business and I guess I've got my marching orders. Nice talking to you, Mr. Rafferty."

When Rafferty walked back around to the front of the mansion, he saw Newman sweeping off the front steps. "'Tis a beautiful evening, is it not?" he said.

Newman nodded, but his impassive face registered no hint that he might actually be enjoying the weather.

Rafferty said, "Your job must be particularly difficult these days in light of all that is being said about Mr. Harriman. May I ask how long you've been in his employ?"

"It will be a year in September, sir."

"And what of Mr. York and Mr. Edmonds?"

"They came on about the same time I did, sir."

"Do you know why the previous servants left?"

"I'm sure I wouldn't know, sir."

"Well, I can't imagine Mr. Harriman is easy to work for. And I don't suppose he has many friends, except for that girl who comes around now and then. I understand he's very fond of her. What was her name again?"

Newman leaned on his broom and said, "You would have to speak with Mr. Harriman about that. Good day, sir," the butler added before stepping back inside the mansion and shutting the door behind him.

When he returned to his saloon, Rafferty telephoned Cuddleton to report on his interviews at Birdwing, including the revelation that Harriman had apparently befriended a young girl in recent weeks. "Do you know anything about the girl?"

"It is news to me," Cuddleton said, "but then again my client is not the most forthright man in the world. I am sure he has other secrets he's keeping from me. You must track down the girl and see what she can tell you."

6
MOUNTING EVIDENCE

A DAY AFTER RAFFERTY'S VISIT to Birdwing, the police arrived at the house with a search warrant, and it yielded evidence that would have sent anyone who wasn't a millionaire immediately to jail. In a basement garbage bin the searchers, led by Chief Gallagher and Detective Donlin, found a pair of boy's shorts and underpants. Donlin was assigned at once to bring the clothes to Freddie's mother to see if she could identify them, and she confirmed that they'd belonged to her son.

A writing desk in the mansion's library produced further evidence in the form of a stack of small blank notecards identical in size and shape to those left behind with the bodies of the dead cats. The cards bolstered the theory that Harriman had hunted down neighborhood cats before taking out his wrath—and his perverse sexual desires—on Freddie. The shattered bedroom window that had supposedly provoked Harriman's homicidal rage was also examined, and detectives immediately spotted the BB on the carpet beneath it.

But it was the discovery of an album of photographs secreted on the top shelf of a closet in Harriman's bedroom that left Gallagher in a state of shocked revulsion. Although Gallagher knew such pictures existed, he had never actually seen the likes of them. "The man is utterly debauched," Gallagher told his men, "and the hangman's rope is too good for him."

Harriman had called Cuddleton as soon as the police arrived to execute the warrant. The attorney rushed up to the mansion and proclaimed the search to be an outrage for which the authorities would be held responsible. Harriman voiced similar sentiments before retreating to the breakfast room with Webster, who let loose a torrent of impolite commentary as he perched nervously on his master's shoulder.

Pressed to explain the incriminating items, Harriman deferred to Cuddleton, who insisted in his usual orotund way that his client had been victimized by someone who wished him ill. Gallagher, however, was unmoved by Cuddleton's protestations, calling them "nothing more than the usual spreading of manure." Yet Gallagher wasn't sure he had enough evidence to arrest Harriman for murder. The chief's usual method was to haul a prime suspect like Harriman to the central police station and extract a confession by any means possible. Unfortunately, Harriman had money and the best lawyer in the city, and that made Gallagher's job more difficult.

"What's the next move?" one of Gallagher's detectives asked when they finally left Birdwing late in the afternoon.

"Why, I believe the press might take some interest in what we found today, and after that I have no doubt our enlightened citizenry will demand Mr. Harriman's head on stick."

* * *

That evening Rafferty received a telephone call from Cuddleton. The lawyer described the search of Harriman's mansion and what they police had found, including the clothing, the notecards, and the BB pellet. "Unfortunately, they found something else," he said, "and it is the most damning discovery imaginable."

"Ah, did they find that scarf?"

Cuddleton said, "No, the scarf was nowhere to be found, thankfully. But Chief Gallagher and his men came upon a boxful of pure dynamite, and when it explodes into public view Mr. Harriman will instantly become the most despised man in St. Paul."

"And what might this dynamite be?"

"Photographs, Mr. Rafferty, of the most vile kind, showing naked young boys in disgusting poses. Gallagher will surely tell the newspapers all about his revolting discovery, and after that it will be hard to find a soul in this city who would decline the opportunity to put a noose around Mr. Harriman's neck and drop him to perdition."

Rafferty knew Cuddleton was right. Only a few years earlier, a man named Frank McManus had been lynched in downtown Minneapolis for allegedly raping a four-year-old girl. After mentioning that appalling incident to Cuddleton, Rafferty said, "I am wondering, does the coroner in fact believe the boy was molested?"

"The body showed no signs of it, according to our distinguished coroner, who nonetheless is not prepared to offer an opinion on the matter one way or the other," Cuddleton said, his voice dripping with disgust. "The police have pressured him, I'm sure, not to rule out an assault. And with no one to tell them otherwise, a jury will be pleased to believe that Freddie was horribly violated by my client."

"So Mr. Harriman has been arrested?"

"Not yet. I managed to keep Gallagher and his gang at bay for a while by making all manner of threats. But once the newspapers have their say, the hounds will be let loose."

"Am I correct in assuming that Mr. Harriman claims to know nothing of the pictures?" Rafferty asked.

"You are. They were found in an album of old family photographs tucked away on a high shelf in his bedroom closet. Mr. Harriman assures me that he has not looked at the album in years. I am now more convinced than ever that someone has gone to great lengths to frame my client. The question is who. As you've said, it had to be someone with ready access to the mansion. What did you think of the servants when you interviewed them?"

"Nothing struck me as unusual, but I didn't have a chance to talk with them for very long. York, the gardener, seemed eager to be rid of me, but it may simply be that he viewed me as a threat to his employer."

"Well, one of them must have planted those photographs unless somebody managed to sneak inside the mansion sight unseen. But why would a servant do such a thing?"

"Somebody could have paid for the dirty work," Rafferty said. "But as to who that would be—"

"Nobody knows, do they?" Cuddleton said. "It is a damnable business, and a very strange one. I am wondering if that Jack Spence fellow could be involved. Mr. Harriman assures me he lied to the newspapers about the cat killings. It would be no great stretch to think he was hired to murder the Whistler boy."

"Rough men like Handy Jack will do most anything, yet killing a child is a line even the worst of his kind are rarely willing to cross," Rafferty noted. "I will see what I can get from him, but do not hold out your hopes. Handy Jack is a hard case, and he will not be easily persuaded to talk."

"Well, see what you can do," Cuddleton said. "Unless we can discover who's setting up Mr. Harriman for a fall, I do not like his chances once we go to court."

* * *

As Cuddleton had predicted, Gallagher wasted no time informing the newspapers of what he and his men had found at Birdwing, and the news was so sensational that the morning *Pioneer Press* put out an extra edition. MURDER CLUES AT HARRIMAN'S MANSION, said the banner headline. A subhead below stated, "Despicable Pictures Uncovered," while yet another announced, "Police Say Harriman to Be Arrested Soon." When the *Dispatch* and *Globe* came out with their editions, they resorted to an array of circumlocutions to describe the pornographic images, but the public was well used to reading between the lines when it came to anything involving sex. Only the most naive readers failed to grasp what Harriman stood accused of or to comprehend that he must be a brute of the worst possible kind.

Speaking for his client, Cuddleton contended that "the disgusting photographs now in the police's possession are unknown to my client, who is a man of decency and rectitude. The pictures were obviously secreted in Mr. Harriman's residence by someone with a deep grudge against him. My client is a victim, just as poor Freddie

Whistler was, of an evil and vicious criminal, and I am confident that when the truth comes out Mr. Harriman will be absolved of all wrongdoing."

The public, however, was unconvinced by Cuddleton's defense, and pressure mounted by the hour for Harriman's arrest. Thurston Whistler helped whip up the frenzy, informing the *Dispatch* that he intended to "deal with Harriman as I would a rabid dog unless the police do their duty." Protesters soon gathered outside Birdwing, shouting "Murderer, murderer" and "Hang the degenerate." Others began throwing stones, rotting fruit, and whatever else was handy in the direction of the house.

A window was broken before the police, led by Gallagher, arrived in force. But they weren't interested in dispersing the crowd. Instead, they pounded on the front door and demanded entry. A few minutes later, Gallagher and his men emerged with Harriman firmly in the chief's grasp as the crowd broke out into a wild mixture of cheers and catcalls.

Wearing his usual kimono, Harriman looked defiant as Gallagher roughly escorted him into a waiting police wagon. Reporters were on hand to witness the spectacle, and Gallagher assured them that justice would be done. "I do not recall a more depraved crime in the history of St. Paul or anywhere else," he said, "but we have the guilty party now and his wealth will not save him."

Dolly Charbonneau of the *Pioneer Press* managed to weave her way through the crowd to the police wagon, where Harriman gazed out from behind a barred window with a surprisingly calm demeanor.

"What do you say for yourself?" Charbonneau asked.

"I say that I am innocent and that if mob justice is allowed to prevail in this city, which is supposedly occupied by lawful men, then there will be no end to terror and darkness. Print that if you dare."

* * *

The *Pioneer Press* did indeed print Harriman's denial. Yet it was a mere droplet in a giant wave of publicity that had all but convicted Harriman of murder by the time he was arraigned the next morning. A hundred or more spectators, Rafferty among them, crammed into the largest courtroom in the new city-county building to witness the proceedings.

Harriman, who spent the night in jail, had traded in his kimono for a shabby suit by the time he was led to the defense table, where Cuddleton awaited him. Spectators craned their necks to glimpse the monster who, according to the *Pioneer Press,* stood accused of "a crime so foul that only a beast could have committed it." Cuddleton and his client whispered to each other "like conspirators," or so the *Globe* later claimed, while on the other side of the well a prosecutor represented the state. Chief Gallagher, looking unusually well-mannered in a new gray suit, sat behind the prosecution table with Thurston and Mathilda Whistler. A cluster of reporters hovered around them, angling for a juicy quote.

The arraignment turned out to be brief and without much drama. Harriman entered a not guilty plea in a firm voice to charges of sodomy, assault, and murder, after which Cuddleton argued that his client, given his standing in the community and lack of any criminal record, should be freed on bail pending trial. The prosecution objected, citing the "heinous nature" of the crimes, but the judge agreed to set cash bail at one hundred thousand dollars, an amount few defendants could afford. After a trial date was set, the court adjourned, disappointing spectators who wanted Harriman to be convicted on the spot and then drawn and quartered on the courthouse lawn.

As Harriman was being taken away by deputies, a slight smile crossed his face and he nodded in Rafferty's direction. A young woman with long blond hair sitting almost directly in front of Rafferty responded with a wave. Only then did Rafferty realize the nod hadn't been for him. Once the crowd began to file out, Rafferty tapped the woman on the shoulder. When she turned around, Rafferty was surprised to see that she was a girl of no more than twelve or so.

"Ah, so you must know Mr. Harriman," he said. "I know him as well. My name is Shadwell Rafferty. May I ask who you are?"

"Anna Jerabek," the girl said without hesitation. "Uncle Ambrose is innocent. I hope you know that. He would never hurt anyone."

"You may be right. But how do you happen to know him?"

"Birds. We both love them. I hope you do, too."

Although Rafferty had shot hundreds of ducks in his day, he said, "Why, I do indeed love birds. Do you think we could talk for a bit? I would like to learn more."

Over the next half hour, as they sat in the empty courtroom, Rafferty heard the tale of "Anna and the Birdman," as he came to call it. Clearly, she was the girl Harriman's coachman had mentioned. Although Rafferty could be perfectly logical if need be—the good Jesuits who taught him, he liked to say, "could speak in syllogisms all day long"—he also believed in the wisdom of the heart. And his heart was now telling him that the gentle man Anna described could not be a vicious killer, despite his supposed misanthropy.

"I should go," Anna finally said. "Mama wants me home by noon. I think you are a nice man, Mr. Rafferty. Will you help Uncle Ambrose?"

"I will," Rafferty promised. "You have my word."

By day's end, Harriman had liquidated sufficient assets to post bail, and at six o'clock he walked out of the county jail with Cuddleton at his side. They slipped into Harriman's waiting landau before passersby had time to notice, and as they wound up the hill toward Summit Avenue, Cuddleton offered his client some advice. "Stay in your house, lock the doors, and hire guards. The public is inflamed and there is no telling what could happen."

"I do not fear the public," Harriman replied.

"Then perhaps you should," Cuddleton said. "In the meantime, I want you to think long and hard about who is trying to frame you. It must be someone you know."

7

JACK SPENCE

THE NEXT AFTERNOON, Rafferty found Jack Spence at Bannion's saloon, a standup joint on St. Peter Street known for cheap beer and the collection of lowlifes who drank it. The place was small and free of charm, offering a bar decorated with brass spittoons, a pine floor marked by stains representing most of the bodily fluids, and a few crude tables at the rear. A group of rough-looking hoodlums were playing cards at one of the tables, while another was occupied by a heavyset man in a red vest who had a pencil in his hand and appeared to be going over some figures. Rafferty, who was acquainted with just about every saloonkeeper in the city, found the establishment's proprietor, Shane Bannion, attending to business behind the bar amid the familiar smells of beer, sweat, tobacco juice, and cigar smoke.

"Shane, top of the day to you," Rafferty said as he caught Bannion's eye. "I trust you are doing well."

"As long as men keep drinking I will make a living," said Bannion. "To what do I owe the pleasure of your company?" Unlike Rafferty, Bannion was a small, slender man who looked more like a dancer than a bartender. Even so, he was a fearless character and kept a 12-gauge behind the bar in the event a customer became too rambunctious.

"I am looking for one of your distinguished patrons, Mr. Spence," Rafferty said.

"Are you now? Well, I have heard many words to describe Jack, but 'distinguished' is not one that comes to mind. What's this about? Does it have something to do with this cat nonsense in the papers?"

"It does, and perhaps other things as well. Unfortunately, I've not had the honor of meeting Mr. Spence, although his reputation precedes him. If you could point him out, I would be grateful."

"Big fellow in the vest at the table behind you," Bannion said. "Just be careful. He's a nasty customer and he always carries a pistol."

Rafferty nodded, ordered a beer, and took it with him as he walked over to Spence's table.

"Mr. Spence," he said, taking a seat across from him. "I would like to have a word with you."

Spence was a broad-shouldered man in his thirties with a pockmarked face, dark eyes behind heavy lids, thick red hair, and a carefully trimmed mustache of the same color that curled around his cheeks like a pair of small, coiled snakes. He was writing figures into what looked to be a small ledger but closed the cover when Rafferty sat down. He glanced up at his visitor and said, in a tone not notable for its friendliness, "And who would you be?"

"Shadwell Rafferty. I see you are at your numbers, Mr. Spence. How is business these days?"

"What's that to you? Now, go away unless you are looking for trouble."

"I am not looking for it, but I am also not the man you wish to make trouble with," Rafferty said, staring at Spence.

"I know about you, Rafferty, but you don't scare me. I got nothing to say."

"Is that so? Now that you are a newspaper celebrity, I thought you would be happy to talk about your exploits with Mr. Harriman and the cats. 'Twas noble of you to turn down his offer, and yet I am reliably informed you would kill the pope in Rome for a suitable consideration. So who paid you to tell the tale?"

Rafferty saw a brief flash of apprehension in Spence's eyes, and his right hand twitched.

Before Spence could reach down under the table, presumably for his pistol, Rafferty clamped a hand on Spence's wrist.

"Now, now, don't do anything foolish, or you will regret it," Rafferty said. "I will ask once again who paid you."

"Go to hell," Spence said, struggling to free his wrist from Rafferty's iron grip. "Do you hear me, you can just go to hell!"

"Where I am sure you, at least, you will receive a warm welcome," Rafferty said, maintaining his grip. "Of course, a few dead cats are the least of your worries at the moment. There is a murdered boy to be accounted for now. Did someone hire you for that work as well?"

Spence responded with a colorful oath directed at Rafferty's parentage just as he managed to free his right hand. He was reaching for his pistol when Rafferty punched him in the jaw, knocking him back in his chair. By the time Spence regained his senses, he was staring down the barrel of the revolver Rafferty always carried.

"You have a choice," Rafferty said calmly. "You can very carefully hand me that pistol of yours or you can try to use it. I would strongly suggest the former."

"You bastard," Spence said, rubbing his jaw. "I will get you for this."

"You can try, but I would not advise it. Now, what will it be?"

Spence knew Rafferty's reputation and decided to beat a retreat. "You've got the drop on me now, but that will change one of these days," he said before handing over a small revolver from his jacket pocket.

"Now then, where were we?" Rafferty said. "Ah, you were about to tell me who paid you to lie about Mr. Harriman and the cats."

Spence, however, was through talking, except for one last statement. "I didn't kill no kid," he said, and for once, Rafferty believed him.

"Does not appear the two of you had a pleasant conversation," Bannion said when Rafferty returned to the bar, where he deposited Spence's revolver for safekeeping.

"'Twould be fair to say we had a minor disagreement," Rafferty acknowledged with a grin. "Well, thanks for the beer, Shane. If I need to speak to Mr. Spence again, I'll know where to find him."

* * *

The phone at Bannion's saloon rang a half hour after Rafferty left. The caller asked for Spence, who was nursing his sore jaw with medicinal doses of whiskey at his usual table.

"Yeah, who's this?" Spence answered.

"You know who," said a familiar voice on the other end of the line. "I have another job for you and there's one hundred dollars in it if you're interested."

"Keep talking."

"I need to take care of a loose end. Somebody might be on to me. I'm thinking you could persuade them to keep quiet."

"Is that so? A hundred wouldn't be enough. I'd need two."

"You're getting rather pricey, Mr. Spence."

"And you're headed for big trouble. I know what you did."

"All right. Two hundred, but not a penny more. Meet me tomorrow night at eleven sharp in the alley behind Bannion's. The man I'm interested in will be at the saloon then—I've arranged it—and I'll point him out to you."

"Sure you will. And you'll have the money with you, won't you."

"I will. Goodbye."

Spence was a little wary, but two hundred dollars was a big payday. Even better, Spence figured it was just the beginning. After all, the caller had asked him to murder Freddie Whistler, only it was now apparent the man had done the terrible deed himself. He'd pay a lot more than two hundred dollars, a great deal more, to keep Spence from going to the police with what he knew.

* * *

The next afternoon, articles in the *Globe* and *Dispatch* delivered the stunning news that Jack Spence had been stabbed to death overnight in the alley behind Bannion's saloon. Under normal circumstances, Spence's murder would have received limited attention. But his connection to the Harriman case made it front-page news. The *Globe*'s article claimed prosecutors "regarded Mr. Spence as a key witness. Now he has been silenced." Despite these ominous overtones, the story eventually got around to mentioning that Spence was "a well-known criminal who may have fallen victim to a robbery, as his wallet was missing."

Rafferty read every word of the stories and then placed a call to Donlin. "What can you tell me about Mr. Spence's untimely demise?" he asked. "Do you really think it was a robbery?"

"Looks that way," the detective said. "Handy Jack was known to carry around a lot of cash, and he didn't have a cent on him when we found the body. Why do you ask? Do you know something I don't?"

"Maybe. Don't you think it odd that Handy Jack was murdered just a few days after Mr. Harriman's arrest?"

"You mean because of that cat business? Well, the papers made plenty of it, that's for sure, but I don't see the connection. Handy Jack was the kind of man born to die in an alley with a knife in his chest. As I see it, there are plenty of pugs who could have killed him just for the money."

"You could be right," Rafferty acknowledged, "but if I was lying in wait for a man like Handy Jack, I'd be very careful. He was a rough brawler, and he usually carried a pistol. He must have been talking up close to somebody he knew when out flashed the knife before he could defend himself. Did you find his pistol?"

"No, but what are you angling at? Who's this mysterious 'somebody' who supposedly did him in?"

"I can't say, Pat, but if I were you, I'd do a little more digging. There may be much more to Handy Jack's murder than you think."

"So you say, but if it's digging you want, I'll give you a shovel and you can have at it. Here's the thing, Shad. Nobody really cares about Handy Jack at the moment. Just another dead crook. Harriman is the only game in town right now."

* * *

After the big news broke about Jack Spence, Cuddleton made his usual appearance at Rafferty's saloon, but he was more interested in conversation than Scotch.

"Let's speak in your office," he said. "I am in need of some quiet and some wise counsel."

Once they'd retreated to the office, Rafferty asked, "How is Mr. Harriman doing?"

"I have instructed him to stay home and shut up," Cuddleton said. "The less he has to say about his situation, the better. Now, what do you think of Mr. Spence's sudden departure from the scene? It cannot have been a mere robbery as the police in their infinite wisdom seem inclined to believe."

"I agree. I am thinking that whoever hired Handy Jack to lie about the cat killings very probably murdered the Whistler boy and framed Harriman for the crime. Knowing what he did, Handy Jack might have become a liability and so had to be eliminated. But I remain in the dark as to who that person might be."

"Well, you know my view of the matter. There is a mastermind pulling all the strings and he bears some godawful grudge against Mr. Harriman. If we can figure out the reason for his unholy animus, I am convinced we will have our man."

Rafferty nodded and said, "It could be a very old grudge, maybe even someone from Mr. Harriman's family. I am curious if you know much about your client's history before he arrived in St. Paul. Family feuds can be extremely bitter."

"They certainly can. I've asked Mr. Harriman about that very possibility but he claims to have no living relatives, and he absolutely refuses to speak of his past."

"I'll have to do more digging," Rafferty said, "and I have an idea where to look. 'Tis a long shot but maybe luck will come my way. Now then, what's this 'wise counsel' you're seeking from me?"

"It's about a girl," Cuddleton said.

"Am I right in guessing the girl in question is Anna Jerabek?"

Cuddleton's face, which was primarily a curtain for disguising his thoughts, registered a hint of genuine surprise. "So you are aware of her."

"Yes. I spotted her at the arraignment, and we had nice talk afterward. She's a very interesting child."

"Well, Mr. Harriman somehow didn't get around to mentioning her to me until this afternoon. The only thing worse than a guilty client, Mr. Rafferty, is one who isn't forthcoming. So now I have a new problem. Mr. Harriman told me he has deep feelings toward the girl but promised not to see her again until this business is over. I only hope he can be trusted to keep his word."

"Ah, so you fear he will continue to meet with the girl and that suspicions will be aroused as a result."

"Yes, that is my fear. Mind you, Mr. Harriman perceives no cause for worry in his relationship with the girl. It's a lovely tale of grandfatherly affection, or so he insists, but it may not appear so to a jury, what with the ugly scent of a dead boy hovering around Mr. Harriman. And so my conundrum. This Jerabek girl's testimony at trial could serve to put a warm human face on Mr. Harriman and allow the jury to see him as a kindly man and not the dyspeptic ogre he appears to be. But cross-examination, as you and I well know, is designed to make mince of meat, and who can say how the girl would withstand it? There is also the fact that for all I know Mr. Harriman's relationship with the girl is not as innocent as he makes it out to be."

"It surprises me you would suggest such a thing," Rafferty said.

"I am a lawyer, Mr. Rafferty, and you are a bartender, two professions that inculcate a healthy skepticism when it comes to the human animal. I do not think anything untoward is going on between my client and the girl, but if I put her on the stand and a clever prosecutor starts clawing away at her, I could be, as the Bard put it, hoisted on my own petard. That is a fate every lawyer dreads above all others. So I must decide what to do about the girl. What do you think of her?"

"I think she's a sweet child, very bright, and she might make a fine witness on Mr. Harriman's behalf. But I agree, there would be danger in allowing her to testify."

"Well, we shall see. I do not mind telling you I greatly fear for Mr. Harriman. I do not think he fully comprehends the gravity of his situation. I will do my utmost to secure an acquittal, but it will be an uphill battle. Everyone despises a man who would murder a child in cold blood, and a jury will require only a few strands of circumstantial evidence to braid a rope around Mr. Harriman's neck. And that is why I am in great need of any exonerating evidence you can deliver."

"I will keep at it," Rafferty said, "but I can make no promises. Our antagonist is a clever fellow and he will be even harder to identify now that Handy Jack is on his way to hell."

8
ANNA INVESTIGATES

ANNA JERABEK MISSED being with Harriman. Her father was a distant man who drank too much and worked long hours at a box factory across the river from their shanty. But Uncle Ambrose was different. He was always sweet, and he spoke to her just like the adult she thought herself to be. And the birds! Oh, how he liked to talk about them and help her learn ever more. He'd given her a fancy sketchbook, and every time they met he helped her with her drawings. In the span of just a month she'd made twenty drawings, and at night, listening to the chug of distant locomotives, she dreamed of the biggest sketchbook in the world where all of God's birds would have a home.

But now she couldn't visit with Harriman because of all the nonsense about him being a murderer. Harriman himself had told her she must not see him for a while, and Anna's mother was even more insistent. "That man is no good," she said. "No good for you or anybody else." Anna knew better, however. She believed fervently that Ambrose Harriman could not, would not have murdered Freddie Whistler under any circumstances. Uncle Ambrose had always treated her with tender regard, and when she looked into his eyes she did not see a killer. Instead, she saw a lonely old man who loved birds because he did not seem to know anymore how to love people. But she'd seen him blossom in her presence, and instead of the bitter crabapple everyone thought him to be, he was extraordinarily kind and caring.

Because she wanted desperately to help Harriman, Anna decided to undertake her own investigation. She recalled that on one of her visits to Birdwing she'd seen a group of children playing in Maiden Lane, the alley behind the estate. She thought one of them might have been Freddie, whose image had been splashed all over the newspapers. Maybe his playmates knew something, if she could persuade them to talk.

On the day after Harriman's arraignment she walked up to Maiden Lane and hung around, looking for children. She soon spotted three boys and a girl playing with a big wooden hoop. The boys, who were loud and obnoxious, looked to be seven or eight. The girl, an obvious tomboy, was a bit older. She wore overalls and had dark curly hair. She appeared to be taking no guff from the boys and gave as good as she got. Anna thought she'd be the one to talk to.

She went up to the girl and said, "Hello, my name is Anna. Who are you?"

The girl said her name was Milly. After telling her how cute her curls were and how much fun the game looked, Anna casually brought up the subject of Freddie Whistler.

"It was so awful what happened to him," Anna said. "Was he a friend of yours?"

"No, he was a nasty boy. I didn't like him. My mama says that mean old man Mr. Harriman did it. Mama says they will hang him for sure."

Anna said, "Did you ever see Freddie with Mr. Harriman?"

"No, but I saw that man in the coat talking to him."

"You mean that man who always wears a maroon coat?"

"Yes."

"Was he mad at Freddie?"

"No, they were just talking, that's all."

"So Freddie knew him?"

"I guess," Milly said as the hoop came rolling her way. Anna intercepted it and sent it back toward the boys, who were busy arguing over something.

"Did you see the two of them talking a lot?" Anna asked.

"Maybe. I don't remember."

"Do you think they were friends?"

Milly shrugged and seemed to be losing interest in the conversation. A woman in maid's clothing came down the lane and said, "Come along, children, it's time for lunch."

"Bye," Milly said and rushed off with her friends.

Anna weighed what Milly had told her. There was only one person at Birdwing who wore a maroon outfit. How and why, she wondered, had Adam Newman come to know Freddie? She intended to ask, as soon as she could find a way to speak in private with the butler.

* * *

Anna had never felt entirely comfortable around Uncle Ambrose's staff. The old housemaid was kind enough, but the three men who worked for Harriman were all a bit peculiar. York rarely spoke to her, but when he did he always eyed her suspiciously, as though she did not belong on the grounds of Birdwing. Once she'd wandered by herself into the carriage house and out of curiosity tried the door to York's apartment, not knowing where it led. He'd reacted angrily, rushing to the door and telling her, "The next time, you must knock, little missy, or there will be trouble. Do you understand?" Then he'd slammed the door in her face.

By contrast, Edmonds was always polite and smiling, but Anna could see that he deeply resented the bowing and scraping that came with being a coachman. He often took Anna back to her home on the river flats after visits to Birdwing, and sometimes he would voice his disgust at how she and her impoverished neighbors lived. "Look at these people scraping like animals in the dirt," he told her, "while rich men gaze down on them from their mansions. Do you suppose they care? I think not. But maybe we'll be rich someday, Anna, and wouldn't that be wonderful."

Newman, Anna thought, was the most inscrutable of the servants. He'd never said an untoward word to her, and he seemed utterly incapable of small talk. Like Edmonds, he was unfailingly polite, but his arctic-blue eyes, devoid of any emotion, made Anna very uneasy, as though they were scanning her for secrets. She'd heard that the other servants disliked and distrusted him, but she wasn't sure why they felt that way.

When she learned that Newman had apparently befriended Freddie Whistler, Anna was surprised, since he hardly struck her as a man who wished to be friends with anyone. But if the butler knew something about Freddie, he might be able to prove Uncle Ambrose's innocence, or so Anna reasoned. Although Anna was forbidden to enter Birdwing, she decided that in her new role as a detective she simply had to speak with Newman.

So it was that she sneaked into the grounds of Birdwing from Maiden Lane and made her way to the front door of the house. She rang the bell, knowing Newman would answer. When he opened the door, however, he looked at Anna as though she was a plague come to decimate the household.

"Go away," he said in a manner that was not the least bit polite. "You are not to be here under any circumstances."

"I know, but it is you I wish to speak with, Mr. Newman. It is about what happened to Freddie. If you could—"

"I cannot," he said and without another word slammed the door shut.

Anna, however, was not easily put off. She was plotting another means of cornering Newman when good fortune came her way. Uncle Ambrose, she learned, wanted to meet with her secretly at the house. She immediately agreed, thinking that when they got together, she could ask him about Newman and maybe even help find the real murderer of Freddie Whistler.

* * *

Eli Tuttle had watched with fascination as Anna Jerabek conquered Harriman's stony old heart. Harriman was normally abrupt, bilious, and cold, a man in every way unhappy with the world, but in the girl's presence he took on a different character. He was kindly, solicitous, and doting, all the hardness in him falling away like rock sliding down a mountain. Indeed, it seemed to Tuttle that Harriman actually loved the girl and found in her some measure of salvation for the old sin buried deep inside him.

Anna didn't know it, but Tuttle had plans for her. Murdering Freddie Whistler had been the middle act of Tuttle's great revenge drama. Now that Harriman had returned home, Tuttle was ready to stage the grand finale, which he knew would haunt the old sinner until his final breath.

9
THE MYSTERY OF AMBROSE HARRIMAN

FOLLOWING HARRIMAN'S ARRAIGNMENT, Shadwell Rafferty decided to spend a day making the rounds of the city's newspaper offices, or more specifically, their morgues, where old clippings rested in small envelopes like relics of the dead. He was hunting for clues—background information in an article, a brief mention in passing, even something Harriman had revealed in one of his diatribes—that might open a window into the old man's past. Rafferty's morgue tour was prompted by something Harriman had said during the interview at his mansion. He'd stated then, after some hesitation, that he was "unaware of anyone in St. Paul" who might be plotting against him. This suggested Harriman might know of

someone with a simmering grievance rooted in events that occurred well before his arrival in the city.

Rafferty's first stop was at the *Pioneer Press,* where he found
nothing of note in the morgue. He then wandered into the newsroom for a talk with Dolly Charbonneau, who'd done crucial detective work for him in the case of the newspaper murders two years
earlier. But she was as much in the dark about Harriman's personal
history as everyone else seemed to be.

"He's the great sphinx of our fair city," she said. "I've been looking for old dirt but so far all I have is the fresh stuff. He seems to
have materialized out of thin air in St. Paul in late 1879. He appears
to have no family, no friends, but these days many enemies. I do
not enjoy hangings the way most of my colleagues do, but I suspect
Mr. Harriman will soon be providing that form of entertainment
to the rude masses."

"I am trying to stop that from happening," Rafferty said, "and
perhaps you can help me. I have run across a clue about his past. I
think he may be from the town of Plattsburgh in New York."

"How do you know that?"

Rafferty cited the map he'd seen mounted in Harriman's mansion. "It could be nothing, but it's the best lead I have. I am hoping
you might be able to make some inquiries there for me."

"I could," Charbonneau said, "but not right now. I'm working
on a big piece about our sainted mayor and his dealings with a certain alderman who qualifies as the most crooked of his ilk in the
city, which is saying a lot. So you'll have to wait a bit before I can
do any digging for you."

"Fair enough," said Rafferty. "If I can't find something at the
Dispatch or *Globe,* I'll get back to you."

Rafferty walked up Fourth Street to the *Dispatch*'s offices. The
morgue there yielded only a single brief article mentioning that
Harriman hailed from New York. But the article was maddeningly
short of detail and didn't identify Harriman's hometown. Nor did
it reveal anything about his family.

Rafferty's last stop was at the *Globe.* After a fruitless hunt through
its morgue, he spotted Joseph Pyle, an old friend, in the newsroom.
Like Charbonneau, Pyle had played a key role in the newspaper

murders, and Rafferty regarded him as among the best reporters in St. Paul.

"Joseph, I am in need of assistance," Rafferty said when he found Pyle at his desk amid the usual accumulation of old newspapers and unsavory luncheon remains. "Do you have a minute?"

"More than that. I am largely unoccupied today, and a reporter without news is a starving man," Pyle said. "If you've got something going on, tell me about it."

After explaining his mission, Rafferty said, "I have found nothing of value in any old newspaper files. Mr. Harriman's past life seems to be blank slate. So now I am down to playing a wild hunch."

"Which is?"

"I was in Mr. Harriman's mansion not long ago and saw a panoramic view of Plattsburgh, New York, very nicely framed and mounted on a wall. It struck me as peculiar because everything else in the house was about birds. So why the picture of Plattsburgh?"

"Could be Plattsburgh is where he was born."

"'Tis what I'm thinking as well. Do you know anything about the newspaper in Plattsburgh?"

"Not offhand, but I could find out. We have an Ayers in the morgue. I'll go fetch it."

Pyle soon returned with a fat volume called *N. W. Ayers and Sons American Newspaper Annual and Directory*. He paged through it until he found a listing for Plattsburgh. "Looks like there's a paper there called the *Plattsburgh Republican*. Editor in chief is Thomas Wisnom."

"Excellent. Now, could you do me a favor? I'd like you to wire Mr. Wisnom and ask if he has any information about Ambrose Harriman or knows of anyone who does. I am playing a long shot, but it's worth a try."

"I can do that. I'll let you know if I find out anything."

"Ah, that would be grand," Rafferty said, rising from his chair. "Your help is always appreciated."

Once he returned to his saloon to prepare for the usual night of merrymaking, Rafferty poured out a shot of his best Tennessee whiskey and sat down to think for a while about Ambrose Harriman and his troubles. Rafferty's theory that an old grievance had prompted the intricate campaign of revenge against Harriman rested on nothing other than the loose sand of speculation. He hoped inquiries in New York might put some bedrock under his idea. If someone out of Harriman's past was indeed framing him for murder, that man had to be in St. Paul now, and he had to be close enough to Harriman to know his daily routine at Birdwing.

But who could that man be? Aside from Anna Jerabek, Harriman had no close friends or acquaintances in St. Paul that Rafferty knew of. The only people who saw him every day and who knew his habits were his servants. Rafferty had talked with all of them to little avail. If one was a masked man with a festering wound, he had covered his tracks expertly, and Rafferty wasn't sure how to pick up the trail. Plattsburgh seemed his best hope, maybe his only hope given Harriman's refusal to open up about his past. But if Plattsburgh turned out to be a dead end, Rafferty didn't know if he could save Harriman from a terrible fate.

* * *

In the days after he posted bail, Ambrose Harriman became a prisoner in his own mansion, and it gave him ample time to contemplate his situation. Cuddleton's words as they rode away from the courthouse were much on his mind. If a terrible thirst for revenge lay behind the effort to destroy him, Harriman could think of only one person who might be responsible. Yet it was a person he barely knew and could not recognize on sight, a ghost from a time long past.

Decades earlier, after a series of tragedies hollowed him out until all that remained was a kind of cold despair, Harrison had done a terrible thing. Furious at the world, he had abandoned his home and family and every vestige of the life he knew. He walked away without fear or hope and with little except revulsion at the very idea of existence to sustain him. He wandered for three days, stopping in New York City before booking a ticket on the Pennsylvania Railroad to points west. He had no destination in mind other than finding some quiet place where he could do what needed to be done.

He detrained for no particular reason at Coshocton, Ohio, and walked out of town until he encountered a dark woodland next to a farmstead. It had taken a few days to screw up his courage, but he was finally ready to do what had to be done. Annihilation—to be erased forever until the last of his remains disappeared into dust—was his aim. He'd brought along an old Colt revolver, and once he was deep in the woods beneath a giant spreading oak, he put the gun to his temple and pulled the trigger, thinking all would be over at last. But the antique Colt failed to go off—the firing pin was too worn to work—and in that instant Harriman experienced an epiphany. Death was as pointless as life, he realized, and unknowable Fate ruled them both.

He tossed away the gun, seeing no immediate point in killing himself. As he stumbled out of the woods, released for a time from the burden of arranging his own demise, he came upon a pitiable sight. A robin's nest had fallen to the ground or perhaps been ripped from its branch by a predator. The mother's body lay beside the broken nest, which held a single blue egg that by some strange chance had not been shattered. Harriman picked up the egg, which had a jagged crack, and heard sounds coming from within. He watched with sudden fascination as a blind chick popped out, its throat wide open, screaming for food.

Harriman wasn't sure what to do, but he somehow knew he couldn't tolerate another death in the world. He walked to the nearby farmhouse, and the elderly woman who answered his knock must have been startled by the sight of Harrison in his long black coat and homburg hat. More startling still was that he cradled a tiny bird in his hands, as gently as though it was his own flesh and blood.

"I found this chick," he blurted out. "Can you tell me what I should feed it?"

Harriman remained in Coshocton for the next month, tending to the robin until one day it simply flew away. The bird's departure inspired Harriman. He could leave, too, he thought, and allow Fate to play whatever hand it had in store for him. By the time he landed in St. Paul many years later, made rich by investments both wise and lucky, birds had become the center of his life and the only anodyne for the ghosts that still disturbed his dreams.

* * *

A week after Joseph Pyle contacted the *Plattsburgh Republican* with questions about Ambrose Harriman, Rafferty was going through his usual stack of mail when he came upon a large manila envelope from the newspaper. Inside, Rafferty found three clippings from back issues of the *Republican* along with a letter from its editor, Thomas Wisnom. He stated that he knew of no one by the last name of Harriman in Plattsburgh but that a man named Ambrose Harriman Tuttle was the subject of a mystery dating back a quarter century. Wisnom went on to say that Rafferty's inquiry was "curious" because only a few weeks earlier he'd received a telephone call from a man who was also interested in the Tuttle family and its history.

The clippings were a revelation. The oldest dated to 1862 and told how Tuttle had been mustered out of the Ninety-Sixth New York Regiment after suffering a serious leg wound at the Battle of Seven Pines while serving with the Army of the Potomac. The story included extensive background information on Tuttle, who was described as "the scion of one of Plattsburgh's most prominent and well-regarded families whose manufactory has long been a mainstay of our community. When his wounds are fully healed, Mr. Tuttle intends to return to the family business, which he has commanded since the death of his parents. In the meantime, he has purchased a fine home on Cumberland Ave. where he will recuperate with his wife and their beautiful young daughter."

The next story, from July 1866, was a tale of heartbreak and loss. It told how six-year-old Elizabeth Tuttle had drowned in Lake Champlain during a family outing: "The little girl was wading with several companions when she encountered an unexpected drop-off and sank suddenly into the depths. When Mr. Tuttle was alerted to her distress, he raced out at once to save her but could not immediately find her in the dark waters. By the time he was able to pull her out, she was already devoid of life. Both Mr. Tuttle and his wife are said to be inconsolable, and the sympathies of the entire community go out to them."

The third story, from just two months after the drowning, was equally tragic but also very strange. It recounted how Tuttle's wife had bled to death after giving birth to a son. Tuttle was said to be "prostrate with grief," but then events took an unexpected turn. Instead of embracing his infant son, Tuttle disappeared. "Mr. Tuttle has not been seen in town for three days," the *Republican* reported, "and there is great concern as to his well-being. The death of his wife was a terrible blow, especially as it came so soon after his daughter drowned, and there are fears Mr. Tuttle may be contemplating self-destruction. The authorities are actively searching for him, and it is hoped he will be found safe. In the meantime, as Mr. Tuttle has no living relatives in Plattsburgh, his son is being cared for at the county orphanage."

After reading the letter from Wisnom and the stories, Rafferty's first thought was: What happened to the son Tuttle abandoned? He also wondered whether Harriman himself had been the recent caller Wisnom mentioned. Was Harriman finally attempting to locate the son he'd left behind in Plattsburgh so many years earlier? It certainly seemed possible. Rafferty sent off a telegram to Wisnom, posing additional questions.

Wisnom's response arrived less than twenty-four hours later on Saturday night as Rafferty was hosting the usual gathering of boisterous, thirsty men at his saloon. The newspaper editor had taken time out from preparing the *Republican*'s Sunday edition to send the wire, and Rafferty would later ship a fine bottle of Scotch to him as thanks. As soon as he read the telegram, Rafferty knew who Ambrose Harriman's nemesis must be. Harriman needed to be warned, and Rafferty went to his office to place a call to Birdwing. There was no answer. Rafferty had the operator try again, with the same result.

As all people do, Rafferty sometimes had premonitions, not of the "this bridge is about to fall" or "this person is about to die" sort, but more like the passing of a dark cloud across the moon. Harriman, Rafferty believed, was in grave danger. Even though it was almost eleven o'clock at night, Rafferty decided he had to act at once. "Boys, you will have to have handle these ruffians on your own for a while," he told his three assistant bartenders. "Something urgent has come up."

Rafferty went out to the Ryan's main entrance and summoned a hack. He gave the driver Birdwing's address and said, "Hurry now! The faster you go, the more there will be in it for you."

Harriman's old stone house was utterly dark when Rafferty arrived at the front gate. He had the hack wait while he tried the gate, which was locked. The walls that protected the estate along Summit were too high to scale, at least for a man of Rafferty's heft, so he climbed back into the cab and instructed the driver to go around to the rear of the property on Maiden Lane. Once they came up on the carriage house, Rafferty saw that it, too, was dark, with no sign of anyone stirring. An adjacent iron gate guarded a walkway leading up to the rear of the main house. To Rafferty's surprise, the gate was open.

"This will do," he told the driver as he added a handsome tip to the fare. "Wait here fifteen minutes, if you would. If I'm not back by then, you can be on your way."

Rafferty walked through the gate and onto the grounds of Birdwing. The night was still, the birds Harriman so adored quiet in their resting places. Above, scudding clouds slipped past a half-moon amid twinkling stars. Despite the peaceful setting, Rafferty felt apprehensive, and his worry only increased when he found that the mansion's back door was also unlocked.

10
A FINAL CONFRONTATION

ELI TUTTLE KNEW that Anna Jerabek went to the public library every Friday afternoon, and when he delivered a message to her there, supposedly from Harriman, she did not doubt its authenticity. The message said: "My Dearest Anna, I wish to meet with you one last time to discuss a matter of the utmost importance. You must come to my mansion tomorrow night so that we can talk. I will have a cab waiting for you at the Upper Landing at ten p.m. Tell no one of this meeting, or my very life might be in jeopardy. Love, Ambrose."

There was no question in Anna's mind that she would do as Harriman asked. He was in terrible trouble, and she was determined to help him in any way she could. And while it was odd that he wished to see her at such a late hour, she assumed he must have some good reason for doing so. All day Saturday she could hardly think of anything except the meeting, and as darkness fell, she could hardly contain her nervous energy.

When the appointed hour finally arrived, Anna sneaked out of her bedroom window and walked east along the levee toward the old Upper Landing along the Mississippi, which flowed by gently in the moonlight. Once busy with steamboat traffic, the landing area was now given over largely to lumberyards and small warehouses arrayed along the busy tracks of the Chicago, Milwaukee and St. Paul Railway. As promised, a hackney cab was waiting for her when she reached Chestnut Street.

"You must be Miss Jerabek," the driver said. "Kind of late, ain't it, for a girl like you to be out all alone?"

"I am fine," Anna said. "Do you know where you're supposed to go?"

"Of course I do," said the driver, who'd been hired by Tuttle and paid in advance. "Now then, let me open the door for you, little lady, and we'll be off to Summit Avenue. I guess you must know Mr. Harriman up there. Are you sure you want to see him? You know what—"

"Yes, I know what people say and it is all a lie," Anna said before she stepped up into the carriage, which was plushily upholstered and seemed very luxurious.

Anna had never taken a carriage ride at night, and she was excited to see all the lighted buildings as they approached Seven Corners, where electric streetcars—still a novelty—rattled along the crooked streets. It was quieter once they'd climbed up the long hill to Summit Avenue. Anna gazed out in wonder, as she always did, at James J. Hill's new mansion, many of its windows still ablaze with light. Once they reached Maiden Lane, the driver maneuvered expertly down the narrow alley until he stopped in front of Birdwing's carriage house, which was pitch dark.

"Don't look like nobody's here," the driver said as he helped Anna out of the hackney.

Anna peered out toward the main house, where a single dim

light illuminated the back door. What looked to be a man in dark clothing stood by the door and waved at her. "This way, my child," he called out.

"I see Mr. Harriman," Anna told the driver. "You may go now."

As the hackney clattered away down the alley, Anna opened the gate next to the carriage house and walked toward the man who had summoned her. When she came up to the door she was surprised to encounter Eli Tuttle, rather than Harriman.

"Anna, I am so glad you could come," Tuttle said, "but we must be very discreet. Mr. Harriman doesn't want you to be seen or there could be trouble. Follow me and everything will be fine."

Holding her hand, Tuttle led Anna up to the back door of the mansion. When they stepped inside the dark kitchen, Tuttle lit a candle and said, "Mr. Harriman is up in his bedroom. He has something to show you there."

Anna thought it odd that no lights were on but said nothing as they climbed the staircase leading up to the second floor. She followed Tuttle down a hallway to a spare bedroom. "Right in here," Tuttle said softy. "Mr. Harriman will be along shortly."

Tuttle had planned everything out with the utmost attention to detail. He knew Harriman, who never stayed up past nine o'clock, would be alone in the house, no doubt fast asleep in his bedroom. The servants had the evening off and would not return until well after midnight, as was their habit.

As with everything else, Tuttle had selected the bedroom carefully. It was at the opposite end of the house from where Harriman slept, and so there was little chance of awakening him. Tuttle knew every corner of the mansion, which he liked to roam late at night when everyone else was asleep. He'd even gone up to the attic once and there he'd discovered a cabinet containing old family pictures from Plattsburgh. One of the daguerreotypes showed Ambrose, his wife, Abigail, and little Elizabeth dressed up in their Sunday finery outside the family's house by Lake Champlain. Blind, dumb fate had taken Elizabeth away and then Abigail had lost her life giving him his. It was all too bad, Tuttle thought, but not nearly as bad as what Ambrose had done next by utterly abandoning his own flesh and blood. Such cowardice and cruelty could never be forgiven.

On one of his nocturnal explorations Tuttle had made another important find—a safe hidden away in the mansion's basement. It hadn't taken Tuttle long to guess the combination, which turned out to be the month, day, and year of Harriman's birth. The safe's contents, he was delighted to discover, included a stash of currency and gold coins easily worth thousands of dollars. Tuttle intended to use the money to bankroll a new life somewhere far from St. Paul once he left Birdwing for good.

But first there was business to attend to. Still holding Anna's hand, Tuttle led her into the bedroom. He intended to strangle her there, quickly and quietly, and leave behind plenty of evidence that no one but Harriman could have committed the crime. Anna, however, grew suspicious when they entered the dark, empty room in the flickering light of Tuttle's candle.

"Where's Uncle Ambrose?" she asked just as Tuttle grabbed her wrist and tried to pull her toward him. But she was stronger than Tuttle thought and managed to slip away from him as his candle fell from his hand. She spun around toward the door, knocking over a table lamp as she tried to escape. The lamp's glass shade shattered with a loud noise as it hit the hardwood floor. "Let me go," she shouted and began to scream as she'd never screamed before.

Anna managed to reach the hallway, screaming all the while, as Tuttle struggled to control her. He finally got an arm around her neck and began dragging her back toward the bedroom when a door at the far end of the hall opened and Harriman emerged, clad in a long nightgown and carrying a candle.

"What is this?" he demanded when the saw Anna and her captor down the hall. "What are you doing?"

"Help me!" Anna shouted as Tuttle pulled her backward, his left arm tightening around her neck.

Tuttle realized that his careful plan had shattered as thoroughly as the table lamp. His dream of a long ruination for Harriman would have to be adjusted. There was no choice now but outright killing. Tuttle produced a pistol, the same one he'd taken from Jack Spence's lifeless body, and put it to the back of Anna's head. "Shut up, you little bitch," he said, "or I will kill you right now."

As the terrible scene unfolded in front of him, Harriman had a sudden realization, and it felt like an icicle plunged through his heart. The worst sin of his life was standing before him and there was no atoning for it. "Don't hurt her, my dear Eli," he said. "I know I have committed a great wrong against you, but killing this girl will not make up for my sins. Take me if it is blood you want."

"A great wrong?" Tuttle echoed as Anna tried to squirm from his grasp. "Is that what you call it? I call it the work of the devil, and now you will rot in hell for it."

"Yes, I suppose I will," Harriman said, suddenly aware of a small light moving through the darkness on the nearby staircase. "But I beg of you to leave little Anna out of this. She has done nothing to you."

* * *

When Rafferty slipped into the mansion, he found himself in complete darkness. He always carried matches for his cigars, and he struck one as he stumbled into the kitchen. He would later say he immediately felt the charge of some great emotion in the air, and it put him on high alert. He struck a second match as he went through the dining room toward the main staircase. A moment later, he heard Anna's screams. He took out his Colt revolver and began climbing the steps. He reached the upper hallway just in time to witness an extraordinary scene.

The man Rafferty now knew to be Harriman's son was holding a gun to Anna Jerabek's head as Harriman, candle in hand, advanced toward them, seemingly oblivious to the danger.

"You shall not have her," Harriman said. "No, no, no, you shall not have her!"

Then Webster came flying out into the hall, his wings beating furiously. "Stupid fellow!" the bird said. "Waste of time!" The bird then began screeching wildly, as though sensing the danger in the air.

Harriman ignored the bird and walked toward Anna and her captor with the fatalistic steps of an infantryman advancing against all odds in battle. He was a few feet away from his son when the first shot rang out. The bullet struck Harriman just beneath his left shoulder, but he kept on coming as blood poured down the front of his nightgown. After that, all was darkness as Harriman's candle tumbled to the floor and went out. Rafferty heard another shot, and then another, and then screaming. He lit a match and peered down the hallway, his Colt at the ready. He saw Harriman and his son lying on the floor, their bodies tangled together. Anna was bent down beside them, sobbing uncontrollably. As Rafferty approached, Webster flew past him and disappeared down the stairs. There was a gas sconce in the hallway, and Rafferty lit it before he came up to the bloody scene.

"It will be all right, child," he said to Anna, gently lifting her to her feet. "Let me help."

Rafferty had seen more bullet wounds than he cared to remember, and he knew at once that Harriman's son was dead. As he'd struggled with his father for the gun, a shot had gone off. The bullet had plowed up through his chin and into his brain, killing him instantly. His arms were outflung and near his right hand a .38-caliber revolver rested on the floor, its work of death accomplished.

Harriman lay on top of his son, face down, his arms stretched out as though he sought a final embrace. Blood had soaked all through his nightgown and Rafferty doubted he could live for long. Rafferty gingerly rolled Harriman over until he lay prone on the floor. His eyes opened wide and he saw that Anna was unharmed.

"Oh, Uncle Ambrose," she said, fighting back a new flood of tears. "Will you be all right?"

He smiled—perhaps for the first time in many years—and reached up to touch her cheek. "Yes," he said, "I am all right now." Then he said to Rafferty, the words pouring out like the blood spreading out across his nightgown, "Do you think it possible one good deed can wipe out the sins of a lifetime?"

"Ah, I cannot answer that. But you have certainly done a fine thing, Mr. Harriman. You saved this girl."

"Yes, yes, I did, and that is all that matters now. Oh, my dear Anna, I—"

Harriman's eyes froze before he could say another word, and when Rafferty felt for a pulse, there was none.

"Come now, Anna," Rafferty said, taking her by the hand and leading her away. "Come with me. There is nothing we can do here now."

"But why did Mr. Edmonds try to hurt me?" she asked, glancing back at the body of the coachman lying next to his long-lost father.

"Ah, that is a long and sad story," Rafferty said. "I will tell it to you once we've called the police."

* * *

By the time two police patrolmen arrived at the front door of the mansion, Rafferty had done his best to explain to Anna the saga of Harriman and the son he'd abandoned so many years before. It wasn't easy for Rafferty to understand how Harriman could have done such a thing until Anna offered an explanation.

"Uncle Ambrose told me once so many bad things happened to him that he tried to kill himself because he was so sad," Anna said. "But then he didn't."

"Did he say why?"

"He said a bird saved him, but I don't know how."

Rafferty knew nothing of Harriman's life-changing moment in the Ohio woods. Yet what Rafferty had learned from Anna and his inquiries in Plattsburgh now suggested a reason for Harriman's seemingly inexplicable act of abandonment. Harriman's heart had been twice broken, by the deaths of his daughter and wife, and Rafferty knew all too well what that could do to a man. A broken heart was a cracked bowl, love draining out of it until it was all but empty. Harriman, Rafferty suspected, had left his baby son because he had no love left in him, for his family, for humanity, for life itself.

Then one day, no doubt to Harriman's vast surprise, Anna had come along and somehow repaired his heart so that love could fill it once again. That could explain why he'd called Wisnom in Plattsburgh in search of information. But Harriman didn't know that it was too late for reconciliation, that his son was already close at hand and bent upon revenge.

When Chief Gallagher and Patrick Donlin arrived at the mansion, Rafferty quickly spun out the story for them. Both men were skeptical at first, but items found in Eli Tuttle's room in the carriage house quickly cleared away all doubts. There were photographs of the Tuttle family in Plattsburgh, Ambrose and his wife and daughter smiling for the camera, not knowing the disasters that lay ahead. There was also a diary, hidden carefully under a loose floorboard, that described in minute detail Eli Tuttle's vengeful campaign against his father.

"We will have to talk to the girl," Gallagher said. "What's her name again?"

"Anna Jerabek. She's shaken up but she'll be a good witness," Rafferty said. "There is iron in her and she is wise beyond her years. I left her downstairs with the two servants who had the evening off, Mr. York and Mr. Newman. They happened to return just after I called the police."

"Well, we will talk to them, too," Gallagher said, still sounding as though he wasn't quite prepared to believe Rafferty's story.

"You can, but I doubt they know much. Eli Tuttle was a man in disguise, or maybe I should say a shadow. He lived in secret and shared his plans with no one, except for the late Jack Spence."

"I take it you think Tuttle killed Spence to ensure his silence," Donlin said.

"Yes, and also, I suspect, to keep from being blackmailed," Rafferty said. "Handy Jack had a fine mind for crime, and he must have figured out that Tuttle killed the Whistler boy. He was probably expecting a blackmail payment when, no doubt much to his surprise, he took a knife to the chest."

"Well, it is a bad business all around," Donlin said. "How could Tuttle murder a boy for no other reason than to blame his father for the crime? What kind of man does such a thing?"

"A man obsessed with vengeance," Rafferty said, "and with no heart left in him. He wanted to do everything possible to humiliate and utterly ruin his father. Think of all the plotting he must have done. 'Twas like a brain fever, I imagine, and it consumed him."

"I guess so, but he'd have been a lot smarter just demanding money," Donlin noted. "Harriman must be worth millions, and if I were his abandoned son, I'd figure he owed me plenty."

"Agreed, Pat, and I wouldn't be surprised if Tuttle managed to steal money or valuables from his father along the way. But I don't think the money mattered all that much to him. It wouldn't have soothed the acid eating at his insides. He wanted something more dear than money. He wanted justice, at least as he saw it."

"Well, it's all over with now," Gallagher said, "and we'll let the papers have their fun with it. I suppose you'll want to play the hero's role, Rafferty, and tell everyone how you saved that girl."

Rafferty shook his head. "No, the hero in the end was Mr. Harriman himself. He could not bear to see the girl killed and he walked straight into two bullets to save her. Only real love could make a man do that. I was merely a bystander and I'd be happy to keep my name out of this."

But the newspapers had other ideas, and Rafferty received much attention in the stories that followed, as did Anna, who was depicted as a stalwart young heroine. It was a week before the press finally began to lose interest in the case and Rafferty could get back to something like his usual life. But Anna Jerabek's life would never return to the one she had known, as she discovered a fortnight after Harriman's death when the terms of his will were made known.

11
ANNA AND HER BIRDS

THE READING OF THE WILL took place in Rutherford Cuddleton's lavishly overstuffed office, which occupied an upper floor of the Union Block directly across from the courthouse. Cuddleton, who served as the executor of the estate, invited Rafferty to the will reading as a witness, along with Anna and her parents, who still seemed dazed by all that had happened to their daughter. Both of Anna's parents spoke limited English, and Anna served as their interpreter as needed.

As they waited for Cuddleton to finish a few final details, Rafferty asked Anna if she had ever been suspicious of Eli Tuttle in his guise as the coachman. She said she hadn't but that she'd wondered about Newman after learning that he'd been seen talking to Freddie Whistler.

"I thought maybe he might have murdered Freddie for some reason and tried to blame Uncle Ambrose," she said. "But when I asked him about it later, he said he'd just been trying to convince Freddie to stay away from Birdwing for his own good."

"Well, I think you're a pretty good little sleuth, Anna," Rafferty said. "It was Eli, of course, who must have persuaded Freddie to trespass on that fatal night. Eli had the devil's gift when it came to lying."

Cuddleton finally returned to the office and said, "I think we are ready now. You may be interested to know that Mr. Harriman, or perhaps I should say Mr. Ambrose Harriman Tuttle, prepared a new will just a week before his most unfortunate demise. His previous will left the bulk of his estate to various charitable and civic endeavors and to a private foundation he intended to establish so that Birdwing could become a permanent bird sanctuary. His final will, however, is quite different."

Cuddleton paused, letting the drama of the moment build, then said, "Mr. Harriman's estate, I have determined, amounts to about five million dollars in all, including real and personal property. As written, the will provides that half of the estate should go to his only son, Eli Tuttle."

Rafferty was now certain that Harriman had been the man making inquiries about Eli Tuttle in Plattsburgh just before the tragic events at Birdwing. Clearly, Harriman had at last come to terms with what he had done and wanted to set things right with his son to the extent he could. Instead, everything had gone very wrong.

Cuddleton continued: "However, as we are all aware, Mr. Eli Tuttle is deceased, and since the will includes a standard sixty-day survivorship clause, the effect is that his portion of the estate will go to the next designated beneficiary, Miss Anna Jerabek. As to Miss Jerabek, the will provides that the other half of the estate, specifically including Birdwing, goes to her minus a few small bequests to servants and the like. When the late Mr. Eli Tuttle's portion is added to that, it means, Miss Jerabek, that you are now worth nearly five million dollars."

Anna's mother, who had a better grasp of English than her

husband, was momentarily dumbfounded before breaking out in tears. When Anna explained the situation to her father, he was even more stunned, and asked her, in Czech, if this meant he could quit his job.

"*Ano,*" she said, and her father, too, began to cry.

"Of course, as Miss Jerabek is only twelve years of age, a conservatorship will have to be established on her behalf until she reaches the age of eighteen, when under the terms of the will she will be entitled to take full control of all that she has inherited," Cuddleton said. "Naturally, I would be pleased to assist you in establishing the conservatorship if you so choose."

Anna, who was about the most self-possessed child Rafferty had ever encountered, was the only member of her family who didn't shed tears over the incredible news. She said, "I did not expect this of Uncle Ambrose, but if he is listening in heaven, I will tell him now that Birdwing will be safe with me, and it will be a splendid place for birds as long as I live."

* * *

Anna Jerabek proved true to her word. With the approval of the probate court, she first arranged to move into Birdwing with her parents. Her father, weakened by years of strenuous labor and hard drinking, died just two years later, but her mother was still alive when Anna turned eighteen a few years before the new century began. By then she had grown into a formidable young woman, and with the financial resources available to her she made numerous improvements to Birdwing. She planted new trees and grasses to attract additional birds, excavated a second duck pond and added walkways and benches for the visitors she welcomed every Sunday, when the grounds were thrown open to the public.

With her beauty and her fortune Anna became the most sought-after woman in the city as young men of all stations feigned interest in her birds while hoping to woo her into marriage with promises of undying affection. But she found little use for such men and their ridiculous pleadings, and she never married. Her mother and Webster were her best companions, but birds in all of their variety remained the great passion of her life. In her late twenties, after both her mother and Webster had died, she began to travel widely and fearlessly. The moist jungles of Panama, the boreal forests of Siberia, and the wild highlands of New Guinea were among her destinations, and on one especially memorable expedition in 1907 she became the first person to photograph an elusive, yellow-throated bird that would one day be named Jerabek's Warbler.

In 1920, she published a magisterial, beautifully illustrated *Guide to the Glorious Birds of Minnesota*. The book's dedication read: "To Ambrose Harriman Tuttle, who discovered the wonder of birds when all seemed lost. May he find peace with them forever in gentle skies." As she grew older, Anna became known, like her mentor, for her eccentricities. She dressed in tattered clothes, let her hair grow down to her waist, and rarely left Birdwing, where she stayed busy supervising new projects, sketching avian visitors, and chasing squirrels away from feeders. As the years went by, many people forgot her real name, but there was hardly a resident of the city unfamiliar with the strange old lady everyone called the Birdwoman of Summit Avenue.

The GOLD KING

A Strange Tale

Not all that tempts your wand'ring eyes
And heedless hearts, is lawful prize;
Nor all, that glistens, gold.

—THOMAS GRAY

1

A MAN OF MYSTERY

THE MAN WHO CALLED HIMSELF the Gold King appeared in St. Paul on the first day of April in 1894, arriving from Chicago on the Burlington Route's afternoon express and then repairing at once to the Ryan Hotel, which in those days was regarded as the city's finest lodging house. His unusual sobriquet came to light when he signed the hotel register as "G. King" and then blithely mentioned what the *G* stood for. Any concern the clerk might have had about one so curiously named was quickly assuaged when the man deposited a pouch filled with twenty-dollar gold pieces on the front desk and announced he intended to stay for "several weeks" in the finest suite the Ryan had to offer. He added, "You may simply call me the King, for as you will discover I am in search of a treasure even Midas would covet."

Little was made of his presence at first, St. Paul then being a great rail hub and thus used to travelers of unorthodox title and demeanor passing through from all corners of the continent. But it wasn't long before the King, as the newspapers soon referred to him, became the focus of intense gossip, the more so because he declined all interviews with the press. "Who is this Gold King and what does he want?" asked the *Pioneer Press* in a story about "the mysterious stranger in our midst." His claim to be in search of treasure naturally aroused all manner of speculation, none of it rooted in the fertile soil of fact, and so idle talk carried the day. Skeptics, meanwhile, contended that he was very probably a mountebank preparing to pull off some cheap swindle, and they warned the public not to be taken in by whatever scheme he had in mind.

Although much uncertainty surrounded the King, there could be no doubt that he was a handsome specimen of manhood. Tall and broad-shouldered, with the bearing of a soldier, he was perhaps fifty years of age. He had a fine head of black hair streaked with gray, a dignified Roman nose, a neatly clipped vandyke beard, and riveting violet eyes. As befitting his regal mien, he was always impeccably attired in a red swallow-tail coat, striped trousers, ascot, and a perfectly starched white shirt accented with gold cufflinks. A splendid gold chain of intricate design draped his long neck, and the fine gold pocket watch he consulted from time to time was reputed to have been custom made in Paris by Cartier. His jeweled array also included, on the middle finger of his right hand, a diamond-studded gold ring of sufficient magnitude to tantalize an heiress.

Not long after his arrival, the King began making daily tours of the city in a brougham carriage rented from a livery stable. His excursions quickly drew yet more attention in the newspapers, for along his route he would toss out one-dollar gold pieces to street waifs who eagerly awaited his daily transits. Two rough-looking men in buckskin jackets and black Stetson hats, both armed with pistols and repeating rifles, always rode atop the carriage, and so fierce was their demeanor that no one dared even think of robbing the King of his gold.

Interest in the King deepened when the afternoon *Dispatch* uncovered a clue as to his business in the city. The King, it was learned, had some weeks earlier acquired the Hopewell Block, a small building on Cedar Street directly across from city hall. How he had managed to do so was unclear, since the building was not known to be for sale. Although undistinguished as a work of architecture, the building was notorious in St. Paul. Its eponym, a financier named Arthur Hopewell, had unaccountably vanished from the building less than six months earlier. The building had been sealed shut since then to keep out trespassers drawn by rumors that Hopewell had secreted a vast quantity of gold bullion in the basement.

News of the King's purchase immediately fueled speculation that he intended to search for Hopewell's supposed treasure. As usual, the King had nothing to say to the press, but his silence was thought to be telling. It was widely assumed that he had by some means become convinced of the treasure's existence and intended to unearth it as soon impossible. This idea gained credence when six men said to be from Montana arrived one afternoon at the Union Depot and casually mentioned to an agent there that they were miners by trade and had come to St. Paul to dig for gold. Station agents in those days earned extra money by serving as tipsters, and within a day the newspapers knew all about the miners.

Reporters went to the King's suite at the Ryan, and to their surprise he agreed to speak to them. "It is true that I have hired some men to work for me," he stated, "but I am not yet prepared to reveal the full extent of my business here. I will say that I am undertaking a small construction project in the building I recently acquired. A basement wall is threatening to collapse, and I must shore it up. That is all I can tell you at the moment."

* * *

The King was much talked about in all the gathering places of the city, none more so than at Shadwell Rafferty's popular saloon, located on the ground floor of the Ryan. Rafferty, who functioned as the city's bartender in chief as well as a part-time private detective, was among those greatly intrigued by the King. A day after the King's brief statement, Rafferty sat at a table in his saloon, working on the giant mug of coffee and bakery roll that formed his usual breakfast. With him was his friend and business partner, George Washington Thomas, who was enjoying a plate piled high with bacon and eggs. Not surprisingly, the King was the focus of their conversation.

"I think we can safely say the King is lying about that supposed problem with the basement walls," Rafferty said after gulping down the last of his coffee.

"Agreed," Thomas said. "He must be after something beneath

the building. Maybe he really believes all those stories about Hopewell's buried gold."

"Who is to say what he believes? But I am firmly of the opinion he's a flimflammer. Yet I cannot say I have seen the likes of him before. He must be embarked upon some bold scheme, but to what end? I do not see how he will ultimately profit from his maneuverings."

"Well, he's already spent a lot of money here, from what I can tell," Thomas noted. "Whatever he's going to do, it will have to be something big if he hopes to come out ahead. But you know as well as I that when it comes to gold, people do crazy things. I'm betting this King fellow will unveil his plans soon enough. Then the gulls will flock around as they always do, and he'll be happy to relieve them of their money."

A story in the next morning's *Pioneer Press* appeared to bear out Thomas's prediction. Written by the newspaper's ace reporter, Dolly Charbonneau, the story claimed the King was in fact trying to unearth "$1 million or more in gold bullion" secreted somewhere in or beneath the Hopewell Block. Charbonneau had not talked to the King, however. Instead, she attributed her information to "an unnamed source," whom Rafferty and Thomas assumed must be one of the supposed miners.

"The King is a treasure hunter," the source told Charbonneau. "No one knows his real name, but he is a remarkable man. I swear he can smell gold from miles away just like a horse can smell water. He would not be in St. Paul unless there were riches to be had. Besides, I am told he knows quite a bit about Arthur Hopewell, so he must have some inside information."

The story created an immediate sensation, and that very night two men tried breaking into the Hopewell Block in search of the precious metal, only to be rudely repulsed by the King's gun-toting guardians. Although the King had nothing to say about the incident, a notice soon appeared in all of the city's newspapers stating that "the Hopewell Block is private property. Trespassers will be met with deadly force. You have been warned!"

* * *

The King's mysterious presence, like the low rumbling thunder of an approaching storm, appeared to set much of St. Paul on edge. The newspapers reported his every movement and badgered him for comment, but he continued to maintain a Delphic silence, which only served to intensify the public's fascination. The King even drew attention from the city's pulpits, where preachers of all stripes suggested that he might well be Satan incarnate come to seduce the faithful with the false idol of gold. Critics of a less pious kind could also be heard, and in letters to the newspapers they ridiculed the King and anyone foolish enough to believe in tales of hidden treasure.

Yet the idea of secret riches held great appeal to many in the city, for gold was very much on the public's mind that April. A severe depression had struck as companies awash in debt began to fail one after another. Stocks tumbled, black ink turned to red, workers lost their jobs, and hard times settled in like a sullen fog. Investors responded by fleeing to the time-honored security of gold, quickly depleting the nation's reserves.

In constricted times, hope expands and so it was that for every person who scoffed at the King, another ten were ready to dream of the gold that had apparently drawn him to St. Paul. What if there really was a million-dollar treasure? And what would it be like to suddenly possess such a prize? By contrast, the city's moneyed men, who preferred tobacco to dreams in their pipes, viewed the King as just another fraudster out to fleece the unwary and so paid little heed to his doings. However, two prominent men of wealth—Harvey Calhoun and Frank Shay—were not as quick as their peers to dismiss the King. They'd been Arthur Hopewell's neighbors on Summit Avenue, and they did not think it entirely impossible that he'd amassed a golden treasure.

"This King fellow is probably a trickster," Calhoun said to Shay one afternoon, "but he bears watching. Do you suppose he's actually going to dig for gold beneath the Hopewell Block?"

"I don't know," said Shay, "but we need to get the police involved to find out more. If the King starts digging, who is to say what he might find? What if Hopewell really did leave behind a stash?"

"It could be, I suppose. That Black devil was capable of just about anything," Calhoun acknowledged as he thought back to the events of the previous year, when Arthur Hopewell had for brief time become the most notorious man in St. Paul.

2

HOPEWELL'S DREAM

A METEOR AFLAME with money and ideas, Arthur Hopewell landed in St. Paul in the summer of 1893, and no one knew at first what to make of him. Some would in time proclaim him a gift from the heavens, while others were convinced he came from a darker realm. But it was his singular appearance that attracted the most attention, for his off-white skin suggested he might be of African ancestry or perhaps even from some exotic Mideastern realm. This would have been no great cause for comment were it not for his wealth, which became evident when he purchased, with fifteen thousand dollars in cash, a mansion on Summit Avenue, where all of the city's grandees lived amid much luxurious tedium.

Those inclined to view Hopewell as a very light-skinned Negro dubbed him the "Mulatto Millionaire" while expressing amazement that a man of his sort could possess great riches. "He is a dark mystery," said the *Globe,* "and no one can as yet explain his sudden appearance here." Nonetheless, a rumor soon spread that he was, in fact, the octoroon son of a wealthy Louisiana plantation owner and had come north to escape the pestilence of yellow fever. But as Hopewell never spoke publicly about his personal history, no one really knew where he had come from or how he had acquired his riches.

Interest in the mysterious newcomer intensified after he bought the mansion. Men of his color, no matter how light the tone, were assumed to be menial laborers at best and were by custom if not by law confined to dwelling in a small section of the city set aside for the "coloreds." To see such a man at home in a big house on Summit was startling. Had the mansion's owner, the elderly widow of a banker, known who the buyer was, she would naturally have refused to sell. Hopewell, however, had arranged the purchase through a third party, and when he showed up to claim his property, trouble ensued.

Most of Hopewell's neighbors on Summit were horrified to learn of the new resident in their midst and called a meeting to consider what to do. "I do not see how I would ever be able to sell my house with a Negro living across the street," said Calhoun, a hardware tycoon who believed fervently in the superiority of the white race. "I also wonder where this Hopewell character gets his money. He must be a charlatan of some kind."

"Perhaps we could buy him out," suggested Morton Rogers, a real estate broker. "There must be somewhere else he would agree to live if there was money in it for him. As it is, he is a stain on our neighborhood and his presence will certainly depress all of our property values."

Shay, a speculator in commodities, agreed that the "damned mulatto" must go but rejected the idea of paying him to leave. "Why give a man of his kind money? Why should we have to do that? I say we confront him and demand he remove himself at once or face the consequences."

"And what would those consequences be?" asked Benjamin Lloyd, a plumbing millionaire who'd lived on Summit for thirty years. "We need to calm down. This is not the end of the world, as most of you seem to think. Besides, if Hopewell is some sort of confidence man, I imagine he will move on before long."

"Well, I do not see how we could rely on that to happen," Calhoun said. "I am with Frank. We must take action."

After much back-and-forth, the neighbors finally agreed to form an ad hoc Committee of Seven, chaired by Calhoun, to deal with Hopewell. As a first step, the committee hired lawyers to challenge Hopewell's mansion purchase on whatever grounds they could dream up. Although a sympathetic judge heard the case, he could find nothing in state law, city ordinance, or in any deed restriction that made the sale illegal. Hopewell, it seemed, could not be removed under color of law, much to the committee's disappointment.

Shortly after he moved into his mansion, attended by a staff of

Swedish servants, Hopewell purchased a building downtown to conduct his business. The nature of his occupation was not immediately apparent. But as time went on it became clear he was a stock manipulator, one of those canny and secretive masters of the markets who bet long, short, and in every other way to create money out of nothing. Despite the stock market's crash in early 1893 and the onset of a deep depression, Hopewell appeared to turn a steady profit. "He is always ahead of the game and how he does it no one knows," an anonymous source told one newspaper. "Every transaction he makes enriches him, without fail. He always buys or sells at precisely the right moment. He can sense even the slightest movements in the market and exploit them."

Although Hopewell reportedly cleared thousands of dollars a week by means of his shrewd investments, he did nothing to flaunt his wealth. He took a cab to and from work, dressed simply, and gave no evidence of a social life, not that he would ever have been invited to any of the balls, cotillions, costume parties, or other galas by which his Summit Avenue neighbors amused themselves. Even after he donated many thousands of dollars to charity—good work only grudgingly noted in the newspapers—he remained an outcast, shunned by the city's leading men as a rank interloper who had no business living as he did.

Hopewell's quiet existence did not last for long. Barely a month after his arrival in St. Paul, he created an instant furor by sending a letter to the newspapers in which he promised to use his wealth to "bring about a great transformation. The ruling class of this city has for too long built its fortune on the backs of laboring men and women. This must change! I am proposing a new social order based on fairness and justice for all, and I will work tirelessly to achieve this end. I ask all the people of St. Paul to join me in this noble endeavor."

The city's leading men read Hopewell's letter with a sense of amazement and dread. How could a man of wealth subscribe to such absurd ideas? Dangerous radicals of all types—agitators, dynamiters, unionists, and worse—were already a growing threat, and now here was Hopewell openly calling for revolution. At the tony Minnesota Club, where men of means met to dine and plot deals, Hopewell became a constant topic of discussion even if he was most definitely not a candidate for admission. Calhoun and Shay, both well-regarded club members, regularly railed against Hopewell.

"He should be run out of town on a rail," opined Calhoun. "His sentiments are outrageous."

"And very dangerous," Shay added. "What if he succeeds in stirring up the masses?"

Other club members were equally alarmed. They feared Hopewell might find an angry army of followers, for misery and want were stalking the streets of St. Paul as the depression worsened and the bleak days of winter approached. St. Paul's version of the chaotic Haymarket Affair in Chicago might well be the result, they believed, if Hopewell was allowed to have his way.

Hopewell offered yet another provocation when he began throwing parties of a most unusual kind at his mansion. Instead of inviting bluebloods, as any decent man would have done, Hopewell sent out teams of servants to bring in people from the poorest neighborhoods of the city. These unlikely guests were then treated to magnificent feasts as well as elaborate entertainments performed by the city's finest musicians, singers, and dancers. It was all more than Calhoun and Shay could stand, and they vowed to be rid of Hopewell by one means or another.

3
MINING FOR GOLD

THE DAY AFTER the King's miners arrived, they set to work building a tramway that led out through the front doors of the Hopewell Block. Crowds gathered to watch as narrow tracks were laid to accommodate cars that presumably would be used to remove soil, stone and miscellaneous debris from the mine. Most of the King's seemingly quixotic enterprise, however, was cloaked in secrecy. No outsiders were allowed into the building, no photographs were permitted, and a newspaper reporter who tried to sneak inside disguised as a workman was roughly removed by the King's guardians.

The King remained mum about his plans until Dolly Charbonneau at the *Pioneer Press* managed to obtain another interview.

"Well, I suppose the cat is out of the bag," he admitted. "I am indeed looking for a stash of gold beneath my building, though whether I will find it remains to be seen. The gold is well hidden, which is why I have brought in experienced men to dig for it."

When Charbonneau asked where the gold had come from and how he knew of it, the King said, "I am, you might say, a prospector by trade, and I go where I believe treasure is to be found. As it so happens, I learned some time ago about Mr. Hopewell and his abiding love of precious metal. As I understand it, he presented himself here as a great man of the people, but I rather doubt that was the case. My sources tell me he was, in fact, something of an actor who enjoyed depicting himself as a noble fellow out to help suffering humanity. But I believe it was the wondrous gleam of gold that enchanted him above all else, so much so that he always kept a large stock of bullion close at hand. With luck, I shall find it."

"Are you sure you are entitled to the gold?" Charbonneau asked. "If it belonged to Mr. Hopewell, might he return to claim it?"

"Oh, I suppose he could try," the King said with an air of nonchalance, "if he ever shows up again in St. Paul, which I doubt he will. Besides, you should know that I intend to donate fully one-quarter of the gold I find to the government of this wonderful city, to be used for good works that will benefit its citizens. I do not think Mr. Hopewell, wherever he is, would be nearly as generous."

* * *

Despite his evident wealth, the Gold King was a dicey character in the eyes of St. Paul Police Chief Michael Gallagher. The King, Gallagher assumed, was running a scam, although he was clearly different from the usual run of fraudsters, fakes, and four-flushers who wandered into St. Paul in search of easy marks. The chief had ample experience with grifters of every type and usually found that what he called "a little lesson in the art of the hickory stick" would convince them to take their underhanded business elsewhere. But the King required a more thorough investigation, and so it was that Gallagher and a team of policemen showed up one morning at the Hopewell Block with a search warrant obtained from a friendly judge.

"Your mine could be unsafe," Gallagher told the King at the front door, "and we must inspect it."

"I assumed you would be coming," the King said with a smile. "Feel free to look around. I am sure you will find there is no problem."

Gallagher and his squad went at once to the basement, which consisted of three stone-walled chambers with dirt floors. The mine, they found, was in the largest chamber. There, the King's men had started excavating a shaft through a layer of gray limestone. The shaft, with a hoist above it, was already about ten feet deep.

"Well, as you can see, there are no problems here," the King said. "My miners know their business and they will take all necessary precautions. But we have quite a ways to go yet, perhaps forty feet or more."

Gallagher asked a few questions, ordered his men to look around the rest of the basement, and then left, apparently satisfied with what he'd seen. When he returned to police headquarters, he went at once to talk with his best detective, Patrick Donlin, who'd already been assigned to look into the King's background.

But Donlin had ended up being flummoxed, for his investigation yielded only a few shreds of information. Donlin was able to establish that the King had stayed two nights at the Palmer House Hotel in Chicago before coming to St. Paul. He'd registered there, as he did at the Ryan, as "G. King" but gave no address. The Chicago police had no record of anyone of his description operating in their city as a confidence man, and inquire as he might, Donlin drew a blank. The King had no known real name, no known address, no known history, no known associates, or as Donlin regretfully concluded, "no known nothing."

Gallagher was stumped as well after speaking with Donlin. "His Royal Highness is either the cleverest fellow around or some goddamn genie," Gallagher said. "I'll have to have a nice long talk with him before long."

A brute of a man who went by the sobriquet "Merry Mike," Gallagher believed that any crime could be solved by beating a confession out of the lowlife who probably committed it. Gallagher would sometimes break out into an eerie giggle while going about his rough business, and the criminal element of the city knew that his laughter was to be feared above all else. Now, Gallagher was wondering whether he might have to amuse himself by shaking the truth out of the King. Gallagher's visit to the Hopewell Block had revealed only that the King was indeed doing some digging. But what was he really up to?

Mayor Thomas Reagan was among those who wanted an answer, and with that in mind, Gallagher went to see the King one evening in his suite at the Ryan. Gallagher was intimately familiar with the hotel, where he regularly used a suite adjacent to the King's to entertain prostitutes, since he did not wish to be seen in the brothels he was supposedly policing. A servant admitted Gallagher to the King's suite and led the way to an elegant parlor with tall Gothic windows and walls painted a rich golden hue. Gallagher found the King lounging on a tufted red sofa, smoking a long cigar and reading the newspapers.

"Ah, Chief Gallagher," he said, directing his visitor to a comfortable chair. "I have been expecting you. We did not have a chance to talk much, did we, when you inspected my mine. Have a cigar and we'll chat."

"Don't mind if I do," Gallagher said. He lit the cigar, and the first puff revealed it to be the finest he'd ever enjoyed.

"Cuban," the King said, noting the look of satisfaction on Gallagher's face, "from the best cigar maker in Havana. I thought you'd like it. Now then, I can only suppose you are here to grill me. What am I doing in St. Paul? Who am I? And perhaps most important, what perfidious plan have I hatched to swindle the good citizens of this city? Does that about cover it?"

"Yeah, it does. So why don't you be a nice fellow and tell me what your game is? Otherwise, I'll have to run you in and persuade you to talk, and you don't want that to happen."

"I certainly do not. As to who I am, it is of little consequence. All you need to know, chief, is that I am not a criminal, nor do I move in criminal circles. I am instead, as I have told the newspapers, a prospector, albeit not of the kind who roots about mountains and deserts, a trusty burro at my side, in search of the earth's treasures. I prefer to hunt for bullion in civilized places like St. Paul. You would be surprised, Chief, how much treasure is there for the taking if you know where to look for it."

"Well, ain't that the sweetest thing I ever heard," Gallagher said. "So you admit you're a thief."

"Oh no, my dear Chief, I am no such thing. I am an honest man of business who happens to have an unusual line of work, that is all."

Gallagher had heard plenty of conmen in his day and he was sure now the King must be a member of that honey-tongued fraternity. "You ain't fooling me," he said. "I know what you're about. So here's some friendly advice. Pack up your bags and leave before I run you out of town."

"I do not think that would be wise of you."

"Why not?"

"Because we can be of use to each other, and I see no reason why you shouldn't share in the wealth I expect to uncover. I am certain now that those stories of gold hidden away in the Hopewell Block are no fairy tales. Perhaps a small gift will convince you that I speak the truth."

"Is that so? What do you have in mind?"

The King summoned his valet and said, "John, be a good fellow and get that satchel in my bedroom and bring it here."

When the servant returned with the satchel, the King instructed him to hand it to the chief. "Go ahead, open it," the King said.

Gallagher was suspicious but did as he was told. Once he undid the latch and peered into the satchel, he was startled to see two gold ingots. He took out the precious bars and noticed that the word "Hopewell" was stamped into them.

"My men just found these this morning in a small passageway they uncovered. I have no doubt they will find many more. Mr. Hopewell, wherever he may be, left this city in such haste that he did not have time to take his treasure with him. I imagine his stash of bullion was simply too heavy to lug about. Poor fellow! But his loss is my gain, and yours. Think of these ingots as a token of my gratitude for the cooperation I know you and Mayor Reagan will extend to me as I go about my work. Naturally, I will want the police of this fine city to ensure that no brazen acts of thievery disturb my enterprise."

Gallagher had always thought a bribe well tendered was a lovely thing, but this was beyond the pale. A single ingot, he knew, was easily worth thousands of dollars. He was left speechless.

"I take it you and the mayor will accept my little gift," the King said with a knowing smile.

All Gallagher could do was nod.

The King stood up and said, "It has been a pleasure meeting you, Chief, and I look forward to working with you in the days ahead. I think we will both have a memorable time. My servant will show you out."

That same evening, Gallagher delivered the second ingot to Reagan, who all but squealed with delight when he held it in his hands. Gallagher also placed a telephone call to Frank Shay, one of his wealthy benefactors, to tell him about the King's "gift." Shay was stunned. "Harley and I thought the man was almost surely a swindler, but now it seems we were mistaken," Shay said. "We must have a talk with him, the sooner the better."

* * *

One Saturday afternoon, a man dressed in livery appeared at Rafferty and Thomas's saloon bearing an invitation. "The Gold King requests the pleasure of your company this evening at seven o'clock in the Ryan Hotel's dining room," the man said. "Will you be able to join him?"

"We will," Rafferty said at once. He had been trying for days to secure a meeting with the King, but all of his efforts had been rejected. "It will be a pleasure to sup with him."

That evening, Rafferty and Thomas arrived at the hotel's sumptuous dining room, which featured stained-glass windows and tall iron columns ornamented in the Gothic manner. St. Paul in those days was hardly renowned for gourmet dining, but it was widely agreed among the trenchermen of the city that the Ryan offered gustatory riches not readily available elsewhere. Rafferty and

Thomas arrived at the appointed hour and were quickly directed to the King's table. To their surprise, he offered a hearty greeting.

"Why, if it isn't the famous Shadwell Rafferty in the flesh!" he said with a broad smile that revealed gold crowns capping two of his front teeth "And Mr. Thomas as well! Come join me, gentlemen, and we shall share a fine repast."

"Very kind of you," Rafferty said. "You seem to have the advantage of knowing us. Have we met before?"

"We have not, but your reputations precede you. I have heard that you, Mr. Rafferty, are that rarest of commodities—an honest man—and that the same can be said of you, Mr. Thomas. I am also told that when the two of you are not tending to your elegant tavern, which I must confess I have yet to visit, you engage in occasional detective work. Are you detecting now?"

"I would say we are merely curious souls," Rafferty said. "You have made quite a stir since your arrival in St. Paul."

"I have and isn't it wonderful! There is excitement in the air, and that is always a good thing in my estimation. But since you are honest men, let us be honest with one another. I imagine you are skeptical regarding my intentions here. Indeed, I think it likely you view me as a confidence man, the very image of a ripe poser out to swindle the good people of St. Paul."

"That thought has crossed my mind," Rafferty acknowledged.

"Well then, let me assure you I have no intention of stealing so much as a penny from the citizens of this city. Indeed, as I have stated publicly, one-fourth of the gold I find will be donated to the city as a gesture of appreciation. First, of course, I must locate the treasure left behind by Mr. Hopewell. My miners have already found a small portion of it, and I have no doubt they will discover the whole of it before long. But why talk of such matters at the moment? I suggest we enjoy our meal first."

Course after course soon arrived, delivered by a platoon of liveried Black waiters, some of whom were surprised to see Thomas at the table. Others, however, knew him, and were pleased that one of their own had broken the dining room's unstated color barrier. For his part, the King seemed far more interested in his dinner than Thomas's race. Little-neck clams, green turtle soup, Atlantic salmon, potato croquettes, larded peas, baked tomatoes, and sweetbreads formed a small mountain of food, all accompanied by the finest wines from the hotel's cellars.

"Help yourself," the King said, "and don't be shy. I am a man of great appetite, as you can see, and I enjoy food of every kind."

Rafferty and Thomas dug into the repast, which was richer and more varied than any they'd ever enjoyed before. "'Tis a wonder you stay so slender," Rafferty observed, for the King appeared to have not an ounce of fat on his wiry frame.

"I am an active man, Mr. Rafferty. Indeed, you might say I have a fire in my belly."

A peach flambé, ignited at the table, culminated the meal. The dessert blazed with such force that Rafferty felt a blast of heat on his cheeks.

"Isn't it beautiful?" the King said. "It is like the very fire of the gods, assuming, of course, that the gods exist. I have my doubts in that regard, but who knows? In any event, the two of you must assist me in eating this delectable dessert."

When the last of the flambé had been dispatched, the King said, "Now, wasn't that lovely! I am really enjoying my visit here."

"May I ask where you're from?" Thomas asked.

"You might say I am traveler from the East," the King replied. "But let us return to the essential question, one that no doubt puzzles both of you to no end. How did I learn of Arthur Hopewell's hidden gold? Well, gentleman, that is quite a story but not one I can relate to you in full, lest I reveal certain secrets. Suffice to say that early this year, while I was in New York, I happened upon someone who knew Mr. Hopewell. This person told me how Hopewell had come to St. Paul to enhance his already substantial fortune, only to vanish without a trace some months later. I was also made aware of persistent rumors regarding a great pile of gold bullion he had amassed before his sudden disappearance."

"And you came out here solely on the basis of a mere rumor?" Rafferty asked. "That seems strange to me."

"No doubt it does, but you must understand that I am a man for whom gold—the sight of it, the gleam of it, the touch of it—is as paradise itself. In other words, I covet it, Mr. Rafferty, as Tantalus did the fruit just beyond his reach, and what you call 'mere rumor' is to me a golden dream I find impossible to ignore. And so here I am, in pursuit of buried treasure. Of course, the two of you know full well how men lust after precious metal, since you were miners once, or so I have been informed. The Comstock Lode, wasn't it?"

Rafferty nodded, struck by how much of his own history was known to the King. "In Nevada, after the war. But it was silver, not gold, Wash and I were after."

"Silver is nice enough, I agree, but it is no substitute for gold. As you can perhaps tell, I have already enjoyed some success as a prospector, but I believe my greatest discovery will be right here. I expect to find a million dollars' worth of gold secreted beneath the Hopewell Block."

"But if Mr. Hopewell had so much gold, why didn't he simply store it in a vault somewhere?" Thomas asked. "Why would he have gone to the trouble of burying it deep underground, as you say?"

"I cannot answer that question, for who knows what goes on in any man's mind? The important thing is that I intend to find every last ounce of Hopewell's gold. Naturally, I must be careful. Where there is gold, there are thieves, which is why I brought along my guardians."

Rafferty and Thomas had spotted the so-called guardians on several occasions. They were lanky, dead-eyed, mustachioed men armed with repeating rifles who wore black Stetson hats, buckskin jackets, black trousers, and finely tooled boots. They were rumored to be former U.S. marshals, culled from some violent backwater of the nation, but no one could say for sure.

"I have seen their sort before," Rafferty said. "They are killers."

"Which is why I hired them," the King said. "Their very presence will, I am sure, deter anyone with larceny in mind."

Rafferty leaned back in his chair and stared into the King's violet eyes, which were mysterious and unreadable. "I must tell you, sir, that I do not believe there is any gold beneath the Hopewell Block. You are running a con and have been all along."

"Ah, do you think so? Then, what do you suppose the purpose of this 'con,' as you so ungraciously call it, might be? Do you know how much money I have already spent on my little endeavor? Five thousand dollars, Mr. Rafferty, and counting. How will I make good on this very substantial investment if I am merely some trickster out to bilk the good people of this city?"

"I haven't figured that out, but I will. You are playing a long game, and the end will come in view at some point."

"I agree it is a long game. Longer, perhaps, than you think." The King removed the napkin from his lap and stood up, signaling that dinner was over, "Now then, I bid you good evening, gentlemen, and Godspeed."

"Well, he is a fine piece of work and a smooth customer if there ever was one," Rafferty said as he watched the King leave. "But no matter what he says, I don't believe for a second that Arthur Hopewell left a million dollars in bullion behind."

"I don't suppose he did," Thomas said, "but what if there is even a chance of it? We knew Mr. Hopewell pretty well, and he really was a remarkable character. I wouldn't put anything past him."

4
LOVE AND ENEMIES

ARTHUR HOPEWELL'S most provocative act, which would stun much of the city, came when he married a white woman. Her name was Meredith Lloyd, and when the wedding was announced, it was widely assumed she had either lost her mind or been cruelly seduced, while still others concluded that she was simply a wanton hussy clothed in silk. The bride was no commoner, being the youngest daughter of Benjamin Lloyd, who'd invented the "Lloyd trap," a clever device found beneath the toilets of thousands of American homes. The device had made Lloyd a very rich man, albeit the butt of much unseemly humor, to which he invariably responded with the tart observation, "Yes, and I'm much richer than you, aren't I?"

Of Lloyd's three daughters, two were considered, in the polite parlance of the time, "plain," and so had been packed off to finishing schools in the East in hopes that excellent manners and household skills, rather than mere good looks, might help them snag a man. Meredith, on the other hand, was anything but plain. Her long blond hair, finely proportioned body, and radiant face made her an object of desire for every randy young playboy on Summit Avenue. When she was sixteen, she began appearing in amateur plays, which invariably attracted crowds of fawning swains whose interest in the dramatic arts was not otherwise evident.

But her good looks came with an even better mind, and her suitors discovered that she possessed an intellect easily powerful enough to discern what a feckless lot they were. Even worse from their perspective was her cutting wit, which she readily directed at the manifest shortcomings of her pursuers. "Men," she liked to tell her girlfriends, "are much like dogs but generally not as interesting." So it was that despite her appeal she was by age twenty-seven still unmarried and therefore regarded as the city's most gorgeous old maid.

Then, while strolling down Summit Avenue one evening, she saw Hopewell outside his mansion, smoking a cigar. Bold by nature, she walked up to him and said, "You must be the mysterious Mr. Hopewell. I have heard much about you, and I must say you do not seem to be very popular with your neighbors."

"Yes, they find me deficient in one key respect," Hopewell replied, looking into her lively blue eyes. "Do you feel the same?"

"I am inclined to like anything or anyone the neighbors do not, so I think it quite likely we shall be friends."

The next day, she confided to one of her sisters, "I realized after only a few moments that he was the man of my dreams."

Her dreams, naturally, failed to accord with those of her widowed father. Although Lloyd had once cautioned his neighbors about overreacting to Hopewell's presence, his liberal sentiments extended only so far, and he could not believe his daughter intended to marry a man who was quite possibly tainted by African blood. He pleaded with her not to stain the family name by such an indecent act and said if she went forward, he would cut her out of his estate, said to be worth ten million dollars. She re-

plied, politely but firmly, that as she was of age, she would do as
she pleased. Lloyd, as all rich men do in times of trouble, fled to
the arms of his attorneys in hopes of stopping the marriage. It required copious hours of billing to determine that because Minnesota inconveniently lacked an anti-miscegenation statute, nothing
could be done.

The marriage was accomplished in a brief civil ceremony at city
hall, presided over by a judge whose reluctance to perform the nup-
tials was greatly assuaged by the placing of one hundred dollars in
his pocket. The newspapers quickly learned of the marriage and
reported on it at great length beneath headlines such as "Hopewell
Weds Blonde Plumbing Heiress," "A Shocking Marriage," and "Mulatto Millionaire Takes White Bride." Other stories followed, built
on one pretense or another, and many of them went out of their
way to intimate, through every conceivable form of circumlocu-
tion, the shameful likelihood that the marriage had been consum-
mated.

The uproar died down as new outrages demanded attention, and
Meredith and her husband fell for a while from the public eye. Even
so, anger lingered in the wake of their union, which was thought to
be unholy before the eyes of God, who was believed to watch such
proceedings closely. As the newlyweds settled into their home,
rumors of the vilest sort began to sprout up around them like nox-
ious weeds. When several young women known to be prostitutes
were seen entering the mansion, wagging tongues concluded that
the Hopewells must be engaged in some awful form of debauchery. All manner of lurid speculation soon followed, some of it duly
reported in the newspapers, which saw no need to temper a good
story with the facts.

A few months after the wedding, Benjamin Lloyd died—of a
broken heart, some claimed—although his doctors pointed to an
infected, suppurating hemorrhoid as the real culprit. Meredith
and Arthur attended the funeral, where they were greeted with
icy stares from other family members. "We all know what killed our
beloved Papa," one of Meredith's sisters told the mourners, somehow forgetting that her father, a man of adamantine rectitude, had
never been very kind to his daughters.

Meredith, however, would have none of it. "Father died because he was an old, sick man," she told her sister. "I feel no guilt, but you should be ashamed that you have turned against me just because of the man I married."

* * *

Hopewell's marriage only served to further enrage his two immediate Summit Avenue neighbors—Harley Calhoun and Frank Shay. Calhoun in particular loathed Hopewell, often referring to him as "the monkey next door" and threatening to give him "a good horsewhipping if he ever ventures onto my property." Known for his violent temper, Calhoun was a distant relative of John C. Calhoun, the great defender of slavery, and like him believed that servitude was the natural lot of Black people.

Calhoun's personal qualities were as harsh and unyielding as his prejudices. It was said of him that looking into his black eyes was like staring into a seething caldron of tar. It was said, too, that his heart was an iron tomb sealed shut to the light of affection, and in every word and deed Calhoun lived up to his fierce reputation. Never married, he satisfied his lust with prostitutes whom he treated with uncommon cruelty. Four years earlier, he'd narrowly escaped public exposure in the scandal surrounding the notorious Anything Goes Club, but even that brush with ruination hadn't caused him to change his behavior.

Born in Georgia to a wealthy family of slave owners, Calhoun had fought with Nathan Bedford Forrest in the Civil War, raiding and pillaging and killing with gleeful abandon. But Forrest, as cruel a man as ever went to war, could not stop Sherman's army on its march through Georgia. The Calhoun family plantation house lay directly in Sherman's path, and his men burned it to the ground before freeing all the slaves.

Calhoun found himself impoverished and adrift after the war until he was invited north by a cousin who owned a small wholesale hardware business in St. Paul. The cousin was in need of a partner and thought Calhoun could help him out. Calhoun discovered that the hardware business suited him far better than running a plantation, although he did miss the distinct pleasure of lording over slaves. He eventually bought out his cousin and by dint of much hard dealing turned the business into one of the largest wholesale houses in the Northwest.

Calhoun occasionally vented his racist beliefs in letters to the newspapers, suggesting in one missive that freeing the slaves had been "a grave mistake." The letter prompted Rafferty, who had fought bravely for the Union cause, to pen one of his own in which he condemned Calhoun and invited him to the saloon for "a nice little talk and a good thrashing if need be," an offer Calhoun wisely ignored. But since most of St. Paul was too busy with the making and spending of money to care much about slavery or the small community of Blacks who called the city their home, Calhoun's hateful views failed to produce any great public outrage.

Like his hot-tempered neighbor, Frank Shay viewed Blacks as inferior beings but largely kept his views to himself, for he was by nature a sly and secretive man. Born to a wealthy St. Paul family, he'd gone off to Yale before beginning work in his father's wholesale grocery firm. But that stolid enterprise bored him, and by the time he was twenty-five he'd entered the treacherous business of commodities trading, at which he quickly excelled. Chilly, inward, and suspicious of all men, Shay lived alone in a towering stone castle complete with embrasures, battlements, and stout oaken doors, past which few visitors were ever admitted.

Gold was Shay's great obsession. He thought of it all day and dreamed of it all night, and a massive vault in his basement was reputed to contain a vast fortune in bullion. His skill as a trader was such that *McClure's Magazine,* in a long article, dubbed him the "Northwest's king of gold, a monarch of the commodities market whose love of the precious metal knows no bounds."

One of Shay's pleasures was flaunting his wealth by riding about the city in his "golden carriage," as it came to be called. Drawn by four white geldings, the carriage was a Chariot d'Orsay said to have been custom built in France and once owned by a Vanderbilt. The carriage's doors were paneled in sheets of gold, while its tall wooden wheels sported gilded rims that flashed and glittered in the sun. Such ostentation did not always sit well with the masses, and mischievous boys had more than once splattered the carriage with tomatoes as it passed by.

Shay was insulted by Hopewell's presence next door and grew even more so when he watched the ragged men and women arriving at his neighbor's doorstep for parties. "Hopewell is a trash collector," he told a friend at the Minnesota Club, "and I am the one who must smell it." But Hopewell's aggressive agitation of the laboring classes disturbed Shay even more. The man was a cancer that had to be excised from the body politic, Shay believed, and with that in mind he secured a meeting with Mayor Thomas Reagan, whose office at city hall, by a nice coincidence, looked directly out on the Hopewell Block across the street.

* * *

The mayor was a florid, outgoing man with a stomach as large as his ego and a gift for delivering lengthy speeches marked by much poetry and little content. He excelled at the chief function of any mayor, which is to circulate like a steady wind among his constituency. No banquet, public meeting, groundbreaking ceremony, or funeral of any consequence lacked his august presence, and he was a master at summoning up whatever false bonhomie the moment demanded. His fondness for pressing the flesh extended to the bedroom, and even though he had sired five children by his wife, he enjoyed occasional romps at the Ryan Hotel in the same luxurious suite where Chief Gallagher regularly entertained prostitutes.

When Shay arrived for his appointment, Reagan greeted him warmly. "Why, Frank, how nice to see you," he said, standing up from his desk. "Have a chair and take a load off your feet. I trust all is well with you."

"You know it is not," said Shay, who had no interest in pointless pleasantries.

Although he presented himself as a friend to the lower classes, the mayor's most prized acquaintances resided on Summit Avenue. The nabobs there expected of him only that he put the full powers of city government behind whatever they wanted, and in exchange for his progressive policies certain favors came his way. Since politicians in those days were assumed to either practice dishonesty or suffer no pangs in its presence, Reagan's underhanded dealings met with little opprobrium.

Shay had moistened the mayor with many small showers of money over the years and therefore expected quick action from him. Yet despite Shay's largesse, Reagan disliked him. Shay, he thought, was a fish so cold not even the balmy waters of the Caribbean could warm him.

"So it is about this Hopewell fellow, I assume," Reagan said. "He seems to have stuck in your craw."

"Damn right he has," Shay said. "Have you seen the people he and that wife of his invite to their home? It disgusts me. Even worse, he is stirring up trouble everywhere, and if he has his way this city will be in open rebellion before long. The laboring classes are already restless, and it will not take much to send them out into the streets. Unless you wish to see a mob ruling this city, you must do something about Hopewell."

"And what would that be? I cannot see that he is breaking any laws."

"I care nothing for the law! What good is it if it cannot protect us from the likes of a liar and fomenter like Hopewell. He is a Black devil, I tell you. You must act."

"What do you recommend I do?"

"Whatever it takes. You have the police at your disposal. Use them! I am sure Chief Gallagher would delight in making an object lesson of Hopewell. But if you do not deal with him, I have no doubt others will."

"Are you plotting something, Frank? I'm not sure that would be wise."

Shay gave the mayor a withering look and said, "Unlike you, there are men in this city who are not afraid to act."

The mayor found himself in a quandary, for Hopewell had of late become a far more generous contributor to his pocketbook than Shay. As a result, Reagan had begun to mute his criticisms of Hopewell. "I will see what I can do, Frank. That's all I can promise."

"And I have a promise for you," Shay said. "If you fail to act against Hopewell, you will not be mayor much longer."

After Shay left, Reagan pondered his options. Hopewell was indeed a troublemaker, but he also seemed to have an unlimited supply of money, and that meant it would be very difficult to silence him. Reagan finally decided that his wisest course would be to string Shay along and do nothing. Besides, the mayor did not wish to create any kind of a fuss. He planned to run for governor the following year, confident that all of Minnesota could benefit from his sagacious leadership.

"Our cowardly mayor will do nothing about Hopewell," Shay said that evening when the Committee of Seven met.

"Then, by God, I will," said Harley Calhoun, rising to his feet and producing a small revolver from his jacket pocket. "I will deal with him myself if need be."

"Come now, Harley, put that gun down," Shay said. "We must not act precipitously. Instead, let us see if we can convince him by other means to leave St. Paul."

5
THE HOPEWELLS AT HOME

SHADWELL RAFFERTY TOOK A DIM VIEW of revolutionaries in general but had to admit Arthur Hopewell was the most unusual man of that ilk he'd ever run across. Still, he wondered whether Hopewell's avowed commitment to social justice was as nobly altruistic as it appeared to be. "I am wary of rich men who propose to rescue the poor," he told Thomas as they relaxed over coffee on a November morning in 1893, "for if they were generous men at heart, they would not be rich in the first place."

"I think you are wrong," Thomas said. "If Hopewell were a poor man, there is little he could do to help the needy."

"True, but how can we divine his real intentions? Besides, you've heard the rumors about him, and for all I know—"

"Oh, come now," Thomas said impatiently. "I've heard all the ridiculous stories, too. Hopewell and his wife stage orgies with girls kept naked and chained in his basement. He has an opium den where he spends long nights of debauchery. And don't forget those satanic rituals at which he summons up spirits from the farthest reaches of hell by sacrificing babies snatched from orphanages. Please don't tell me you believe any of that nonsense."

"Of course not. I am merely saying that we don't know the man. 'Tis possible he is indeed a noble fellow, but as I have never met him, I can make no judgment in that regard. Until I've had a chance to size him up, I must take his pronouncements with a grain of salt."

Thomas smiled in a way that suggested he knew something Rafferty didn't. He said, "Well, you'll be able to take Mr. Hopewell's measure soon enough. You see, I have some interesting news. I met him last evening. He was speaking to some folks up on Selby Avenue and I decided to have a listen. Afterward, I introduced myself. Turns out he knows about me and you, and he invited us over to his mansion for dinner tonight."

Rafferty could only shake his head in amazement. "Wash, you are the real thing. Dinner it shall be."

* * *

After lazing away the rest of what was a raw November day, Rafferty and Thomas took a cab to the Hopewells' mansion for their dinner date. The home was not one of the city's great ornaments. It had been built of the local gray limestone in the 1860s by a dour banker named Jedediah Hobson, who saw his fortune dissolve into dust in the panic of 1873 and escaped ruin by hanging himself from a rafter in the attic. Like most big houses of its rough-hewn era, the mansion was tall and ungainly, offering rockbound solidity but little in the way of decorative solace.

As Rafferty and Thomas approached, they passed Frank Shay's enormous castle, which rose behind a spiked iron fence bristling with "Keep Out" signs. Harley Calhoun's home was also visible in the distance, its grounds surrounded by an imposing brick wall. By comparison, the Hopewells' mansion was small but welcoming, its window and door trim newly painted in a warm red hue. A tall butler with blond hair, blue eyes, and a Swedish accent greeted them at the front door.

"*Ja,* right this way," he said, leading them past a grand staircase and down a dark hallway toward the rear of the house, which opened up into a solarium that served as an oasis from the November chill. A garden of red, white, and black roses bloomed by the windows next to a gurgling fountain, while small trees of many varieties reached toward the ceiling. Rafferty and Thomas barely had time to look around before Hopewell and his wife came through a side door to greet them.

Both were stunning human specimens. Hopewell was tall and muscular, perhaps thirty-five years of age, with strong facial features of the type usually described as "chiseled." A tightly curled mass of hair formed a dark halo around his head, and his very light brown skin seemed to possess no visible flaw. His eyes were a curious bluish brown and commanding. One newspaper had called him "a dusky Apollo," not meaning it as compliment, but Rafferty begged to differ. Hopewell was just about the handsomest man he'd ever seen.

Meredith Hopewell was equally beautiful in a long gown of pink silk. She was tall and slender, with delicate features and china-doll skin as white as skin could be. But it was her eyes, large and round and a remarkable Delft blue in color, that riveted Rafferty. It was no wonder she'd inspired so much male desire, all of it apparently unrequited, before marrying Hopewell.

"Gentlemen, welcome," Hopewell said, then turned to his wife and took her hand. "I think you know Meredith."

"We do," Rafferty said with a slight bow. "A pleasure to see you, Mrs. Hopewell."

"And you," she said. "Isn't this a lovely room? Most of this house is as dark and gloomy as an old man's dreams, so Arthur and I spend as much time here as we can."

"Indeed we do," Hopewell said as he gave his wife an adoring glance. "Well, gentlemen, dinner awaits. Come along and we'll talk more."

The dining room, thick with mahogany and the scent of old money, would have succumbed to gloom were it not for a pair of French doors that offered a view of the rear garden, its flowers dor-

mant beneath the weak sun. Two large portraits—one depicting
Hopewell in a gold velvet suit and the other showing Meredith in
a beautiful dress of gold lamé—hung on the walls. The dinner itself was a gourmand's feast organized around a perfectly prepared
beef tenderloin. A uniformed cadre of young Swedes and Germans
served the food, course after course of it, along with the best wine
Rafferty had ever tasted.

Like almost everyone else in St. Paul, Rafferty and Thomas were
eager to learn more about Hopewell. And so, midway between pear
compote and creamed asparagus, Rafferty said, "I am curious how
you came to settle in St. Paul, Mr. Hopewell. The newspapers have
offered all manner of theories but, as far as I can tell, little in the
way of bothersome fact."

"Very true. I will simply say that virtually everything you've read
about me is a lie."

"But you are from New Orleans, are you not?" Thomas asked.

"Yes, that is the one truth in all of the nonsense that's been written. As to the circumstances of my arrival in the world, that is a matter I prefer to keep private. But I will tell you that I found my way
to Philadelphia some years ago and went to work for Jay Cooke.
You've heard of him, I'm sure."

"Ah, who has not?" said Rafferty. "He makes and loses fortunes
at the drop of a hat. The Northern Pacific was his dream and then,
it seems, his undoing."

"I guarantee you he will not die a poor man," Hopewell said. "In
any case, it so happens I am very good with numbers, and a man
who can follow the numbers as they wend their way down Wall
Street is a man who can make a great deal of money. I did so in New
York after leaving Mr. Cooke's employ. But in time my presence
made the titans of Wall Street uncomfortable."

Rafferty did not have to ask why. "So you decided to relocate."

"Yes. I have no doubt you know Mr. Elijah Rose of this city."

"Of course. The banker."

"And also, as you know, an old-time abolitionist who will tell
you to this day that John Brown was the greatest of American he-
roes. I ran across Mr. Rose in New York, and he suggested I come
to St. Paul. He claimed I would be welcomed here by the business

class. I have learned he was mistaken. Be that as it may, I intend to stay in St. Paul for a while and do what good I can. You see, my most fervent desire is to change the world."

"A hard job, that," Rafferty said, "unless you can figure out a way to change people."

"Agreed, but I have found that if there is one thing that can change people and soften even the hardest hearts, it is money. I suppose you could even say money is magic," Hopewell said with a smile as a gold coin suddenly materialized in his right hand and spun between his fingers as if propelled by some unseen force. The coin vanished as quickly as it had appeared.

Rafferty grinned and said, "Nicely done, but you will need more than a sleight-of-hand trick to accomplish your goal."

"True, but gold possesses the power to do almost anything if you have enough of it," he added, looking past Rafferty's shoulder toward the far side of the dining room.

Rafferty and Thomas turned around to see two young women in white dresses who had apparently come in through a hidden door. Between them they held a small wooden chest. They walked up to the table and carefully set the chest atop it.

"These are Beth and Anna, our wards," Meredith said. "I'm sure you're aware of all the absurd rumors about our relationship with them. The truth is that they were abandoned by their families and were working on the streets when they came for one our parties. We were so touched by their terrible circumstances that we decided to take them in. Now, I suppose you could say they have become our apostles. We give them shelter and safety, and all we ask in return is that they spread Arthur's revolutionary gospel of change wherever they can."

"Pleased to meet you," Beth said to Rafferty and Thomas with a curtsy.

"Me, too," Anna said.

After the girls left, Hopewell said, "I imagine you're wondering what's in the chest. Let me show you."

He opened the lid to reveal a glittering pile of gold coins. "The stuff of men's dreams, is it not?" he said, digging his finger into the coins as though scooping out dirt from a garden, "and I will not deny that I desire it. But I also care for what wealth can create. If fortune favors me, the money I have been amassing since my arrival in St. Paul will effect magnificent transformations. It will flow like holy water into the hands of the poor and powerless, and it will stir a mighty uprising against all those who would lord over and beat down their fellow men."

Rafferty had to admit he was moved by Hopewell's words. The man sounded utterly sincere, even if his dream seemed as unreachable as the stars. But was he really a great reformer? Rafferty had known a few speculators in his day, and what they had in common was a voracious greed beyond all satisfying. A desire to help their fellow man, on the other hand, was rarely in evidence.

"Isn't Arthur amazing?" Meredith said.

"I believe that would be an understatement," Rafferty replied.

As the meal went on, Hopewell described how he and his wife had also rescued several other girls from the city's most horrid brothels. "Naturally, the newspapers, which exist only to serve their rich masters, have suggested I am keeping a harem here."

"Dear Arthur has taken much abuse on account of our girls," Meredith said, "and it is very unfair. The real abuse is the suffering these girls endured at the hands of so many men, including our beloved mayor, Mr. Reagan, who I am told is particularly fond of young girls like Beth and Anne. The man is an ogre, and I cannot even begin to describe the hideous things he has done to gratify his lust. But he will soon face a well-deserved reckoning. Arthur and I shall see to that."

Rafferty had heard rumors about Mayor Reagan's taste for pubescent flesh. "What is it you intend to do?" Rafferty asked.

"We intend to expose his vile behavior," Arthur said. "But he will not be the only one to feel the sting of justice. Our esteemed neighbors, Mr. Calhoun and Mr. Shay, are also long overdue for a fall. I have obtained a wealth of evidence that Mr. Calhoun's business is built on a foundation of lying, cheating, embezzling, and outright thievery. Mr. Shay, meanwhile, has gone deeply into debt and is one margin call away from disaster. I have arranged to be the one who makes that call. Ruin awaits them both."

"You are taking on very powerful men," Rafferty said, "and fighting them will not be easy. I trust you know that."

"I do, but I also believe that the truth must be served. I will go to the newspapers first, and if they refuse to print what I give them, I will do so myself in a thousand broadsides distributed to every corner of St. Paul. These men have hidden behind their money and power for too long, and they must be held accountable for their actions."

Rafferty was struck once again by Hopewell's fervor. Perhaps the man really did believe in his power to right wrongs and shine a light into every dark corner of the city. It was bracing to see such naked idealism in a world clothed with lies. Then again, Hopewell might be the one wrapped in a garment of falsehoods. Confidence men, after all, could be very convincing.

"Well, I wish you the best of luck, Mr. Hopewell, I truly do," Rafferty said. "But I would also advise you to be careful. You know what they say about poking at a nest of snakes."

"I know there is danger, but if I were a fearful man, I would not be where I am today. So I will take my chances, Mr. Rafferty. I believe with all of my heart and soul that a revolution is coming, here and all throughout the world. You shall see that I am right! You—"

Meredith interrupted. "Now, now Arthur, you are lecturing our poor guests. I think coffee and dessert are in order. Our chef makes a marvelous chocolate torte, and Mr. Rafferty and Mr. Thomas simply must have a taste of it."

The torte was indeed superb, and the dinner ended with pleasant small talk. By the time Rafferty and Thomas said their goodbyes, they were left with full stomachs and many questions.

"As good a meal as I ever ate," Rafferty said as they rode back downtown in a cab. "As for Mr. Hopewell and his wife, I am at a loss about what to think. They sound too good to be true. But if they are sincere, I do not like their chances. They are brewing up a big storm and I wonder what will happen to them once the wild winds start to blow."

6

AN UNEXPECTED GUEST

A FORTNIGHT AFTER the Gold King's arrival in St. Paul, a striking woman checked into the Ryan. The callow desk clerk, a relative newcomer to the city, took no special note when she signed in as "M. Lloyd, New York" and requested any available suite on the fourth floor, where the Gold King was staying.

Although the clerk didn't realize she was Arthur Hopewell's wife, the bellboy who took her up to the suite recognized her and spread word of her arrival with all due speed. What made her return so surprising was that she had left St. Paul in utter disgust following her husband's mysterious disappearance the previous year. Saying she believed her husband had met with foul play and that the police had conducted "no more than a sham investigation," she'd sold the Summit Avenue mansion and all of its furnishings, then boarded a train for the East Coast. Her final comments, as recorded by the press, were brief and enigmatic: "Arthur's story is not over. Lies are mere dirt covering the bedrock of truth, and the people of St. Paul would be wise to remember that."

Now she was suddenly back, a guest at the Ryan occupying rooms just a few doors down from those of the King. Within an hour of her arrival reporters from every newspaper in the city were camped outside her suite clamoring for interviews. She readily obliged, and when the news hounds were ushered inside, they found her seated on a dark red divan, looking serene and beautiful in a dark silk dress accented by a stunning gold necklace. What she had to say, however, defied all expectations.

"You are no doubt wondering why I have come back to St. Paul," she began. "The answer is simple. I wish to reclaim the fortune which my lying, thieving husband tried to hide from me. Like many others, I was fooled by Arthur Hopewell. I thought he was a man of dignity and honor. How wrong I was! Even his name was a lie, for it appears he used many different aliases as he went about his deceitful business. It was only after he disappeared, without so much as a parting word to me, that I discovered his true nature. I inspected his books, which in his rush to escape he'd left behind, and discovered that his liberal sentiments and occasional good works were all a false front, designed to disguise the greed that motivated his every action."

As the reporters scribbled away furiously, knowing they had hit upon a front-page story of the most delicious kind, she continued: "Gold was Arthur's grail, and his true genius was not as a financier but as a swindler who had mastered the art of deceiving gullible investors. His business was a game of shells, and his only intention was to amass enough gold that he might one day be the richest man on the continent. But his shady dealing finally caught up with him and that is why he fled St. Paul."

Another woman now spoke up. "I am confused," said Dolly Charbonneau of the *Pioneer Press.* The city's only female newspaper reporter, Charbonneau had written numerous stories about Arthur Hopewell's puzzling disappearance. "You said last year you thought your husband had been murdered. Now you are saying he fled the city on his own accord. What caused you to change your mind?"

"I came into possession of new information when I moved to New York City," Meredith said. "I learned there that private detectives hired by a very rich man Arthur had cheated were hot on his trail. They tracked him here and intended to take him back to New York, by force if necessary, to stand trial for his crimes. Arthur learned they were in St. Paul and about to lay hands on him, so he fled at once like the coward he is."

"Do you have any idea where he is now?"

"I suspect he is somewhere in South America, perhaps Bolivia, chasing after gold. I doubt any of us will ever see him again."

"What about the treasure it is now claimed he left behind?" Charbonneau asked.

"Ah yes, the treasure. It appears that in his haste to escape Arthur had no time to take his stash of gold with him. I knew nothing of the bullion supposedly stored somewhere in his building, for Arthur was very secretive about everything. Do you remember those young women he took in and claimed to be saving from a life degradation? Well, he was, in fact, taking his pleasure with them behind my very back. There was no end to his deceit, and that was especially true of the gold he hoarded."

Charbonneau said, "It sounds as though you believe the King really has found a store of gold bullion that was amassed by your husband."

"I do, and that is why I have returned to St. Paul. I am here to tell you that this man who calls himself the Gold King will not enrich himself at my expense. He will not have a single ounce of the gold unless he first settles with me, as I remain Arthur's only heir according to his last will and testament."

"And yet he bought your husband's building, did he not?" Charbonneau pointed out. "It must have been you who sold it to him."

"No, that is not true. I suspect he used some subterfuge to gain control of the property. My attorneys are looking into the matter."

"Have you been in contact with the King?" another reporter asked.

"I will be, and I am confident we can come to terms."

"What if you can't?"

"Then he will leave this city a very disappointed man. Now, that is all I have to say for the moment. I will let you know if I have any further comments to make."

Since the King's suite was close at hand, the reportorial scrum went at once to pound on his door. After a long wait, he cracked it open, peered out, and said, "You have talked with Mrs. Hopewell, I imagine. I learned only within the last hour of her arrival. I will—"

"She says she is entitled to the gold you're digging for," an impatient reporter cut in. "What do you say to that?"

"I say only that it is a matter to be resolved, in a court of law if necessary. But I am hopeful an accommodation can be reached without the bothersome expense of engaging lawyers. I will talk with Mrs. Hopewell at the first available opportunity. That is all I have to say."

When Shadwell Rafferty read the next day's newspapers, he was as surprised as everyone else by Meredith's comments. He wasn't sure what to believe and wanted to speak with her as soon as possible. But when he went up to her suite, the maid who answered the door said, "Miss Lloyd isn't talking to anybody right now" and politely asked Rafferty to leave.

* * *

Meredith Lloyd's stunning interview with the press greatly heightened interest in the Gold King's activities. She had lent credence to the King's treasure hunt, and the gold he sought began to gleam ever more brightly in the public's imagination. Meanwhile, digging beneath the Hopewell Block continued under the strictest secrecy, illuminated only by the flickering light of rumor.

By the third week in April, however, Dolly Charbonneau at the *Pioneer Press* managed to shine a far brighter light on the King's underground activities by means of a spectacular scoop. Her front-page story began with a simple declaration: "The Gold King is telling the truth. There is a treasure in gold beneath the Hopewell Block." The story went on to reveal that the King's miners had excavated a pit, about twenty feet deep, into the rock below the building. "A rickety wooden staircase leads down into this pit, which is illuminated by electric arc lamps powered by a generator in the basement," Charbonneau reported. "The miners first dug through a thin layer of limestone and then into the fine white sandstone below. There, they broke through the roof of an old tunnel that was apparently excavated years ago for some unknown purpose."

What Charbonneau wrote next left all of St. Paul in a state of wonder. "Along the walls of this tunnel, which is about five feet high and not much wider, are narrow shelves dug into the stone. It was on these shelves that Arthur Hopewell stored his treasure in the form of gold ingots and bags filled with twenty-dollar gold pieces. It is believed the miners have thus far found no less than a half-million dollars' worth of gold and that a like amount, or perhaps even more, remains to be discovered in another passageway only recently located."

The Gold King expressed displeasure at Charbonneau's revelations and told the *Globe* and *Dispatch* that she "should be held accountable for her criminal behavior, as I believe she must have broken into my building in the dead of night like a common burglar.

If the police do not detain her, then I shall look into the possibility of a lawsuit against the *Pioneer Press*." Yet despite being pressed, the King would neither confirm nor deny Charbonneau's account of what his miners had uncovered, and so it was widely assumed that the story must indeed be true.

At least one newspaper reader, however, found a curious feature in Charbonneau's story. "'Tis odd, don't you think, that the King's men would be digging a big hole to uncover this supposed secret tunnel," Rafferty told Thomas after they'd pored over her account. "How would Hopewell have gained access to the tunnel in the first place if it was hidden under twenty feet of rock?"

"There must have been an entrance someplace," Thomas said. "Maybe the King couldn't find it, so he decided to dig straight down until he hit the tunnel."

"Ah, I am not so sure about that. The King told us he learned of Hopewell's stash of gold from someone in New York. This same person must have known about the tunnel. So why didn't the King search long and hard for the entrance before going to all the trouble of digging a big pit? There must have been a shaft somewhere in the basement leading down to the tunnel, assuming this whole business isn't just a big cock-and-bull story."

"Well, we know that Hopewell was a very smart customer. Maybe he found a way to completely seal off the shaft before he left town so that he could later reclaim the gold."

"'Tis a possibility," Rafferty admitted, "but I remain on the side of the skeptics when it comes to everything about this business, and we certainly can't rely on the King to tell us the truth. If only Meredith would talk to us, we might finally get some answers."

But Meredith remained steadfastly inaccessible, taking no telephone calls and rebuffing anyone who came to her door, including Rafferty. Then, one evening her maid gave Rafferty cause for hope when she answered his knock. "Miss Lloyd says she will speak to you one day soon, but not now. She will be in touch when the time comes."

* * *

The day after Charbonneau's story appeared, the King invited Harley Calhoun, Frank Shay, and Chief Michael Gallagher to his suite. Calhoun and Shay were surprised by the invitation. They had been trying for weeks to secure a meeting with the King, only to be curtly rebuffed. Now, he'd suddenly changed his mind, or so it seemed.

"I will be blunt," the King said after passing around his Cuban cigars. "I have a problem and her name is Meredith Lloyd. She is after my gold, as you know, and it is possible she will get her greedy little hands on it if she goes to court. I am hoping you gentlemen can help me stop that from happening."

The King then outlined an audacious scheme to make the gold his own, without so much as an ounce going to Meredith. "However, it will take some time before I can effect my plan," he said. "I cannot act until all the gold has been discovered. Now, I know you gentlemen were bitter enemies of that scoundrel Hopewell and therefore can be relied upon. If you agree to help me, there will be ten thousand dollars in it for each of you. What do you say?"

"I am all for it," Gallagher said.

Calhoun and Shay, however, were skeptical. "I would have to see the gold first," said Calhoun.

"I thought you might say that," the King replied. "I will make arrangements for all of you to do so. I promise your eyes will open wide with wonder when you see what I found thus far."

The King was as good as his word, and the three men soon received a private tour of the mine, which was as described in Charbonneau's story. At the bottom of the newly excavated shaft there was indeed a tunnel where gold ingots and bags of coins lay ready for the taking. The three men were astounded by what they saw.

"Why, there is easily a million dollars or more worth of gold down there," Shay said afterward as he, Calhoun, and Gallagher shared drinks. "But why should we settle for a mere ten thousand dollars when all of it could be ours?"

"So you have a plan?" Gallagher asked.

"Let us just say I am beginning to form an idea, Chief, and if I'm right, we will share in the prize of a lifetime. As for the King, he might just end up buried in that mine of his."

* * *

With Meredith Lloyd still out of reach, Rafferty decided to speak
with another, equally interesting woman—Dolly Charbonneau.
Four years earlier she'd helped Rafferty and Thomas solve the so-
called newspaper murders. Since then, she'd been a reliable source
of information, while Rafferty in turn had tipped her off to a number of good stories.

"Ah, Dolly, 'twould seem you've once again seized the front
page of the *Pioneer Press* as your very own," Rafferty said when he
reached her by telephone. "I think a gift of gold from the King is
now out of the question for you."

"Well, I was not counting on it anyway," Charbonneau said. "But
it would be nice, wouldn't it, to see just how much gold he's found
down there."

"It would. Am I right in thinking, by the way, that you were
never in that tunnel you described? Or did you actually sneak inside somehow?"

Charbonneau burst out into a great snorting laugh and said, "No,
I didn't want to deal with the King's gunmen. They look like the
kind of men who would shoot first and probably second and third,
too. But I did try to make it sound like I was there in the building."

"You had a source, I take it. Someone who's been down in that
tunnel. One of the miners, perhaps?"

"If you want to know the truth, Shad, it was an anonymous
source, but the information was so precise and detailed that I had
no doubt as to its accuracy. "

"Ah, but do you really believe the King has found all that gold?
'Tis possible, is it not, that he is playing you just as he is playing
everyone else. Have you considered that he could be your secret
source?"

"The thought occurred to me, I'll admit, but I put it aside. The
public wants to believe there's a treasure and why not? It's a great
story, no matter where it came from. That's about all I can tell you."

Rafferty had hardly hung up the phone when a call came in from
his old friend, Detective Patrick Donlin, who'd also read Charbonneau's story with a critical eye.

"So, what do you think about her story?" he asked. "Do you believe a single goddamn word of it?"

"I am withholding judgment," Rafferty said. "But if you know something, Pat, I would be pleased to hear of it."

"Officially, I don't know nothing," Donlin said. "Merry Mike was all for investigating the King at first, only now he's not, and that means I ain't either. But it so happens a stagehand I know at the Metropolitan Opera House told me a little story yesterday that you might find interesting. There was a play there last night called *Innocent as a Lamb* starring an actor named Roland Reed. Ever hear of him?"

"No."

"Well, it seems he happened to see a sketch of the King in one of the newspapers, and guess what? He said he looked familiar."

"Is that so? And who did he look like, according to Mr. Reed?"

"That's the problem. I don't know. The stagehand only heard the story in passing from somebody who heard the story from somebody else. You know how that goes. As for this Reed fellow, he's touring with the play and he's already on his way to Chicago from what I've been told. Merry Mike would have my head if he found out I was investigating the King behind his back, so there's nothing I can do. You, on the other hand, might want to make some inquiries."

"I might indeed," Rafferty said. "I appreciate the tip."

"Just keep my name out of whatever you do," Donlin said.

"I will, and the next time you're at the saloon, Pat, a bottle of my best Tennessee whiskey will be waiting for you."

The Metropolitan Opera House on Sixth Street was but a few steps from the Ryan Hotel, and after his talk with Donlin, Rafferty walked over to the theater to see what he could find out. But no one there, including the stagehand Donlin had mentioned, could recall Roland Reed saying who he thought the King might actually be.

Knowing Reed was in Chicago, Rafferty tried to contact him there. He sent off one telegram and then another, but neither yielded a reply. "I am at sea, as usual, and there is no wind to drive me forward," Rafferty reported glumly to Thomas.

"Well, if this Reed fellow really did recognize the King, maybe he ran across him in a theater somewhere," Thomas said. "That could mean—"

"He's an actor. 'Tis what I am thinking, Wash. An actor hired to put on a spectacular performance. If that is true—and we have no proof of it—then who hired him and what is the final act to be?"

"Well, I guess we'll find out soon enough. The way I see it, this whole business can't go on much longer."

"I agree. And when the King finally leaves town, I have no doubt he'll have a pile of money to keep him company."

Thomas said, "I still don't see how that will happen. Where is all this money you say he intends to walk away with? Who will he steal it from, if that is his plan?"

"I don't know," Rafferty admitted, "but his story of hidden treasure must be a lie. I refuse to believe otherwise."

7

A MOB AND A SPY

THE GIRL'S NAME was Gwen Jacobs, she was seventeen years old, and she had quite a story to tell when she appeared one morning in October 1893 in the offices of the *Pioneer Press*. She claimed that Arthur Hopewell had assaulted her and other "virginal young white girls" in a most brutish fashion at his mansion. She went on to say that he had not only cruelly violated her but that he'd regularly taken his fiendish pleasure with even younger girls. "He is a monster," she stated, tears rolling down her dewy cheeks, "and I am sorry I ever went to his mansion." The next day, screaming headlines announced her accusations. Hopewell and his wife responded in an interview that the allegations were "ridiculous" and that Jacobs was "obviously a liar paid for by those who seek to stop the movement for economic justice we have started."

But their response was as a cup of water tossed at a house fire, and much outrage ensued. Harley Calhoun was particularly incensed, and in a letter to the editor he called on "all red-blooded men of this city to take action against the monster in our midst." Calhoun did not specify the sort of action he had in mind, but most readers knew what he meant. A decade earlier, a man had been lynched in Minneapolis after being accused of raping a four-year-old girl. Hopewell, it was assumed, deserved a similar fate.

As though on cue, a small mob formed a few nights later near the cable car stop at the top of the Selby Avenue hill, just a few blocks from the Hopewells' mansion. There was, however, nothing spontaneous about the gathering, and anyone familiar with St. Paul's criminal underworld would have recognized many of the faces in the crowd. They were the sort of rough, desperate men who for a few dollars and a barrel of cheap whiskey would happily storm the gates of hell. But hell was not their destination.

Curiously, not a single police officer could be found within a mile of the Hopewells' mansion that night, a circumstance Chief Gallagher later attributed to an "unusual number of calls for help elsewhere in the city." This was untrue. Careful arrangements had, in fact, been made to ensure no police would be in the vicinity of the mob, whose leader was a strong-arm robber named Shamus Doherty. Although Doherty rarely had occasion to puzzle out the mysteries of mathematics, he counted twenty ruffians in his ragtag brigade and told them, "We are going to have a mighty fine riot tonight, boys, and catch a darky at the end of it."

Armed with clubs and stones and whatever makeshift weapons could be found, the men made their way—"quietly now, quietly," Doherty instructed—along backstreets toward Hopewell's mansion. When the house loomed into view, its windows dark and its resident grandfather clock ready to chime the midnight hour, Doherty gave a loud whoop. His worthies surged forward at once, shouting vile racial epithets and brandishing their crude weapons. Their intention was to forcibly remove Hopewell from the mansion, threaten him with lynching, and demand that he leave St. Paul at once or face dire consequences.

Although no policemen were nearby, news reporters had been tipped off that something big was about to happen. So it was that four of the city's most distinguished scribblers, Dolly Charbonneau among them, were on hand to watch the unfolding mayhem. She'd tipped off Rafferty and Thomas at the last minute, and they were just coming up on the scene when events took a stunning turn.

Unbeknownst to the mob's instigators, word of their scheme had leaked out like a small but steady drip, and Hopewell spotted the puddle. His business was intelligence, finding minute bits of information that could lead to an advantage in the markets, and upon arriving in St. Paul he'd quickly established a network of well-paid informants in every corner of the city. One of his tipsters got wind that a mob would be formed, and when the hired army of thugs arrived on Hopewell's fine green lawn, he was ready for them.

In an instant, the hunters became the hunted. Huge electric arc lamps mounted on the mansion's parapets suddenly let loose powerful rays of light that swept menacingly across the mob. Then several of the mansion's windows were flung open to reveal black-clad sharpshooters, who immediately opened fire. The rioters, whose courage had been fortified by the usual combination of bad whiskey and even worse ideas, instantly lost their nerve as bullets slammed into the ground at their feet. Doherty tried to rally his charges but to no avail, and when a bullet knocked the shovel hat from his big bearded head, he saw much wisdom in running away. A general retreat ensued, and by the time the police finally arrived on the scene, the mob had vanished into the night.

"'Twas like watching Pickett's men on Cemetery Ridge," Rafferty later said. "The mob had no chance of breaching Mr. Hopewell's defenses."

Both Frank Shay and Harley Calhoun witnessed the assault and agreed it had been a debacle. Shay, as usual, made no public comment, but Calhoun told reporters that it was "a sorry business all around. I watched from my front door and never have I seen a more ridiculous group of fellows." When asked who might have instigated the attack, he said he doubted it was "an organized affair. I suspect some men got to drinking and one thing led to another."

Calhoun, however, knew otherwise and was stunned by how quickly Hopewell's hired guns had routed Doherty and his rag-tag mob. "That black devil knew they were coming," he told Shay. "How do you suppose he found out?"

"I wish I knew," Shay said. "Maybe he is smarter than we give him credit for."

* * *

The assault on Hopewell's mansion quickly became the talk of the city. The press, which depicted the mob as a scruffy group of thugs and drunkards, blamed the attack on Doherty, who was arrested the next morning on charges of public rioting. "Doherty is a well-known ruffian," the *Globe* reported, "and it must be assumed that some hatred toward the Hopewells motivated the attack. He will now have a stretch of time in the county jail to contemplate his folly."

Yet most of the press made no effort to dig more deeply into what lay behind the attack, satisfied that it was little more than an alcohol-fueled misadventure. Dolly Charbonneau, however, had her doubts. She quickly learned that Doherty, who rarely dipped a toe in the limpid waters of sobriety, was hardly capable of organizing a mob. "Most of the time Shamus has trouble finding his way out of the door," said a bartender at the dive on Washington Street Doherty frequented. "He couldn't plan nothin' if his life depended on it."

If Doherty was merely a hired hand, as Charbonneau suspected, then who was in fact behind the attack? Charbonneau's suspicions led to a breakthrough when she tracked down Gwen Jacobs. The girl's heart-wrenching account of being raped by Hopewell, told with a kind of mechanical precision, had never quite rung true to Charbonneau. After being pressed, Jacobs finally admitted that she'd fabricated the story. She said she'd been paid twenty dollars to lie by a man she could identify only as "Mr. Smith." Charbonneau believed the mysterious "Mr. Smith" was in all likelihood an agent in the employ of Hopewell's enemies, but she was never able to identify him.

Charbonneau also spoke with Doherty at the county jail. "I got nothing to say to you," he said before reversing himself and stating, in obscene terms, what she could do for him. After informing Doherty that he should do to himself what he had in mind, Charbonneau went looking for other members of the mob. The ne'er-do-wells she found readily acknowledged that they had been paid, albeit a pittance, to march on the mansion.

Hopewell himself was certain who set the mob in motion. "Some of my neighbors have formed a committee with the intent of forcing me from my property, and I do not doubt they paid the poor Jacobs girl to spread her scurrilous story," he told Charbonneau. "You may be sure as well that they are behind the mob that attacked my home. But it will take far more than a collection of drunkards culled from the gutters of this city to make me leave."

Charbonneau's revealing story appeared four days after the riot and created a new sensation. But she was never able to follow up on her scoop by showing who'd ordered the attack, and the story soon faded from view. Still, it was enough to convince Rafferty that more troubles were in the wind.

"Dark passions have been unleashed, and I cannot say where we are headed next," he told Thomas. "There is a wildness about the city now, the likes of which I have never seen before, and I have grave fears for Mr. Hopewell's well-being."

* * *

Two days after the unsuccessful storming of Hopewell's home, the *Dispatch* offered an intriguing portrait of the financier, claiming he had devised "a secret formula for making money day after day despite the downward trend of the markets." An unnamed source went on to state that Hopewell "is a genius when it comes to money. There is no other way to describe him."

Most of Hopewell's wealthy neighbors read the story with disbelief. "The man has Negro blood," Harley Calhoun said that evening at a meeting of what had become the Committee of Six after Benjamin Lloyd's death. "It is ridiculous to think he is some kind of genius. Perhaps he is simply lucky."

"Or just lying," said Morton Rogers, the real estate baron who'd seen his business ravaged by plummeting property values. "Then again, I have heard that a few very clever short sellers have managed to do reasonably well, at least up to now."

As usual, Frank Shay had little to say other than an occasional murmur of agreement with the prevailing viewpoint. Yet he wasn't as sure as the others that the *Dispatch*'s story must be wrong. Shay's own portfolio had become a disaster of plunging prices and urgent margin calls, and even his precious cache of gold was at risk. Was it possible Hopewell really had devised a brilliant means of making money while everyone else was struggling to stave off bankruptcy? If so, what was his secret?

In hopes of answering that question, Shay turned to one of his few trusted employees, an operative named Albert Johnson. The plainest of men—in name, appearance, manner, and speech—Johnson moved through the world as a ghost, unnoticed wherever he went. Small pieces of intelligence, sometimes no more than motes of dust in the wind, were of vital importance in commodities trading, and Shay periodically used Johnson to infiltrate the offices of other brokers to learn what he could. More than once Johnson's efforts had led to a windfall for Shay.

So it was that Shay assigned his operative the task of worming his way into Hopewell's employ. Johnson accomplished this with his customary skill and was soon at work in Hopewell's downtown office as a junior clerk. But Johnson, who was clever when it came to figures, found himself as baffled as everyone else by Hopewell's uncanny financial legerdemain. After a fortnight on the job, Johnson feared he would have little of consequence to report. That changed, however, when Hopewell's bookkeeper revealed a startling secret, which Johnson shared hours later with Shay.

"I was just sitting there in the office, trying to look busy, when the bookkeeper comes up to me, puts a hand on my shoulder, and says, 'Albert, do you ever wonder what Mr. Hopewell does with all his money? Well, I'll tell you.' "

Shay was dubious. "He really said that? Why would he reveal such a thing to a mere junior clerk?"

"I don't know, sir, but it is God's own truth. You know I would never lie to you," said Johnson, who had learned never to underestimate the value of obsequity.

"All right, go on."

"So I says to him, 'I suppose he reinvests his profits to make more money.' Well, the bookkeeper looks at me like I'm an idiot and says, 'Mr. Hopewell knows that only a fool tries to play the markets forever, and that's why most of what he makes is turned straight into gold. Why, not twenty feet below you in the basement of this very building there is enough bullion to satisfy a king.' "

Shay's hard gray eyes lit up, for gold tantalized him like nothing else. "Does he have a vault down there?"

"That I cannot say. I did my level best to sound out the book-keeper, but he would say nothing else about the gold. Of course, I will try to learn more in the days to come."

"You do that," Shay said and dismissed Johnson with a ten-dollar gold piece.

That night, alone in his castle, Shay could think of nothing save Hopewell's stash of gold and how he might make it his own.

* * *

By the bleak December of 1893 Arthur Hopewell's ideas were gaining traction as the depression sank to new depths, with no relief in sight. Destitute men thrown out of their jobs haunted the downtown streets and nightly filled the gospel missions that offered food in exchange for sermons extolling the distant glories of God. Other of the city's charitable enterprises were equally overwhelmed, and one newspaper reported that "so many laboring men of this city are without work that this winter is sure to be exceptionally bitter."

Hopewell's business, however, seemed miraculously unaffected by the financial collapse, and he soon took the unprecedented step of establishing what he called the "people's dining room" in a large downtown hall. There, he served free meals around the clock, gave away clothing, and passed out chits that allowed impoverished families to obtain desperately needed coal. In exchange, he did not issue promises of eternal salvation but instead offered the prospect of a new world in the here and now.

In nightly speeches to his diners, Hopewell spoke of equality and justice and the need for "a true and lasting revolution" to achieve these ends. In one especially rousing speech, he referred to city's business leaders, by name, as "leeches" who "suck the lifeblood" from their workers and then dispose of them "like trash" at the first sign of trouble. "Let all men profit fairly from their labor,"

Hopewell told the cheering crowd, "and let those who would oppose justice be ousted rudely from their undeserved thrones."

Inevitably, naysayers questioned Hopewell's sincerity, for it was noted that he himself was the very definition of a capitalist, a man who lived by manipulating money for personal enrichment. One prominent newspaper editorialist wrote that since Hopewell himself appeared to possess vast wealth, he should be "among the first to be dethroned." And when Hopewell began collecting donations at the dining hall, supposedly to help the downtrodden, suspicious minds began to wonder where the money actually went. Was it not possible he was simply running an elaborate confidence game, and that one day he would vanish with his ill-gotten gains?

Harley Calhoun and Frank Shay, as much as any men in the city, hated Hopewell for his supposedly radical ideas. Yet they also found themselves increasingly tantalized by his wealth. "I have become convinced that he is no more a revolutionary than I am," Calhoun said to Shay one afternoon at the Minnesota Club. "He is just out to make a fortune."

"True, but unlike you and me, he seems to be doing very well at it."

"What do you mean?"

"Come now, Harley, you know that both of us are in trouble."

This was true. Although Calhoun presented himself as a shrewd businessman, his hardware company had always been heavily leveraged, and Shay had heard it was teetering at the brink of insolvency. The situation was aggravated by Calhoun's long history of embezzlement for personal gain, of which Shay was also aware. Shay's financial affairs were in equal disarray. The commodities market had become a dicier game than ever, and of late Shay had made all the wrong bets, leaving him without nearly enough money to cover his losses.

"So what are you thinking?" Calhoun asked.

"I am thinking we could both use a large infusion of cash to keep the wolves at bay, and I have an idea how we might get it."

8

THE KING HAS A QUEEN

SHORTLY AFTER Meredith Lloyd's surprising return to St. Paul, another women who produced an even greater stir checked into the Ryan Hotel. She gave her name as Mirabella Luray, but told the desk clerk, "You may call me 'Queenie,' dear fellow. All my gentlemen friends do."

The clerk found himself momentarily at a loss for words, for everything about the woman was startling. She was of such statuesque beauty that the clerk, a reedy young man who had little experience with women, felt at once the fierce tug of lascivious thoughts. The clerk was further mesmerized when he looked into her azure eyes, which seemed to promise the wonders of paradise. Her apparel only served to intensify her ripe carnality. She wore a shockingly short red skirt, finely tooled boots, a low-cut black blouse, and a small black hat tilted at an enticing angle. But her most extraordinary feature was her red hair, which tumbled down past her shoulders like tongues of fire.

Lost in lustful fantasies, the clerk was snapped back into reality when Luray said, "I will require a large suite, as I intend to stay for several days. Number four fifteen is available and that will do nicely. Now, be a fine chap and have someone fetch my bags."

"Certainly, ma'am. Your desire is all that I wish," said the clerk, whose tongue had taken on a life of its own. "I mean, I desire you . . . ah, you know, to be well served here at the Ryan. If there is anything else I can do—"

"At the moment, no. But I am sure you will be ready and able to perform if I need you."

"Of course. And may I ask, ma'am, why you are called Queenie?"

"Because that is what I am. You might say I am the Queen of Men's Dreams, and that is the largest realm on earth, is it not?"

"Well, if you say so, ma'am."

"Aren't you the dearest young man!" she said and reached over the desk to squeeze the clerk's wrist. "I so look forward to seeing you again."

Her touch, the clerk would later say, felt as "soft as warm velvet." When she took her hand away, he felt a wave of disappointment. "Touch me again," he desperately wanted to say but didn't have the nerve to do it. Instead, he watched silently as she turned away and walked toward the elevators. As she did so, every eye in the hotel lobby followed her as though she were some magnificent being come down from the heavens.

Meanwhile, rational thought began reemerging out of the clerk's foggy brain and a question occurred to him. How had she known about suite 415, which was adjacent to that of the Gold King, and that it was available? It seemed very odd that she would have such intimate knowledge of the hotel and its occupancy. The clerk, however, had no time to ponder the matter, for once Luray had disappeared into an elevator, he was immediately besieged by lobby loungers, mostly old men who'd seen her arrive. Who is she, they demanded, and what can you tell us about her?

"Her name is Luray," said the clerk, "but she calls herself Queenie. As to where she is from and why she has come to St. Paul, I cannot say. She is a mystery woman, I guess."

* * *

The fact that Mirabella Luray had taken a suite next to that of the Gold King occasioned much speculation among the idlers who populated the Ryan's lobby. A consensus soon emerged that she and the King must be lovers, but the truth was that no one really knew why she had suddenly appeared in St. Paul. Did she have some business in the city or was she merely an adornment whose only purpose was to pleasure the King? Luray managed to avoid the press for several days, but finally agreed to speak to the city's most persistent reporter, Dolly Charbonneau.

When Charbonneau arrived at Luray's suite, a maid answered her knock and ushered her inside, where Charbonneau found Luray draped languorously across a daybed as though preparing to pose for a dirty-minded French painter. She wore red harem pants decorated with orange flames, a broad red sash, and a ruffled orange blouse, its upper buttons left open to reveal her striking cleavage. A gold chain around her neck held a diamond-studded pendant in the shape of a Latin cross, which rested incongruously, or so it seemed to Charbonneau, between her breasts, like a sacred relic enveloped in sin.

"Ah, Miss Charbonneau, do come in," she said in voice that rustled like silk and seemed to promise all the wonders of Eros. "Please have a seat and we'll talk. You wish to know, I'm sure, why I have come to your fair city."

"I do, as do many others. You have made quite an impression in your brief time here."

"Yes, it seems many men in particular have taken an interest in me. Indeed, more than a few have already invited me out to dinner, presumably to discuss the issues of the day." Luray offered a sly smile before adding, "Or perhaps their intentions are not entirely honorable."

"Oh, I doubt they are," Charbonneau said with a smile of her own. "But tell me, why are you here in St. Paul? Did the Gold King invite you?"

"No, but he and I are acquaintances, and I decided to come up for a visit. That's all there is to it."

"I don't believe you," Charbonneau said in her usual blunt way. "There must be more to the story. Why don't you start by telling where you're from and who you really are?"

"So you doubt my word, do you? Well, good for you. I like a woman with a skeptical mind who isn't afraid to think for herself. Yes, there is more to the story, much more. It will all play out soon enough, and when it does, you will be the first to know. Tell me, do you have tipsters here at the Ryan?"

"I may."

"Excellent. Keep in close touch with them and you will be rewarded."

"I would rather be rewarded now with the truth from you."

"Patience, Miss Charbonneau, patience. A day of reckoning is at hand, and it will make for a truly memorable story. That I can promise you. Now, my maid will show you out, since there is nothing more I can tell you at the moment."

9

A GLITTERING PROMISE

WITH CITY HALL and the police department snugly in his pocket, the King went about his mysterious business free from any official interference even as reporters continued to hound him for more information. He grew so tired of their constant inquiries that he stopped speaking to the press altogether and kept largely out of public view. His miners, however, became familiar figures in the city's saloons, taking refreshment nightly in one establishment or another. Most of the miners were burly laborers of the usual type, hard-drinking but taciturn men who had little to say to anyone.

One man who claimed to be employed in the mine was of a much different character. He was short and skinny, possessed a prodigious appetite for alcohol, and spoke with the glib fluency of a carnival barker. He appeared one evening at Rafferty's saloon, where he downed glass after glass of bourbon and proclaimed to anyone who cared to listen that he was about to become a very rich man.

"The King has promised all of us a share, and if you have seen what I have, then you would not doubt for one second that I will soon be a man of wealth," said the man.

"And what have you seen?" asked a drinker standing next to him at the bar as Rafferty listened in.

"Why, I have seen enough gold to gild the streets of this city. There are three hundred ingots or more down there and more coins than you could count. And we haven't even found it all yet. Not even the Spanish galleons of old held more treasure than we've discovered, and that is God's truth."

Rafferty had learned from his years tending bar that men who invoked God's truth were as often as not telling the devil's own lies. As a regular reader of the Sherlock Holmes mystery stories, Rafferty had also learned how to be a close observer. Fred, he noticed, had no calluses on his hands as would a man who wielded an axe or shovel all day long.

"I have been looking you over," he told the supposed miner, "and if you are indeed digging for gold, then you must be holding your pick axe with your toes, as your hands look as soft as a baby's. Now, why don't you tell me who you really are, although I can guess. You are booming for the King, I imagine, and trying to incite the public's lust for gold."

"The King needs no one to boom for him, as you will find out before long," the man replied evenly. "But you are free to doubt, if that suits you. You will change your mind when the King shows off his treasure." The man then finished off his bourbon, deposited a five-dollar gold piece on the bar, and departed without another word.

Thomas watched him leave, came over to Rafferty and said, "I overheard a little bit of that. You're right in thinking that fellow is no miner. More like a shill, I'd say."

Rafferty nodded and said, "I am of the same mind. Con men like the King tend to travel with a team whose job is to drum up excitement for the big swindle to come. But I am still at a loss to explain the King's game. How does it all end?"

"With the flock being sheared," Thomas said.

"'Tis a distinct possibility," Rafferty acknowledged, "and yet I wonder. What if this whole business is about something more than money? A confidence man, after all, is nothing if not a great deceiver, and I am thinking the King may have a few more tricks up his sleeve before he is done with us."

* * *

By the time May approached, the King had been digging for nearly a month without providing solid proof that a golden treasure lay beneath the Hopewell Block, and the press grew restless. The newspapers had become believers in the King after Meredith Hopewell's comments, but enthusiasm melted into doubt when no gold seemed to be forthcoming. FOOL'S GOLD? asked the *Dispatch* in an outsized headline, while the *Pioneer Press* editorialized that the King's "only claim to royalty may be that he is the Crown Prince of Deception. Haven't the good people of St. Paul served as his ignorant vassals long enough? Show us the gold, dear King, or find some new realm of fools to rule over."

The King at first made no reply to the newspapers, but a few days later his workers began erecting a small stage in front of the

Hopewell Block. Behind it two curtains were mounted to create a narrow space hidden from public view. Curiosity deepened when a late-night passerby spotted one of the King's armed guardians carrying a draped object up to the stage before disappearing behind the front curtain.

The next morning, the King appeared on a balcony that extended across the upper floor of the Hopewell Block. Two trumpeters in gaudy costumes accompanied him and immediately delivered a stirring fanfare. When the trumpets went silent, the King extended his arms in the manner of the pope welcoming the faithful and said, "Come, gather around, my people, and hear what I have to say. I am here to tell you that today is a most exciting one for me and for all of you. It is time for you to enjoy a taste of what my hunt for gold has yielded."

Whooping and hollering greeted the King's announcement, but when the noise died down a voice from somewhere in the crowd shouted, "Where's the proof? Show us the gold!" The crowd immediately took up this challenge and cries of "gold, gold, gold" filled the air.

An amused smile appeared on the King's face as the chant grew louder. He gestured for silence, then said, "If it is proof you want, I have it." He nodded down toward the stage, where his two armed guardians were stationed along with four muscular members of his mining crew. One of the men pulled on a rope to open the curtain behind them. Cries of astonishment erupted from the crowd as they saw a gleaming pyramid consisting of twenty-one gold ingots, stacked six layers high, resting on a heavy table. Next to the ingots was a treasure chest sufficient to hold a pirate's booty. A glass pane built into the front of the chest revealed that it was filled with gold coins.

"I promised you treasure and now you can see it for yourself," the King declared. "This is just what we discovered yesterday, in a hidden chamber along the tunnel we have been exploring. Even more, I am certain, remains to be found."

"It's a fake," shouted the same skeptical voice that had been heard earlier.

"O ye of little faith," said the King, who promptly invited the scoffer, a beefy teamster, to step up on stage and remove the top-most ingot from the pyramid. "Go ahead, put it in your hand and feel the weight of it," the King said. "You will have no doubt that it is real. But if you are still uncertain, you may take it to Mr. McGuf-fin, who runs a well-known gold and jewelry business on Prince Street. He will do a fire assay, at my expense, to prove to you that the ingot is indeed of the purest gold. Of course, one of my guard-ians will go along. I trust you, sir, but not entirely," the King added, drawing laughter from the crowd.

After the teamster left, with the guardian and several reporters in tow, the King once again addressed the crowd: "My men are on the verge of finding the last of the bullion, and I expect to make my final announcement regarding the treasure within a week. It will be a glorious day when I do so, for I now expect I will be able to donate over one-quarter of a million dollars in gold to you, the noble citizens of St. Paul. Think of all the good that treasure will do! Until we meet again, my friends, be assured that everything I have told you is true."

With a wave to the crowd, the King left the balcony to the sound of another trumpet fanfare as his miners picked up the treasure-laden table and carried it with some effort down from the stage, escorted by the remaining guardian. They hauled their heavy load into the Hopewell Block and closed its massive iron doors behind them with a convincing clang. The show was over.

The newspapers duly reported every word of the King's speech in a manner that suggested it might be foolish to put any faith in his promises. Disbelief turned to astonishment the next day when Mc-Guffin, the assayer, reported that the ingot brought to him by the teamster was "99.9 percent pure gold" and as fine as any he'd ever seen. "It is close to perfect," McGuffin stated. "It is truly a wonder."

* * *

As the King's great unveiling neared, he became as the sun, shin-ing brightly over St. Paul with the promise of vast treasure. All of the city's newspapers employed men around the clock to watch his every move, and one newsroom wag remarked that the King would "never pee alone again" so long as he remained in the city. So great was the public's interest in his enterprise that the King attracted a crowd every time he walked the short distance between his suite at the Ryan and the Hopewell Block. He was also frequently seen dining with Mirabella Luray at the hotel.

The King himself had no additional comments for the press, but Luray briefly made herself available again to Dolly Charbonneau one afternoon. "You must know that the King is a man of great principle," Luray stated. "Dare I even say his word is gold?"

"Perhaps now would be a good time to tell me more about him," Charbonneau said. "Where does he come from?"

"Oh, I will let the King do that, if he pleases. But there is really no mystery about him. He is simply a prospector looking for gold, and now he has found it. I am here to share in his moment of triumph."

"So you are lovers, I take it," Charbonneau said.

"We are friends, as I have said. I will let you decide how close our friendship may be. The truth is, I have many gentlemen friends, here and elsewhere. But I am not the story, and so what do my words matter? No, the King is the story, and when you see what he has discovered, you will be utterly amazed. It will be in every sense a revelation."

"And also a day of reckoning, as you told me earlier?"

"It will be that, but I can say no more."

Meanwhile, the woman the press really wanted to speak to had nothing to say at all. Meredith Lloyd remained stubbornly incommunicado, refusing all interviews. With nothing of real substance to offer, the newspapers were therefore forced to engage in their usual business of wild speculation.

Most of the theorizing centered on what sort of accommodation the King may have made with Meredith to divvy up the treasure. Based on a conversation supposedly overheard by an elevator operator at the Ryan, the *Pioneer Press* informed its readers that Meredith was to receive "one half of all the gold found by the King." The *Globe,* perhaps consulting a different elevator operator, reported that the two had, in fact, made no deal and that "lawsuits will decide the matter." Not to be outdone, the *Dispatch* made the wildest claim of all, stating that "the King and Mrs. Hopewell are said to have formed an instant attachment, and it is entirely possible they will soon be man and wife."

10
THE MAYOR HAS AN ADVENTURE

THE DEARTH OF REAL NEWS gave way a few days later to a story so delightfully titillating that it might have been the stuff of a ribald vaudeville skit. It happened on a Friday night after Mayor Thomas Reagan received a telephone call from Mirabella Luray saying she wished to speak with him in her suite at the Ryan. "There is something about the King you need to know," she teased. "Why don't you come up around ten tonight? Perhaps we can become a little better acquainted when you do."

As she occupied the very rooms where the mayor liked to frolic with girlish prostitutes, he wondered what she might have in mind. Telling his disbelieving wife that he had a late dinner to attend, he reached the hotel a few minutes before ten and went directly up to Luray's suite. He was pleased to see that the hall outside her suite was deserted, since witnesses might initiate unseemly gossip about the nature of his visit. He knocked lightly on the door and was surprised when Luray herself, and not her maid, answered.

"Why, Your Honor, please come in," she said. "I have so been wanting to meet you." She was dressed provocatively in a plunging black gown that fit her long, lithe body perfectly. "Let us have a drink—I am guessing you are a Scotch man—and then we can talk."

She led Reagan to a divan upholstered in red velvet and told him to get comfortable while she poured drinks. When she returned with two glasses, she handed one to Reagan and said, "Here is to a wonderful evening. Skoal!" Those were the last words Reagan remembered.

Just before eleven, as the hotel's house detective made his rounds, he came upon a naked man in the hallway outside Luray's suite. He was pounding on her door, creating a ruckus that had aroused nearby guests, who looked out from their rooms with disbelief. As the detective drew nearer, he was shocked to see that the man at the door was the Honorable Thomas Reagan.

"What the hell are you looking at?" Reagan said, doing his best to shield his privates. His speech was slurred and he looked drunk. "The damn woman has locked me out without my clothes. Open the door and let me in."

The detective, who was too cowed to challenge the mayor, used his passkey to unlock the door. Reagan rushed into the suite and the detective followed. "Come out, you damned whore," Reagan shouted but received no answer. He found his pants, shirt, coat, and tie neatly draped over a chair, which also held his underwear along with his shoes and socks. After Reagan managed to dress himself, he stumbled into an adjoining bedroom in search of Luray. The detective trailed behind and saw that the room was empty and that the bed covers had not been turned down.

"Well, Christ," Reagan said. "She must be here." But she wasn't, and all the mayor could do was stagger back out into the hallway, where other guests were still peeking out their doors.

"Go to sleep!" Reagan shouted at the startled onlookers. "And mind your own goddamn business."

When they reached the elevators, Reagan told the detective, "Not a word of this to any anyone! Understand? They'll be something in it for you if you keep your mouth shut."

The detective nodded, eager for a little hush money to pad his meager salary. "I won't say nothing," he said, "but there's people out in the hallway who saw you."

"Bribe them for their silence," Reagan said. "I'll see to it that they get paid."

* * *

Although the house detective did his best to carry out Reagan's orders, the cover-up was doomed to fail because, unbeknownst to the mayor, someone had managed to take photographs of his naked escapade. These pictures were soon sent to every newspaper office in the city. Even before the unseemly photographs surfaced, rumors of the mayor's inebriated adventure had leaked out from the Ryan like a pungent aroma, wafted two blocks down Robert

Street to the *Pioneer Press* newsroom and into the receptive nostrils of Dolly Charbonneau. The photographs, delivered anonymously, reached her desk not long thereafter. Copies, it was later learned, had also gone to Reagan's wife.

"A public servant caught displaying his privates," Charbonneau said to her editor. "Could there be a better story?" There could not, and Charbonneau made sure to give the mayor all the publicity he so richly deserved. MAYOR REAGAN CAVORTS IN THE BUFF read the headline above her front-page story. "Found Naked at the Ryan Hotel," said the subhead. "Seen Outside Miss Mirabella Luray's Suite," added another.

The newspaper wasn't able to print photographs in those days, but Charbonneau gleefully made note of their existence, adding that the mayor had "no possible hope of denying last night's shocking occurrence." Charbonneau couldn't get any immediate comment from Reagan, who reportedly was hiding out at a friend's house. Luray, however, was happy to talk.

"I did not invite the mayor to my suite," she said, "and in any event I prefer that my callers wear clothes. It is very strange that the mayor, whom I do not know, was found frolicking outside my door in such a condition. Whatever do you suppose possessed him? Still, it must have been quite a spectacle. I only regret that I was out for a night on the town and so missed his most unexpected appearance."

The good citizens of St. Paul had no trouble tolerating a reasonably dishonest mayor, but public nakedness was beyond the pale. There were immediate calls for Reagan's resignation along with much derisive laughter at his expense. When Reagan finally spoke to reporters, he apologized profusely for his behavior. "I was intoxicated," he stated, "and I have no memory of how I ended up at Miss Luray's suite."

But the mayor could not as easily avoid the public eye or the amused tittering that followed him everywhere he went. Two days after the episode at the Ryan, his reputation in shatters, he resigned, saying he did so for "the good of the city." His wife, meanwhile, demanded that he move out of their home, and he was forced to rent a small apartment. There, in the long hours of the night, alcohol became his only solace. Yet the real story of his encounter with Luray was far stranger than anyone realized, and as Reagan brooded over his fate, he felt a growing need to unburden himself, and so late one night he went to Rafferty's saloon to talk with the best listener he knew.

* * *

Rafferty had known Reagan for years. At first glance he appeared to be just another well-spoken Irish pol who specialized in slapping backs, kissing babies, evading trouble, and managing whatever graft he could. But Rafferty had heard that Reagan, when pushed, could erupt into volcanic outbursts of anger. There were also unpleasant rumors that he had a fondness for rough sex with the young prostitutes who regularly served him at the Ryan. In his role as mayor, he'd always been the halest of fellows well met, the kind of man who did not so much enter a room as overwhelm it. Now, he was a defeated man.

"Well, Thomas, you have had a bad week, haven't you?" Rafferty said. "I am sorry to hear of your troubles." It was two o'clock in the morning, well after closing time, and they had the saloon to themselves. The mayor, looking glum and ashen, was working on a bottle of Old Overholt, but there was no dulling his pain.

"You don't know the half of it," Reagan said, gulping down a slug of rye. "Someone must learn the truth, and it might as well be you. There is not much to be done now, but perhaps one day you can expose that Luray woman for what she is—a seductress who set out to destroy me."

Whiskey in Rafferty's experience had an exaggerated voice all its own and he thought he was hearing it. "Come now, why would she do that?"

"That is for you to discover if you can. All I know is that she lied to that damned Charbonneau woman. The truth is, she asked me to come up to her suite, no matter what she said to the newspapers."

Rafferty was intrigued. "I am listening, Thomas. Tell me what happened."

"I'll tell you, but you have to believe me. I will swear to you on my mother's grave that I speak the truth." He then recounted how

Luray had asked him to come to her suite so that she could share some information about the Gold King.

"Did she hint what this information might be?"

"No. But I was naturally curious and decided it might be worth talking with her."

Rafferty was instantly skeptical of the mayor's story. As a resident of the Ryan, Rafferty had heard rumors about numerous men being attracted to Luray's suite. "Was it really information about the King you were after?" he asked. "Or were you just hoping to have a good time with Miss Luray?"

"And what if I was? There's no crime in it, and as I said, she's the one who invited me. In any event, I went to see her, and when she opened the door she was wearing a tight black dress that didn't leave much to the imagination."

"Ah, so you thought you'd be in for a night of romance. Didn't that strike you as odd?"

"Why should it?" Reagan demanded, sounding aggrieved. "Many women seek my company."

"Of course," Rafferty said, even though Reagan—with his big ruddy face, crooked nose, and outsized ears—was no one's idea of a handsome lothario. "But you do have a wife and family."

"Yes, but I don't see why a man can't have a little fun now and then."

"Your wife, I have heard, disagrees, but that is not my business. What happened next with Miss Luray?"

"She offered me a drink and then, lo and behold, the next thing I know I'm standing naked in the hallway."

"So you are thinking, I take it, that Miss Luray slipped something into your drink."

"Had to be. Knockout drops of some kind, I figure. She also must have hired someone to take that photograph. Gallagher is trying to track the fellow down but hasn't had any luck so far."

"Ah, and what about Miss Luray herself? What does she have to say?"

"Wouldn't I like to know. I sent Gallagher up to get the truth out of her yesterday, only it turns out she's gone. She checked out of the Ryan at two in the morning and vanished just like that. Some-body apparently picked her up in a carriage but that's all we know."

"Well, that is a most peculiar tale, Thomas. Why do you think Miss Luray went to so much trouble to make a fool of you?"

"I wish I knew. I certainly did nothing to her. But that witch has fixed me good, hasn't she? I am staring into the void, Shad. Every-one is laughing at me, and my wife has left for good. I do not see that I have any future is this city."

"It will blow over if you give it time," Rafferty said.

"Will it?" Reagan said, standing up. "I'm not so sure. Once a man becomes an object of ridicule, how does he regain his place in the world? Pray for me, Shad, for that is my only hope now."

"I will do that," Rafferty promised, even though he was not a religious man.

"Well then, it is goodbye," Reagan said with note of finality and shook Rafferty's hand before he walked out into the night.

11
MISS LURAY SPEAKS

WOULD YOU LIKE TO LEARN MORE? 6 P.M. TOMORROW. GARDNER HOUSE, HASTINGS. ASK FOR MISS MOORE. COME ALONE. M. L. Rafferty studied the telegram, which had been delivered to his sa-loon on the afternoon following his late-night conversation with Reagan, and quickly concluded who "M. L." must be. "It seems Mirabella Luray has surfaced in Hastings," he told Wash Thomas, "and wishes to speak with me."

"You'd better be careful," Thomas said. "That woman is trouble, and you don't want to be the next scandal."

"Ah, do not worry, Wash. "I am too old and too fat to be turned into a naked spectacle. I intend to keep all my clothes on, no mat-ter what. But I will be interested to find out what she has to say."

Hastings was only twenty miles south of St. Paul and easily reached via the Chicago, Milwaukee, St. Paul and Pacific Railroad. It was quarter to six when Rafferty walked into the Gardner House

Hotel, which was said to be the finest establishment of its kind in Hastings. He lounged briefly in the lobby before telling the desk clerk he wished to see a guest named Miss Moore.

"Yes, she is expecting you," the clerk said. "She will meet you in the dining room."

Rafferty secured a table in the crowded dining room, keeping an eye out for Mirabella Luray. But he hardly recognized her when she arrived to join him, for the provocative attire she'd presented in St. Paul had given way to a simple, high-buttoned gray dress and a black felt hat with a veil. All traces of her sultriness had also vanished. Her breasts were strapped down under her dress, which was so long that not even her ankles were exposed. She looked, Rafferty thought, like the entirely proper wife of a small-town banker.

"Well, I must say you are not the same woman you were in St. Paul," Rafferty said as he rose to greet her. "It is quite a transformation."

"It is, but I have my reasons, as you can imagine. It seems the police there are looking for me, but I doubt their efforts will succeed. Now then, let us order a light dinner and I will tell you some things of interest, as I have been instructed to do."

"Instructed by whom?"

"That will become clear in due time. Now then, I imagine you are curious about what happened with the mayor—or I suppose, I should say—the former mayor."

"I am. He claims he was invited into your room, drugged, and stripped of his clothes solely in order to embarrass him. And he wonders why you would do such a thing."

Luray smiled, mysteriously, and said, "Perhaps it did happen that way. Or perhaps not. We'll never really know, will we?"

"We will if you tell the truth."

"The truth, Mr. Rafferty, is that the former mayor, despite what he says, came to my room because he was eager to share his seed with me, as were many other men in St. Paul. Indeed, you may be surprised to learn that during my brief stay in your fair city I had intimate relations with a number of men, all pillars of the community. You may also be surprised when I tell you that no money changed hands."

"So you simply seduced them for you own pleasure, is that it?"

"Hardly. Men of their kind know nothing of pleasuring a woman, for that does not interest them and never will. So you see, I was not after pleasure, Mr. Rafferty."

"Then what were you after?"

"Why, I was after those men, of course. They all have a price to pay, and it will be paid very shortly. I cannot tell you more at present."

"Well, you have left me thoroughly confused, Miss Luray. What is this price you speak of?"

"It is the price of injustice, for I believe, as does the King, that men who lie and cheat and steal must answer for their behavior, in this world and not in some other one that may or may not come. They must be ruined just as they ruined the lives of others."

"You are sounding like a vengeful goddess," Rafferty said, and the "goddess" part didn't seem a stretch. Luray was like no woman he'd ever met before.

"I am no goddess, Mr. Rafferty, but I am the woman every man wants and yet every man must fear. I am a weapon, and I am the terrible truth. Men, as you surely know, are used to having their way with women. It is, they believe, the natural order of things. You might think of me as the unnatural order of things, for I am a hunter in the night, and men of a certain kind are my prey."

Luray's remarkable eyes now began boring into Rafferty, and even in her modest clothing her sexual allure was so powerful that he felt like a man caught in a burning house. Still, there was more he wanted to know. "I am curious about your relationship with the Gold King," he said. "Did he invite you to St. Paul?"

"I was invited, but I cannot say by whom. The King and I are mere players in a drama, Mr. Rafferty, and our work in St. Paul is nearly done. In fact, I will be leaving tonight for Chicago and points East. The King will also be moving on shortly."

A waiter brought their food—Rafferty's idea of a light dinner was a slab of rare steak buttressed with a massive baked potato—while Luray dined on a green salad of the kind Rafferty had spent his entire life avoiding. After she'd taken a few bites, Luray said, "I imagine you are asking yourself why I invited you here. The reason is simple: you are to be our official witness, the one man in St. Paul who will be privy to the truth of all that is about to happen."

"Well, I am flattered. But why me?"

"You will find that out in due time. For the moment, however, there are two other things you need to know. The first is that the King has now set a date to reveal his treasure."

"Ah, and when will that be?"

"Saturday the nineteenth. The unveiling will be in every way an event to remember, and you must be on hand to observe."

"I would not miss it for anything," Rafferty said.

"Good. The second thing you must be aware of is that great danger lies ahead. Under no circumstances should you or any associate, such as Mr. Thomas, enter the Hopewell Block at any time before or during the unveiling. You must give me your word on this."

"Is that so? Is there something in the building you do not wish me to see?"

"Perhaps, but there are good reasons for what I ask of you. I know you have been investigating the King and are eager to discover the truth about him. But as I said, you cannot go into the Hopewell Block. Now, do I have your word you will not do so?"

Rafferty wasn't sure he wanted to make such a promise. Clearly, the Hopewell Block held a secret that might unlock the mystery of the Gold King. Why should he not try to go ahead and find it? Yet he sensed that Luray's warning was genuine and that, in her own way, she was looking out for him.

"Very well," he finally said. "You have my word."

"Excellent. Then let us be at ease and finish our dinner. I do so enjoy talking with a man as interesting as you are."

Over the next hour Rafferty did his best to learn more about Luray, but she skillfully deflected all of his questions. When she was ready to leave, she gave Rafferty a kiss on his bearded cheek that, he later told Thomas, "was like a touch of fire." Then she said, "You will never see me again, but I hope you will always remember me in your dreams."

"Oh, I will," Rafferty said. "Of that, you may be certain."

* * *

The "price of injustice" Luray had spoken of was soon exacted. The day after her dinner with Rafferty, letters she'd sent to the wives of four prominent men in St. Paul arrived in the mail. The letters described, in shockingly graphic language, her encounters with their husbands. "I greatly enjoyed my time with your husband, Morton," began a typical missive. "Let me tell you all about the many interesting things we did together."

The "Morton" in this case was Morton Rogers, the real estate broker who'd been a member of the committee formed by Arthur Hopewell's Summit Avenue neighbors with the aim of forcing him from St. Paul. The wives of his fellow committee members—except for Calhoun and Shay, who were bachelors—received the other letters. To make sure the public did not miss the riveting news of her secret sexual liaisons, Luray sent copies of her letters to Dolly Charbonneau, who could scarcely believe what she read. How could supposedly sober men of wealth act so foolishly? Or had Luray simply made up her lewd allegations in order to destroy the men's reputations. And if so, why?

The letters were so replete with pornographic detail that Charbonneau knew they could never be published in the *Pioneer Press*. Nonetheless, Charbonneau wanted to write a story about the letters in which she could cite Luray's allegations in circumspect language without necessarily naming the four men. But her managing editor nixed even that limited step. "The lawyers will be released from their kennels if we so much as hint at the existence of these naughty letters," he said, "and that could expose us to expensive libel suits. Some things are just too hot to handle. Burn the letters and move on."

Yet Charbonneau, who was inclined to believe Luray's claims, couldn't bring herself to destroy the letters. They were too juicy and too revelatory of hypocrisy in high places to meet such a fate, and so she decided to leak word of the letters to a number of notable gossips, and within a matter of days Luray's missives were the source of much talk, especially in the salons and ballrooms of Summit Avenue. The afternoon *Dispatch,* less fearful than its morning rival, soon picked up on the story, running a short piece under the headline "Rumors of Romance." The story didn't name names, but the public lapped it up anyway, for there was general delight in seeing high-hat men of wealth brought low by their own base desires.

Meanwhile, the wives felt profoundly embarrassed as word of their husband's uncouth rutting spread. They confronted their wayward husbands, whose uniform strategy of denial did not serve them well, and households that had once been peaceful and orderly descended into angry chaos. Within a week, the first divorce petition was filed, by Morton Rogers's wife, and others would follow as the identities of Luray's surreptitious lovers became widely known.

Rafferty managed to obtain steamy excerpts from one of Luray's letters, and even he was stunned by her uninhibited candor. Clearly, as poor Tom Reagan had told Rafferty, she was on a mission to destroy men's lives. But even after his talk with her, Rafferty still didn't know why she had embarked upon her campaign of seduction and ruin. And to what extent was the Gold King involved? Had he, in fact, directed her activities? Rafferty didn't know, but on the nineteenth, when the Gold King was supposed to unveil his treasure, Rafferty hoped he'd finally have some answers.

12
THE DISAPPEARANCE

CHRISTMAS EVE 1893 dawned with swirls of snow in the air and a mystery that would rivet all of St. Paul for days on end. Newspaper headlines told the story. HOPEWELL VANISHES, said the *Globe*, while the *Pioneer Press* led with a question: WHERE IS ARTHUR HOPEWELL? An answer would prove elusive.

The stories that unfolded beneath the headlines more or less agreed as to the facts of the case. Hopewell had gone to his offices, as he usually did, on Friday the twenty-second. At three o'clock he sent his small staff of assistants home to enjoy the long holiday weekend while he stayed behind to finish some work. "There did not seem to be anything wrong," one of the assistants later said. "He was in a good mood and gave us all a Christmas bonus, but he said he had to balance his year-end accounts and would be working very late."

Hopewell later called Meredith to say he might be working until midnight, and so she did not wait up for him. But when she awoke the next morning, he was not at their mansion and she became very concerned. She placed a call to his office but received no answer. A second and third call produced the same result. By nine o'clock she became so worried that she instructed her coachman to take her to the Hopewell Block.

The building's front door was locked, as Meredith expected it would be, and she used her key to enter with the coachman. They went straight up to Hopewell's office but found no sign of him there. "We must search the building from top to bottom," Meredith said. "I am beginning to fear something is terribly wrong."

Her premonition proved correct, for when she and the coachman descended into the basement—the last stop on their search—Meredith felt a sharp, cold dread piercing her heart. The basement consisted of several rooms, including a central chamber built around an abandoned well and an old cistern still partly filled with water. The coachman, who'd found a kerosene lamp by the basement stairs, swung it around to illuminate the far corners of the chamber. There was no sign of Arthur, but the lamplight did reveal a low doorway cut into a wall near the cistern. When Meredith went over for a look, the coachman right behind her, they discovered that the doorway opened into a vault-like room, no more than eight feet square. A heavy safe, its door ajar, stood in one corner. Meredith went over to inspect the safe and found that it was empty.

"Maybe some thieves got into it," the coachman said. "Did Mr. Hopewell keep a lot of valuables inside?"

"Not that I'm aware of," Meredith said, "but Arthur is my only concern now. Where could he be? We must contact the police at once."

* * *

Despite a thorough search in and around his building, Arthur Hopewell could not be found, and initially the police suspected foul play. Chief Gallagher took personal charge of the investigation, assigning Patrick Donlin to trace Hopewell's movements on the day he vanished. But as Donlin later told Rafferty, he wasn't able to generate any leads as to Hopewell's whereabouts.

"Once his assistants left for the day, not a soul saw him after that, as far as I can tell."

"What about the open safe? If burglars broke in, perhaps Hopewell confronted them and was murdered for his trouble."

"Well, we didn't find no evidence that yeggs got at the safe. The door was open, but it didn't look like it was forced. It's possible the safe wasn't even being used. Besides, there was another safe up in Hopewell's office that his wife opened for us. There were some legal documents in it but no valuables. Of course, we combed through every inch of the place looking for Hopewell. Didn't find a trace of him. Not so much as a drop of blood. So if Hopewell was murdered, the burglars must have hauled his body away along with the loot, and that don't make no sense."

"Do you know if anything at all was taken?"

"Not that we could find."

"So what's your theory, Pat?" Rafferty asked. "What do you think happened to Hopewell?"

"If you ask me, he just up and left for some reason. That's about all I can figure."

Donlin's boss, it was soon revealed, had come to the same conclusion. As the new year approached, Gallagher called in reporters to say that he believed Hopewell had staged his own disappearance for nefarious purposes. "It is clear Hopewell was simply a confidence man all along. We have talked to some prominent businessmen who say they gave Hopewell many thousands of dollars to invest and now it's gone. We started an investigation, so he knew we were on to him. I figure he cleaned out his safe and left town to find new pigeons somewhere else. I have received reliable reports that he passed through Chicago a few days ago, but I cannot say where he is now."

Most of the press happily swallowed the chief's claim, but Dolly Charbonneau demurred. To her, it didn't make sense. If Hopewell was merely a swindler, why had he spent so much time, energy, and money to establish himself in St. Paul? After all, he'd bought an office building and a mansion, among other things. He'd also spent many thousands of dollars to assist the city's neediest residents. And while he'd wed a woman who came from wealth, Meredith supposedly had been cut off from her inheritance and therefore brought little money to the marriage. As Charbonneau saw it, Hopewell would have needed to engineer a gigantic fraud to come out ahead of the game. But where was the proof of it?

When Charbonneau put her doubts to Gallagher, the chief asserted that the full extent of Hopewell's scheming might never be known because the businessmen who were taken in by his lies did not wish to be identified. "No one likes to be played for a fool," the chief added, "but Hopewell was a very clever fellow. I would not be surprised if he got away with half a million dollars or more."

Mayor Thomas Reagan joined the chorus of critics. "I suspected Hopewell all along of bad intentions." Harley Calhoun, in a venomous letter to the *Pioneer Press,* wrote that "everyone knows Negroes are not to be trusted" and suggested hanging Hopewell "from the nearest available tree" if he ever dared set foot in St. Paul again. The great unwashed public was also quick to condemn Hopewell for his unknown sins, and his charitable works were all but forgotten in the rush to paint him as a charlatan of the worst kind.

Meredith Hopewell responded to the outpouring of bile by labeling Gallagher a "liar and a fool," while dismissing Reagan and Calhoun as "men who hate my husband for no other reason than the color of his skin." She also insisted that Arthur had almost certainly met with foul play. "He was doing his best to help the poor people of St. Paul, but the rich men who run this city did not like how he challenged their greedy ways. Now I fear he has paid the ultimate price for his courage."

* * *

Rafferty called Meredith a few days after her husband's disappearance to offer his help. "If he has been the victim of foul play, I am ready to do what I can to find out what happened."

"That is kind of you," she said, "but I must do some things first. Arthur left behind many interesting documents that I am still going through. You might even say they are eye-opening, and I believe they may eventually point the way to some surprising truths."

"Truths about your husband?"

"Perhaps. I have found that the truth can be like a child in hiding, and sometimes you have to look in unexpected places. As for Arthur, I will only say that he was complicated and contradictory to some degree, and he may not have been all I thought he was. He loved gold, perhaps inordinately so, and yet he also believed wealth could never be its own end and that it was not fair for a few rich men to hoard so much of it. Do not get me wrong, however. Arthur was the only man I ever loved or ever will love. Now I do not even have his body to bury and mourn over."

"Ah, I know how terrible it is to lose those we love the most," Rafferty said, thinking of his wife and son lost years earlier in childbirth. "There is no medicine, I fear, for the heartache it brings. You have my deepest condolences, and as I said, if you find yourself in need of any help at all, please call on me."

"I may take you up on your offer at some point, Mr. Rafferty. For the time being, however, I prefer to be my own detective, as it were. Women, I have found, too easily rely on men to act on their behalf. I would rather act for myself."

"Well then, I wish you good luck. Am I safe in assuming that you intend to remain in St. Paul while you go about your work?"

"Yes, I will be here for a while, but then I will probably go to New York. I cannot stay indefinitely in this suffocating city, with its prim hypocrisy. Perhaps we will talk again soon. Goodbye, Mr. Rafferty, and keep me in your prayers, if you believe in such things."

Three weeks later, in the midst of a brutal January cold spell, Rafferty spotted a small item in the *Pioneer Press.* It stated that "Mrs. Arthur Hopewell has sold her mansion on Summit Avenue and will spend the remainder of the winter, and perhaps longer, in New York City. The wife of the missing financier did not say when, or if, she intends to return to St. Paul."

* * *

In March 1894, three months after Arthur Hopewell's disappearance, a man with a briefcase appeared one evening at the door of Albert Johnson's apartment in St. Paul. The man was tall and slender, with a fine head of black hair streaked with silver, and he possessed the dignified bearing of a gentleman well bred. A hint of New England lurked in his rich baritone, but what Johnson found most notable about the man were his violet eyes, which had an almost hypnotic effect.

"I take it you are Albert Johnson," the man said. "I have a lucrative proposition for you if you will give me give me a few minutes of your time. May I come in?"

"All right," Johnson said and directed the man to a ragged old couch. "Now, what's this all about?"

The man smiled, then opened his briefcase and removed a leather pouch, which he placed on a table in front of Johnson. "Go ahead, open it," he said. "Inside you will find fifty double eagles, worth one thousand dollars. If you tell me what I wish to know, this pouch will still be on the table when I leave. Shall I go on?"

It was a stunning offer. A thousand dollars was more than Johnson usually earned in a year. "Sure, tell me more," Johnson said, trying not to sound too eager. "What do you have in mind?"

"What I have in mind is the truth," the man said. "The question is whether you are willing to provide it."

When the man made known the "truth" he sought, Johnson felt a sharp spasm of anxiety. A thousand dollars would do him no good if he did not live long enough to spend it.

"Well, I don't know," Johnson said. "It might not be healthy for me to tell you such things."

"Then perhaps this will help persuade you," the man, taking a document from his briefcase and setting it next to the pouch. "I offer you, in addition to gold, an employment contract from Mr. Edgar Wallace with the Pinkerton Agency in St. Louis. I imagine you have heard of him, as his work has been much publicized. You are from St. Louis, as I understand it, and would no doubt enjoy moving back there. Mr. Wallace has been informed of your peculiar talents as a spy, and he would be pleased to take you on at twelve hundred dollars a year, per this contract."

Johnson could hardly believe what he was hearing. "Who are you?" he asked, "and why should I trust you?"

"My identity is of no consequence. As for trust, you may regard the gold as my word. Now, what will it be? Do you want to continue your precarious life here or would you prefer to go to St. Louis with a thousand dollars in your pocket and the prospect of steady, remunerative employment?"

Johnson made his choice. The money and job were too good to resist, even if he had no idea who might be behind his good fortune. He wrote out a statement detailing everything he knew, keeping a carbon copy. The visitor thanked him, shook his hand, and left. As promised, Johnson kept the gold coins and contract.

In early April, as Johnson enjoyed a day off from his Pinkerton duties in the big, sunny apartment he'd rented in St. Louis, he came across an intriguing article in the *Post-Dispatch*. It concerned the activities of a man in St. Paul who called himself the Gold King. The article included a woodcut illustration, and Johnson was shocked when he saw it, for he recognized the figure in the drawing as the same man who'd come knocking at his door a month earlier in St. Paul.

"Well, I'll be damned and double-damned," Johnson said to himself. "I wonder what this fellow is up to now."

13
DIVIDING THE SPOILS

ON MONDAY, the fourteenth of May, a full six weeks after the Gold King's arrival in St. Paul, a full-page announcement appeared in all of the city's newspapers. Beneath a headline stating TREASURE TO BE UNVEILED, the announcement said: "The Gold King requests your presence at a once-in-a-lifetime event, to begin at noon on Saturday, May 19, outside the Hopewell Block at 366 Cedar Street in St. Paul. One million dollars in gold bullion recovered from said building will be displayed for all to see. A lottery will be held as part of the festivities. Buy a numbered lottery ticket for $1 at the front door of the Hopewell block by 5 p.m. Friday and you will be eligible to win a prize of $10,000 in gold. Do not miss this opportunity! I look forward to seeing everyone on Saturday. Your friend, the Gold King."

"Ah, so now the truth is out," Rafferty said to Thomas after they'd read the announcement. "The lottery is how the King intends to fleece the public. You can bet that the 'lucky winner' will never see a cent."

"I guess you're right," Thomas said, "but it's still the craziest con game I've ever seen. It's taken him an awfully long time to pull it off, and he's spent a lot of money."

"Ah, didn't your mother tell you, Wash, that patience is a virtue? But you are right, it is a strange business. That Luray woman is the wild card. As far as I can tell, she was after revenge, not money, and we still don't know how closely she was working with the King."

Rafferty's expectation that the lottery would attract many eager ticket buyers was quickly borne out. Hardly had the King's announcement appeared in the newspapers before a line began forming outside the Hopewell Block. By that evening, more than a thousand hopefuls had already purchased tickets, sometimes buying ten or more each.

Not everyone saw the lottery in a positive light. "Gold, gold, and more gold is all men talk about," declared the Reverend Samuel Smith from his pulpit in the People's Church. "But it is a false idol, just as Baal was to the Canaanites. The one true treasure is the shining light of God, not the insidious glitter of gold. Securing a place in heaven is no lottery, and gold will be of no help to you on the Day of Judgment."

* * *

The day after the King announced his lottery, he invited Meredith Lloyd to a luncheon meeting at the Ryan Hotel's café. She reacted with surprise when she saw that Harley Calhoun and Frank Shay were also at the table.

"I had assumed it would just be the two of us," she said. "Why did you bring these two gentlemen with you?"

"They are sober businessmen whose judgment I have come to admire, and they are here to support me."

"Very well, I have no objections. As I do not suppose it is the pleasure of my company you seek, tell me why you asked me here."

"That is what I like about you, madam," the King said with a slight smile. "You get straight to the point. Very well, business it shall be. A great day is at hand, and I would hate to see it ruined by any unseemly disagreements. Therefore, let us see if the two of us come to a satisfactory final arrangement."

"I will need a ninety percent share," Meredith said without hesitation, looking directly at the King, "and not a penny less. I am entitled to all of it, of course, but in order to avoid protracted legal proceedings, I am willing to provide you a finder's fee, as it were, of ten percent. If you have found a million dollars' worth of my departed husband's bullion, as you claim, then you will leave St. Paul with one hundred thousand dollars, plus whatever you make from that silly lottery you're staging. I believe that is a fair settlement."

"I don't think it is fair at all," the King said with some heat. "Without me, Mrs. Hopewell, there would be no gold for you. A fifty-fifty split is what I have in mind."

"Then we shall end up in court after all," Meredith said, rising from her chair. "Good day, gentlemen."

"The lady drives a hard bargain," Calhoun said as he watched Meredith leave.

"Perhaps, but she may not be as clever as she thinks herself to be," said the King. "The time has arrived for me to take the gold, with, of course, your help, as we discussed earlier. Here is what I have in mind. Listen carefully, gentlemen, and do not reveal these plans to anyone, or it could go hard for all of us."

After the King outlined his plan, Calhoun and Shay signaled their enthusiastic support. But that evening, when they met with Gallagher at Calhoun's mansion, they finalized a scheme of their own. "We shall have every last piece of the gold," Shay said. "The King thinks he'll fool that damned Lloyd woman, but he's the one who will be in for a very unpleasant surprise."

* * *

The day before the King's great unveiling, Rafferty sent yet another message to Roland Reed, the actor he'd been trying to reach for nearly a fortnight. INVESTIGATING CRIMINAL CASE IN ST. PAUL RE "GOLD KING," the telegram said. DO YOU KNOW THE MAN? REPLY URGENTLY REQUESTED. He signed the message, SGT. S. RAFFERTY, ST. PAUL POLICE. Rafferty hadn't claimed to be the police in his earlier messages but now thought it was worth a try.

Rafferty held out only modest hope of a reply—Reed had already ignored messages sent to him in Chicago—but at six in the evening a response was delivered to Rafferty at the Ryan Hotel. POSSIBLY GORDON GREENE, ENGLISH ACTOR. ONLY MET HIM ONCE SO NOT SURE. WHAT IS HE ACCUSED OF?

"By God, I knew it," Rafferty crowed when he showed the telegram to Wash Thomas. "The King is an actor."

"Well, it doesn't sound like this Reed fellow is all that certain," Thomas said.

"'Tis a start nonetheless. If Greene is our man, we have a chance to unravel this business."

"Maybe, but if the King is an Englishman, how do we prove his identity? It could take weeks, and I don't think we have that much time. I doubt the King will stick around for long after he puts on his big show tomorrow."

"Then we must confront him at once and put his feet to the fire," Rafferty said. "Let's see if we can catch him in his suite upstairs."

A knock at the suite's door yielded no response, so Rafferty decided on a bold expedient.

"Go ahead and open it," he told Thomas, who was a skilled locksmith. "We must have a look inside."

But when they stepped inside, they found the suite empty, without so much as toothbrush left behind by its occupant. They went back downstairs to the front desk, where a clerk told them the King has checked out that morning.

"Now that is mighty strange," Rafferty said. "He is supposed to have his big reveal tomorrow. Did he say where he was going?"

"I wasn't on duty then," the clerk said, "so I don't know."

A bellboy proved more helpful. "The King checked out at eight," he reported. "Said he was going to stay at friend's place for the night. But he told me not to worry, that he'd be unveiling the treasure tomorrow just like he said. Gave me a ten-dollar gold piece. How about that?"

"Now what?" Thomas asked when they returned to their saloon, which was already filled with thirsty men.

Rafferty scratched at his beard and said, "I guess we'll just have to see what happens tomorrow like everybody else, assuming our friend the King hasn't made a getaway already."

14
THE REAL TREASURE

"THE DAY OF DAYS," as one newspaper described it, dawned as bright as a May morning could be, the sun climbing into a flawless blue sky. All of St. Paul, or so it seemed, arose in eager anticipation of the big event. By nine in the morning a crowd had already begun to gather around the Hopewell Block, even though what the King called "the great unveiling" would not take place until noon. The crowd rapidly grew, swelling into a restless mass of humanity that enveloped the Hopewell Block so tightly there was scarcely room to breathe. Rich and poor alike intermingled, forming a handsome source of revenue for the city's pickpockets, who busily plied their trade on the theory that a dollar in hand was worth more than dreams of gold.

Clocks and watches now seemed to lose their usual momentum, and the minutes ticked by with agonizing slowness while the crowd awaited the promised revelation. By quarter to twelve the crowd had become a bottle of champagne with its cork ready to pop. Ten to arrived, then five to. Unable to contain its intense expectations, the throng surged forward toward the line of police protecting the Hopewell Block. The line bowed backward against the force of the masses but held.

A chant now slowly began to make itself heard above the din. "Gold, gold, gold!" was the cry of the people, and it grew ever louder and more insistent. Fearing the crowd might storm the building, a line of police on big black horses did their best to maintain order, wielding their batons with crisp efficiency. Curiously,

Chief Gallagher was not present, a patrol captain assuming command in his place.

Rafferty and Thomas were among those taking in the spectacle. With the help of a well-placed bribe, they'd secured a prime viewing spot at a second-floor window in city hall. Like everyone else, they were eager to hear what the King would have to say, even though they remained deeply skeptical about the treasure he claimed to have discovered.

At precisely noon, the doors to the Hopewell Block's balcony flew open amid the beating of a powerful gong from somewhere inside the building. Twelve times it rang out, each stroke seemingly louder than the one before. The crowd became silent as the gong's last beat echoed like rolling thunder. Then the Gold King stepped out on the balcony to the sound of applause that quickly built into a mighty crescendo. The Stetson-hatted guardians, holding Winchester rifles, were at his side and gazed out over the crowd with "dark-lidded eyes almost reptilian in character," as one news reporter put it.

The King himself had never looked more resplendent. His entire outfit was of a deep golden hue, accented by gems of every kind. Even his shoes, which resembled a genie's slippers, were of the same color. "The King presented a celestial vision," wrote one reporter, "as though enveloped in the very radiance of the sun."

"My dear friends, we have at last reached the moment we have all been waiting for," the King began. "Below me, in the depths of the earth, I have found what was once lost. But it may not quite be the treasure you expect. For what is gold, after all, but a dead thing, and of what does it avail us in the end? No, my friends, there are only two real treasures in this world. The first is love, and if we find it, then what else really matters? The second is justice, for without it there can be no peace and happiness."

A low murmur rose from crowd. What was all this crazy talk of love and justice? Where was the gold that all had come to see? "Show us the treasure," a man shouted, "or there will be trouble."

"Yes, yes, the treasure," said the King. "You will see it momentarily. But first let me introduce someone you all know. Please welcome Mrs. Arthur Hopewell, who would like to say a few words."

The crowd buzzed with confusion. Why had the King called her Mrs. Hopewell? Hadn't she renounced her husband? Was she going to unveil the gold? The buzzing turned to stunned silence when Meredith stepped out onto the balcony, for her appearance was riveting. She wore a black mourning dress, a black hat, and a black veil, and when she spoke her voice was as clear and hard as ice.

"The truth is a sacred and mighty thing," she said, gazing down on the eager multitudes, "and when you see what the King has wrought you will scarcely believe your eyes. The moment of revelation is at hand!"

* * *

What happened next would be remembered for days and weeks and years to come. "You are wondering, I suppose, where the treasure is," Meredith said. "Well, let me show what has been unearthed beneath this building. I am sure you will be amazed." She clapped her hands and the two guardians went back inside the building. They reemerged moments later, wheeling a tall object covered by black drapery out onto the balcony. A collective gasp could be heard as Meredith removed the drapery to reveal an open coffin, mounted vertically like those used to display the bodies of dead gunslingers in the Wild West. The coffin held a papier-mâché skeleton painted bright gold.

"You have all been fools," she said as the crowd stared up in wonderment at the coffin, "and here is your false idol. Worship it, for there will be other gold. Now, hear my words. I returned to this city of liars and hypocrites not to seek a hidden fortune but to find my murdered husband and obtain justice, which is dearer to me than all the gold in the world. My men found Arthur, as I feared they would, buried under rock and debris at the bottom of an old well under this very building. His mortal remains are now resting in peace somewhere far away. But the three men who murdered him will soon be where they belong, with the damned in hell!"

The expectant crowd reacted to Meredith's word with a kind of stunned awe, unable to fully comprehend what had just occurred. Was she serious? Was there really to be no gold after all? And who were the murderers of whom she spoke? Then came another surprise. Thick smoke suddenly enveloped the balcony, and when it cleared Meredith, the King, and the guardians were gone. Only the golden skeleton remained, forming a scene so strange and grotesque that many in the crowd began to experience a sense of deep unease.

"Oh my," said Wash Thomas, who was otherwise at a loss for words.

Rafferty was equally astonished, but before he could respond klaxons began blaring out a warning as the guardians emerged from the Hopewell Block's front door and fired their rifles into the air. "Back! Back!" they shouted to the crowd as the police cordon in front of them dissolved into confusion. "There is danger! Back away! Back away!"

The crowd began a slow retreat, but panic broke out when some men began to run, although they couldn't say what exactly they were running from. In the chaos that followed, a woman and two children were nearly trampled as shouts and cries could be heard all down Cedar Street. Most of the crowd was still clustered near the Hopewell Block by the time a series of short, sharp reports came from inside the building.

Rafferty and Thomas had used dynamite as miners, and they knew the sound of explosives being detonated. They ducked just as a tremendous blast rocked the Hopewell Block. The entire building seemed to lift itself up. Then, its upward momentum spent, the building came apart in a flying tangle of brick, wood, and plaster. Amid a billowing cloud of dust, the building finally collapsed with a roar into its own basement.

Blinded by the dust and gasping for air, many people in the crowd fell to their knees. Others tried to run, only to trip over unseen bodies and tumble roughly to the ground. Although no one realized it at that moment, the explosion had been so carefully managed that no portion of the building fell on the crowd, and so there were no serious injuries. When the dust cleared away, a remarkable scene presented itself. The Hopewell Block was gone, not a single wall left in place

"I do not believe what just happened," Thomas said as he and Rafferty looked out over the ruins.

"We must believe it," Rafferty said, "hard as it may be. I'm wondering now what happens next."

* * *

Searchers immediately began combing through the rubble, unsure what they would find. After hours of careful digging, they located the shaft dug by the King's miners. As they peered down into it, they heard a man's faint voice. "Help me, oh God, help me," said the man, who presumably was somewhere at the bottom of the shaft buried under chunks of limestone, splintered wooden beams and other building material. A hoisting mechanism was soon put in place, and strong young men were lowered into the shaft on ropes to clear away the debris even as the voice went silent.

It was nine o'clock, with darkness settling in, when the first body—that of Harley Calhoun—was recovered, his hand and feet tied, a gag over his mouth, and his eyes frozen open in terror. Frank Shay was the next to be found, in a similar condition. Michael Gallagher, still improbably clinging to life, was the last to be pulled out, but he died shortly thereafter without regaining consciousness. All three bodies were terribly battered, and the coroner later determined that they had been crushed and suffocated as debris from the explosion rained down on them. The men, however, did not die without the gold they coveted. Draped around each man's neck was a solid gold medallion engraved with the word *vindicta*— Latin for "vengeance"—and the date of May 19, 1894.

With Merry Mike Gallagher no longer around to be amused by crime, Patrick Donlin was put in charge of the investigation that followed. His assignment was to find and arrest the Gold King, Meredith Hopewell, the guardians, the miners, and anyone else who might have had a hand in the killing of the three men. Donlin quickly established that the King, as Rafferty and Thomas already knew, had checked out of the Ryan the day before. So had Meredith Hopewell. A search of their suites yielded no useful evidence, while inquiries at the Union Depot failed to turn up anyone who had seen them boarding a train. The two dead-eyed guardians and the miners were also in the wind. With no clues to be found, Donlin's investigation slowed to a crawl within a matter of days, despite a nationwide alert.

Meanwhile, another crime manifested itself. When policemen arrived at Frank Shay's mansion to look for clues, they discovered a basement vault that had been blown open. Its contents—said to include cash, bonds, and a great stockpile of gold bullion—were gone. The thieves, however, left behind a note that read, "A dead man has no use of gold. Let it now help the living."

The newspapers, having been presented with a story for the ages, did not wish to let it go, and so they eagerly joined in the hunt for Meredith and the Gold King, filling many column inches with speculation as to where the miscreants might be. Sightings of the fugitives were reported in Chicago, Omaha, Pittsburgh, and other cities, but were soon discredited. Rafferty read the news accounts as faithfully as everyone else but expressed doubts to his friend Dolly Charbonneau that the culprits would ever be tracked down.

"'Tis as strange a business as I've ever seen," he told her one afternoon, "and yet also the work of a brilliant and meticulous mind."

"That person being?"

"Why, it can be no one other than Meredith Hopewell," Rafferty said. "She was playing with us from the start, and she put on a magnificent show. I was taken in like everyone else."

Charbonneau said, "Do not tell me the mighty Shadwell Rafferty admits to being hoodwinked?"

"Hoodwinked, hornswoggled, and played for a fool, as was this entire city. Why, not even Irene Adler deceived the great Sherlock Holmes more skillfully! I do wish I could speak to Meredith, but who knows where she has gone to? She will have planned her escape as carefully as everything else."

"And what of the Gold King?"

"I have evidence he could be an English thespian by the name of Gordon Greene, and I have passed that information on to the police. Meredith hired him, of course, and he played his role superbly. He, too, must be long gone by now."

15

VENGEANCE

By JULY, the search for Meredith and the Gold King had gone cold, all leads exhausted. Then, as pleasant September days arrived in St. Paul, so too did an envelope addressed to Rafferty at his saloon. It was postmarked from New Orleans, with the initials M. H. in the upper left corner. Rafferty knew at once who'd sent it. He opened the envelope and found a four-page letter, written in a clear hand without a single cross-out or correction. He called over Thomas, who was inventorying liquor behind the bar, and said, "Well, I think we will have some answers now, Wash. Why don't you read it aloud and we will see what Meredith Hopewell has to say?"

"My Dear Mr. Rafferty," the letter began, "by the time you receive this missive, I shall be out of the country, never to return. But as you and Mr. Thomas have been true friends, I feel you should know the truth of my recent adventures in St. Paul. As you surely have guessed by now, I planned everything once I became convinced that Calhoun, Shay, and Gallagher—as evil a trio of devils who ever trod this earth—had cruelly murdered my dear husband. I suspected all along that they had killed Arthur and hidden his body beneath the Hopewell Block, but I had no proof of it at first and, of course, I could expect no help from the police. Gallagher saw to that.

"I finally gained the proof I sought from a man who later told me he had been hired by Shay to infiltrate Arthur's business and spy on him. Arthur figured out at once that the man must be working on behalf of Shay or Calhoun or possibly both. As a kind of joke, Arthur let it be known to this spy that he had a vast fortune in gold hidden in the basement of his building. In truth, he kept no gold there, but he enjoyed tantalizing his enemies, for he knew how much Shay in particular coveted gold."

Rafferty said, "'Tis odd Mr. Hopewell didn't realize it might be dangerous to play such a joke on the likes of Calhoun and Shay. He knew they were greedy, disreputable men who had already formed a mob to attack him in his own house."

Thomas sighed and shook his head. "I can't explain it either. Maybe after he headed off that mob, he figured Calhoun and Shay wouldn't dare go after him again."

"It must be so. All right, Wash, read on."

"Arthur's little joke, as it turned out, had tragic consequences," the letter continued, "for Shay, Calhoun, and their lackey Gallagher decided they would steal the nonexistent treasure. I learned of their scheme after I came across the name of the spy in Arthur's papers. By then I was in New York, so I decided to hire someone to go to St. Paul and investigate on my behalf. It was the same man who later took on the role of the Gold King and, I think you will agree, performed brilliantly in that capacity. I dispatched him to St. Paul to sound out the spy, who for certain considerations agreed to tell all he knew.

"The details of Arthur's murder are too painful for me to recount in full, but here is what I learned from the spy. On Dec. 23, last, he drove Calhoun and Shay to the Hopewell Block at one o'clock in the morning. There they met Gallagher and a safecracker he'd brought along to open the basement vault. The conspirators believed the building would be unoccupied, but Arthur was in fact working exceptionally late to clear his year-end books. Although the spy waited outside the building and so did not witness Arthur's murder, it is clear nonetheless what happened. Arthur confronted the burglars and was shot in the head, probably by Gallagher. I know this because my diggers found a hole in Arthur's skull when they recovered his remains.

"After committing their awful deed, the conspirators threw Arthur's lifeless body down the old well in the basement and then covered his corpse with large blocks of stone and other items found in the basement. It is even possible they subsequently hired men who would ask no questions to throw additional debris down the well to eliminate any chance that Arthur's body would be found. I believe that after murdering Arthur, the conspirators went to blow open the vault, only to discover the door ajar and nothing inside.

"Once I became convinced who had murdered Arthur, I began to plot my revenge, and gold lay at the center of my plans. As I told you once, Arthur did in fact love gold—it was his one great weak-

ness, he told me—and he kept a large store of bullion in a vault at
our home. I had removed all of it before selling our property and
moving to New York, and I saw how it could be used to good effect.

"I think you will agree there is a certain delicious irony in the fact
that it was indeed Arthur's gold the King 'discovered' beneath the
Hopewell Block. Only it was I who put it there, to lure the murderers to their doom. The miners I hired were in fact Montana men,
and good enough fellows, but they never actually saw the gold,
which the King and I took great pains to secure until the proper
moment. The old tunnel, incidentally, was pure serendipity, since
the King and I had no idea it existed until the miners encountered
it quite by accident.

"As for the King himself, I can say only that I chose him carefully
to be my agent of retribution. I will not share his real identity with
you—does it really matter, after all?—but he proved to be a magnificent performer, and he was paid very handsomely for his services. I
have no idea where he is today, but I will always be grateful to him.

"You may well wonder what led me to embark on such an elaborate and costly scheme. The answer is that I wished, in some sense,
to make all of St. Paul both my audience and my target. Although a
few people—you and Mr. Thomas most definitely among them!—
treated Arthur kindly during his brief time in St. Paul, a far greater
number despised him and worked in every way they could to un-
dercut him because they resented the idea that a man of his ancestry could, or should, be wealthy. My own late father shared this
sentiment, and that will always leave me deeply saddened.

"As to my great scheme, you saw with your own eyes how it
ended. What you do not know is how carefully I devised it. For
example, I became an anonymous source for Miss Charbonneau at
the *Pioneer Press* so that the public in general, and the three murderers in particular, would come to believe in the hidden gold. But
the key moment came when I met with Calhoun, Shay, and the
King a few days before the treasure was to be unveiled. The King
and I staged an argument over who should receive the lion's share
of the gold, after which I left in an apparent huff. The King then
informed the two men that he intended to take the entire treasure

for himself but would need their help, along with Gallagher's, to accomplish this feat.

"Greedy men always want more, and when the King outlined his supposed secret plan, Calhoun and Shay agreed to it at once. He told them that on the Friday night before the big reveal, they and Gallagher were to meet him in the basement of the Hopewell Block. There, he would show them how he intended to spirit away the gold with their help, for which they were to receive ten thousand dollars each. I knew, however, that they would try to double-cross the King in order to take the gold for themselves and that they were ready to murder him just as they had Arthur. I should tell you, by the way, that the King knew nothing of my real intentions on that fateful night, and he had no hand in the deaths of the three conspirators.

"I imagine you can guess what actually happened that night in the basement. When Calhoun, Shay, and Gallagher arrived, thinking they were about to enrich themselves, they fell into a trap. The King was not there, but I was, along with the two so-called guardians in my employ. They waylaid the conspirators at gunpoint, then bound and gagged them, after which I explained to them that they must pay for murdering my beloved Arthur. Their eyes begged for mercy, but I would have none of it.

"You must think me coldhearted, and I will not deny it. All warmth and tenderness rushed out of me like a great exhalation after Arthur's remains were found, and so I could muster no sympathy for his killers. After I told the murderers to say their prayers, as that was the only hope left to them, they were lowered into the mine shaft. There they waited—in abject terror, I can only presume—until the building was dynamited, and they died as Arthur did, in the cold, melancholy depths of the earth.

"Now, before I bid you farewell, I must mention Mirabella Luray. That is not her real name, of course, and she is, in fact, a high-priced woman of the evening much sought after by society men in New York. I hired her to sow chaos among a certain breed of men in St. Paul who believe no girl is too young to satisfy their lust. Arthur and I, as you know, took in some of their victims, and I thought it only right they should face shame and ruin for their actions. I singled out the despicable Michael Reagan for particular attention because I thought it possible he knew what happened to Arthur but made no attempt to bring his murderers to justice. I can only hope all of his remaining days will be filled with misery and pain.

"I know what you are thinking, Mr. Rafferty, which is that vengeance is best left to the Almighty and not to a mere mortal such as myself. You may be right, but I make no apologies for what I have done. When I lost Arthur, I lost the only man I will ever love. He was my sun, and without him the heavens will always be dark to me. But at least I will take to my grave the satisfaction of knowing that his murderers received all they deserved. And if on Judgment Day I am sent to join them in the eternal fires of hell, I shall burn in peace." The letter was signed, "Your Friend, Meredith."

The letter included three postscripts. The first said: "You undoubtedly heard that Frank Shay's vault was burgled on the night of his demise. It contained a quarter of a million dollars' worth of bullion, which I have converted into currency. This money has already begun to flow back to St. Paul in the form of charitable gifts to help the city's neediest citizens. It is what Arthur would have wanted, and it gives me great satisfaction to know that Shay's gold is being used for good works."

The second said: "I recently met a traveling man from Minneapolis named Louis Menage. You have perhaps heard of him, as he left that city last year under a cloud of suspicion after his loan company failed. He is an interesting gentleman, and I learned from him that Guatemala is a beautiful country that has no extradition treaty with the United States. Perhaps I will visit there one day and see if it suits me."

The final postscript was the shortest: "I have sent to you and Mr. Thomas two small items to remember me by. Expect to receive them shortly."

"Well, ain't that just about the damnedest thing I ever read!" Thomas exclaimed. "Yes, sir, just about the damnedest thing."

"I cannot argue with you," Rafferty said. "It is a murder confession without a trace of remorse. We didn't know Meredith

Hopewell, did we? She is a blue-eyed lioness, and when she found her prey, she did not hesitate to kill. Well, we will have to give this letter, perhaps minus the postscripts, to Pat Donlin, but I doubt the authorities will ever find Meredith."

"And what of the Gold King?"

Rafferty shrugged. "We will have to wait and see. If is in indeed the actor Gordon Greene, the authorities will catch up with him soon enough."

* * *

Rafferty's prediction proved true, for in late September Scotland Yard detectives located Greene, who turned out to be a minor figure on the English stage. And while he did look a bit like the Gold King, it was soon established that he'd been in London during all of April and May and so could not have been putting on a performance in St. Paul.

By this time, Rafferty and Thomas had received their gift from Meredith Hopewell in the form of two gold medallions like those found on the bodies of Calhoun, Shay, and Gallagher. But instead of *vindicta,* they were engraved with another Latin word, *veritas.*

Every time he looked at his gift, Rafferty thought of Meredith and her harsh quest for justice. "She found the truth all right," Rafferty said late one evening as he and Thomas shared a nightcap at their saloon. As Rafferty rolled the medallion between his fingers, he felt a sudden twinge of sadness.

"They say the truth will set you free," he said, "but I wonder. Meredith has achieved her revenge, yet at what cost to her own well-being? She is all alone now, roaming somewhere in the tropics, and I would not be surprised if one day she concludes there is nothing left for her in this life."

"You think she will kill herself?"

"Ah, who can say? We are all mysteries, Wash, and we occupy a mysterious world."

"Speaking of which, what about the Gold King? Do you think he'll ever be identified?"

Rafferty shrugged. "I am no better at predicting the future than

I am at explaining the past, so I will not try. But here we are, in the long hours of the night, a bottle of fine Kentucky bourbon before us, and that is not a bad place to be. So let us have a toast," he said, raising his glass. "To the King and his vengeful Queen!"

"Yes," said Thomas. "To the King and the Queen, wherever they may be!"

LARRY MILLETT was a reporter and architecture critic for the *St. Paul Pioneer Press* for thirty years. He has written more than twenty books, including nine mystery novels featuring Sherlock Holmes and Shadwell Rafferty published by the University of Minnesota Press.